BY SARAH ADAMS

The

RULE
BOOK

The
RULE
BOOK

A NOVEL

SARAH ADAMS

DELL BOOKS
NEW YORK

A Dell Trade Paperback Original

Copyright © 2024 by Sarah Adams

Published in the United States by Dell, an imprint of Random House, a division of Penguin Random House LLC, New York.

DELL and the D colophon are registered trademarks of Penguin Random House LLC.

LIBRARY OF CONGRESS CATALOGING-IN-PUBLICATION DATA
Names: Adams, Sarah, 1991– author.
Title: The rule book: a novel / Sarah Adams.
Description: New York: Dell Books, 2024.
Identifiers: LCCN 2023040033 (print) | LCCN 2023040034 (ebook) |
ISBN 9780593723678 (trade paperback; acid-free paper) |
ISBN 9780593723685 (ebook)
Subjects: LCSH: Romance fiction. | LCGFT: Romance fiction. | Novels.
Classification: LCC PS3601.D3947 R85 2024 (print) |
LCC PS3601.D3947 (ebook) | DDC 813/.6—dc23/eng/20230908
LC record available at https://lccn.loc.gov/2023040033
LC ebook record available at https://lccn.loc.gov/2023040034

B&N special edition ISBN 978-0-593-87316-8

Printed in the United States of America on acid-free paper

randomhousebooks.com

2   4   6   8   9   7   5   3   1

Title page art by jan stopka © Adobe Stock Photos

Book design by Sara Bereta

This one's for my girls:
Dream even bigger.
Reach impossibly higher.
Don't you dare ever settle.

AUTHOR NOTE AND CONTENT WARNING

Dear reader, thank you for wanting to spend time with Derek and Nora. Although this book is written in such a way that it feels light and comedic, please be advised that there are heavier topics and themes portrayed such as late diagnosis of dyslexia and parental neglect. The story also contains adult language and sexual scenes. If you prefer to keep the bedroom door fully closed, please skip chapter 34.

The
RULE
BOOK

1

Nora

Sometimes life is like a box of chocolates, and sometimes life is like a box of chocolates left out in the sun all day.

Today, it turns out, is a melty, disappointing chocolate sort of day. Not only did I step in gum while wearing my favorite shoes on my way into work, but I also fired up my email to find some wonderfully disturbing information.

"Knock knock," I say to my boss, Nicole Hart, as I step hesitantly into her office to address said email.

Truthfully, I'm always a little hesitant to step into her office because, whew, this woman is a force to be reckoned with. There's a reason she's CEO of the agency. She's kind to me (in her own way), but she's like a tornado of confidence. You need a helmet and a safe place to take shelter when she focuses her attention on you.

Like now, she's sitting at her desk in her immaculate gray pin-striped skirt and silk blouse—red lipstick painted perfectly on her full lips, blond hair pulled back into a sleek, perky ponytail that has a magical flip on the end. But all those surface-level attributes are nothing but a misdirection. It's in her eyes you see the truth. The alert, bone-chilling, feline ferocity. Her keen mind is why she's the top agent in our industry and lands enormous deals for clients like Nathan Donelson, famous quarterback for our city's NFL team, the L.A. Sharks. The woman is all sharp edges and absolute dedication. She's an inspiration.

"Please tell me you're asking to come in and it's not the beginning of a joke."

"I could tell you that, but then I'd be lying."

She cuts her eyes to me, and I smile. She's worked with me long enough to know I'm not going anywhere until this is over.

"Who's there?" she asks like she's in the middle of a root canal.

"Needle."

"Needle who?"

"Needle little smile to brighten your day?" I give her one as I shuffle into her office.

She looks up from her keyboard—posture ramrod straight—and her eyes bounce from my reddish-brown hair, down to my yellow sneakers, and back up to my face. Nicole misses nothing. She's an assassin who's just identified her target's weak spot. *God, I want to be her.*

She discards my fabulous joke. "How many pairs of those shoes do you own?" She's referring to my bright yellow sneakers.

"Four. I was wearing my red pair this morning, but I stepped in gum and had to change into these." I raise my foot and wiggle it proudly. "Smelled delicious but left a nasty squelching trail."

"I'm guessing Marty had something to say when he saw those. Do I need to humble him?" Her attention is on her keyboard, somehow still able to talk as her fingers fly across the keys. The thing about Nicole is she's all bark and . . . an even worse bite. But she only bites those who threaten her people. And even though she likes to pretend I mean nothing to her—she's made it clear I'm one of her people.

I wrinkle my nose at the mention of the worst man in this office. They're all pretty unspectacular and seem to dislike me joining their boys' club no matter how many fun-size packs of Skittles I leave in the break room, but Marty is by far the most awful. *Male chauvinist number one.*

I shrug a shoulder. "Only that the yellow is somehow more offensive to look at than the red and I should spend my paycheck on a professional wardrobe one of these days."

"He's not wrong about the color," she says, giving me brief side-eye. "But only I'm allowed to criticize your style choices. Not a man who wouldn't know a good-looking suit if it smacked him in the face."

"And on that note, you're absolutely correct," I say cheerfully. "But that's not why I'm here actually."

When I first started working here as Nicole's intern two years ago, she was very vocal about how much she disliked my playful wardrobe. But I've since been promoted to her associate agent over the last year, and I've more than proved my capability in this industry, miraculously earning her respect. Now she never tells me what to wear. Instead, she tells everyone else to piss off on my behalf since I have a tough time saying mean things to people.

Currently I'm sporting a fitted, three-quarter-length yellow-and-white herringbone blazer with a baby blue pleated skirt and a Rolling Stones T-shirt underneath to really pull it all together, and even though I know she must hate it, she keeps quiet. I sort of miss the days when she'd say something like *You look like a librarian attempting to be cool.* Sassy Nicole is a pleasure to study.

"Let me know if Marty says anything else about your wardrobe. I'll be happy to jam those yellow shoes right up his ass."

"And this is why I fear you as much as I adore you, my glorious workplace warrior goddess. However, I think I'd rather keep my shoes away from Marty's nether regions. Actually, I'm here because I want to talk about the email I just got."

Nicole finally stops typing and swivels her chair to me with a sigh of long suffering. She crosses one sleek (waxed . . . I know because I used to make those appointments for her when I was an intern) leg over the other and then leans her elbow on the desk. She delicately rests her chin on her fingers.

"I think it might be a mistake," I continue, shifting on my little feet hugs (that's what I call these dream shoes) as her gaze narrows on me.

"Stop second-guessing yourself, Mac. You're ready for this step. You've worked hard to get here and deserve the promotion," she tells me in her no-nonsense kind of way.

She's right. I have worked hard, and not to blow my own trumpet too loudly, but I do feel that I've earned this promotion. In fact, I've been reaching for this dream ever since I was a kid and would go visit my dad for the weekend and sit with him on the couch and watch whatever sport was on TV at the time. During those few hours, he would let me into his life, and I felt close to him. My relationship with my dad didn't last, but my dream of becoming a professional sports agent has endured through high school, college, grad school, postgrad intern positions, and lately, working as Nicole's associate agent.

No, the promotion to full-time agent without training wheels is not the issue.

The mistake is that she's assigning me to Derek Pender, tight end for the L.A. Sharks.

"I'm not second-guessing," I tell Nicole. "It's more like third- and fourth-guessing. I could be a professional guesser at this point. Are you sure Mr. Pender and I would be a good fit?"

I'm not asking what I really want to ask. But I'm not sure if I should come out with the whole truth or keep it to myself. If Nicole has taught me anything, it's that this industry is all about playing your cards right—and the key to doing that is to not show them too early.

Nicole senses my half-truth, though, and taps her red-tipped nails on the desk. "You're practically vibrating with nervous energy—what is the real question you're not asking me?"

"I'm just concerned that Derek was told he was meeting with *Mac* and not *Nora Mackenzie* and might be expecting someone else entirely." It's the truth. Just not all of it. I tuck my cards a little closer to my chest.

"You're wanting to make sure he's not expecting a man?"

Not exactly. Although, that too. Everyone around the office calls me Mac because of my last name. I don't particularly love it, but I've learned to tolerate it because the sad truth is, in our industry, people on the other end of email correspondences tend to say yes more often when they have the incorrect assumption I'm a dude. The most misogynistic men live in the world of sports (ahem Marty), and women work twice as hard as men to gain the same amount of respect. It's messed up.

"I guess I was just wondering if you could tell me exactly what you told Derek—er, Mr. Pender about me. It . . . it just seems too good to be true that he'd be willing to sign with a brand-new agent, and I want to make sure he knows the whole story."

She waves a dismissive hand. "Don't worry. I used your pronouns and told him that you're new, but that I was the one who trained you, so he can be assured you have been taught by the best"—*the confi-*

dence on this one—"and that if he were smart, he'd snatch you up before you have a chance to go skyrocket someone else's career."

My heart quivers with delight. Did she really say all of that? Does she mean it? Nicole is not flippant with compliments, so I had no idea she thought any of that about me.

"Wow . . . thank you," I say, trying not to get emotional but not entirely successful. I press my lips together and she knows why.

Her nose crinkles in distaste. "Are you about to cry?"

I keep my lips sealed and shake my head even though pools are settling over my eyeballs. Oh no, they're clinging to my lashes. We're going to have a runner!

She groans and turns her face back to her laptop. "No emotions in my office, you know that. I believe in you, and I'm happy to propel you toward success, Mac." She's typing and talking again. How does she do that? "Derek Pender has a lot of obstacles to face in the next several months. His career is completely up in the air, and you could be looking at a trade or a contract renegotiation as well as controlling any weak narratives that the media will undoubtedly try to throw at him as the season approaches. Are you up for it?"

See, now this whole situation makes me want to nervous-cackle, because, *no*, I'm not up for it. But not because I don't feel I can handle any of those things. In fact, the idea of jumping major hurdles at the start of my career fills my stomach with twinkling stars of delight. *Anticipation.* I love a good challenge. And since Derek Pender—the most legendary tight end in professional football of our time—is returning this season from an epic ankle injury that should have killed his career, it's the mother of all challenges.

No, the problem is, I'm not ready to face the man himself. The man I still dream about when I absolutely shouldn't.

I blink back my tears. "Thank you, Nicole. I'm excited for the opportunity. I owe you my undying love and friendship." I'm embarrassed to admit just how much I wish she'd reciprocate the friendship part.

Except she says, "Save the love and friendship, please. I'm not doing you a favor; you've earned this all on your own. Do you know in the history of this company we've never had an associate close as many deals as you have? And you're definitely my first one to ever scout and land a player on my behalf." That one was technically an accident. I ran into a popular college basketball player at the grocery store, and I complimented him on his super cool sneakers and phenomenal game the previous week. One thing led to another and he was in Nicole's office Monday morning signing a contract. Super nice guy. Bumped his head on the doorframe on his way out.

"But now," Nicole continues, "we'll really see what you're made of because you're on your own in the cutthroat world of athlete representation and there's no room for screwing up."

Ominous. Don't love that.

"Okay, so not a favor, but you do want to be best friends. Got it," I add with a salute, and then feel thankful that she was staring at her computer and missed that gesture because it would just annoy her even further. And the truth is, I really do want Nicole to like me. Because although I love having my mom as my BFF (she's truly awesome), I'm starting to feel it's time to make some friends.

Admittedly, the making friends part is easy. It's the keeping them that's proved tricky.

I slip out of Nicole's office and miraculously make it down the hall and back to my office—if you can even call it that since it more resembles a broom closet with a window the size of a porthole—without being confronted by Marty or his minions. In my office, I press my back to the wall and scoot around the desk to get to my chair just like I always do.

With a determination to take this melty chocolate day and turn it into delicious hot chocolate instead, I begin reorganizing my desk, because nothing lifts my spirits more than putting things in order and sorting them by color. Once my world feels a little steadier, I crack open my inbox and reread The Email once again. I am still convinced this is a mistake. A hallucination. A nightmare.

Any moment, I, Nora Mackenzie, will wake up and my favorite red sneakers won't be marred with Juicy Fruit and my big career break will not hinge on *him*.

Mac,

Exciting news. Nicole and I have been very impressed with your work as of late (especially regarding the athleisure deal you facilitated on Nicole's behalf while she was out sick) and we feel that you are more than ready to move up into the position of full-time agent.

Derek Pender, tight end for the Sharks, who I'm sure you're already aware is a client of ours, needs a new agent. Bill Hodge has repped Derek during his seven years in the NFL. Unfortunately, Bill is facing medical issues, the details of which we will not go into at this time, and has resigned effective immediately. We need to place Mr. Pender with a new agent ASAP. Nicole cannot currently take on any other clients but has communicated to him her faith in you as an agent, and he is willing to meet with you to see if you two would be a good fit. He'll be here at one o'clock today. Although we are all aware of the obstacles he will be facing at the start of the season, he is still an excellent first athlete for your roster. Congrats!

—Joseph Newman,
Owner and Director,
Sports Representation Inc.

The email itself is lovely, affirming and everything I've ever dreamed of happening in my career. The problem is, I'm convinced Derek doesn't know who he's actually supposed to meet with later. If he did, there's no way he would have agreed to it.

Because the last time I saw Derek, my college boyfriend, was when I was breaking up with him.

2

Derek

I step into the house, set the container of to-go soup on the counter, catch one look at the whiteboard in the corner of the room, and turn right back around.

"Nope," I say, heading for the door.

Sick my ass. My friend and teammate, Nathan, sent me a text this morning saying he and his wife, Bree, were really sick and wondered if I could drop off some soup—knowing I'm hardwired to show up when someone needs me. But he looks healthy as a clam standing by the whiteboard with my three other friends wearing a shit-eating grin on his face.

Lawrence steps in my path as I try to retreat, giving me a taste of what it's like to face him—our left tackle—on the field. "Hear us out, Derek."

"Like hell. I'm here under false pretenses—not for whatever that intervention is," I say, pointing to the whiteboard behind me.

"Dude, come on. It's time." Jamal loves the sound of his own voice. "Besides, after what we found in your bedside table, you can't deny you want this."

"It is not time, and I don't want it." I stalk over to rip the dry-erase marker from Jamal's hand. Next, I aggressively wipe away the words *Find Derek A Wife* from the top of the whiteboard. The whiteboard that has become a staple for every important life planning session in our friend group over the last two years ever since we used it to help Nathan get out of the friend zone with his best friend (now wife), Bree. And listen, I'm happy to sit around with these guys and meticulously plot out each of their sappy love-life plans all day, but try to use it on me, and I'll burn it to the ground.

"I don't want a wife. And this is the last time I'll warn you not to bring up my bedside table before there's real consequences in the form of your face looking a little less pretty at the start of the season."

I should have never given these guys a key to my place while I was out of town, even if my plants needed watering. Of course they would snoop. It's in their DNA to overstep.

But this shit with the whiteboard is too much. I know why they're doing it—can see right through their nervous pity-smiles. I've been hermitting myself away too much, declining more and more dinners, never going out to clubs with them, and definitely not dating. I'm basically a one-eighty of who I used to be, and they think a relationship is going to pull me back out. And maybe their fears are valid. They don't know who I am anymore or how to handle me. I don't know who I am either.

I haven't felt this uncertain of myself since I was an awkward, gangly, eighth-grader who was once again sucking at school, struggling to make friends who didn't tease me mercilessly after they heard me read aloud, and only lived in the shadow of my older sister. Ginny who was everyone's favorite. Achieving straight A's was effortless for her, and probably why she's now a practicing doctor. Where she thrived, I struggled twice as hard. I fought relentlessly with my parents over grades and heard *Why can't you just apply yourself, Derek, and stop goofing off* more times than I could count.

It wasn't until a few months ago that I was finally diagnosed with what my supposed *goofing off* was . . . dyslexia. One night while lying in bed and scrolling through social media, I came across a video where a guy was describing what living with dyslexia was like for him. I was shocked—because everything he described, those were my experiences too. I got in with a learning specialist quickly, and after testing, it was confirmed.

I'm dyslexic.

It's why reading and writing were so damn hard for me and took me twice as long as other students. Why I struggled to process certain words. Why I fell behind. I wasn't tested in my adolescence because I come from a very firm "he just needs to try harder" family. But in reality, I was working the hardest. I could never understand why it wasn't enough. Why I couldn't comprehend what I was reading in my textbooks like everyone else. And that wedge just grew between me and my parents until I hated learning altogether.

But then . . . I found football my ninth-grade year. I stepped onto the field and it was like every puzzle piece fell into place for me. I was *good*. A natural. And I only got better and better as the years went on and I grew into my six-four body and filled out in a way the other guys around me did not. Girls suddenly really liked me. Teachers gave me more slack. My parents were proud, because like Ginny, I was making a name for myself. A new reason they could brag to their friends. No one really cared too much that my grades sucked or that I was struggling with academics—because I was clearly going to play college football and then go on to the NFL, so what did it matter anyway?

And that's what happened.

I just barely graduated high school but shattered varsity records as a tight end. I got more handouts in college courses from my professors than I'd care to admit, but I graduated, and then went first round in the draft. I've played in two Super Bowls and have been named MVP. I've dated movie stars, bought my parents their new house, and paid off my sister's med school loans as her graduation present.

It wasn't until I snapped my ankle on the field at the end of last season and needed surgery that my identity altered. I've leaned on this career for security and acceptance for so long that I don't know who the hell I'd be without it. What will all these people think of me when I can no longer do the *one* thing I was good at. *Worthless.*

It would be the worst time to try to find a relationship. Especially when Collin Abbot—the rookie backup who stepped in for me while I was out during the last two games of the season—blew everyone away. The rumors circle me like piranhas now. *He's going to take my place this season.* I have everything to lose—and nothing permanent to offer.

"Derek, quit being a dipshit and let us help you find love and happiness," says Nathan.

"It's not the right time," I tell him instead of snapping at him that love and happiness are not synonymous in my head and that he can shove his opinions up his ass. I've only contemplated the idea of marriage with one woman. The only woman that I've ever felt really loved me for who I was outside of football. It was before I ever met these four buffoons that I call teammates—less affectionately known as friends—and let's just say I got enough of a taste of being loved and left to never want seconds. They don't know about her. They don't know she's the reason I chafe at the idea of a long-term relationship now.

"Why not?" Nathan Donelson is the quarterback of our team, the Los Angeles Sharks, and we've affectionately nicknamed him *Dad* because of his leadership and wisdom. Which is why after he married his best friend, Bree, two years ago, the rest of the guys followed suit shortly after. Jamal married Tamara and Lawrence married Cora—both couples even going so far as to elope in Vegas just like Nathan and Bree because they made it look like a damn fairy tale. But marriage is where the sheeplike following ends for me.

I'm the last of our five-man crew without a wedding ring, and I'm going to keep it that way.

"Pender's just scared," says Jamal Mericks, our team's running back and self-designated pain-in-my-ass, taking the dry-erase marker from my hand again and using it to draw a big baby with a pacifier on the board. In case there was any question as to who the baby was supposed to represent, he writes my name with a big arrow pointing down to it.

I give him the bird.

"Real mature. You're only proving my point." He taps the marker against the cartoon baby.

"That's enough bickering for the day," says Lawrence, who is undoubtedly the biggest softie of the group but also the most aggressive on the field—you'd never guess it by the way he bristles when we fight. He's also the only one in here who makes me look short. I'm six-four and Lawrence towers over me.

He pushes past me and Jamal to erase the board again. "Jamal, it's a miracle you managed to land a wife with your big ego. And Derek, I'm starting to doubt that you could get one even if you tried."

"Rude," Jamal and I say in unison, and then turn mirroring glares at each other. We're a love-hate situation. As in, I mostly love to hate him.

"How about you guys do something constructive and come help

me instead of trying to force romance down Derek's throat?" Price shouts from the living room, where he's sprawled out with a million tiny little plastic rainbow-colored parts on the floor. I think they are eventually supposed to resemble some sort of baby-jumping-play-saucer-thing.

Jayon Price is our curmudgeonly wide receiver. He shocked the hell out of us all by becoming the first in the group to announce a pregnancy. My money was on Nathan, but no. Hope, Price's wife, is in her last trimester, and I've never seen the guy so happy.

Well, he doesn't currently look happy as he tries to shove a plastic springy thing into another plastic part, but it won't click together. His bicep is about to burst from how much force he's using. "Why the hell don't they sell these things already assembled?"

He chucks the offending piece across the room, and I duck—just narrowly missing a plastic bumblebee to the face.

"Better question," says Jamal, stepping up to look at the box the parts came in. "Why are you putting this together now?"

Price looks dumbstruck. "Why not? Hope's due date is like two months away."

I grunt a laugh. "Man, your baby won't be old enough for that thing for a while." I point at the box. "It says on the back that it's to strengthen a baby's legs and back to start walking."

Price drops the instructions and levels an ominous look at each of us. "Tell Hope about this and you're all dead. She's already freaking out that we don't know what we're doing, and I don't want her to worry more when she finds out she asked me to piece together a toy for an eight-month-old."

I really do love getting to walk through all these seasons of life with my friends. Which is why I have to make a full comeback. Because part of me is worried that if I get cut . . . *never mind*. I don't want to think about it right now.

Nathan nods. "We'll help you put it together, but mainly because your pregnant wife truly terrified me last week when she threatened to stab her fork's prongs into my hand if I took the last brownie. If that woman wants her baby's exersaucer built several months early, we'll build it." He faces me again. "But first . . . we're not done talking about your relationship status yet."

"Oh yes we are," I say, backing into the kitchen and aiming for my keys on the counter. "Leave me and my bachelorhood alone and go eat your soup, you lying asshole. I'm outta here."

"No one is going anywhere!" comes a feminine voice from the kitchen threshold. I look up to find that Nathan's wife, Bree, has appeared out of nowhere and is using her body as a human barrier—arms stretched out and gripping the trim around the door so I can't exit. She must have just come from her ballet studio because she's wearing a black leotard with gray sweatpants. Her usual look. "Did you guys talk to him about the plan yet?"

Nathan yells from the living room. "Yeah, he doesn't want to get married."

Bree's mouth falls open. "Ever?" She sounds personally offended by this choice. It's not like I have anything against marriage for other people, though—it's just not for me. Not anymore at least.

I shrug and toss my keys around my finger, staring at the woman who now feels like my little sister. "Sorry, Bree Cheese—it's just not for me."

"Okay, okay . . ." She waves a hand. "So you don't want to get married—that's fine. At least let us set you up with someone."

"Thanks, but no. I'm all set on that front." I walk toward her, but she doesn't move out of the threshold.

"No, you're not! Don't think we haven't noticed how you—Derek Pender—have not even been on a single date since your injury. All those overgrown toddlers peeking from behind the corner might be too chicken to come right out and say it . . . but it's worrisome that you're not going out anymore. Not dating. Not even hooking up with anyone!" She says all of this like my name should be synonymous with those things. And . . . well, I guess it used to be.

I look over my shoulder and sure enough, everyone is watching. They duck back a little, though, when I make eye contact. "Nothing to worry about, guys. I'm just focusing on rehab full-time right now."

"At what cost?" Bree asks, shoulders sagging a little.

I look her in the eyes. "Quit worrying. I'm fine—I swear."

She drops her arms and rolls her eyes. "You're annoying is what you are. But I guess I'll still let you have this anyway." She reaches in her purse hanging off her shoulder and I know what's coming next: a Breenkit. Bree shows her affection by occasionally giving out little presents that made her think of her friends. We each have at least a few. I have a skull coffee mug that she said looks like the tattoo on my forearm and a magnetic *82* she stole from her little nieces' fridge number-learning stash in honor of my jersey number.

Today, she pulls out something that stops me in my tracks even though there's no way she could know why this particular item has so much impact on me.

Bree sets a little key chain onto my palm and all I can do for a solid three breaths is stare down at the miniature bowl of ice cream topped with cereal bits. The skin of my face heats like I've been caught red-handed.

"Why did you give me this?" My tone is accusatory. Like she's been snooping around inside my brain without permission. Like she knows all my secrets, and this is part of the intervention.

"Because . . ." Her smile turns questioning. "Remember? At Lawrence's wedding reception when you got drunk? You gave that funny speech about how all you ever want to eat for the rest of your life is ice cream and cereal and you were so sad thinking you couldn't? I saw a shop online that makes custom ice cream resin key chains, so I had them make you this one with cereal on top."

Right. Because of the speech. My shoulders relax a little in relief that she doesn't know about *her*. About Nora.

To this day the group still laughs about that "funny little speech" I gave at the reception. They thought I was so incredibly drunk that I was just spouting pitiful nonsense. And it's true—I was drunk. But only because I couldn't get Nora—the woman I wanted to marry from the day I met her—off my mind through the entire ceremony. I couldn't stop thinking about where she is now or wondering for the thousandth time why I wasn't enough for her. Yes, we were opposites. Her being incredibly smart and driven and academically focused whereas I was a jock with an undiagnosed learning disorder who was great at partying.

But we were also compatible in a lot of ways. We loved to compete—turning everything into a pointless, fun game and thriving off it. We had chemistry that I've never felt with anyone else. The kind that slips into your bloodstream and alters you. And if that wasn't enough—we both loved sports. In fact, she was aiming to become an agent. *Did that ever happen?*

And Nora's favorite snack: ice cream topped with cereal.

Apparently, I never gave any hints that the speech was actually directed toward my broken heart or the woman who brought the hammer down on it. They just assumed I had a serious sweet tooth that night. I've let them believe it because I prefer my history with Nora to remain buried.

I close my hand around the key chain and force a smile. "Right, I completely forgot. Thank you—this is funny."

She frowns and probably would say more about my unamused demeanor if Nathan didn't turn the corner behind her and wrap his arms around Bree's waist. These two will make you puke. They're too damn sweet for their own good.

"We're all going to lunch. Want to join?" Nathan asks me while still holding on to Bree.

"Can't. I have a meeting at one o'clock. Bill had to retire—something health-related he didn't want to talk about—so I'm meeting with a brand-new agent that Nicole recommends."

And that's another thing. You know that my agency isn't putting too much stock in my career when they try to stick me with the new kid on the block. Imagine being the number one tight end in professional football, only to get tackled in a way that snapped my ankle like a twig and required surgery to repair it, and now I'm stuck with the agency rookie who's never had a client in her life. The only reasons I didn't turn down the idea immediately are (1) I'm not so sure I'm worth it anymore either, and (2) Nicole—who has been Nathan's agent from the start of his career and is known as the best in the business—recommended her.

"Nicole wouldn't steer you wrong. If she says to sign with him, do it," says Nathan, still holding Bree like she's his lifeline and he'll keel over if their physical contact is severed.

I envy them.

"Her," I correct, looking away from the happy couple to spin my keys around my finger again. "The agent is a woman."

"Ooh, maybe she'll be gorgeous and single, and you'll fall madly in love," says Bree with hearts in her eyes.

I shake my head. "I seriously need you guys to give it up. I don't want a relationship."

"Sure . . . you think that now. But what about after you go meet the most incredible woman in the world?"

I look at Nathan. "Can you please ask Cupid to stand down so I can leave?"

3

Nora

I touch the door handle to the conference room, and my stomach leaps off a cliff. And as it free-falls, it drops directly into a space-time continuum portal where I continue to fall with absolutely no relief from my misery. But not because I'm unprepared to do my job. It's because I'm unprepared to be face-to-face with Derek Pender again.

Simply put: Derek was my everything that was never supposed to be. I had my life all organized in a nicely laid-out plan. A plan I'm still hyperfocused on. Meeting a wild, fun, sexy football player and falling madly in love with him my senior year of college was never supposed to be part of that plan. We had both attended University of Southern California for three years without bumping into each other.

But then, like a ripple in the universe, there he was . . . at the same party as me with eyes as blue as a hot flame. Inexplicably, he was just as drawn to me as I was to him. He noticed me hanging on the outskirts of the party, not because I'm introverted or shy, but because I didn't want to be there. It was keeping me from finishing a presentation I was excited to work on, but my roommate forced me to go.

Apparently I hadn't blinked in several days. And that was when Derek came over to talk.

After a while, he coaxed me out onto the dance floor, and my cheeks ached at the end of the night from how much I laughed. I also got rip-roaring drunk, and since my roommate left with a guy and we were off campus, I didn't have a ride. Derek (who was way more sober than me) called us an Uber and made sure I got back to my dorm safely. And then he slept on my floor all night to make sure I didn't aspirate in my sleep.

The next morning, I felt terrible that he had gone through all that trouble for me, so I wrote him a little IOU that could be redeemed at any time. He never did, though, and it didn't take long for us to fall head over heels for each other. Didn't take long for me to lose sight of my goals and dreams either. To replace them with my addiction to his smile, his touch, the way he looked at me as if I were the greatest thing in the world. We understood each other in a way no one else did. Even our need for constant competition. It was normal for us to randomly declare a race to wherever we were going. Who could balance a cup on their head the longest. The floor is lava. Ridiculous little competitions all the time.

We had that silly, soul-wrenching young love that can only exist in a bubble full of skipping class, staying out all night to see the sunrise while eating gas station donuts, and ignoring my textbooks in favor of watching him practice or play a game.

Until I realized Derek didn't understand one of the most important parts of who I was. So just before we graduated college and he was drafted into the NFL, I ended it. Abruptly and cold as ice. I've never stopped regretting that part.

The most likely scenario of seeing my ex again, however, is this: Derek will take one look at me, smile a slow smile, and then give me a platonic hug. He might even call me by my old cute nickname once for old times' sake. *Ginger Snap.* Because we're both adults now. Because even though it nearly killed me to break up with him, he moved on a week later. And judging by all the press and tabloids, if there's one thing Derek hasn't been doing, it's sitting around and pining over me. That thought used to bother me, but today it brings me comfort. If he moved on so quickly, there's a chance that I'm barely a memory for him.

And so, with great bravery I twist the door handle and step confidently into the conference room—exuding power and poise. *Just kidding.* Someone else opens the door from the inside while my hand is still on the handle, and it drags me in. I stumble through the doorway, past the intern who opened it, and accidentally shoot the pen resting on the top of my pile of contracts like a cannonball onto the conference room table. It lands smack-dab in the middle, and Nicole (oh goody, apparently Nicole will be in this meeting too) looks absolutely shocked.

I right myself and tug down the end of my blazer with all the dignity of a queen. Possibly a toddler playing a queen in a dress-up outfit, but the dignity is there all the same.

"Hi. I'm here!" I will my voice to come out steady.

"Yes, you are." Thankfully Nicole was the only one who witnessed my clumsy entrance, because Derek (oh my gosh, there's Derek) still has his broad back to me, facing the table. "Let's get the introductions started, shall we?"

Oh no. This is where it all falls into ruin, and Nicole will be here to witness it. I should have just told her the truth in her office. The truth is always the right choice. Always. I know this, because I'm the captain of the Rule Followers Club. And yet . . .

Derek reaches forward and plucks the pen from the middle of the table. With it clutched in his hand, he pushes his chair back and stands. I gulp down a thousand butterflies at just the sight of his back. It's . . . expansive. I don't remember there being this much terrain before. The muscles are so obscene they're rippling through his shirt. That poor cotton tee is straining with all its might, but it barely stands a chance. And then he turns and the floor falls out from under me.

Sharp, cornflower-blue eyes connect with mine—so beautiful they're nearly cruel, and I feel an old glimmer of something tug between us. And then a thought grips me before I can banish it. *I'm not over him, and I'm scared I never will be.*

His sun-kissed brown hair plays around his temples and nape, highlighting his bring-you-to-your-knees bone structure. Honestly, he and the quarterback of his team, Nathan Donelson, look like brothers with their size and jawlines. But Derek is Nathan's worldlier counterpart. Derek's face is broodingly, fascinatingly handsome.

My gaze bounces, nervous to fully land on any one part of him. He was broad and strong in college, but . . . goodness, this man is overwhelming now. He belongs to a time when people needed warriors for their safety. And all of his tattoos . . . individual ones dotting but not quite connecting on both of his arms; those are new to me too. I've seen them on TV when I've watched him play, but something about witnessing them on his flesh in person heightens the experience.

When I look to his face again, he does not seem happy to see me.

Nicole clears her throat. "Derek, this is—"

"Nora Mackenzie," I say at the same moment he does in order to hide his voice. I stick out my hand with a bright, pleading smile and resist fainting from my sudden peak of adrenaline. "It's nice to meet you, Derek."

Nicole can't see me. Derek's massive frame is blocking her view. His cool gaze sweeps down to my hand extended toward him and his frown etches deeper. I silently beg him to accept it. To go along with my charade just until Nicole leaves. But I don't think he's going to.

Just as Derek opens his mouth to say something, the conference room door opens behind me, and our receptionist peeks her head in. "Nicole, sorry to interrupt you but you have an urgent call. I have him on hold in your office."

Nicole rounds the conference table and looks from Derek's stormy face to my bright and peppy expression that's clearly trying to compensate for his. "If you will both excuse me," she says, hesitation marking her tone. "I'll be back in a moment."

Yep. Take your time, ma'am! All day if you need!

Nicole leaves the room and graciously shuts the door behind her. I'm left alone staring into Derek's chilling eyes. He wastes no time before shaking his head and turning away from me to retrieve his keys from the table. "Nope. Not happening."

Wait, what?

I'm shocked. Stunned and blinking like someone just shined a bright spotlight in my eyes. It's been years since we've seen each other, and that's all he's going to say?

"Derek, wait!" I round him to stand in his path before he makes it to the door.

He eyes me, jaws flexing. "I was told your name is Mac." He scoffs—disgust clouding his vision. "Congrats. If your aim was to epically play me, you hit your mark. You won."

Even his voice is different now. Deeper.

I'm struggling to find my footing because I severely underestimated what it would feel like to stand face-to-face with Derek again. Every cell in my body is humming like they're coming back to life. I would be lying if I said I hadn't imagined running into him before. I've always known that Derek was Bill's client—but I didn't think we would actually have a chance to see each other because Bill always met with Derek offsite, and I had no reason to reach out to Derek and announce my presence within the agency.

But still, I imagined it. Imagined bumping into him in the hallway one random afternoon and sharing a second glance. However, in my fantasies, it always started with a slow mischievous smile spreading over his mouth and ended with us making out in a supply closet.

His reaction now is justified, though. I hurt him—and I need to apologize for it. But this is definitely not the time.

"No—please listen. I wasn't trying to play you. In fact, I was afraid you didn't know who I was when I heard that Nicole presented the idea to you. Everyone in the office calls me Mac. It's short for—"

"*Mackenzie,*" he says thunderously as if he can't believe I have the audacity to insinuate he didn't already know. "Yeah, I damn well remember, Nora." And then he lets out a short disdainful laugh. "And I also remember how easily you can drop a person out of nowhere, which is why I will never sign with you. I prefer my agent to be trustworthy and dedicated."

Ouch.

Without a backward glance, Derek walks by me, careful not to touch any part of me lest he catch the cooties I'm carrying before he storms out the conference room door.

"Well, that certainly could have gone better," I tell the empty chairs.

So it turns out Derek does remember me. And he hates me. Which, I can't say I blame him for, even if it confuses me.

It seems I have two options here. (1) I tell Nicole about how I already lost the first client she practically spoon-fed me. *Embarrassing.* (2) Rip this knife out of my chest and use it as a dart to hit my career goals instead.

I'm going with option 2, which means it's time to clear the air with my ex-boyfriend.

4

Derek

"Derek! Derek! Wait!"

This cannot be happening. I'm on the sidewalk outside the agency, trying to get away from this place and that woman as quickly as possible. *Mac.* I should have asked for more details. But how was I supposed to know that my ex-girlfriend got a job with the sports agency that represents me? *Oh god—how long has she worked there?* How long has she known that there was always only one degree of separation between us but never chose to enlighten me about it?

There's no way in hell I'll let her represent me.

"Derek! Please—*ugh*. Will you slow down a minute? Jeez, your legs are huge now. You're like one of those giant trees in *Lord of the Rings*." She's running after me yelling this for the whole city to hear. My SUV is just around the corner in the private parking lot, and I plan on getting to it before she gets to me. Am I being petty? Yeah. Do I care? Hell no.

"You're not my agent, and never will be, so stop chasing me," I tell her over my shoulder. I get a glimpse of her rosy cheeks and her deep auburn hair blowing around her face as she jogs to catch up. The wind keeps whipping up her skirt and showing more of her legs than she wants, judging by the way she's trying to keep a hand pressed to the front of it like a Marilyn Monroe poster. Looks like I finally have the answer to my question: She did become a sports agent.

She overtakes me quickly and does this little hop-skip maneuver to walk backward while looking at my face. "Will you just give me a second to explain?"

"Pole."

"Huh?"

"There's a pole," I say, grabbing her arm and tugging it just enough to maneuver her safely around it. I let go immediately after. *Should have just let her run into it.* Instead, she's at my side again in a second. "Derek, please! I want to talk about this. And to apologize."

"I don't want an apology. In fact, I don't want anything from you." And that's the truth. There might have been a time when I would have given anything to have her begging me for a chance to explain and apologize, but not anymore. My heart is permanently iced over. I clearly wasn't enough for her, and that's all there is to it.

I keep my face forward, trying to block her out as she continues that backward walk. "Stop following me. And watch where you're going or you're going to trip."

"See! I'm already such a devoted agent there's nothing I wouldn't risk for you!"

This makes me unreasonably angry. She's joking around like we're old friends rather than exes with a history so convoluted that I can only see red when I look at her. "You are not and will never be my agent. We're done here."

I want to shut my eyes. I want to close her out and pretend she's not right here beside me—because this moment, it's going to set me back again. Just the sight of her rips open old wounds that I felt would never heal in the first place. I'm having flashbacks of Nora poking me in the cheek to get me to smile. Nora's nervous wide eyes as she sneaks with me into our college rec center after hours to skinny dip in the pool. Nora's soft smile as she sits beside me in class frantically writing notes and I draw an invisible heart over and over on the top of her thigh.

When I enter the parking lot and click the key fob to my electric SUV, the headlights blink and the door handles pop out. Nora notes which vehicle is mine and shuffles ahead of me to plaster her back against the door—breathing heavily. Why does she have to be so damn pretty still? "I'm not moving until you hear me out."

"Move or I will move you. This is your only warning." *Don't look in her eyes.*

She tips her brows. "Not to taunt you, but I think you might be underestimating my impressive five-seven height and sheer determination to remain rooted until you—"

I set my hands on her waist, refuse to acknowledge the way she smells like a sweet tropical pink drink, and lift her off the ground, setting her down away from my door. *Obstacle removed.*

She gasps in outrage.

"I warned you." I open my door and the audiobook I was listening to resumes playing at max volume. It's something the learning specialist told me to try—apparently listening to an audiobook is an easier way for my brain to comprehend information. I thought I'd give it a try with a fantasy series that everyone loved in high school, whereas I hated it because it was so difficult to read. I wanted to see what I was missing out on. But now, hearing it blast over the speaker with Nora right beside me makes me feel like I'm standing naked in a hurricane.

I reach in quickly and click the control on my steering wheel, turning the volume all the way down. Once it's silent again, Nora's voice cuts through my cloud of anger.

"Derek . . . *please*." Her tone is so soft and pleading. I don't want to feel anything for her. No sympathy. No heart tugs. Nothing.

But dammit, I do. Because this is Nora. *My* Nora. And this is why I told myself not to look in her eyes, because then I'll see everything we once were reflected in them. I'll see that she's more gut-wrenchingly beautiful than ever, and no matter what she does or where she goes, in my heart she'll always be mine. And I hate her for it.

I shut the truck door again and face her fully, crossing my arms and wishing I had an actual shield to cover me. Her eyes drop briefly to my tattoos, and she studies them. I'm sure it's startling to see me with them since I didn't have a single tattoo when I knew her. There's a lot about me that's changed since we were together.

She pulls her gaze up to meet mine, and determination flares in her eyes. "I'm not sure . . . that is . . . I want to—" She licks her lips and I let her flounder. She deserves to drown in awkwardness. "It's been a while since we've seen each other."

"Really? Because it feels like just yesterday you were telling me you didn't want me in your life anymore."

She winces. "Do you want to talk about what happened back then?"

I couldn't want something less. "If you want to talk, I'd rather hear how long you've known."

"About the birds and the bees? My mom gave me the talk when I was—"

I shut my eyes and she cuts off. Deflecting with humor is so classically Nora it hurts. "We haven't talked in eight years and you're making jokes?"

Her smile falls. "You're right," she says in a different, more reasonable, genuine tone. "No more argle-bargle. You're asking how long I've known that I work for the same agency that represents you?"

I give a curt nod.

"Well . . . I've known since I first started here about two years ago. But I didn't realize it until after I already had the job and was sitting in on a meeting where agents were discussing their athletes. Your name came up—and I've heard about you from time to time since then but never in a lot of detail."

My blood boils. "And you didn't think it would be appropriate to tell me? You just thought it would be more fun to surprise me randomly one day instead? And what the hell is argle-bargle?" I really don't want to ask that last question, but it'll eat at me if I don't.

Nora looks a little too eager to answer. "It means 'copious but meaningless talk or writing.' My mom got me a Weird Word of the Day calendar and *argle-bargle* is today's word. I didn't think I'd get a chance to use it, but . . ."

When I shift toward my truck again, Nora's eyes widen frantically. "Wait, Derek—I'm sorry. I'm handling this so wrong. I wasn't sure what to do or if it would matter to you. For all I knew you and Bill were going to happily live out the rest of your lives together. I didn't rule out matching tattoos! And I had zero idea they were going to pair me with you until this morning—I promise you I would have given you a heads-up if I'd had one myself. And no one in the office knows about our history, I swear. It's not been some big joke on my end."

I believe her. I think that's what sucks the most—I fully buy that she didn't think our proximity to each other would matter one shit. A flashback pierces my memory of the last time I saw her when she was standing in the hallway outside my apartment shoving a box of my stuff into my arms out of the blue. *"I'm so sorry, Derek. I thought*

I could do this with you, but I can't. I want to break up. You're going your way and . . . I can't go with you. This never should have happened between us. It was a mistake." The cold way she looked at me with eyes shuttered and heart closed—I'd rather have been physically stabbed.

I wanted to spend my life with Nora, and it turns out I was only ever a brief distraction for her.

All these years of trying to forget her, trying to get over her and not compare every woman I meet against her, and here she is . . . asking to be my agent. Asking to step right back into my life as if nothing of significance ever happened.

"I can't, Nora. It won't work for me."

Her golden-green eyes blink up at me. "I, however, am determined for it to work. You just haven't given me a chance to prove that I can be the best agent you've ever had. And I know we have history between us, but—"

"I took your virginity," I say bluntly, and watch as red splotches rise on her cheekbones. "In your dorm room on your pink comforter. You cried after and told me that having sex with me was going to be your new favorite hobby." She opens her mouth and closes it when I press on. "I know that you have a pattern of freckles on your right ass cheek that looks like the Big Dipper. And that you make a soft little noise right before you—"

"Okay, I get it," she says, her face the color of a ripe strawberry.

I shake my head firmly and edge a little closer, crowding her. I lower my voice. "No, Nora. I don't think you do. Because I'm trying to tell you that there are some things you can't look past or forget, and you don't seem to be listening."

Like wanting to marry her because I was so in love with her it physically hurt, only for her to break up with me before I ever got the chance. I can't forget that, and I can't look past it. Especially not right now when my career is on the rocks. She would be the physical manifestation of all I've lost and all I could lose at the same time.

"Believe me, I know all of this," Nora says, putting her hand on my door to keep me from opening it with a raw grit in her voice that wasn't there a moment ago. It's a complete contradiction to her watermelon-pink nail polish—but a quick flashback of the deeply competitive Nora I knew and loved. "But I'm willing to put it all behind us. Actually, I have put it all behind us because it was years ago. And I know you have too, judging by all the . . ." She lets that sentence dangle and doesn't bother finishing it. I want her to. I need to know what she was going to say and why she thinks she has the right to tell me what I'm over.

You don't know anything about it, Nora.

Unspoken words and old pent-up frustrations beg me to let it all out right here in this parking lot. I never thought I'd see this woman again. Never thought I'd have the chance to tell her how badly she wrecked me. But here she is . . . begging me to let her be my agent like our time together left me with nothing but a paper cut.

I keep my arms firmly set across my chest and stare at her.

She doesn't waver under my glare. "Maybe it would help if I told you some of my ideas to help grow your image over the next year?"

"No."

She crinkles her nose. "I could tell you how I think you're missing out on bigger endorsement opportunities?"

"No."

"A joke, then? A song and dance? Do you need your truck washed and cleaned?"

I'm already rolling my eyes and wrenching my door open because I'm not doing this. It's time for me to go. But when I feel warm fingers close over my bicep, I freeze. My gaze drops to her pink fingernails, gently holding on to my arm. I feel burned.

When she sees me staring at our point of contact, she pulls her hand away. "Don't go yet," she says softly. "I'm just asking for a chance that I know I don't deserve, Derek. *Please*. I get that you don't want to be friends, and that's fine. I'm only asking for one chance to show you that I'm a good agent. That I could even be a *great* agent for you, because you have a lot of obstacles coming at you in the next few months and I'm confident that you're going to hurdle all of them effortlessly. I believe in you and I'm asking for you to believe in me too."

What a touching speech.

It can go to hell.

Now my anger is mounting to something palpable. Her words did not move me to sympathy. They moved me from anger straight into wanting revenge, because she seriously has no idea how much she wrecked me.

I feel like making her life as miserable as she made mine just so she'll finally understand. After she broke up with me, I couldn't eat, I couldn't sleep, I couldn't focus for weeks. The one person I thought loved me for who I was and not for the sport I played or my fame on the horizon broke up with me on a random Tuesday without warning or so much as a guilty excuse. It was torture, and I've just decided to give her a little taste of it.

I angle toward Nora with a look in my eyes that should serve as a warning for what's ahead. "Fine," I say, taking a small step closer to her. She doesn't waver or retreat. "You want a shot, rookie? I'll give you a shot. But that's all you get. I won't hesitate to dissolve our contract at any point if I'm unhappy with your representation. And I'll make damn sure that clause is added to the contract."

"Really?" Her eyes are bright and brimming with naïve hope. Those same eyes I used to get lost in. I refuse to let that happen again. "Great. Perfect! Thank you! You're not going to regret this, Derek."

She's right. I won't regret it one bit. But she sure as hell will, because I plan on making Nora's career a nightmare until either she quits or I fire her—whichever happens first.

"Do you want to go back inside and sign the papers now?" she asks.

"Today's not good for me. We can meet tomorrow," I say, purely because I feel like being a dick. "And if we're going to work together, we're going to lay down some rules first. Because over it or not—we have a history. A physical history. And I want clear parameters for how we can and cannot interact in a working relationship."

Nora closes her eyes and at first, I think it's because I've hurt her feelings. But then I remember this is Nora I'm talking to and she's simply having to breathe through her surge of excitement. Her pupils are dilated when her eyes open again. "Derek—after this, I will stop asking you for things—but please . . . I'm begging you. Will you let me color-code the rules?"

5

Nora

I step back into the office building and immediately encounter the last person in the world I want to see right now: Marty Vallar. The man seems as if he's had fire ants in his underwear since I met him judging by the scowl he always gives me. He's one of those midforties men who think feminism is a dirty word only attributed to man-haters. I pity him his sad, narrow mind.

"Excuse me, Marty," I say, attempting to step around him.

"Meeting not go well?" he asks, stepping in front of me so I can't pass. "I saw Pender storm out of here like you bit him. I thought maybe he wasn't too keen on the idea of having a . . . newbie as an agent."

Newbie is not what he was going to say.

"Working on your detective skills, Marty? Impressive. I'll keep you in mind for my next murder mystery dinner party." In actuality, I know that Marty pays attention to every move I make at all times. Not because he's attracted to me or anything . . . but because he genuinely hates that I'm here and wants to see me gone.

There's not a single agency meeting where he doesn't try to under-

mine one of my suggested marketing strategies or make a crack
about something I've said, trying to lure me into a public argument
that will make me look hotheaded and irrational. But I don't take the
bait because my stats always speak for themselves. My ideas are
good—and he's threatened by them. By me.

So every day that I step into this office, I remind myself not to
waste my mental energy on a man who has his head so far up his own
butt he can't even see that his tactics are outdated. That his marketing ideas are unoriginal. And that if he doesn't learn to adapt his
thinking to a more progressive approach, I'm going to run him out
of business. He thinks he hates me because I'm a woman in a world
that supposedly belongs to men, but why he should really hate me is
because I'm smarter than him and will smile while I steal his clients.

"Well, anyway," he says with an annoying fake chuckle. "I only
came out here to say that if things aren't going well with Pender, I'll
be happy to take him on for you. Save you the embarrassment of not
knowing what you're talking about in front of him."

Am I seething inside at the way he condescends to me? Yes. Have
I learned by now that it's more fun to prove someone wrong by succeeding than by blowing smoke in a hallway? Also yes. But will I
absolutely mess with him because it's the only joy I find in this situation? Again, a resounding yes.

I put my hand over my heart. "Thanks for that, Marty. But I
think I'm all good since he already agreed to sign with me, and we
were only outside to look at his cool electric SUV. Besides, how difficult can it really be to manage one basketball player?" I laugh purposely sweet. "Enjoy the Skittles I left in the break room before
everyone eats them! They're the tropical flavor this week just to mix
things up."

As I walk past Marty I hear him begin to correct me that Derek is
a *football* player and not a *basketball* player, but then he shuts his

mouth, probably in hopes that I'll embarrass myself in front of Derek at some point. Pitiful that he would so easily believe that I don't even know the sport of the athlete I'm looking to represent. But that's Marty for you. It also makes me grateful I never told anyone that Derek and I used to date. Not that it matters much in the great scheme of things, but I know that Marty will find a way to spin it so that it seems like it does. Like I'm getting special treatment or something. If anything, our history has done nothing but hinder my chances at being Derek's agent. I'm glad I listened to my gut, even if it means keeping a secret from Nicole.

Maybe one day it won't feel like such a struggle to simply exist as a woman in my field, but today is not that day. So I'll continue to fight with all I've got to prove I belong here. Even when that means representing my ex-boyfriend.

"I got our drinks," I say, carrying two iced coffees over to the little table in the corner of the café where Derek is waiting for me. He wasn't too happy when I told him I'd order and pay for the drinks, but since he clearly would like to interact with me as little as possible, he didn't fight me on it. But now he looks for all the world like a grumpy giant sitting among Barbie furniture. He's wearing a maroon-colored hoodie that manages to make him look even more broad somehow (but sadly hides his tattoos other than the ones on his hands), black athletic shorts, and tall white socks with limited-edition Nikes from his partnership line with them. And a hat that casts an ominous shadow over his face. The man looks hot as hell even though I'd rather eat a rock than admit it.

He fidgets in his seat when he sees me, and his knee bumps the tiny table, threatening to knock it on its side. His hand splays flat against the top—steadying it. *Goodness, he's a big guy.*

"First task as your agent . . . complete," I say dramatically, while setting down the drinks.

I could almost swear his eyes flicker with amusement from under the bill of his hat. "What was that voice supposed to be?"

I take my seat across from him. "A video-game announcer."

He looks confused.

"You know? Like when you unlock the next level and the godlike voice booms over the speaker?"

He raises an eyebrow. "It's clear you don't play videogames."

"True. But why would I need to when I could organize my sock drawer by color, size, and patterns instead?"

Zero expression from Derek. He's stone cold over there. Somehow his sharp cheekbones and jawline look even sharper today.

I think he'd rather be having dental surgery right now than sitting across from me. And honestly, I'm struggling to keep the smile on my face too. It's painfully tense. And I think it will stay this way until we clear the air between us. Until I tell him the full truth of our breakup. That it had very little to do with him and everything to do with me.

"You know . . ." I take a sip of my vanilla cold brew and let the sugar throw a party in my veins. "I was reviewing your file earlier today and I noticed you haven't done a single interview or endorsement deal since your injury last season. I have a few friends in—"

He holds up his hand like he's a king and I've just been summoned to silence. "I don't want to discuss endorsement deals or my injury or anything concerning my career today. We're writing rules for conduct and then signing. That's it."

What a dingle-berry. I know we have a beef between us, but . . . this isn't at all the man I used to know. Not only is this one a mountain and covered in tattoos and has a scowl that marks his face like a bloodstain on a white shirt, but he's so snippy. The Derek I used to know was a world-class flirt. He could have charmed you naked in ten seconds with one strategic smile. I would have thought that Famous Football Player Derek would be the guy I used to know but on steroids. (Not literal steroids, though, because that shit is illegal.) The guy sitting in front of me more resembles a muscular cactus.

I swallow my retorts because I need to find peace between us if we're going to make this work. I'll let him throw his hissy fit and then we'll get down to business.

"Okay, let's write the rules, boss man."

"Don't call me *boss man*," he grumbles before finally taking a drink of his coffee.

"No? Not flashy enough. How about Your Supreme Football-ness?" I eye him with lifted brows and he just glowers. "We'll keep workshopping it."

I fish a sparkly purple pen with a giant pom-pom on the top from my purse followed by a little spiral-bound notebook that I had lying around my office (read: neatly placed in a drawer in its own organizational container and lined up against six of its multicolored pals). I fan it out in front of my face, and the breeze of it tosses my hair like I'm standing on the beach.

"Nothing excites me more than getting to crack open a fresh three-by-five top-bound memo pad." I pretend to snort its scent. Fine, I really do snort it.

Back in the day, Derek would have quipped that I'm such a nerd. And then he would have pulled me into his lap right here in the middle of the café and made out with me until my lips were bruised and there was a hickey on my neck. It's the kind of thing I would only ever do with him.

Now, he looks at me like I'm offending his senses.

I glance down, mainly to give myself somewhere else to look so he doesn't see whatever emotion I'm trying not to feel. I'm split down the middle. Part of me is still guilty over how I broke up with him in college—knowing full well that I was callous and hurtful. That part of me really wants to apologize and make amends. But the other half of me is balking at his rude reaction to me after all this time. After he brazenly moved on from me so easily back then like I was a crumb he could flick off his shirt. It seems at odds with his "I will make you pay" attitude.

I get comfy in my seat and force my gaze up to him again, willing myself to be serious when it doesn't come easily for me. "Derek. I feel like we have some things we should talk about. Namely . . . the way I broke up with you. If you're up for it, I'd like to explain everything."

"*Rule number one . . .*"

My eyebrows fly up at his sudden assertive tone.

"No discussing our history."

I gawk at him. "You can't be serious. A little communication would go a long way between us."

He smiles but it's not a nice one. It's vicious. "I'm communicating to you now that I don't give a shit about your reasons for breaking up with me because I'm over it. And if you have a problem with it, feel free to walk now."

I grit my teeth and write the rule into the notebook. "As tempting as that offer is, I think I'll make like the gum stuck on the bottom of my favorite sneakers and stick around."

"Number two . . ." snaps Derek, making me jump.

"Someone's an eager beaver."

". . . No prying into personal lives," he says, and by the way he's whipping these rules out so quickly, I imagine he has been rehearsing them all the way here. They're meant to remind me of my place—

which is not in his arms, in his bed, or in his heart. They're meant to hurt me. And suddenly, I can see into the future. I can see exactly what this list of rules is meant to accomplish.

And because I don't want him to see that he's gotten under my skin already, I point my pen at him. "That's good. Surface friends only. Gives us more time to focus our conversations on your career."

"Rule number three, no friendship." His arctic blue eyes are frosted over with hatred.

I imagine I look like I've swallowed a lemon. The more time I spend with this new Derek, the less inclined I am to be his friend anyway. I hurt him back then and he wants me to pay for my transgressions now? Fine, I can see the fairness in it. But I don't have to look like I'm paying for them while I do.

I smile sweetly the entire time I jot down his no-friendship rule. "It's good you mentioned this one because I was just about to knit us matching BFF Christmas sweaters, but now you've saved me the effort."

"Number four . . ." He holds up each of his fingers except his pinky.

"Goodness, you're taking this seriously."

Derek sits forward, eyes catching mine. A zing pulses down my back. "No kissing."

Now see, the problem is not with this rule itself. I can appreciate it. We used to kiss and although we don't plan to kiss again, it makes sense to put it on the list because if I remember correctly, we used to do that particular activity quite well and as often as possible. The problem is with the challenging glint in Derek's eyes as he delivers it. This glint implies that I want to kiss him but he's going to withhold his gorgeous brooding mouth from me as torture. And although I might have imagined his lips on mine again at one point, not anymore. Not after the way he's treating me today. Not after realizing he's grown into an oversized baby.

And that's why I sit forward too—until we're a few inches apart and I can feel his knee press into mine. "Fantastic rule. But I'd like to take it a step further." I hold his sharp gaze for one beat before looking down and speaking as I write. "Rule number five, no unnecessary touching. Because, you know, we wouldn't want anyone"—I add special emphasis on that word so he knows I'm meaning him—"getting their emotional wires crossed at any point." I remove my knee for extra emphasis.

His jaw tics and then I see it . . . the slightest tug in the corner of his mouth. He might as well have painted the words *Game On* across the wall. It almost excites me because challenging each other was what we enjoyed most. We played little games all the time. But this feels different because it's not for fun or for the sake of flirting. It's laced with cruelty—I can taste it.

"Just so we're both on the same page, could you expound on what constitutes unnecessary?" He pauses and his eyes drop to my mouth for a split second—inspiration sparking in his eyes before they slide back up to mine. "For instance, let's say you're walking, and I can tell you're about to step on a snake, should I reach out and pull you away or leave you to the snake?"

I set down my pom-pom pen because I take all snake queries very seriously and he knows this about me. "That should be filed under *necessary touching.* As in, me about to step on a snake necessitates you picking me up and allowing me to stand on your freakishly large shoulders until I can grab hold of a nearby tree branch and climb it all the way up into the clouds where I will never have to see that damn snake ever again. Got it?"

"Got it."

He waits until my pen is once again in hand before dropping

his voice like dark silk. "Now let's say we're in an important meeting with the GM and I look over and notice that you have some chocolate on your mouth left over from the candy you snuck off his desk on the way in. Not wanting you to feel embarrassed from said chocolate, I lean over and drag my thumb across your bottom lip, cleaning off the chocolate and then licking it off my thumb." He pauses long enough for that scenario to permeate my brain. And permeate it does. "Would that be considered necessary or unnecessary contact?"

A vivid fantasy of the whole thing plays out in my head. I imagine what his callused fingers would feel like dragging across my lips. And then staring at me the entire time he licks the chocolate off his own thumb as a blatant reminder of late nights in his apartment, tangled up in sheets and blocking out the world for as long as possible.

I don't even realize my fingers are gripping my pen so hard it's in danger of shattering until Derek reaches over and removes it from my grasp, laying it gently on the table. He sits back with a grin.

It's entirely possible that it's been too long since I've been touched by a man and that's why my body is breaking out in a hot flush all of a sudden. It has nothing to do with Derek and everything to do with basic biology. Unfortunately, because of my body's sabotage, Derek is winning whatever random competition we've started. Who can rile the other person the most? Who can show the most indifference? I don't even know now. But judging by my painful heartbeat and the goosebumps lining my arms, I'm losing.

"Unnecessary!" I practically shout like I'm throwing down the gavel along with a guilty sentence in a court of law. I retrieve my pen once again. "Rule number six . . . no flirting."

His eyes narrow slightly with wicked amusement, but he doesn't smile. "Rule number seven, always wear pants in meetings."

"Okay, buddy, now look! I'm obviously going to wear pants in meetings. What kind of a hooligan do you think I am?"

He shrugs, looking smug. "As my memory serves, you used to live pantsless as much as possible."

"That's when I was at home! I would never consider going to a meeting in my underwear. Comfy though it may be." Apparently, Derek doesn't just remember me, he *remember-remembers* me.

He shrugs like I'm a nudist who lives a reckless, pants-free life and he's just at the mercy of my naked whims.

"Fine! I'll write it down. But you better believe that rule number eight is going to be *Derek must always wear a shirt*. So, ha!"

"Just a shirt? Okay, I always thought the Winnie-the-Pooh wasn't an attractive look but if you're okay with it . . ."

"Rule number nine." I state with magnificent authority. "Wear all clothing at all times in all places. No exposed skin."

And on and on this list goes. We lob insults in the form of rules back and forth like a Wimbledon tennis match. I'm not sure exactly what the heck this list is supposed to be—all I know is what it winds up as: a cathartic breakup. When I ended it back then, I said what I needed to say, and Derek never fought me on it. If anything, his eyes only shuttered before he turned his back and walked away from us without a second thought. Even though I had no right to—I expected him to fight for me. To at least question me. He never did.

But today . . . today we went one by one through every perk our relationship ever had and ruthlessly slashed them all. *No sleeping in the same bed. No watching TV together. No sharing the bill. No riding in the same car. No holding hands.*

And by the time we finish the list on number twenty, our eyes are feral, our breathing heavy, and I know exactly where Derek stands. *He hates me.* It perplexes me, even as the feeling is quickly becoming mutual.

He pushes his chair back from the table and stands after finally (unhappily) signing the contract. "I think that covers it."

I watch Derek snatch up his keys and throw his sunglasses on his face before walking with sure strides out of the coffee shop—not once looking back at me.

After all of this, my only question is: Will he let me do my job now that he got that out of his system?

And in tiny invisible ink subtext scribbled on the bottom corner of my heart: I miss my Derek.

6

Derek

I need a drink. But not the kind anyone would expect me to go for.

I toss my keys onto my kitchen counter and bypass the beer that's been sitting in my fridge for months only to turn on my electric kettle instead. I started drinking a lot of chamomile tea after surgery to help me sleep, and somehow, I've become addicted. Throw some honey in that shit and feel the warmth as it heats you from the inside out. It's good on a lonely night or when I feel the weight of the world pressing in on me.

After the water boils, I submerge the tea bag to let it steep, and while I wait, I look around my big empty house. It's enormous. Somehow growing in vastness by the day. I bought it a few years ago so I could throw big parties and have more than enough room. And yeah, it was perfect for that. But when it's empty, it's really freaking empty. The thing is, I don't miss the parties at all. This silence, however, is starting to wear on me.

Pulling out my phone, I dial my mom, which is how I know I'm really in a low spot.

"Derek! This is a pleasant surprise. Everything okay?" Her soft voice is colored with concern. In times like this, I have to block out memories of our loud fights in the kitchen when she would tell me how disappointed she was about my grades after looking at my report card. *Why can't you just apply yourself like Ginny?* Where was this concern for me back then when I was telling her school wasn't as easy for me as it was for my sister—and she'd roll her eyes. Maybe that's why I haven't told my parents yet about my recent diagnosis. There's still a wound that hasn't healed, and I'm not ready for my parents to comment on it in any way.

I hop up on the counter, take a drink of my tea, and lie to my mom. "Yeah. Everything's good."

On the way home, I turned on a sports talk radio show and wouldn't you know it, those two shitheads Glenn and Brenn or Jim and Jam . . . I don't care other than they were spouting off once again about how a guy my age might not be able to come back from the injury I sustained. *Compound fracture to the ankle is a career death sentence.*

It doesn't help that our team's medical personnel have been keeping the media informed of my recovery only in the most basic of regards: "We're optimistic he will have a full recovery and be ready by the time the season starts. We'll evaluate him further when he returns to the facilities."

But they're not exactly saying anything to help put these guys' faith in me again. They predict I'll play game one like a rusty old wheel. *It's sad to see greats like Pender fall, but in the end, it's gotta happen to make room for the new generation like Abbot.* I haven't even had the chance to play yet and they've already got me with one foot out the damn door. *My* door. The Sharks are *my* team full of *my* brothers and they are trying to hand my position over to Abbot on a silver platter.

It's not Abbot's fault, though. He's a good guy and a great athlete.

The problem is, I used to let negative talk fuel my fire. Right out of surgery, I did everything I could to rehab correctly and efficiently. I thought my fans were on my side, and that helped. But over the months since then, I've seen how quickly an entire fan base can turn and grow hearts in their eyes for another player.

Abbot isn't out to get me or anything, but he sure isn't hiding away either. On his social media, the kid's been posting daily workout videos showing how he's staying in shape in the offseason and doing live sessions so his fans can train with him. Lots of other shit like that too.

I always knew my days on the field were numbered, but now it's getting real. I imagined that I'd be married with maybe a kid or two when retirement came for me. I'd be ready for the next chapter. Right now—I'm not even close to ready. I'm terrified.

"You sure you're okay? You sound off," my mom says, pulling me out of my miserable thoughts.

I clear my throat and smile like she can see it through the line. "Yep. All good. Just wanted to see what's up with you and Dad." And to hear my mom's voice because there's lots of books out there to help you cope with over-the-top toxic parents, but few that help you navigate a complicated relationship with parents you very much love but still carry some childhood hurt from.

"Nothing much going on here!" my dad chimes in. Apparently, they're old enough now to have entered the stealth speakerphone era. "We had lunch with your sister yesterday. She's thriving at the new hospital."

"I'd expect nothing less from Ginny." My sister really is great. I don't have anything against her—and we stay in contact for the most part. I just hate that her name is often a reminder of my shortcomings. Lately, I've been wondering if I get cut from the team, if my parents will look at me again like they used to. *Disappointment.*

Frustration. Or have I finally proved myself enough to them that we'll continue on like normal.

This call is doing the opposite of what I hoped it would do. So we talk for a few more minutes about nothing in particular and I hang up and set my phone down.

The house is so silent that the click of my phone case against the marble counter echoes like a penny dropped down a well. I already worked out today—but I'm considering going out to my home gym and doing some extra rehab exercises. Mainly because there's nothing to do and I don't feel like seeing friends. But instead of going right to the gym, I lie back on the counter and stare up at the ceiling and let my thoughts travel to the one place I shouldn't.

Nora Mackenzie.

I smile, realizing I know the perfect way to fill my time and the silence.

7

Nora

I'm just getting home from the office after having scanned all the contract papers and digitized them post-atrocious-coffee-meeting with Derek. Of course Marty dropped by my door with his favorite man-minion, Joe, to talk down to me. *Be careful, Mac. You wouldn't want Pender to see you frowning like that. I'd keep that smile up if I were you, sweetheart.*

Right, because my beauty is what got me where I am. Because a woman is only as good as her smile. But here's the thing, I refuse to let these absolute corn nuts take the wonder out of smiling for me. To taint it. If I want to smile every damn second of my life, I will. If I wake up tomorrow and decide to never show my pearly whites again, it's my choice. But what I won't do is be manipulated one way or the other. So I just pretended to get a call and ignored them until they walked away.

It was an exhausting day, but now I'm home in the comfort of my lovely little abode and I sigh with relief as I unzip my jeans and drop them the second I step through the front door. They hit the ground with a satisfying *thunk*. I shed my hot pink blazer next and then scoop them both up and deposit them in my laundry hamper (sorting by color because I like to have fun in my off time).

Now I'm alone in my apartment with my polar bear undies and *Let's Go Girls* graphic T-shirt and everything is right with the world. I refuse to allow Derek's comment about my pantslessness to permeate my brain, because despite what he thinks, he doesn't know me anymore. Like everyone else, he sees the flashy colors and my pinky-pink lipstick smile, and he underestimates me and what I've gone through to get to this place in my career.

I decide to call the one person who truly knows and understands: my mom. I wait for the line to connect while removing a pint of ice cream from the fridge along with a box of cereal from the pantry so I can make my ultimate feel-better dish: a scoop of vanilla ice cream with a dash of cinnamon sugar squares on top. I should eat dinner first, but honestly, my day was such an emotional roller coaster that I doubt even the strictest of nutritionists would blame me for counting this as my meal.

The line connects just as I'm hopping my polar bear butt up onto the counter. (No one judge me, I live alone so there's no one here to complain about the countertop butt germs that I'll most certainly sanitize away before bed.)

"Hi, Mom."

"Hey, sweetie pie!" Mom says, brightly toned and out of breath.

I shove the cold spoonful of ice cream and crunchy cereal into my mouth. "Are you answering my call in your exercise class again?" I ask, my words littered with crumbs.

The instructor in the background sounds over a grainy microphone. "And kick, kick, and step, step! Faster this time!"

"Yes—but I'm still doing the moves."

I smile down into my bowl of ice cream, imagining my mom holding her phone to her ear while attempting a high kick in a

YMCA exercise class. Ever since I was little my mom has been throwing herself into every group activity under the sun. *I don't need a man to enjoy my life! That's why community activities were invented, sweets.*

She's one of those infectious souls you can't help but come to life around. Honestly, I have no idea how she's still single. I'm starting to believe it's because she genuinely prefers it. She's had a few men come and go from her life after I hit my teenage years—but they were never anything serious. Just someone fun to spend time with now and then, but it's always been very clear that Mom was the one holding them at arm's length.

Because when a man doesn't encourage you to reach for the stars, Nora Bug, he's putting you in a glass jar to contain your light. We don't have to settle for air through holes poked in the top of a lid. We get to become stars ourselves is what she'd say to me with a wink after I asked why she and so-and-so broke up.

My mom has had many different career seasons in her life. Times of really going for something and times of working for my school simply so she could be home with me in the afternoons. But one thing is for certain, she's approached each of her careers with equal drive and passion. She's shown me that every season of life is important and that no one path is more meaningful than another.

"Anything specific you want to talk about?" she asks, panting for air.

"Uh . . . let's see . . . was there something I wanted to talk about? Oh yeah—just one. *I signed my first client today!*"

My mom squeals with delight just like I knew she would. She's always been my biggest champion—never once letting on that she resented the load that single parenting put on her. We couldn't count on my dad to be a dad, but my mom was parent enough for both of them.

The instructor reprimands her in the background and tells her she has to leave the class if she wants to talk on the phone. She calls him a fuddy-duddy and then walks out of the class.

"Mom! Don't leave. I can talk to you about it later."

"Oh please. And pass up an opportunity to miss out on high kicks? No thank you. This way I still get my postclass donut but can also move and sit down on the toilet tomorrow without screaming in pain. Now, back to your client—would I have heard of him or her?"

Hmm. *He was pretty much all I ever talked about senior year of college. He came home with me for Christmas and helped you make waffles. He sent you flowers on your birthday, and oh, yeah, took your daughter's virginity in her college dorm room* (not that my mom knows that last part, but Derek brought it up and now it's on a constant loop in my mind).

"Yep," I squeak. "You might have. It's . . . Derek . . . Pender."

"Oh."

"Yeah."

"That's . . ."

"Uh-huh."

"And you haven't . . . ?" *Seen him since you broke up* is what she doesn't have to voice.

"Correct."

We both marinate in this for a second. And to be honest, I think it's the first time I've really let myself sink into the painful parts of it since seeing him again yesterday. I looked in his eyes. And I watched those eyes shutter when they looked at me.

My heart hurts.

"It wasn't my idea," I tell my mom. "The agency paired us together last minute. They obviously don't know our history and I plan to keep it that way as long as possible, so things don't get weird." Or weirder . . .

"And how did it go? How did Derek act when he saw you again?"

"Umm . . . it could have gone better." I pause, thinking of the frown between his brows. He never used to frown at me. "I just can't stop thinking of how ironic it is that I ended it with him to pursue my career, and now my career is hinging on him."

"It's not hinging on him, Nora. Your career will go forward even without him. But through him might be the easiest way to make it happen sooner. So . . . you'll just have to decide what this new working relationship is worth to you."

More than I want to admit—but maybe not for career advancement reasons.

Wait, no!

I'm in this with Derek for career advancement only.

"I'll figure out a way to make it work."

"I know you will. You always do, sugar peach!" Somehow my mom rarely calls me the same pet name twice. "I have complete faith in you and will show up to your cheering section with a bedazzled sign any time you need me."

I smile because I know she's not kidding. Would probably appear outside my office building like that if I asked her to. Because that's the thing about my mom—she's supportive. Even back in the eighth grade when on a whim I told her I wanted to cut off my long hair I had spent years growing, she didn't ask me a thousand questions and make sure I knew what I was doing. She simply made an appointment and let me chop it to my chin. Her motto has always been to encourage me to listen to my inner voice. To trust myself and learn from my choices as I go.

And so, when out of the blue I broke up with my college boyfriend who I had been hopelessly in love with, she didn't question me or my logic. She said: *Come home this weekend and let's eat ice cream and watch movies and you can tell me about it.*

Ugh, why does my brain continue to run toward Derek every chance it gets. It needs to be put on a leash.

"While I've got you," my mom starts, giving me the distraction I need. "I want to give you a heads-up about some news I just saw on Facebook."

"Why do you still get on Facebook?"

"I love the drama. Especially when the neighborhood gets their panties in a wad about whose dog pooped in whose yard. Gets really juicy . . . the gossip, not the poop."

"That was both disgusting and hilarious. I loved it."

"Good, because you might not like the next bit." She pauses, and I tense. "Your dad is getting married again."

My lungs deflate in a rush.

The subject of my dad is a tricky one. My parents were never a couple, and so in between his visits, I started keeping journals full of stats on teams and players just so I could wow my sports-loving dad over on his next visit, and then maybe . . . just maybe he'd want to spend even more time with me. (And then fall in love with my mom and we'd all live happily ever after like in the Disney movies.)

It worked in some seasons of my life, and in others it didn't. And the older I got the more I realized it wasn't that my dad wasn't choosing my mom—it was my mom who didn't choose my dad because she had good standards, and god love him, my dad would never meet them.

But the reward of his attention was enough that it kept me hungry to learn everything I could about sports. And then when I was ten, my dad married someone—not my mom, the woman he got pregnant in college and never bothered trying to deserve. Someone with a daughter of her own that he seemed to completely trade me and my mom for.

But I let go of that anger toward him a long time ago, because if anything, I can thank my dear ole dad for instilling in me a passion and a dream. I rarely talk to him these days, but somewhere along the line of trying to impress him, I truly fell in love with sports. I'll always feel thankful to him for that at least.

I drop my spoon into my quickly melting bowl of ice cream and set it aside. "Of course he is! He probably heard I haven't had a good excuse to wear my wedding cocktail dress in a while," I say with a fake laugh that I really hope is convincing.

"That's your dad, always so conscious of your closet!"

We chuckle. Both of us knowing the other is full of shit.

My smile falls. "You know, I wouldn't care that it's his third marriage if I felt like he was going to put some effort into this one. But he's not—we both know it. It feels like he'll never grow up. Never put anyone before himself."

I dread the uncomfortable phone call on my horizon where he expects me to be happy for him and his new soon-to-be wife. I dream of not answering and letting it go to voicemail. But in the back of my head, I know I never will. Because no matter how hard I try to resist it, I'll always be the girl hoping this is the time he decides to stick around in my life instead of trading me out for a new family—only circling back around again when the other one fizzles out.

My chest constricts with a memory of the last time I put misplaced faith in my dad, only for him to stand me up at dinner. The night before the college exam I failed. The exam I put off studying for so I could go on a vacation with Derek to visit his parents—and then should have spent the night I was home cramming for the test instead of agreeing to meet my dad for dinner an hour and a half away from school because he *missed me so much and wanted to see me.* Only to sit at that damn restaurant for an hour before finally leaving without so much as a returned text or call from my dad. As I found out later, he was swept up in the moment and decided to propose to his girlfriend that very night—which is why he forgot about our dinner. I failed the test and a few days later I broke up with my boyfriend.

That was the day I realized no one would care about me as much as I cared about myself—and I needed to fight for my dreams because no one else would.

"I agree," my mom says. "And . . . I'm sorry he's your dad, Nora. I'm sorry you don't have someone who invests in your life and stays put like you deserve."

My mom has always partly blamed herself for conceiving me with my dad. Which is infuriating because she's been present in my life enough for a mom and a dad.

"I'm not sorry one bit. He ignited my love of sports and gave me my fabulous auburn hair. Just imagine how weird I would have turned out as a blonde or something. I love you, Mom, and you continue to reign supreme in my life. Just under Dolly Parton."

"It's because of her bedazzled outfits, isn't it?"

"Her boobs actually. I'd give anything to have a pair of glorious melons like hers."

My mom laughs. "Maybe one day after you make tons of money from endorsement deals with your ex-boyfriend-slash-client."

After a few more unholy conversational turns, we hang up so my mom can return to her class. I go settle onto my couch and turn on *The Great British Bake Off* for background noise while I review Derek's contracts and deals because I don't like to be alone with my thoughts and therapy is too expensive. British people kindly competing in a low-stakes baking competition to win a plate is the next best thing. I just need something to drown out the thought of my dad getting married again. And that's why I'm a little too excited when I hear my phone ringing.

"Hello?" I ask even though I don't recognize the number. It might be a telemarketer, but honestly, I'm ready to talk about my car's extended warranty if it means I don't have to sit here and think about the sadness creeping into my chest after that conversation with my mom.

"Nora, it's me."

There's only one man who still calls me by that name, and I was not expecting to hear from him so quickly. Unjustified butterflies surge at the sound of his rumbly voice on the other end of my phone, and I don't quite know what to make of that. Shouldn't I hate the sound of his voice after everything? Must be muscle memory.

"Hi, me. It's nice to meet you." I hop up from the couch and run back to my room so I can dig through my dirty clothes and find my pants again. Probably ridiculous, but somehow, I feel like he'll hear it in my voice that I'm mostly naked and then claim I'm breaking a rule.

"That was a terrible dad joke."

"No such thing." I shimmy into my jeans and pull up the zipper.

"Did I give you enough time to get your pants back on before asking if you're wearing any?" His tone is not teasing or playful. It's smug.

My jaw drops but I'm careful not to make any sounds that indicate my surprise. "We can file that one under inappropriate questions. And I've had my pants on the whole time, thank you very much," I lie through my teeth.

"I heard the zipper."

Damn.

"What can I do you for, client of mine?" I ask extra chipper, more than ready to change the subject.

His voice is low and muffled when he speaks, sounding like he's lying down. "You can start by being fifty percent less happy all the time."

"Got it. Writing it down. Fifty percent . . . less . . . happy," I say like I'm taking studious notes. "And now I'm wadding it up and throwing it in the garbage where it belongs. Anything actually productive I can help you with?"

He sighs deeply on the other end and for some reason, that has me grinning. "Well . . . I was calling because . . . I need you."

There's a deafening silence after those words and my body pulls taut. If I were a cat, each of the hairs on the back of my neck would be standing at attention. "You . . . ?"

"Sorry. I choked on some water and had to mute you for a second so I could cough." He clears his throat one more time. "I need you to come to my house and help me with something. It's important."

My shoulders droop. With relief! And no other reason. Definitely not disappointment at his wording mishap. "Oh. Sure. Yeah. Whatever you need. Should I plan to come by tomorrow around—"

"Now," he says in that sharp demanding tone I've already heard from him too much.

I look at the clock. It's already six, which means traffic going anywhere in L.A. will be horrendous right now. More than that, I just got home from work and haven't eaten dinner yet. Ice cream doesn't count because my stomach is already growling again. I'm one of those people who eat eight small meals a day (read: medium to large), and I need every single one of them or my chipper turns into a chip on my shoulder. And when I have a chip on my shoulder . . . well, no one knows it because I'm not great at expressing frustration, but still! I feel rough internally.

"Are you sure it can't wait until tomorrow?"

He barely waits for me to finish speaking before he replies curtly. "Are you my agent or not?"

I blink and grip the phone tighter. "Yes. You know I am."

"Then you'll have to act like it. I need my agent to be available to me 24/7. If that's too difficult for you . . ." I hear the arrogant smile in his voice and instinctively know that this entire agreement is one big trap. I see it now for what it is. He's going to be as annoying as possible until I quit. Maybe he never really planned to let me be his agent in the first place. I can feel it in my cheery little bones that this is going to be our next competition. *Who can outlast the other person.*

"Of course that's not an issue. I was only thinking of how tired you might be at the end of the day. I will always keep my client's very best interests at heart." And make him eat crap when I'm the best damn agent he's ever had. Which is why I'm running to my cupboard to shove my half-empty box of cereal into my oversized purse and steal my keys off the counter. "Text me your address, Dere-Bear. I'm on my way."

"Never cutesify my name again," he says and then hangs up without another word.

Well, now a new nickname pops into my head. *Derek the Dickhead.* At least this attitude of his will help me get rid of these pesky feelings I've been carrying around for him.

But first, I change his contact in my phone to Dere-Bear.

8

Nora

I pull up to Derek's gated community and check in with the very serious-looking security guard. This neighborhood is known for housing some of the most elite celebrities and athletes in L.A. It's highly guarded and no one is getting in here without special access. Which is why I'm really hoping Derek added me to the list as I hand my ID over to the guard. A few seconds later, he buzzes me through and I'm driving past the most jaw-dropping homes I've ever seen.

Not a single house in this neighborhood goes for under eight million dollars. And as I pull into Derek's curved driveway, cresting the small privacy forest planted strategically in front, I get a good look at his enormous home and know exactly how Elizabeth Bennet felt pulling up to Pemberley. There's no way he bought this thing for under twelve million.

This is where Derek lives.

Too bad he's a meanie now.

I park my car on the designated guest parking slab, and then just sit here and stare for goodness knows how long, taking it all in. The monstrosity is built in an L shape and the exterior is a mix of gray stone, charcoal siding, and black iron trim around all the windows. There's some sort of lion statue in a little pond off to the side shooting water from its mouth. And the windows are so large I wouldn't be surprised to find out they're the same size as an entire wall of my apartment. This place is easily ten thousand square feet.

Why does he live here? It seems like too much house for one man.

Or . . . oh shoot. Maybe he's not one man. Maybe he has a girlfriend right now and she lives in there with him? Maybe he has a girlfriend that he's deeply in love with and only seconds from popping the question to! Maybe I'm about to interrupt a proposal!

Maybe I need to put a lid on my imagination and set my burners to simmer.

I give myself a stern look in my car's rearview mirror. "Now, listen up, you. Derek Pender doesn't matter to you anymore. Even if you interrupt a proposal, it has no bearing on your life. He's free to marry whomever he wishes. You can do this. You are a strong, smart, sexy muffin of a woman and you can do this." One firm nod, and I'm out of the car and walking under the stone portico that leads to his front door.

I ring the doorbell and wait for him to answer. I wait, and I wait, and I wait. Finally, as I'm about to get my phone out to call him, the door opens.

"Took you forever to get here," Derek says in lieu of a greeting and gestures for me to come inside.

I don't know why I was expecting a *Downton Abbey* butler to be on the other side of that door, but I definitely wasn't prepared for the sight of Derek in athletic shorts, sweating and chest heaving under a white, sweat-soaked L.A. Sharks T-shirt. It's clinging scandalously to his body, and I can see a perfect outline of each ripped muscle on his torso. He's got tattoos under that shirt too. They're dotting his pecs—though I can't make out what they are.

I want to pause and admire the ones on his arms, but I don't dare let myself stare long enough to identify them. My gaze has already been lingering on his massive shoulders too long.

"Yes, well, all of L.A. decided it was a good night to take a drive. And the sunset was gorgeous, so they weren't wrong." *And you also didn't give me any heads-up about this impromptu drive.*

Ripping my eyes away from his body, I find his face. That's no better. It's honestly unfair that any human can look this sexy. I always thought Derek was manly and grown up back when we dated in college. This version makes past Derek look like a little baby boy in a diaper. I mean, holy crap. The forearms on him. The muscles at the base of his neck. He has crowbars for collarbones. If I lock myself out of my car, I'll just have him ram those bones of steel into my window and it'll break in an instant. But it's the sheer heftiness of his muscles that are the most shocking. Last I heard, the NFL used weights in the training facility, but I think they're lifting cars.

Everyone who's ever cracked open a magazine knows that Nathan Donelson is the most beautiful man in the NFL. He's got Clark Kent Superman looks. A pretty smile and dimples and dark eyes. But Derek Pender is attractive in a different way. He's just so . . . well, he's virile and dangerous-looking. His masculinity rolls off him in waves, making me want to bite my bottom lip and then his. It's a desire that I haven't felt in a long time.

Speaking of bottom lips, that mouth of his is turned down into a serious frown and I assume he knows I've been ogling him.

I clear my throat and hitch my thumb over my shoulder. "Your house is incredible. And I love the lion out there. Please tell me you named him Simba?"

"I haven't named it anything."

I press my hand to my heart. "How will he know you love him?"

Looking annoyed, Derek opens the door further. "Just come inside, Nora."

He turns around for me to follow and thanks to his nearly see-through sweaty shirt, it looks like he's got some tattoos on his back as well. I'm itching to ask if there's any meaning behind each of them, but I'm also trying to stay as mentally detached from the man walking in front of me as possible. I can't let myself wonder what this Derek is like. If he still hates popcorn. What his favorite show is these days? Does he still talk in his sleep?

"Everyone calls me Mac now, you know?"

"I noticed."

"But you're not going to?" It still feels so strange to be in the same room as him. A quiet energy hums under my skin. Like it's trying to resuscitate itself.

"It's tempting . . ." I can hear the smirk in his voice. "Since I remember how much you hate that nickname. But no, I don't think I will."

My steps falter a beat from my shock—thankfully, he doesn't notice. And also doesn't ask me any questions about why I'd go by that name (probably because that would be breaking rule number two). So why isn't he jumping at the opportunity to call me by a name I dislike? Especially since he seems to hate me so much.

I follow Derek's sexy back all the way through his enormous lofty foyer (omg his staircase has a glass railing, making it look like it floats to the top floor), through a gorgeous living room decorated in a Scandinavian design, which opens into a breathtaking kitchen that overlooks his backyard. And oh my gosh, don't even get me started on how incredible a backyard it is! Through the floor-to-ceiling glass doors, I see a mix of a courtyard and pool complete with white canopied cabana. Behind all of that is his completely glass-encased home gym.

"Wow," I say, doing a half spin to take it all in. "This is . . ."

"A kitchen."

I level a flat look at him. "Oh please—it's an ode to paradise and how dare you call it anything else."

"Well, it's lucky you feel that way because this is where you'll be for the next hour or so." He plucks a kitchen towel off the island and rubs it over the back of his sweaty neck and hair. The tight muscles in his arms flex under his tattoos and I tear my gaze away as quickly as possible.

I toss a hesitant glance around the kitchen island and find ingredients littering the counter. His Important Work is feeling less important by the second. "What exactly am I doing here, boss?"

"Don't call me *boss*."

"Okay, Derek-bo-berek-fe-fi-fo—"

He groans, cutting me off while running his hands over his face. He's already exasperated with me, and I've only been here five minutes. It's these small comforts in life that bring me joy. "Just don't call me anything," he says impatiently. "You're here to make fettuccine Alfredo for my date. That's all."

I laugh once. "I'm sorry, I think all those extravagant muscles of yours are pulling too much energy from your brain, because it sounds like you just told me I'm going to be your personal chef, and surely that's a mistake?"

Derek's blue eyes narrow on me and I could swear a hint of a smile sneaks into the corner of his mouth. "No mistake. I need you to make dinner. I have a date coming over later and my chef is indisposed."

Indisposed is what someone says about a person they've killed and stuffed in the basement. Did Derek kill his cook so that he could torture me in a culinary fashion?

I put one hand on my hip, trying to appear as authoritative as possible. "I truly dislike bursting your bubble, but I don't think fettuccine Alfredo is in my job description."

His eyes zero in on me, intense enough to make me waver on my feet. He takes one step closer. "Isn't it, though? My last agent made sure I knew he was always at my service whenever I needed him. And I distinctly remember you saying you have your client's best interests at heart."

He's giving Darth Vader right now—wholly committed to the Dark Side.

And okay, so technically it's true that we agents are supposed to fulfill our clients' appropriate needs, but they're never actually so rude to ask us to do this kind of work. Well, except for that time Nicole played Elsa. But again, she offered to do so because she liked her client and wanted to help. I don't particularly care for Derek these days, nor do I relish the idea of helping him get lucky on his date tonight. (Forget I added the last part.)

I inch into his space. "You're abusing your power."

He inches into mine. "Am I? You're welcome to quit at any point if the work is too difficult for you. The contract can be dissolved in no time." His smirk is antagonizing. I hate this Derek. He looks different, he sounds different, he acts different. I'm feeling lucky I didn't attach myself to him in a more permanent way back then, because clearly professional football has jammed a splintered stick right up his ass.

However, I'm not in the business of giving up. I'm the CEO of taking a lemon and squashing it between my bare hands and then adding a boatload of sugar to the juice because I don't like tart lemonade. *You're going to have to try harder than fettuccine Alfredo to scare me off, bucko.*

I angle my chin higher—so close to him I can smell his sweat and notice the new fine lines beside his eyes—and then . . . I lower my gaze until I'm staring right up into his nostrils. Nicole wears heels to get on men's eye level as an intimidation tactic. This, however, is my preferred strategy. "I'm happy to help. Where's the recipe?"

"Over beside the ingredients." His brows pull together slightly, clearly concerned that I'm staring relentlessly at his nose, but he doesn't retreat yet. But *oh* he wants to. Especially when I take it up a notch and bounce my gaze from his eyes to his nose, back and forth.

He's so tall and broad it feels like eyeing a skyscraper, but I continue staring up the gold mines of his nose, waiting for him to withdraw first. And to really put it over the top, I sniff lightly. Just once to worm my way into his head a little further.

It takes him all of two seconds to crack.

"Dammit," Derek finally mutters under his breath before sniffing and turning his head to wipe quickly at his nose and the nonexistent booger. I turn my back to him with a satisfied grin, knowing that this small win will float me for the rest of the night.

Once he's regained composure, certain there are no bats in the cave, he faces me again. "I'm going to go get a shower." *Not picturing that.* "Everything you need should be on the counter or in the fridge."

I nod and then bury my face in the recipe so I don't allow myself to remember what it was like to stand under the hot spray of water with Derek's arms around me. Kissing my shoulder and neck and then . . .

"Hey, Nora?" Derek asks, and the tenderness in his voice hooks me. For a split second, it's like the man from my past is calling out to me. I wonder if it's because he's having the same memory I was.

"Yeah?"

He licks his lips with a small frown, making me think something truly earth-shattering is coming. "Umm. Just . . . don't overcook the noodles." His smile is a snake. "I hate when they get sticky."

You're sticky, I want to say to his retreating backside.

9

Nora

I've never made fettuccine Alfredo before, but where there's a will there's a way. Because if Derek thinks I'm going to be easily driven off by a bit of cooking, he must not know me at all. I'm going to make this pasta so good—so delicious he'll weep. And then I'm going to make him sit down at the table and talk career strategy with me. He'll have no choice but to comply once I put him in this food coma. I'm also convinced he doesn't have a real date coming over. I have access to his Google Calendar now and when I just checked it, there was nothing on it that mentioned a date.

Which means it was yet another intended torture device for the night. He thinks I care if he has a date? *Ha!* Well, I . . . do, yes very much actually. But he will never get the satisfaction of knowing it.

I spend the next hour sorting ingredients, making the dough for the noodles and then cutting them out (yes, he required homemade noodles). I watch a YouTube video from a sweet angel who really holds my hand through the whole process, and by the time I'm finished with the noodles, I feel like Julia Child's offspring. Next up is the sauce and it requires browning butter in a pan with garlic. My stomach growls so loud I'm sure it'll be reported as an earthquake on the news later.

Before I know it, it's time to add the chicken broth to the pot. So after measuring out two cups of disgusting-smelling liquid into a glass measuring cup, I lift it from the counter and turn toward the stove. Unfortunately, my hand collides with the chest of the man I never heard enter the room, and I dump the entire contents of that smelly chicken stock all over my shirt and jeans. The glass cup falls to the floor and shatters into a million pieces because gravity is not slacking on the job today.

I yelp and drop to the floor to pick up the glass shards so we don't step on them, but before I can, Derek grabs me around the waist and hauls me up onto the counter. His look is pure thunder, and I think maybe this new Derek is a yeller and he's about to lay into me for making a mess in his kitchen. But then he says something unpredictable. "Please tell me you did not just try to pick up that glass with your bare hands?"

He takes my hand in his, turning it palm up and studying it closely. My awareness zeroes in on the warm, rough skin of his fingers. How big and sure and capable his hand is. I notice other things too—like how clean he smells after his shower. How I think his body-wash smells so delicious I would consider drinking it. But it's the fact that this scent is mixed with his natural smell—the smell that's so Derek—it makes my insides twist and melt.

"It was a gut reaction. I'm so sorry about the mess. I promise I'll . . ."

Derek's hand drops mine to trail down my calf, forcing my leg to extend out where he can take my bare foot in his hand (because I'm not one of those people who wear outside shoes inside). My lips part and I suck in a soft breath at the feel of his hands gliding delicately over my ankle and the arch of my foot. It's such an intimate touch.

Kind and tender. Like some part of him remembers that he used to think I was precious to him.

It takes a second for my brain to catch up, but finally, I realize what he's doing. He's making sure I'm not cut.

"I'm fine." I try to yank my foot away because I can't handle the swarm of hot dragonflies that the touch of his hands has released in my stomach. I'm not supposed to feel this way toward him anymore. My body should not react to his body.

The pinched lines between his dark brows intensify when those bright blue eyes flick to mine. "Hold still. There's glass stuck in the top of your foot."

"There is?" I look down and then the room goes woozy. There's a little trail of blood gliding down the top of my foot along with two small pieces of glass sticking out.

This is the end for me. Tell my mom I love her. Please send all my money to the Knitters of America Association because I feel like it's an underappreciated operation and I've always wanted to learn to knit.

"Hey, whoa," says Derek, stepping closer and dropping my foot to cradle the back of my head with his hand. I want to say it's romantic, but really, it's that he can see I'm seconds from passing out and doesn't want my skull to crash back against his counter and cause an even bigger mess. Then he'd have glass and pieces of bone to clean up and that sounds like too much to do before a date.

"You still pass out at the sight of blood?"

I nod because that's all I'm capable of doing at the moment.

He learned this about me the hard way in college when one of our friends took a Frisbee to the face and had a gushing bloody nose. I fainted on the spot and hit the ground. He had to take me to the ER because I had a mild concussion, and after I was discharged, he stayed awake with me all night watching *The Office* and feeding me candy.

The medical term is vasovagal syndrome, and it's a heart condition where certain stressful triggers (mostly the sight of blood for me) can make my heart rate and blood pressure drop, which causes me to faint. But what most people hear is: a condition where Nora is a drama queen. In high school, girls thought I was faking it to steal the boys' attention by fainting on my desk when Kathleen accidentally cut her hand during dissection week. It was so deep she needed stitches, and no one in her friend group forgave me that her crush—Cody—comforted me that day instead of her.

But my most recent ex-boyfriend just thought it was another *over-the-top thing* he could put on the mental tally sheet he was apparently keeping for how extra I am. *As if I can control what my heart does.* Involuntary or not, it was the final straw for him. He was playing a scrimmage basketball game with his friends and he took an elbow to the face that knocked out his front tooth and busted his lip. He ran over to me at the bleachers and showed me his mouth to assess the damage. There was *so* much blood. I fainted, and later when it was all settled, he broke up with me. He just said our relationship was too much. But what he meant was *I* was too much.

That's all right. My mom taught me early on that I would never be everyone's cup of tea, but that doesn't mean I should change my flavor for anyone either. I let that boyfriend go—I wish I could let the sting of his rejection go too.

Derek is not treating me like I'm extra, though. His eyes and hands and voice are all gentle, which honestly surprises me.

He bends slightly to catch my gaze. "Focus on me. Forget you saw anything, okay?" His eyes look so soft right now—a stark contrast to his size and tattoos. Gone is the scowl from earlier, and for this brief moment, I'm looking into the face of the man I once loved. Who once loved me. Who worried more about me when I fainted than me making an embarrassing scene for him.

I nod again and now my attention is away from the blood and slipping to the place where his big hand is woven in the back of my hair. His other is gripping my hip. Does he realize he's holding me so affectionately? Possessively? It's not the kind of touch a stranger would give. It's the kind that says *You were mine once.*

He leans over me then, his chest brushing mine as he snatches a magazine from the opposite side of the counter and then plops it in my lap. "Here. Look at this to distract yourself while I remove the glass."

I must look pale all of a sudden because his hold on me tightens again.

"Breathe, Nora," he reminds me gently before deciding I'm not safe sitting up. He takes a dish towel and folds it over until it's a nice cushion and sets it a little way behind me.

"Lie back," he commands, and really, it's fine the way those words erupt over my skin. It's fine and dandy and not at all concerning that my brain is so overloaded with ideas now I can barely think straight. I'm blaming it on the drop in my blood pressure.

I try to focus on the images in this junk mail department store magazine and block out the sensation of this man gingerly holding my foot as if I'm Cinderella. I'm aware of a tiny tinge of pain, but it's nothing compared to the waves of heat bursting up my leg from Derek's calluses lightly scraping over my skin. It's been so long since I've been tenderly touched like this. *Held.* I mean, other men have held me since Derek, but . . . not in the way Derek ever did. Part of me has always worried that no one ever will either.

"Do you need a new three-piece suit?" I ask him, trying to get my thoughts to surface from the sexual-tension-filled pit they've fallen into.

"Huh? No." He's not paying attention to me. All his focus is on the glass removal. I feel a slight tug on the top of my foot, and he hisses in through his teeth. "Did that hurt?"

I shake my head and furiously flip through pages, desperate to not think about the cuts. "How about a new blender?" My voice is a squeaky toy. "An ornate glass vase thingy? *Oh*—look at this deal: Buy three pillow shams and get the fourth a whopping ten percent off. *Wow.* How do department stores even stay in business just giving things away like that?"

His hand squeezes around my ankle.

"Just a little more. Doesn't look like it'll need stitches." He's all compassion when another tug makes me shut my eyes. "Don't pass out on me, rookie. I'm done with the removal. You can breathe."

His hand stays fixed on the outside of my thigh as he reaches down the island to open a drawer, and I wonder if he even realizes he's still holding me. He pulls out a little red-and-white first-aid kit, and pauses, frowning at the drawer. "Nora. Did you organize my junk drawer?"

"I did, yes."

He continues staring at it and I can't tell for sure but it looks like he's fighting a smile. "According to color, though?"

"Well . . . yes. It makes the most sense that way, don't you think? Because we can easily spot the color of something we're looking for but it takes more brainpower to think of what category it would belong to." I pause. "In full transparency I also organized your dish towel drawer. You were folding them the wrong way."

His gaze slides to me. "And?"

I scrunch my nose. "Aaaand . . . your container drawer."

He looks up at the ceiling and now I could swear it's because he doesn't want me to see him smile. Or maybe that's wishful thinking. He clears his throat and closes the junk drawer. "I would tell you not to organize anything in my house from now on, but it's no use, is it? You'll do it anyway."

"That's the most likely outcome, yes." Another thing that really bothered my ex-boyfriend. My brain sits happier when things are in nice little rainbow rows.

He begins doctoring up my foot with antiseptic spray and bandages. "I guess that part of you hasn't changed."

Has he been assessing me for changes and similarities to my past self just like I've been doing with him? From the way he's been treating me, I'd have suspected he never contemplated me beyond what task would be most annoying for me to complete.

"Okay, you're all set," he says, gently releasing my foot. It falls back down beside my other foot, all cold and bored now.

Derek extends his hand to help me sit up. But once I'm on his level again, he doesn't step back. He's standing closer than we've been since we broke up. In fact, he's right between my legs. Legs that suddenly burn to wrap around his waist. His chilling blue eyes meet mine and flare as that old glimmer pulls taut between us. The air shifts entirely and it's like we're two different people. Or rather, two people we once were.

I don't know who closes the distance, but somehow, we're closer and his hands find my waist, shifting me more toward the edge of the counter. My inner thighs press against his hips, and our faces hover centimeters apart.

"Nora, are you . . . seeing anyone now?" Derek whispers so quiet it's like he didn't even want me to hear it. Like if the words are silent enough they don't count.

"No." My breath trembles out of me.

Derek's gaze drops to my parted mouth, and without meaning to, I sink my teeth into my bottom lip. His expression shifts to one of agony now, and I remember the rule I just broke.

Reality suspends, the world narrows, and it's just us. Me and Derek. His face angles lower and mine lifts, removing that small gap between us. Our lips brush softly—not quite a kiss but more of a refrain. There's no pressure or commitment to it, only a gesture laced with torture. Maybe this is our next unspoken competition: Who can withstand the tension the longest?

I want to snap and let go. I want to kiss Derek—this Derek—more than I've wanted anything in a long time. It's like I'm split down the middle, with half of me running as quickly away from him as possible, and the other considering climbing him and holding on for dear life. But most startling is the realization that when I look at Derek, some corner of my heart still says *mine*. Will that ever go away? Do I want it to?

I smell him and I need more pressure. I need to taste his mouth and see if it's the same. He's always been a drug that zips through my veins and alters me. This moment is no different.

His hands flex at my waist and my thighs tense around his hips. I breathe out and he breathes in like it's what he's been waiting for. Like he's also struggling against the need to have just a little sample. But god help me if this happens . . . if we really give in to the tensions gripping us—there will be no stopping. No going back. We'll still have to work together through whatever consequences our actions bring after the dopamine wears off. And as far as I remember, Derek Pender hates me these days.

It's a sobering thought.

And just as I'm not sure who instigated this closeness, I'm not sure who pulls back first either. I just know that one second I'm drowning in desire and the next, Derek steps away as I push back farther onto the counter, putting much needed space between us. I press my hands to my overheated face and Derek watches me, taking one last look at my mouth. When his eyes meet mine again, I can tell he feels the same way I do. *This was a mistake.* And one we will never acknowledge.

Derek roughly rubs the back of his neck and then walks away. The glass crunches under his shoes. "I'll get the broom." He glances back at me and his eyes snag on my top before quickly darting away. He clears his throat. "And you can . . . borrow one of my shirts . . . if you want." He must also be feeling pretty off-kilter from that almost-kiss to be showing me any kind of consideration.

"I'll be fine until I get home. Besides, I think the smell of chicken broth suits me. Maybe it'll become my new perfume, what do you think?" I attempt a joke, but my voice still sounds thick with . . . well . . . desire.

"Up to you. But if you change your mind, my room is upstairs. Second door on the right."

"Really," I say with a small laugh. "I'm not so high-maintenance that a little chicken broth smell is—" But I cut off when I finally look down at my broth-soaked T-shirt, and I realize why he's avoiding looking at me now. The material has gone pretty much see-through against all my good bits. What a day to wear a thin rainbow print bralette. And there's definitely a nipple situation happening now too.

"On second thought, you should never shit where your gift horse lies." I slide around to the opposite side of the island.

"That's definitely not how the phrase goes."

"Close enough." I hightail it upstairs, ready to shed my soaked shirt along with all this pesky sexual tension.

10

Derek

I blow out a heavy breath as I sweep up the last of the glass. I think it's safe to say this night is not going at all how I anticipated. No—I don't have a date, but I wanted Nora to think I did because apparently I'm petty AF. Why do I even want her to feel jealous? That wasn't part of the revenge plan.

Except this whole night has backfired because Nora is Nora. I forgot she never backs down from a challenge, and instead, she bends it to her will before painting a rainbow on it. And that has me remembering her sexy rainbow print bra. *Awesome.*

Nora wasn't even miserable cooking. She hummed the entire time, and even talked to the ingredients like they were her friends—*she was sorry to cook them, but they were dying for a noble cause.* That woman brought so much life to my house in such a short period of time.

I lingered at the top of the stairs just listening to her buzz around my kitchen before realizing I was sinking into dangerous territory. That was when I took a shower. A cold shower. But then I made her drop that glass measuring cup, and that's when it all really went to hell. I had my fingers in her hair again. My hands on her thighs—her hips. The feel of her skin under my fingertips. Her mouth against my lips. I can't quite call what happened to us against that counter a kiss, but it sure wasn't not-a-kiss either. All I know is whatever it was, it was devastating. Memories, emotions, and desire all rushed me. And then quickly leveled me until I thought I was going to lose control and *really* kiss her. That can't happen. At the last second, I thankfully found my senses and enough willpower to pull away before that brush of lips became something much more.

And now, in an ironic turn of events, Nora is upstairs putting on my clothes while I'm down here doing the job I invented to annoy her. Somehow, she's taken everything I planned and flipped it on end. Typical Nora. I need to get her out of here so I can get my thoughts in order again. I'll annoy her more tomorrow—but tonight, she's got to go.

There's a knock at the front door followed by a rapid ringing of my doorbell. It's enough to prepare me for my worst nightmare.

"Shit." I turn the heat down on the stove so the pasta stays warm before going to the front door.

Through the frosted glass, Jamal's glittering eyes peer at me. "Honey, we're home! Don't leave us standing out here in the frigid cold!"

It's sixty-two degrees outside.

"Go away," I tell him and the other guys who are now pushing into view beside and above Jamal's head. Not a chance I'm letting them inside right now. They can't know that Nora is upstairs or who Nora is or even what Nora has been doing here tonight. It's all bad. It's all going to end with them roasting my ass into oblivion.

"Dude, let us in," says Nathan. "I smell something garlicky."

"We're gonna need some of it," Price adds.

I brace a hand on the door, afraid they'll push their way in some-how even though it's locked. "Not tonight. I'm busy."

"With what? You don't have a life anymore. Don't even pretend you have a woman in there." Jamal has his face pressed fully against the glass to get a clear view of my house and then the look on my face. "Wait . . . you *do* have a woman in there?" He howls an excited laugh. "Nah—we for sure need to come inside now."

He smiles a warning before his finger hovers over the doorbell. "Last chance. Either you let us in, or we get her to."

"No, you can't—"

He mashes that doorbell over and over in rapid succession.

"Assholes!" I grunt, and then flip the deadbolt to let the leeches in. "There, are you happy? You're inside. Now don't pee on the carpet or chew up any of the furniture. My date isn't here yet, so you can only stay a few minutes."

"Maybe we wouldn't have to force our way into your life like this if you would simply answer our texts or invite us over during the week." Lawrence has his offended eyes on.

Nathan thumps the back of his hand against my chest. "You've been more aloof than usual this week. What's up?"

I shrug and close the door behind them. "Just been busy train-ing."

It's not a lie. It's just also not the whole truth. Because I *have* been avoiding them. Distancing myself in case the idiots on sports talk radio are right and I'll get cut at the start of the season so Abbot can take my position. If that happens, there's no reason for these guys to keep me in their friend circle.

"Dude, you're training too much. You need to get out once in a while or else you're going to start thinking your weights are talking to you."

All four men shuffle around my foyer and living room with narrowed eyes. Their inspections are in full swing. If Nathan were using a magnifying glass, I wouldn't be surprised. I half expect Lawrence to pull out a little notebook and pencil and take down clues. His eyes drop and a smile tugs his mouth when he finds one: Nora's yellow sneakers. Lawrence nudges Nathan like he's being discreet and then nods toward the shoes.

"Yeah, I saw them too," Nathan half whispers.

I tense. "You've all had your look. Now leave me in peace."

Jamal comes to stand in front of me, right eyebrow climbing slowly toward his hairline. "The question is, Derek ole boy. Why are you so adamant we leave? Hm? What are you hiding?"

I should have shown less interest. I try to backtrack with a cocky grin. "Truth is . . . I'm worried my date is going to run away screaming when she gets a look at your ugly-ass face."

Jamal sniffs the air. He sniffs again, his nostrils flaring. He looks over his shoulder and makes eye contact with a contrite Nathan. "You smell what I smell, boys?"

Nathan nods slowly. Meaningfully. "Pasta."

"Right." Jamal puts a finger to my chest. "And we all know, pasta gives you the bloats and gas. You would never be caught dead eating pasta on a date. Therefore, you're lying. Admit it."

"Objection," I say, and Jamal and I both look to Nathan.

He crosses his arms. "Overruled."

Dammit.

"Answer the question." Jamal is too joyful about this. "And also tell us why you're trying to hide the fact that a woman who wears a size nine shoe is already here somewhere? Did you put her in the closet? I swear we raised you better than that."

"Fine." I shoot a nervous glance to the staircase, and the guys all follow my gaze. "Would y'all just keep your voices down. I don't have a date, but I want my agent to think I do."

"Why the hell would you want Bill to think you have a date?" asks Price while folding his arms and leaning against the wall.

Lawrence, who was just peeking out the front window, turns to us. "That's not Bill's car outside. You've got a new agent?"

They all four gasp, and I roll my eyes again. "Yes, okay? I have a new agent. And why are you gasping, Nathan, I already told you about her?"

"I like to be involved in group emotions," he says, like that's a normal answer.

"You guys are making way too much out of this. It's not a big deal."

Jamal holds up a finger. A point-making finger. "You texted us when you bought a new duvet for your bed. That was no big deal, and you still felt the need to mention it over dinner. The fact that you're hiding this confirms it's a very big deal. So, we're not leaving until you explain why."

"You're not gonna leave even if I tell you."

"Well, sure, but tell us anyway."

They all four cross their arms and narrow their eyes. Before I get a chance to say anything else, a female voice filters down the stairs. "Hey, Dere-Bear, don't be mad but I tidied up your bathroom drawers a little while . . . Oh! Sorry! Didn't mean to interrupt."

Well shit. Nora is standing in the middle of the stairs wearing one of my T-shirts that absolutely swallows her whole and has paired it with my athletic shorts—drawstring pulled tight just to keep them from sagging off her hips. She looks so damn cute.

A slow smile spreads over each of the guys' faces as they register a gorgeous woman dressed in my clothes who they now know is my agent. Yeah, this isn't going to go over well for me. I can already see Nathan creating a mental wedding registry in his head.

Jamal speaks first, sidling closer to the stairs. "Not interrupting in the least! Our friend Derek here was just telling us you're his new agent. So lovely to meet you."

"Why are you talking like that?" I ask, and Jamal just swats the air behind him like he's telling me to get lost. *This is my house, asshole.*

"I'm—"

"Jamal Mericks," says Nora with a bright smile. "I know. And you guys are Nathan Donelson, Jayon Price, and Lawrence Hill." She laughs and it sounds almost nervous. "I know it's super unprofessional to say this, but I'm seriously starstruck right now. The Sharks are my favorite team. But of course, that's off the record because it's about as unprofessional as a clown in the courtroom to admit you have a favorite team as a sports agent."

"Really?" I ask her with a frown.

"No, it's true. Clowns don't belong in courtrooms. Ask anyone." Well, I fell right into that one. She grins playfully at me. "But yes— I love the Sharks."

"Is that so?" says Jamal, extending his hand for her to shake and then guiding her toward the living room.

"You're acting creepy," I tell him.

He flips me off behind her back. "So . . . Derek's new agent . . ."

"Mac," she says with an easy smile.

"Nora," I correct, just to piss her off. And also maybe because I hate hearing her go by a name I know she hates. I shouldn't care. But I do. I don't want my friends to call her by that name. It doesn't even suit her.

She glares at me over her shoulder. "Mac is what I go by professionally." She turns back toward the guys, who are all now settling in with her on the couch looking as excited as a bunch of babies at story time. "My full name is Nora Mackenzie. Call me whatever you like."

"So everyone except Derek calls you *Mac*?" Lawrence asks, sounding innocent, but I hear the unspoken fishing in his voice. He's trying to get some answers to why I was hiding her. Why she's in my clothes. Why she's here at night in my house. Even I can admit it looks incriminating. It looks like I'm having a fling with my agent.

Which I'm not and never will.

I step forward. "Guys, let her be. My agent has work to do." I add extra inflection on the businessy term, so they'll lay off.

"What work?" Price is normally the quiet one, but even he's invested in this mystery.

Nora perks up and looks over her shoulder. "The pasta! Shoot. I bet it's burning." She stands up and jumps over the back of the couch, sprinting toward the kitchen. All the guys' eyebrows fly up, and I get it. Nora is not like any of the other agents we're used to.

Nathan has Nicole, who is the epitome of sharp professionalism. And the other guys' agents are all stuck-up dudes that are so unmemorable I can't hold their names in my head. But Nora has a realness about her that sort of grabs you by the collar and says you have no choice but to like her. I can't tell if she just hasn't been scarred yet by the industry or if she's truly unapologetically herself. Either way, it makes me mad. I want to forget her once and for all—even as I know that'll never be possible.

The second she's out of view, the guys' smiles drop, and they shoot accusing glares at me. We all whisper-argue at once. They want to know why I'm having her make me pasta and why she's in my clothes and what the hell I'm not telling them. I remind them it's none of their business and to get lost.

She turns the corner again and our whispers die. They flash beaming smiles at Nora. I scowl.

"Derek, by the way, I know you didn't ask me to, but I found a better outfit for you to wear on your date tonight, so I laid it on the bed. It'll go with your personality better than what you have on." I don't even want to look at the scowls the guys are sending me. "Oh, and the pasta is ready. Hope you don't mind; I stole a to-go container and took some for myself since I didn't get to eat dinner. And I moved the pot to the back burner so it doesn't get sticky which you don't like—but the directions said if you wait too long to eat it, it will turn into cement. So, I'd get to cleaning my plate sooner rather than later." Her kindness is grating on me. I'd much rather she give me the middle finger so I don't feel like such a dick.

Her smile somehow widens and her hazel eyes glitter. "If you don't need anything else from me, boss man, I'll just be on my way! I'll call you tomorrow about an endorsement opportunity you received earlier. Already working on the details because it's a good one." She does a weird pistol *pew, pew, pew* motion and then walks to the door and toes into her shoes, careful to not agitate her bandaged foot.

I give it three seconds before—

"Mac!" Jamal yells, standing in indignant outrage. "I feel you should know that Derek is being a jackass for some unknown reason. I'm sure you're already aware but none of us make any of our agents do any of this shit, and he shouldn't be making you do it either. He doesn't even have a date tonight!"

I swear, I will beat him as soon as that woman leaves.

I turn cautious eyes to Nora, hesitant to see the hurt look on her face. I don't find it because she's smiling. Ear to ear, blinding, pearly white smile over those pink lips I almost got a taste of earlier.

"Oh, I know," she says cheerfully. "I may be a little unconventional, but I'm a damn good agent, and I plan on sticking it out until Derek gets over his temper tantrum and lets me prove it. When he's ready, I'll take his career to a height he didn't know existed." She winks and opens the front door. "'Night, boys. Enjoy the pasta for me, it was nice meeting you!"

The door shuts behind Nora, and the silence that follows swallows me up. All of us stare at one another like we're in a shootout in the Wild West. Who will pull the trigger first? Except, all at once, the guys spring from their seats and take off running for the stairs. When they make it to my room, I hear a crow of laughter.

I give up and follow them to my room, where I find the chicken suit that I wore for Halloween five years ago laid out on my bed. There's a note beside it. *"Wear this, you'll look clucking irresistible,"* with a little laughing smiley face drawn beside her corny joke.

Nathan—Dad—looks at me with disappointment in his eyes. "She's incredible. And you didn't even say thank you for making your dinner. You have five seconds to explain your ass, or we sic the wives on you."

"It turns out," I begin, every word a struggle to get out. "Mac, as Nicole referred to her when she presented the idea of her representing me, is . . . my college ex-girlfriend. And also . . . who the thing in my bedside table belongs to."

They respond in a choir of *ooh*s.

"And I'm assuming by the way you're treating her, it didn't end well?" asks Nathan.

I jump back to that moment standing in front of my apartment, seeing her pale frown as she walked up holding a box of my stuff. The whole breakup took a minute at most. Almost a year of love and commitment and she ended it in sixty seconds.

"No." I clench my teeth. "It didn't. And I was miserable after, because I . . . I really loved her."

Lawrence scowls. "So now this is all some sort of revenge play? To make her miserable too by doing your chores? That's a shitty move—and nothing like you."

It sounds pretty awful hearing it out loud. I'm not even sure how to respond. Because I don't intend to stop. Especially not now that my old feelings for her are resurfacing. I need her to quit.

"I call bullshit," says Jamal, plopping down on my bed and making himself comfortable. "You wouldn't have said yes to her if there wasn't some part of you that actually wanted her as your agent. I think the revenge aspect is just a cover. I think you still love her but wanted a way to be near her again without risking anything."

Yes.

I mean no.

God, I don't even know anymore.

I slap Jamal's foot. "Get your shoes off my bed."

"For the record," Price says in his usual gruff tone. "I think you're making a mistake. Nora seemed nice. And very capable. I bet she'd make a good agent—and you really need one of those right now."

"You're right about one thing. She's the nicest," I admit. "Until she decides she's done with you. And then she's the coldest person you'll ever meet." I'm not sure I could ever trust her again even if I wanted to. Or trust her fully with my career. Better to get her to quit and then I'll find a different agent afterward. An agent that I can trust to help bring my career back from the pits if I really do overcome this injury . . .

Lawrence shifts beside me. "You could get your petty revenge, or you could just sit down and talk to her and find some real closure. Get whatever answers you need, then maybe even find your way back to each—"

"Don't finish that sentence," I say, going to my bedroom door and standing beside it to make my intentions clear: I want them to leave. "I know you guys are trying to help, but I didn't ask you to. You have no idea what happened between us, and for me, this isn't a matter of miscommunication. I don't want to know what her reasoning was. I don't care. It won't fix what happened or the pain I felt after. So now—I plan to get even for a few weeks until she quits and then I'll go about my life, and I really don't give a shit what you guys think about it in the meantime."

And because they're my best friends and know me way too well, they share a look that says they can see something in my future that I can't. They leave without any further questions or comments, which is concerning. And also makes me feel guilty as hell.

Once everyone is gone, I go back out to my home gym for the third time today because my body is restless and angry, and this is the only place—the only part of my life—where I don't feel lost and out of control. This is the only place I can shut out my thoughts and fears and make myself believe that I'm actually working toward something good.

This is all I have to offer, so I'm going to put everything into it.

11

Nora

God, I miss him. More than I've missed anything in my life, and this aching won't stop. I made a mistake—that's all there is to it. I never should have ended things with Derek, and definitely not as coldly as I did.

And I'm going to get him back.

It's late and I probably shouldn't be here right now, but I don't even care if I look desperate. I am desperate. Desperate to have him back and mend what I broke. I turn the corner in the little breezeway of his apartment complex and freeze. There he is . . . Derek. My chest tightens just from the sight of him. My mind drinks up the image of his broad shoulders. Shoulders I used to run my hands across, but never will be able to again if I don't mend this break.

I'm one step from emerging out of the shadows when I realize Derek isn't alone. He shifts slightly and there's a woman standing there with him. Her little black dress barely covers her underwear and her long tan legs go on for miles. She is . . . opposite of me. I watch with a knife in my stomach as she angles her face up to Derek and plants her hands against his chest—blond wavy hair sliding off her shoulders down her back. Nausea builds in my stomach as I realize they're going to kiss. No. We only broke up a week ago . . . how could he move on so quickly? How could he—

I open my mouth to yell his name as the woman rises on her tiptoes to kiss him. He bends his head to accommodate her, but no words will come out of my mouth. Nothing but hot air releases as I try again and again to yell his name.

And now he sinks his hand into the back of her hair, and I want more than anything to say something or run to him, but heavy sand is growing over my feet and legs, keeping me from moving. My voice is still a whisper no matter how hard I yell his—

BURRRR. BURRRR.

My head shoots up from my pillow, hair curtaining my face.

"Derek!" I yell into my dark room, clutching my arms protectively around myself until I register the soft, worn fabric of the sweatshirt I'm wearing. *I'm in my bed . . . not back in that hallway.* And the sound is coming from my phone about to buzz off my nightstand.

I sag a bit and wipe my eyes with my hands, wishing I could wipe that dream out too. The dream that continues to slice me in two every time I experience it again.

Finally, I slap my hand onto my phone and drag it to my face. "What? Hello?"

"Nora."

It's Derek—calling almost as if he knew I was dreaming about him.

Please tell me this man isn't calling in the dead of night to ask me for something.

"It's not the dead of night," he says, because apparently I said that out loud.

I roll over onto my back. "I can't be held responsible for anything I say at the hour of"—I pull my phone away to look at the time—"four A.M.? Are you freaking kidding me, Derek?"

I swear I hear a devious smile in his voice when he says, "Not a joke. I need you to meet me in my gym in an hour."

I want to cry. In fact, I might be already. Tears are quite possibly melting down my cheeks. "It's too early! What could you possibly need me to do for you at the gym? It's been ten years since I've attempted a push-up."

"That's not good. Building muscle is important for your overall health."

"Know what else is important for your overall health? Sleep!"

"There's a lot of complaining coming from my agent who's needed to film my workout for social media."

Okay, I'm torn. In one regard, I'm happy to hear him actually doing something for his career—because so far, the last few days (after fettuccine Alfredo night) Derek has had me doing nothing but running back-to-back errands for him and cleaning out his truck. Not a *Thank you* or *Good job* in sight. So the prospect of doing something that actually pertains to his career is tempting. Derek desperately needs to be focusing on building a strong positive narrative around his name for the upcoming season. He needs to be giving interviews, taking endorsement deals, and showing up to the events he's invited to. And he needs a good agent to be leading the parade of his success, but I'll never get to be that for him if he won't let me do my real job.

So yes, I want him to film his workouts for social media. The issue arises in that my bed is oh so warm and cozy.

"Can you set your phone up on a tripod or something? Film it all and then I'd be happy to edit and post it for you later."

"No thanks," he says while definitely smiling. "It'll be better if you do it. My agent."

"Listen. I'm going to level with you in my moment of weakness, Dere-Bear. I only went to bed three hours ago."

"*Why?*" He sounds appalled but not sympathetic.

I hesitate to tell him it's because I've been staying up late putting in extra hours doing actual work on his behalf. This week, I've reviewed all of his contracts and put a plan in place for future renegotiations on a few bad deals I spotted, as well as been in contact with his financial advisor, familiarizing myself with where all of his money is going to ensure that he has a good long-term strategy for when his income doesn't stem from football anymore. But last night, I learned something startling:

Derek is a founder of one of the biggest foundations that helps struggling single moms pay their rent or mortgage, but he funds it anonymously. When I read that email, my heart stopped. Because I happen to know that Derek does not have a single mom. In fact, he comes from a family with a mom and dad very much in support of each other. But I was raised by a single mom . . . and Derek knows this. He knows it because I talked to him repeatedly about how much I admired my mom and all she sacrificed for me. That I wished there were more funding for single moms to lessen their financial burdens so my mom could have been working toward her own dreams while also trying so hard to make mine possible.

I told my silly heart not to look too deeply into this. But it won't stop jumping to assumptions that he did this for *me*. For other women like my mom. I can't ask him about it, though, because then he'd know I've been working extra hours. And if he knows that, he might start finding a way to keep me busy at night too.

My stomach clenches at the thought.

Not busy like that, you traitorous body!

"I couldn't sleep because I was too busy expunging all the bad press about you from the Internet to sleep." I deliver the over-the-top lie to distract him from the truth.

He laughs for maybe the first time since I've seen him again and my heart leaps. I wish more than anything I were there to see his smile paired with that laugh. "If that were true—you'd still be working. Get your ass up and meet me at the gym, rookie." He pauses for a minute, and when I don't respond, he prompts, "Nora?"

I breathe in sharply through my nose. "Hm?"

"You went back to sleep, didn't you?"

"No," I whimper pitifully. My eye sockets hurt. I want to slip right back into dreamland. The dreamland where I get to go to work at a normal hour. Work with a normal athlete who lets me do normal sports-related work instead of this monster who seems hell-bent on making my life a living nightmare. Or maybe not a nightmare, but definitely on an annoying loop where my talents are wasted, and I'm made to do chores 24/7 like Cinderella before she became fabulous.

"Better sit up so you don't fall asleep again."

"You're mean," I say, reluctantly tossing off the covers and throwing my legs over the side of the bed. The sun is not even close to perky yet. It's still snug as a bug in a rug.

"If you're so miserable, feel free to quit. Or would you rather go back to sleep and have me fire you? I'm content with either option." He's enjoying this way too much.

"Monster," I say.

"What's that?" He definitely heard me the first time.

"I said: Mister! I'll be there lickety-split."

"Do you have to say catchphrases like that all the time?"

You used to love my catchphrases.

"Yes—or I'll die. Catchphrases are my lifeblood. Do you really want all that mess on your hands, Your Bossiness?"

He grunts. "It would seem you're awake now."

"I'm so awake I could charge the whole city with my brainpower. I'm going to take over the world, Pinky."

"Can you just record my workout instead?" he says, not even acknowledging my wonderfully old-school *Pinky and the Brain* reference.

"Sure, sure. But after that—I'm going to be *so* ready for world domination. We're going to have a blast together, just you wait." I click brew on the coffeepot I thankfully preloaded with water and coffee grounds last night.

"Super," he says, and I can't figure out his tone. Is he angry or is he trying not to laugh? Probably angry.

"Okay, gotta go. Be there in a flash, mustache."

He grumbles, "On second thought . . . maybe I don't need for you to film for me."

"See you soon, raccoon!" I smile into the phone because now that I know he doesn't like these phrases, this job is going to be a little more fun.

12

Nora

I tap my pencil on my desk, anticipating that my phone will buzz at any moment. How do I know it will buzz? Because apparently when Derek puts his mind to something, he really commits. He rarely lets me have any downtime before calling with a new command. It's only been two weeks on the job, and I'm exhausted.

I've figured out his tactic by now: Never allow Nora time during the day to accomplish actual work. Keep her busy with annoying stuff at all costs.

Which is why I've been working until the early hours of the morning getting the important stuff done like responding to email inquiries, researching interview and appearance opportunities, and talent-scouting online for potential clients. My nights are full of agent productivity, but my days . . . not so much.

I've washed and detailed Derek's SUV, run busy errands for him all over California (yes, sometimes going so far that I'm forced to make a day trip out of it), reorganized his closet (which was actually really fun and also gave me the chance to use my emergency sewing kit to mend a few articles of his clothing—specifically raising the hemline an inch on only the right leg of each of his pants). And of course I've had to unsubscribe him from all junk emails he's ever received in the last several years because isn't that every professional agent's responsibility? At this rate, I'll never grow Derek's career or have time to scout other clients. He's making sure I want to quit.

And any of the endorsement deals Derek's been offered and I've brought to his attention? Forget it. He never lets me finish pitching them before he cuts me off with another chore to accomplish. Which is really starting to stump me, because even though I know this is all a ploy to make me so miserable I supposedly quit, he hasn't truly intended to go through with it, right? I guess I thought this would be something he'd get out of his system and then we could all move on happily into the grown-up realm of business. He needs a good agent. He's a smart guy—and should know that he's at the point of jeopardizing growing his income with how many opportunities he's passing up. It's starting to feel like there's something else at play I haven't considered.

There's even a top-of-the-line suit company, Dapper, that wants to pay Derek an enormous amount of money to represent their brand and star in their next commercial. But Derek said no immediately because he was too busy and couldn't take a day off from training. I can't quite explain it, but I'm starting to get the feeling that excuse is nothing but BS.

I'm supposed to give Dapper an answer by the end of the day today, but I'm dreading severing that lucrative connection.

Another problem is the tug of my traitorous heart in the rare moments when Derek does something unexpected. Something like handing me a water bottle if we've been outside too long. Always making sure I'm fed when he keeps me busy with tasks. Pretending he doesn't see me if I accidentally nod off on the job from the super early mornings combined with my sleepless nights. Yesterday, I could have sworn I fell asleep sitting at his kitchen island while going through his emails, but when I woke up, I was lying on his couch with a blanket. I asked him if he knew anything about that and he shrugged and said I must have sleepwalked. *Not likely.*

And it's in these small moments when I realize that the old Derek—my Derek—is still in there somewhere. The Derek who would blow me a kiss from the field before every game in college. The Derek whose hands felt like the first day of summer when you've been seasonally depressed for too long. Who would wink and make my stomach dip. And let me tell you—no one can wink like Derek. Most people try and it makes them look like a creep who might follow you out to your car. Not Derek. It looks so effortless and genuine. Like you're both in on this extravagant, delicious secret together.

Against all odds, I'm still enormously attracted to him. I need to get a lock on my feelings. Because if there's one thing I'm certain of after working closely with Derek all week: He doesn't like me, or at best doesn't want to.

A knock sounds at my office door.

"Come in," I say in complete despair.

The door opens and I peek up through my lashes to see Nicole lean her pencil-skirted hip against my doorframe. Today she's in her gorgeous black power suit. It wraps around her body tightly and screams *Don't mess with all this!* It's hard not to have a girl crush on her.

She crosses her arms and lifts a brow. "Napping at work?"

"No," I groan into the crook of my arm. "I'm giving up. This is my giving-up position."

"So soon?" She pauses and then casts a disgusted glance around my office. "Then again, I would too if I had to work in here every day. Gross. How do you have a window but still no natural light?"

"The sun only comes through for five minutes sometime between two-thirty and two-forty-five each day."

"It's oppressive."

I lift my head. "You know I think you're a powerful, beautiful goddess in all ways—but you are not great at pep talks."

She raises both eyebrows now. "Oh. Is that what I'm supposed to be doing? I was only here to see if you knew where the paper clips are kept."

I'm already standing up from my desk and tugging her into my office. "Well, you're here now, so might as well stay awhile and impart your all-knowing wisdom to me."

"But I really need to—oh, no, don't shut the door. It's so musty in here."

"You get used to it quickly," I say, practically shoving her into the chair in front of my desk. She looks at the armrests like if she touches them, she might come away with sludge on her sleeve. I turn to face her and hop up on my desk. Her lashes lower to assess my chambray daisy-printed overalls, with a yellow short-sleeve shirt underneath.

"Did you just come from milking cows?"

I gasp in offense and hook my thumbs around the straps. "These are stylish. I got them from the most fashionable store in the country."

She looks skeptical. "Where?"

"Target."

She rolls her eyes away from me. "Hopeless."

"Baby, if this hopeless, I never want to be hopeful." Nicole makes like she's going to stand and leave. I hold out my hand. "No, wait! Stay. Please. I need your advice."

"You have one minute of my time. Go."

It's a good thing that I've been training to go on *Supermarket Sweep* my whole life and therefore turn on stopwatches periodically in my day just so I'm used to the sudden time crunch. I thrive under pressure.

I fill my lungs with so much air it makes Nicole cringe. But I need all the air I can get if I'm going to come clean and unload my entire romantic history on her. "I haven't been able to do any real work for Derek yet because he's sort of hazing me by making me do all this busy work instead. And it's all because—"

"Let me stop you there and save us both the next fifty seconds," she says, holding up a hand. "I've dealt with his type many times before. And the answer is simple: You need to beat his ass at his own petulant little game."

"But how—"

Apparently, Nicole is feeling benevolent today because she continues right on talking. "You're a grown woman with a career, and you don't have time for men like him to mess around with it. If he wants a fight, give him a fight. But you play by your rules from now on." She stands up with the authority of a commander addressing an army. "Believe me, Mac, sometimes the only way to gain a person's respect is to demand it. You're his agent. Act like it. Do your job regardless of what busy errand he tries to send you on, and if he fires you, his loss."

I want to slow clap for her, but I refrain because she hated it when I did that to her last time. Plus she's already standing up from the chair and walking toward the door. There's no time to play around.

"It won't look bad on me if he dissolves the contract?" I ask.

"Not if you explain the situation." She pauses and hesitates before saying the next bit. "Plus—you have me on your side. I'll make sure you're not penalized."

This changes everything.

"Okay," I say with a grateful smile. "Thank you, Nicole. For everything."

She nods and almost smiles. "And for the love of fashion and pro-fessionalism, please stop wearing clothes like that."

"Never." I hop off my desk and pat my thighs. "It has pockets."

A look of agony crosses her face. "It keeps getting worse."

"Careful, you're starting to sound like Marty."

Nicole grunts a dismissive laugh. "The difference being I have im-peccable fashion sense and want to see you succeed. Marty wears out-of-date suits two sizes too big for him, still thinks he dresses like a god, and only criticizes your fashion to cut you down." She pauses. "But I see your point. Wear what makes you happy, I suppose."

The look on her face as she delivers that last line while walking out of my office tells me how painful it was for her to say. I chuckle while rounding my desk and take my seat again, this time pulling one foot up into the chair with me to think. I have to find a way to beat Derek at his own game. But how?

I pick up my pencil and tap it against my lips. Just as that five-minute sliver of sunlight bursts through my office, my phone starts ringing. Derek's name flashes across my screen and I growl before answering.

"Hello, Derek Pender's personal minion, how may I be of ser-vice?"

"Why do you keep answering like this?" By this he means in a cutesy way. I've been changing the tagline each time, but the gist of it is always the same.

"Because it annoys you, and it's the only way I can fight back against your malicious hazing."

"I don't know what you're talking about," he says deadpan, but I hear a note of mischievousness in there. "I'm going out tonight. I need you to pick up my suit from the dry cleaners and bring it to my house."

I drag in one deep breath through my nose and release it slowly.

"Hm, that sounds like a lot of fun, but I happen to know you have several killer-looking suits in your closet. And rumor has it, they're feeling pretty lonely and forgotten. I bet if you wore one of those, it would boost morale for your entire closet."

He's not having it. "I need my dry cleaning by six."

"By *six* . . . ?" I draw out the word and then let it dangle in a question.

"Yes. By six."

"No, I'm saying, by six what?"

"Six on the dot. Not before, not after."

I groan and refrain from banging my head on my desk. "No, Derek! You're missing the word *please*! I need for you to at least say the word *please* when you're being a demeaning poop-nugget."

"And I need for you to use real insults like a grown-up, but we can't both get our way. Feel free to quit if—"

"Yeah, yeah, yeah, I know the speech. I'll have your suit to you by six."

I hang up before he has a chance to not say thank you.

Nicole's advice pings in my brain, but how can I be expected to turn the tables on him when he's in the offseason and seems to have all the time in the world at his fingertips to boss me around? And don't even think I haven't noticed the way he's been avoiding his friends. Never hanging out with them or returning their calls and texts. It seems Derek's entire life is devoted to training and ruining my life. Which at first, I thought was simply because he hates me . . . but now, I'm thinking it's for an entirely different reason I've been overlooking.

And then it hits me. The most glorious plan ever. But I'm going to need to recruit some help.

If it's a suit Derek wants . . . it's a suit he's going to get.

13

Derek

She's late. It's six-thirty and she's not here with my suit. I need her to be here. And I need that suit. Actually, I don't need the suit, because like she said, I have plenty of suits to wear. But how can I annoy the shit out of her if she's not here? She's supposed to be here.

I pace by my front door.

Back and forth, back and forth with my phone pressed to my ear. The call rings repetitively but never connects. Now I'm not just pissed, I'm concerned. Nora's been answering my calls and texts promptly every day for the last two weeks. What if something happened to her? What if she got in an accident on the way here? On the way to bring me a suit that I don't even need.

I run a hand through my hair, considering calling the hospitals, but just as I think it, I hear the sound of a car coming up my driveway. I look through the window just long enough to confirm that it's her, and then without thinking, I charge out the front door and meet her in the driveway.

She steps out of her car and a breeze whips her hair into her face. Even though she has no reason to, she smiles when she spots me barreling toward her. She is sunshine parting the clouds in my miserable day, and it makes me angrier.

It's how I've felt the entire two weeks working with her. I'm supposed to hate her. I'm supposed to find her smile irritating. And those weird quirky catchphrases? Really supposed to hate those. But do I? *No way.* If anything, I have to fight with everything in me to not smile when she banters at me. To not wrap her in my arms every time she's within reach.

Which leads to the familiar anger—but not with Nora, with myself.

Irritated that I'm once again having a positive reaction to the sight of her, I put my hands in my pockets. "Why haven't you been answering my calls?"

Her smile widens and she steps past me with a suit bag draped over her shoulder. "Sorry, Dere-Bear. My phone died about an hour ago. And I forgot that I took my charger into the office." She peeks at me over her shoulder. "You weren't worried, were you?" There's a teasing spark in her green-gold eyes and I have to turn away, so I don't kiss it off.

"No. Just need my suit." Jeez, I'm tired of acting like an overbearing dick. I really thought she'd have quit by now. I don't know how much more of this I can take.

Her smile falters a smidge, but she recovers it quickly. "Well, here it is! The suit of your dreams."

Something about the way she says this sounds suspicious. It's then that I really notice the garment bag. It's not the usual clear one from my dry cleaner—this one is sleek and black and opaque. This one is from a designer.

"What the hell is that?" I ask her, even though I know what it is. She has the look of a person who just bested me.

"This is your requested suit."

"Not my suit from the dry cleaners." I don't phrase it like a question because it's not one.

She grins and taps my chest once—sensation zipping right through to my spine. "Astute. You're not going to be needing that one—or any of your old suits anymore either," she says in a little too chipper a tone before carrying it into my house toward the stairs. The stairs that go up to my room. Why is she going up to my room?

And why am I now following her like a lamb to the slaughter?

"Nora . . . please tell me that you did not take the endorsement deal with the suit designer?"

"I could tell you that, but since I subscribe to the idea that honesty is the best policy, I better just tell you that I did agree to it, and you are now the front man for one of the most popular American suit makers in the biz. I only need you to sign on the dotted line tonight."

I stop in the middle of the stairs and watch as her sassy bubble butt sways up ahead of me, and against all reason, I'm not thinking about the suit deal. My thoughts dive to wondering if Nora still wears days-of-the-week underwear. At first, I thought it was just a cute fluke in college. But then I started noticing that every day she wore the correct day. I asked her about it once and she said she liked the habit of it. Her beautiful ass became my calendar, and—yeah, that's not something I should be thinking about anymore.

"You did that without my consent. I could fire you on the spot," I say, jogging the last few stairs to catch her.

She turns into my bedroom. "You could. But you're really going to need an agent in a few days while you're on set. And I doubt you'd be able to find someone to fill the position before your flight out on Friday morning."

I'm sorry, my *what*? And what set? "I don't have a flight on Friday morning," I say with a measured calm that should alert her to how frustrated I am in this moment.

She lays the garment bag across my bed, and I try very hard not to stare as she leans over to unzip it. Those overall shorts she's wearing should be unattractive. They're not. Nora pulls my suit from the bag and holds it up, assessing it for any damages, and then carries it primly into my closet like she owns it.

I stand in the middle of my bedroom, arms crossed, feet firmly planted because there's something going on here and I have a feeling I'm going to need all my willpower to withstand it. There's a new energy humming around Nora. *Don't let her smile fool you, she's covered in yellow daisies but she's dangerous as hell.*

The woman emerges from my closet, still not making eye contact, arms loaded down with clothes. I watch with narrowed eyes as she dumps them on my bed mumbling something about socks and how many pairs I'll need. Next, she drags out my suitcase. The big one. She heaves it up on the bed, making a squeak of effort before it lands.

"Do you have any packing preferences? I like to do socks and underwear in a neat little corner and then build a fortress of rolled shirts around them. But I'm open to suggestions . . . *to a certain degree.*" She starts loading my clothes in.

"Stop," I command, but she doesn't. "Nora, stop packing."

"Sorry, can't do that! We're on a tight schedule here. I need to start *your* packing tonight so I can do *my* laundry and packing tomorrow. Because as of now, my favorite leggings are dirty and there's no way I'm sitting in a plane all day in jeans."

I cross the floor in two strides, and once her fingers are clear, I close the lid of the suitcase. "Explain what is going on."

She squares her shoulders at me like she's been hoping it would come to this. The blaze in her eyes swarms through my veins. She's so close to me I could take one step forward and we'd be pressed together. The no-touching rule hums between us. Taunting me. "We have a flight Friday morning. Bright and early. First flight out in fact, so we're going to get to the airport around five-thirty A.M."

"Like hell we are."

I don't mean to, but my eyes drop to her mouth. This is the first time she's really fought back against me at all since we started working together, and it reminds me so much of how we used to play-fight just for the fun of it back when we were together. And when my gaze drops to her arms, I find chillbumps lining her skin. She's not unaffected by this moment either.

She clears her throat and turns away, rushing off to the closet again while I'm back here losing my mind. I shove my hands into my hair and tug just to relieve some frustration. But it's not about this damn job. I'm angry that I want her. And frustrated that I can't have her.

And I really can't.

Even if Nora wanted me back, I won't ever let myself trust her again. Not after loving her so thoroughly and then having her back out on us with zero warning or hints. Not even a week of fading us out. One day she loved me and dreamed of a future with me while ditching her public speaking class so we could go on a hike to a waterfall, and the next, she sent our relationship to the guillotine.

"Where is this flight going that I won't be on?" I ask, meeting her at the closet and leaning my hands on either side of the doorjamb, blocking her in there until she gives me a straight answer.

She grins. "Las Vegas." And then she and her arms full of socks and underwear easily dart under my blockade.

A boulder drops into the pit of my stomach. She's serious. She really booked us plane tickets to Vegas.

"I am not going to Vegas. And I'm not participating in this endorsement deal. End of story."

She's a little bee buzzing around my room, still gathering everything she needs for a trip I am not taking. "Oh, I think you are. Because number one, I already booked the flights and confirmed with Dapper that you'll be on set Friday, bright-eyed and bushy-tailed and ready to star in their main commercial spot of the year."

My nostrils flare. "You didn't."

"And number two, I've been instructed to tell you by the guys that if you resist, they will tell me about the thing they found in your bedside table a few months ago."

My smirk drops.

They wouldn't.

"I had a group call with them earlier to explain the situation and get their input. Turns out they side with me and think it's time you get back to work. So Jamal instructed I read you this note from him if you resist." She pulls a piece of paper from her back pocket and shakes it out like it's an old-fashioned newspaper. *"Derek, you're the biggest dipshit I've ever met if you thought we wouldn't use this against you. Get your ass on that plane or I'll tell her what we found."*

I groan because that's all the response I can manage right now. Needing space, I pace the floor once and turn back sharply to Nora. "Did they already tell you what it was they found?"

"No. Although—I'm very intrigued. It must be really embarrassing to get a reaction like this. I think as your agent I should know—"

"Absolutely not."

She licks her lips on a smile and steps even closer, tilting her chin up and angling those perfect lips at me. "Does that mean you're coming with me to Vegas?"

Nora is chipper and basking in the glow of a solid win. But I'm not.

I push my hand through my hair and pace away from her. "You shouldn't have done this, Nora. This was too far."

Her gaze cuts through me. "Is it really? You've been hazing me for two weeks, and you just expect me to sit back and let you miss out on huge career opportunities because of something that happened between us in college? No more. From now on, we're taking the deals. You're giving the interviews."

I should keep my mouth shut. Should let her think that all of this avoidance is only because of her. But suddenly I feel like I'm in a runaway car I can't get control of. Panic wells in my chest at the thought of putting myself out there with so much on the line. Without permission, my mind replays the announcers on sport talk radio and ESPN saying there's no way I'll bounce back. That they've seen plenty of athletes fall to this sort of injury and it's going to be sad to watch it happen to me. I'll be a spectacle.

Everything swirls endlessly around me. My breathing goes shallow. Sweat gathers on my neck. And suddenly, I'm back in elementary school standing in the front of the class watching them all laugh mercilessly at me when I couldn't get through the passage I was asked to read.

And that's when I snap. "It's not about you, Nora!"

She doesn't flinch at my raised voice. She looks relieved. "Then what is it about? Tell me, Derek, or I can't fix it."

My hands clench at my sides. "I don't want to go off and act like some hotshot for a designer when there's a big chance I'm going to get cut before the season even starts! Everyone—and I do mean everyone, thinks that the Sharks are going to give my position to Abbot, and when that happens, I'll look like the idiot who didn't realize he had egg on his face. Dapper—and anyone else you've made deals with—will come back and dissolve our contract. So no thank you. I prefer to keep laying low and focusing on my game and nothing else. I won't get distracted, and I won't preen around in a suit when I might not even have a job this year!"

Nora blinks, the energy my outburst shot into the room fading. And then she frowns. "So . . . all the hazing . . . all the keeping me from doing any real work . . . it was because of this? Because you're scared you're going to fail and look silly trying?"

I sigh, finding it impossible to fully explain how I never again want to feel like the kid whose supposed failure was everyone else's entertainment, without telling her the truth of my past and my recent diagnosis. "Yes and no. I guess . . . you were a good excuse to put a pause on all the outside stuff so I could just lay low and train. So please . . . call and cancel the deal. I don't want to do it."

Silence blankets the room for a minute, and I really think I've gotten through to Nora. But then her eyes flash. If I thought she looked determined before . . .

"You know what, Derek? That makes me angrier than a hornet stuck in a sweaty person's shirt. I wish it had been that you just wanted to make me miserable. But throwing your career away because you're afraid of what people might think if you try really hard and still fail?" She walks closer and pokes me in the chest like she's someone my size rather than almost a foot shorter. "That breaks my heart, and I'm not going to allow it. You deserve good things no matter the outcome of your injury. You've worked hard your entire career and earned it. And you know what else? Not everyone thinks your position is going to go to Abbot. I believe in you. *I do*, Derek." She presses a hand firmly to her chest.

Intensity rolls off her in waves. "I know what you are like when you put your mind to something—evidence being the way you've committed fully to my misery. And beyond that, I've been the one sitting in on all of your workouts these weeks. You're not washed up.

You're not rusty. You're a freaking ox, Derek, but you have to believe in yourself too or no one else is going to."

She pauses long enough to take a breath. "Get your muscled ass out there and bet on yourself. Take the endorsement deals. Do some interviews. Post your training content that shows you working hard and crushing it. Don't give up just because a few narrow-minded people say you should! And *stop* using my career that I've worked my ass off for as a play toy. It's not fair to me and frankly it's beneath you."

I can hardly breathe my chest is so tight. I can't decide if I'm pissed, sad, embarrassed, or encouraged. "Anything else?"

"Yeah." She pokes me again, but this time in the center of my chin. "You don't smile enough anymore."

"What?"

"You heard me," she says like a bite, but there's no teeth to it. Her eyes soften. "You used to smile all the time—and you never do now. I thought in the beginning it was because you hated me, but you don't smile at anyone else either. I miss it, that smile. It was so warm I would feel it all the way in my toes."

I stare down at Nora—a million questions and apologies swirling in my head, but I can't pick a single one over the big one I've avoided for so long. "I'm ready to know what happened," I say quietly—no fire left in my veins.

I've spent long enough telling myself that I didn't care. That she broke it off and she didn't love me anymore and that's all there was to it. I didn't need details or even want them. Because any explanation she would give me would hurt too much, and I was already hurting so much I thought I'd break.

But now, I have to know. Because something about how she just described the way I've basically given up on my career out of fear resonated with another area of my life too. Nora might have been the one who walked away from us, but I let her. I didn't fight for her even once because I was afraid I genuinely wasn't enough for her.

Nora stares at me in shock. "Wh—what?"

"What happened back then? To us," I ask slowly and carefully in case I spook her away. "What made you end it? And end it so damn coldly. What did I do wrong, Nora?"

14

Nora

I shut my eyes and let out a breath. "It's against the rules to—"

"Tell me. Please. I need to know." His voice is more desperate than I've ever heard it.

I look into his eyes and transport myself back to when I was a senior in college looking at changing her whole life for an up-and-coming athlete. I let in all the feelings I've spent years trying to block out. Partly from pain, partly from guilt.

"I was scared," I say honestly.

His brows furrow and he takes a tentative step forward. "Scared of what?"

"You," I breathe out. "Of how I felt about you."

He watches me like I'm changing shape before him.

I move a step toward him too, feeling like the room is slowly being zapped of oxygen. "You weren't supposed to happen, Derek. I had a solid plan for my life, and love wasn't supposed to factor in until much later."

But one look at Derek at that party and I was a goner. I remember it like it was yesterday. The jolt to my nervous system. The grip of my body that said, *Him . . . he's important.*

"When I met you, and I fell hard for you, it terrified me. And then suddenly my grades were dropping because I was spending so much time with you, and there was all this talk about where you were going in the NFL, and your fame was building quickly." I'm talking fast but I can't bring myself to slow down now that I'm finally saying the words out loud. "And if all of that wasn't scary enough, the day I broke up with you, I learned that I got an awful grade on my econ final, which almost made me fail the entire class. It was a huge wake-up call for me. Especially if I wanted to get into grad school."

Seeing that grade felt like a blow to who I was as a person. I had a 4.0 in high school and was valedictorian. I wasn't someone who slacked in her classes. But suddenly, I had become that person all for a guy, and I hated it—was afraid of what other parts of myself I'd give up if I stayed with him.

Besides, if my dad taught me anything, it's that men are not worth pinning your future happiness on. They leave when they're bored. And I had no way of knowing how long it would take for Derek to get tired of me. It was all such a big risk to take on at the cusp of my career. I needed to keep fighting for myself.

Now, I study the sharp angles of Derek's face, which somehow looks even more cruelly beautiful when he's frowning like this. He shakes his head, but the motion is tense. "I . . . I didn't know your grades were even suffering. If you'd told me, I would have done more to help—studied with you or something."

"You would have?" I ask honestly, remembering the way Derek's main mission in life seemed to be getting me to put away my text-book and play with him instead. "I definitely think the Derek you are now would have helped me. But the fun-loving, play-all-the-time Derek I was dating . . . yeah, he would have told me not to worry about it. I think you would have offered to marry me and support me instead, promising I'd never have to work a day in my life."

Derek's eyes flash with something I don't recognize, but a second later it's gone, and he just looks sad. "I still wish you'd told me this when you were breaking up with me. Even if I didn't understand then—it would have helped to know later. It would have helped . . ." He shifts on his feet like his vulnerability is literally killing him. I'm shocked when he actually finishes his sentence. "It might have stopped hurting sooner if I'd known."

This time, I feel the hit.

The word *sooner* implies that he'd been hurting for a long time. But that can't be right. He moved on with that other woman so fast. Then again, maybe just like how there was more behind my stone-cold breakup that Derek never saw, maybe there was more he never let me see too.

"You're right. I should have been honest with you back then, but I felt too selfish choosing myself over us, and I couldn't find a way to explain that I didn't want to put my dreams on hold at such a young age to chase yours." I roll my lips between my teeth, hating that sting of guilt I still feel. "I'm so sorry I hurt you, Derek—and for the way I ended it. I wasn't ready or mature enough for the kind of love we had."

"You don't think we would have made it?" he asks, and the hope I hear in his voice breaks me. But I can't lie to him.

I shake my head softly. "No. As much as I loved you—there were a lot of things I needed to experience in life that I wouldn't have been able to if I had followed you after graduation. I think we would have tried very hard for a while, and then we would have felt the pull of two different dreams ripping us apart. That was something I couldn't stomach the thought of. And maybe none of those reasons are good enough for you to forgive me but—"

"They are," he says gently, but still the force of those words hits me like a boulder to the chest. I can't breathe. Can't do anything besides blink at Derek's face as I watch the harsh lines soften. This time, he's the one taking shape in front of me. This isn't Derek the young reckless boy—this is Derek the man.

He moves even closer to me, and my skin vibrates with awareness, disappointed when he stops a few inches away. He doesn't make any moves to touch me, but it's clear in his burning sapphire eyes that something new is unraveling between us. A truce. Maybe even empathy.

Whatever baggage we carried into this room, we're not leaving with it.

Derek's chest expands with a breath. "It might not have been a good enough reason for me back then when I was twenty-four and immature, but now . . ." He shifts on his feet. "It makes sense to me, Nora."

"Really?" I ask, my eyes misting over. I had no idea until this moment how much I needed to hear that from him. Needed to hear that he understands the choice I made and maybe doesn't hate me for it.

His eyes run over my jaw and mouth like a caress. The look he's giving me now reminds me we were something special once. That I was something special to him once.

"I think . . ." He takes a breath, eyes floating back up to mine. "I've been holding on to a hurt that maybe I should have let go of a long time ago."

I want to tip forward. There's an invisible string tied from his lips to mine and it's tugging hard. The pull is almost too much to withstand, so I inch closer. "I never even realized I hurt you, Derek. You just walked away when I ended it. You took the box from me and turned around without another word. So I knew you were angry—but hurt? You didn't show it."

"That's apparently what I do best." His smile is achingly sad. "I'm sorry, Nora. I'm sorry for all of it—including treating your career like a pawn in my stupid game." His hand brushes mine and I can't tell if it's intentional or not. But my body feels that small touch in every corner.

"It's okay. We had a messy start," I say, nearly breathless.

"No." His voice is stern. "It's not okay. I was an asshole to you these last two weeks, and I'm very sorry."

My lips part but I barely know what to say. This feels like a dream. "I'm sorry too."

We both stand in silence for a few moments, absorbing this new reality and what it means for us. We're so close that my face has to angle up to see him, and with every inhale, our chests nearly touch. Neither of us moves away—and when I feel that familiar glimmer between us pull taut, I'm struck with the realization that I never want to be separated from Derek again. I want him to touch me. To put his hands on my hips and tug me to him until there's zero separation between us. My body is craving a pressure that only he can satisfy.

But now our careers are tangled up together and a relationship could get messy very quickly. Not only that, but I've seen the way athletes go through relationships like water. The way *Derek* has gone through relationships. I might still have feelings for him, but I'm not sure I have trust. And I definitely don't have it in me to just hook up with him and go about life business as usual tomorrow.

So it looks like our only option right now is . . .

"Can we be friends?" My voice is embarrassingly full of hope.

I see the exact moment Derek's eyes shutter closed, and I know my hope was misplaced. He takes a large step away from me and rubs the back of his neck. "No. I'm sorry, but . . . I can't be friends with you again, Nora."

Because he doesn't want to be? Because there's too much history between us? I can't bring myself to ask—and furthermore, I get the feeling he's putting up a boundary by not immediately explaining why.

"Right. And that's okay. Perfectly good actually." I shift awkwardly on my feet. "It's understandable and noble and . . . other adjectives that I can't think of at the moment."

Derek stares at me as he sighs. I would give anything to get inside his head. "But . . ." he begins, jaw flexing against the word. "I will pick you up before our flight Friday morning."

I blink, wide-eyed at him. "You're going to go to Vegas with me?"

He presses his lips together and instinctively I know this choice is costing him. "Yeah. I won't get in the way of your career anymore, rookie. And I do need help with mine since it seems you're not going to let me tap out early." He smiles tentatively. "I'll sign the deal and go with you to Vegas."

15

Derek

Bam, bam, bam.

I pound my fist on Nathan's door. I know all the guys are in there because Nathan posted a story an hour ago with a photo of a stack of board games and tagged the guys.

The door opens and there's Nathan in his gym shorts and T-shirt looking immediately guilty. "Derek, we weren't expecting—"

I cut him off when I push my way in past him. "What the hell were y'all thinking messing with my life like that today?"

"Whoa!" he says, throwing his hands up as I storm by. "I guess Nora told you about your plans for the weekend?"

"Yeah, she told me. And she relayed your blackmail information too. That was way too far." I freeze in the living room at the sight of Jamal, Price, and Lawrence all sitting on the floor around a game. "Monopoly?" I say, in outrage.

Lawrence blinks at me. "Derek . . . it's not what it looks like."

"Oh, really? Because it looks like you pricks have the audacity to play my favorite board game without me while simultaneously plotting with my ex-girlfriend-slash-agent behind my back."

Price grimaces. "Okay, it's a little bit how it looks, then. You want to be dealt in? It's not too late."

"No. I do not want to be *dealt in*. I want to know what made you guys think it was okay to side with Nora?"

Nathan sets down his glass of wine. "Simple. You were being an ass and toying with her for weeks. Honestly you deserve more than a little blackmail that forced you to do the work you should have been doing the whole time."

"I didn't toy with her." *I pissed her off on purpose.*

"You sure as hell didn't value her or treat her with respect," says Lawrence, standing up from the floor and using his height to make me pay attention. "You've been a huge jerk. And not only to her—but to us too, by not returning our calls or coming around anytime we invite you. It's hurtful."

"I didn't mean to . . ." *To what?* Because I *did* mean to shut them out. I *did* mean to hide away. But I didn't mean to hurt them in the process. Part of me didn't think they'd notice or care that much. Is it wrong to say I'm happy to hear they do?

Price scrolls on his phone. "I'm going to order some dinner. What do you guys want tonight?" He looks back at me. "Derek, I assume you're too full to eat since you've got that massive stick up your ass?"

The tension that's been building in my body all night snaps. I take his phone out of his hand and walk it with me to the coffee table, where I drop it into a full glass of water. It makes a dramatic *plop* sound. I regret it instantly.

"*Pender . . .*" Price drawls ominously as he strides over and removes his phone from the glass. He dries it with his shirt. "You're lucky this is waterproof, because if Hope tried to call me to tell me she was in labor and I missed it due to you acting like a petulant child, your life would have ended. *Apologize.*"

Damn, what is happening to me?

"I'm sorry, man," I say, actually meaning it. My hands scrape through my hair and the height of my anger dissipates. "The truth is . . . I'm going through a lot. But I haven't wanted to talk about it."

Like spending the past few months looking back on my adolescent memories with new light. How would things have been different for me if I'd been supported through my learning differences instead of shamed for them? And then there's Nora and everything she told me tonight. She was right—the Derek from college hated his studies and textbooks and classes because of how they made him feel. So inadequate. So lacking. Having to buckle down and study more with her would have driven a wedge between us like it did for me and my parents.

"I've been pulling away from you guys because . . . *shit* . . . I've just been scared, okay? Scared I'm going to lose you all as friends if I get cut and I'm not a Shark anymore."

"I wish you'd told us," says Nathan. "We could have punched you in the balls a long time ago and left Nora out of it completely. Bottom line, you're not getting rid of us."

Lawrence grunts a laugh. "We're all getting older, man. Injuries are going to happen. Retirement is on the horizon for all of us. Except for Nathan because he'll probably play until he's eighty."

Nathan nods. "It's true."

"Which is why our friendship isn't contingent on our contracts. We're like the Sisterhood of the Traveling Pants." Lawrence settles back down on the floor.

I raise my eyebrows. "Have we been sharing pants and I don't know about it? Is that why they've all been fitting me wrong lately?"

"I was going to say something the other day. Your pants have looked weird, man." Price looks to mine now and sure enough . . . one side is a little shorter than the other.

"No," Lawrence interjects before we get off the rails too far. "I mean, we'll always be connected no matter how far apart we are."

Nathan squints at my legs. "It's like an inch difference. Have you only been drying one pant leg or something?"

I shrug. "I really don't know. Maybe one of my legs is still growing and the other stopped?"

Jamal hits me in the face with a pillow. "I don't give a shit about your ugly pants, Derek. What about the *woman*?"

"What about her?" I shrug.

His eyes widen in annoyance. "Are you still in love with her?"

For once I'm too tired to fight with him. "Yes, I am. Deeply. Terribly."

Everyone is just as shocked by my honest answer as I am.

Jamal sits up. "Well, damn, this is bad if you're not threatening to kick my butt out the window over calling your pants ugly."

That's when the weight of everything topples over me and I sit heavily on the couch, dropping my face in my hands. "I do still love her. I think I always will. And even more pathetic, I think part of why I've been hazing her with chores around my house all week is because I just like having her near me. I like hearing her laugh and her silly quips and the glares she shoots me when she pretends to be upset with me. I like her—more than I've liked anyone or anything in my entire life."

Nathan blows out a heavy breath, making his cheeks puff out. He leans his elbows onto his knees. "I didn't see that coming. Now I almost feel bad about the blackmail."

"I don't," Jamal says, and we all turn a flat look at him.

Nathan joins me on the couch. "Now that you realize this, what do you want to do about it?"

"What do you mean?"

Price sits forward. "He means you must have come here for some other reason than to drop my phone in a glass of water. Do you want to get her back?"

"*No,*" I say firmly, meaning it.

Jamal rolls his eyes and pushes off the ground, disappearing into the kitchen. He hates my answer.

Nathan levels me with a look that I feel in my soul. "Then what do you want?"

What do I want?

"I want to get over her for good and move on. I think I've been so resistant to relationships because part of me has still been holding on to her. I've got to let her go, and . . . I don't know, maybe I'll finally let you guys set me up with someone."

Lawrence stands up. "Okay then, if you want to move on, you're going to have to act like an adult from now on. Quit hazing her, and just be honest with her. Tell her that after this Vegas trip, you guys have to part ways. It's not healthy for you to work so closely with someone you love like that."

"I agree with Lawrence," Price adds. "She deserves more respect than what you've been giving her, and you deserve to move on. Tell her the truth."

I breathe deeply. He's right. Nora has always treated me with respect and kindness. I realize for the first time that her straight-to-the-point breakup was even merciful in a way. She saw we weren't compatible anymore—she needed to focus on school and study, and my personality rebelled against those things out of self-preservation. Where everyone else in my life was quick to tell me to shape up and try harder, Nora never did. She loved the man I was, and also realized she needed something different for herself and moved on without ever presenting me with a "you need to change to be with me" ultimatum.

And I've hazed her because of it.

"You're right. I'll tell her on the plane on Friday."

Jamal suddenly scoffs and emerges from the kitchen with a goblet full of a berry-colored drink that almost matches his shirt.

"First of all." He points to Nathan. "*You* didn't tell me there was sangria!" His finger swivels to Lawrence. "And *you* gave out the worst advice I've ever heard. Clearly the man needs to win back his woman, not let her go."

I cross my arms and sit back heavily against the couch. "You're wrong, man. Nora's not mine. She made that clear years ago, and it's time I respect that. Now, deal me in for Monopoly and I'll take a glass of sangria. Throw a piece of ice in there while you're at it."

Jamal sits back down on the floor. "Get your own drink, you unromantic piece of shit." He hands me some rainbow-colored cash. "And you have to be the top hat—that's all that's left."

16

Nora

Wow, do you feel that? It's hope! Radiant. Light. Expressive, hope! Why am I skipping around my apartment like a teenager who's never experienced disappointment in her lifetime? Because the other night, Derek and I cleared the air, and I think he's finally going to let me do my job. He didn't even call me once yesterday or send me on any silly errands.

Not only that, but the guilt I've been carrying for so long is gone. He understands. More than that, he thought it was the right decision. The real difficulty now has been erasing the memory of his eyes softening. Of him telling me he was glad I took care of myself back then. If wild and fun Derek was enticing, stable and mature Derek is terrifying. I can't deny how much I still . . .

Never mind. None of it matters. Because in the next breath he said he didn't want to be friends again and that gutted me like a trout at the fish market, but it's okay. I get it. (I hate it with all my heart—but I respect it.) We're going to put our careers first. Good, good, good.

My luggage is packed, my backpack is loaded down with my laptop full of work projects (real projects and not just obscure errands), which I stayed up all night working on because I was too excited to wait, and when I blinked, my alarm was going off. I've been doing nothing but working an endless stream of hours since he decided to quit hazing me because I have so much lost time to make up for.

I feel triumphant. Like I should run around my apartment with an American flag strapped to my back like I just won the Olympics. I'm living off hopes and dreams and coffee and I'm sure there's a slightly rabid look in my eyes, but I don't even care. For the first time, I feel things are really moving in my life. My dreams are attainable. And even if I don't get to have Derek romantically or as a friend . . . at least I won't be completely out of his life again. I don't have to say goodbye to him. Is that pathetic? Choosing not to answer that question.

Just as I'm pouring my fourth cup of coffee, there's a knock on my door. I know it's Derek because there's a ripple down my spine. Just kidding, it's because he said he and his driver would pick me up here at five A.M.

I race to the door and throw it open. "Good morning, Dere-Bear!" I tell him with a huge smile because I refuse to allow any lingering awkwardness after my vulnerability dump and our eye sex. Because yes—upon replaying it over and over in my head since that night, I've officially determined it was eye sex. "Come in for a second while I grab my stuff."

Derek frowns slightly, hesitating at the door. "Uh, Nora—"

"No." I point at him. "Don't start all that. We're going to the airport. I am going to make you a load of money. And we will not have any weirdness between us because of the other night. We can both be professional adults and double down on all our rules." I go to my bedroom and grab my backpack and suitcase while still talking to him, raising my voice so he can hear me in the next room. "Not to toot my own horn, but I've really nailed the agent gig over the last few days. I doubt there's a single thing that could happen on this trip that I'm not prepared for."

When I'm back in the living room, Derek frowns deeply at my face. "Nora, did you sleep at all last night?"

I point my airplane pillow at him before I shove it into my backpack. "Good question. The answer is: No. But luckily, I don't need sleep anymore. Unrelated note, did you know if you drink enough coffee, you can hear the color purple?"

I heave my bag up over my shoulders and try to walk to the door. *Try* being the key word because I'm suddenly snagged backward by a hand on my backpack. I squeak as I stumble into Derek. He looks down at me over my shoulder with stern blue eyes. "So you haven't slept. Have you eaten anything today?"

"Yes—I've eaten about four thousand milligrams of caffeine, and I've gained spidey-senses. It's great, everything is swirling and tingling around me."

"That's called a panic attack."

I make a *psh* sound and try to walk away again, but he snags me once more. I swallow when I feel his hands sliding under the straps of my backpack and removing it from my shoulders. "Derek, come on, we've gotta—"

"Listen to me, rookie. We're not going anywhere until you eat something." He sets down my backpack and I slump. "Do you have any eggs in your fridge?"

"Well . . . yes . . . but I don't have time to make them."

He's already striding away from me to the kitchen—that confident mountain of a man acting as if time and space will bow before him. And with an ass like his, maybe they will.

"I'm making you eggs, you're going to eat them, and then we're going to go to the airport and you're going to sleep the entire flight. I mean it, Nora, if I even see a sliver of your green eyes, I'm going to call it all off, understand?"

Bossy, bossy, bossy. Why don't I hate it? Better question: Why am I feeling hot and bothered by it? Probably because I'm suddenly flooded with memories of his shoulders hovering over me, silhouetted by only the moonlight when he would whisper other bossy things to me.

He opens the fridge door and pulls out a carton of eggs. "Now, while I'm cooking, go put some damn pants on. You broke rule number seven."

I grunt a laugh. "I did no—" I look down and somehow gasp and shriek at the same time. "Derek! I'm not wearing pants!"

"I noticed," he grumbles, not looking at me. "I tried to tell you when I walked in, but you were too busy seeing into a different universe with your new caffeine-induced powers."

"I'm so sorry! This is really unprofessional." I snatch a fuzzy turquoise blanket from my pink couch (perks of the single life) and wrap it around my lower half as I start inching toward my bedroom. "I promise I didn't realize I wasn't wearing pants. I just never wear them when I'm home and I've been so preoccupied with work that—"

"Nora." Derek turns and levels me with a look so full of memory and emotion that my knees nearly buckle. He doesn't say a single word, but his warm eyes say everything: *I know you don't wear pants at home. And I already know exactly what you look like without pants. In fact, I know what you look like completely naked in my bed.*

"Just get dressed, please," he finally says, and I nod before dipping into my room to change, trying to hide a smile I have no business wearing.

We get through security quickly, but I'll be honest, I'm struggling. My sluggish legs are trying to keep up with Derek's extra-long, extra-awake ones, and I'm feeling pretty delirious from my lack of sleep and mix of caffeine. At this point, I'm seeing the world through a fishbowl. Everything is hazy, and Derek is right, the intense amount of caffeine is giving me loads of anxiety. It could also be the large number of onlookers making me nervous.

We're both wearing hats and sweatshirts, hiding as best we can. But even if people don't know specifically who he is—though I'll bet you that seventy-five percent of these people do because the man is the most famous tight end in the NFL—they see his size and muscles and expensive athleisure wear and they know he's someone important. Someone to snap pictures of. I think I'm supposed to be keeping him safe right now, but I keep tripping on my own feet and feeling dizzy. Derek evidently notices because before I know it, his arm goes around my shoulders—pulling me in close to his side to stabilize me.

The problem is, Derek is so strong and warm and smells like Moroccan mint bodywash (yes, that's the exact scent . . . I might have peeked in his shower once) and it's getting too difficult to fight my body's urge to close my eyes while I walk. At some point, I realize that Derek is practically holding me up. He's not even complaining. His hand is firmly gripping my side like he wants me to know he's got me. And every now and then, when we stop to wait in a line, I allow myself to fully lean against him and take little catnaps. Professionalism starts tomorrow.

I've never been so tired in all my life. I think two weeks' worth of sleeplessness plus an entire night without ever closing my eyes is catching up to me in a bad way.

"Almost to our gate," Derek says, leaning down to whisper against my ear. Tingles erupt across my body and I'm too tired to fight them off. All I can think is *God, I miss him like this.*

When we finally make it to gate ten, Derek guides us to a secluded corner, but it doesn't really help. People still take note of us, and he has to spend several minutes signing autographs and taking pictures. I ask him if he wants me to keep the crowd away, but he says he doesn't mind and that he's happy to do it. And I think he really is, judging by the way he takes a little extra time with a few teenage boys, asking what positions they play in varsity football and where they want to go to college. The boys ask him if his ankle is going to be okay to play and Derek just grins at them and says, "I'll be ready for game day, don't worry."

I think he needed this, honestly. He's been hiding himself away too long in the offseason, mentally preparing for the call that he's been cut. That call is never going to happen if I have anything to do with it.

Soon enough, we're settled in our chairs in the terminal waiting to board the flight and I'm staring at Derek's massive knee just a few inches from mine. I can't look away. My peepers are glued to this bendy extremity of his that suddenly feels so erotic I can't stand it. Has he always had these knees? His hand is resting on his thigh and when I see him squeeze his leg once, I feel the shift in the air before he even says my name.

"Nora . . . we need to talk."

I don't think that leg squeeze was a good one. I think he caught me staring and saw the raw longing I was too sleepy to cover up. Oh no . . .

Derek is about to fire me.

I know it. I know it in the pinch of his brows and the softness of his eyes. Something significant has changed in Derek since the other night. I can't put my finger on it, but now, after he made me eggs and protectively guided me through the airport—I can see it clearly. He's being tender because he's going to cut me loose. Maybe he thinks I'm too much of a rookie to take him on for real after convincing him he needs to stop hiding behind his training and protect his career. Or maybe it was the lack of pants this morning. Or the fact that I was falling asleep walking through the airport.

But—no! I can't let him fire me before I even get to prove myself for the first time. I can hide my longing better! I can wear pants at all times! I swear!

"Not yet," I say quickly before he gets the chance to give me the boot. "Just—I know what you're going to say . . . but . . . can you wait until after this weekend? Please?"

Derek opens his mouth to respond, but I'm saved by the nice lady over the intercom telling us that our gate is now boarding. My dreams get to live on another hour at least.

We both stand, and I pick up my backpack, but Derek takes it from me before I can strap it on my back and hoists it over his shoulder instead. A few minutes later, we board the plane and once seated in first class living like a queen and king, I conk out. And thankfully, Derek doesn't wake me up to fire me—he doesn't even wake me up to tell me my head is lying against his arm.

17

Derek

A dramatic southern accent perks up behind me. "Excuse me, kind sir, could I bother you for an autograph? You see, I'm your biggest fan in all the world! And it would mean ever so much—"

"Why the hell aren't you sleeping?" I ask Nora as she slips onto the barstool beside me, looking . . . *damn she's so pretty.* Her hair is all up on her head in a messy bun that drives me literally wild. She's in her same outfit that she changed into at the airport after our flight— bright pink leather sandals, light blue flowy pants, and a white short-sleeve button-down tucked into the high waistline of the pants. I can't quite describe it, but just looking at her you know she smells good—sweet and delicious. Like a dream.

She has no business looking this good after the insane day we've had. We got into Vegas around nine-thirty A.M. and were immediately driven to the set of the commercial—which took place in a casino. They threw me into an indigo suit that fit me like a glove and the crew shot a few different moody, ritzy-looking scenes of me playing blackjack, roulette, and pool. Turns out, pool is difficult to play in a skintight suit when you're a person my size. On the last take of the night, the fabric couldn't handle the strain any longer and split down the back of the jacket.

Other than leaving the jacket behind, I didn't bother changing when we made it to our hotel, where I deposited Nora at her room and told her I'd tie her down if she didn't sleep. We finished filming about eleven P.M., and Nora hung on set with me the whole day even though I tried multiple times to get her to go back to the hotel and nap. She wasn't having it. She's by far the most thorough agent I've ever had—which makes it even tougher that I've decided to dissolve our contract.

I really don't want to. Not only do I need a good agent and think she'd fit the bill perfectly, judging by how she handed me my ass the other night when I was all but giving up on my career, but I'm dreading letting her out of my life again.

It's not like all the pain I've been carrying from losing the woman I loved magically disappeared when I learned the truth, but it did take on a new light. I respect Nora for the decision she made for herself. And dammit if respecting her doesn't make me love her that much more.

In order for me to move on, I can't be faced with her day in and day out. It'll hurt too much.

Nora doesn't even bother looking guilty for popping up beside me at the bar now. "I tried to sleep. But it's too noisy."

"I can get you some earplugs."

She scrunches her nose and wiggles her fingers beside her head. "I mean it's too noisy in my brain. I can't stop thinking of all the potential endorsement deals you'd be incredible for—especially now knowing you can act. What do you think about—"

"Nora." I interrupt her while looking down at my empty glass. She can hear the change in my voice and knows what I'm about to say.

Her smile fades. I hate that I'm the reason for it dimming.

I grip my glass and stare into it as I say the words I know are going to hurt her. "I . . . I can't do this. I thought I could, but I can't. I need to dissolve our contract."

There's a beat of silence between us where only the sounds of Vegas fill the lull. From the corner of my eye, I see her shoulders rise and fall. "Is it . . . was I . . . did I not do a good job with the commercial?"

I look sharply at her. "What? No. You are incredible at your job and under different circumstances . . . I'd be lucky to have you." Those words felt thick in my mouth. "But . . ." *Damn, I don't want to say it.* "Because of our history, this is too much for me. I'm glad we talked the other night and cleared the air. I meant everything I said about understanding your side of things, but . . ." *I can't get over you.*

Her usual smile is nowhere in sight. "You don't think with time . . . ?"

I laugh once. "It's been eight years. I think if time was going to fix this, it would have already."

I feel like I'm being pretty transparent here. That she's understanding what I'm saying without me having to say the awkward words *Hey, I'm still in love with you and unless you love me back, we can't do this because it hurts so damn much to be near you and not have you.*

But then she says, "Is it . . . do you . . . do you still hate me?"

My heart rips down the middle.

Do I hate her? *I hate that when your mouth curves into a smile, I can't kiss it. I hate that you hold my heart in a vise grip and you have no idea. I hate that I've never been able to move on from you—not for a single day. I hate that if I were to tell you all of this, you'd leave, and I'd be left vulnerable and bleeding out at the bar.*

"No. *Hate* is not the right word for it," I say, because I can't bring myself to lay my heart out on the line in the middle of a Vegas bar. It's time to move on and just let her go.

We're interrupted when the bartender steps up and asks Nora what she wants, leaning over the counter toward her so he can hear—or maybe because he notices how beautiful her eyes are and wants a closer look.

"What can I get you?" he asks, and then with an obnoxious smirk, he tacks on, "My number maybe?"

And now I have the strongest urge to slam his face down into the bar and break his nose. Which, yep, this only solidifies why I can't work with Nora. I can't be around this all the time. Everyone seems to want her—with good reason.

She laughs at his flirty comment, and I bite the insides of my cheeks not to say anything. But then her hand juts out and lands on the side of my neck where it meets my shoulder. She grips it once, possessively, and I cut my eyes to her. *What the hell?*

"Sorry—I'm taken," she says, and my heart—my pitiful little sad sap of a heart—rockets against my sternum.

"Ah, too bad," says the bartender, turning to me with unapologetic eyes.

I keep quiet as Nora rattles off her order—a gin gimlet—all the while keeping her hand fixed on my neck. Her thumb glides up and down my skin and I doubt she understands how completely she's torturing me right now. Also how confused she's making me. Did I not just essentially fire her? What the hell is happening? And why am I contemplating sweeping her into my arms and carrying her straight up to my hotel room?

The bartender walks off and the moment his back is to us, Nora drops her hand away along with her smile.

"I'm so sorry!" she says, turning wide-eyed at me. "He hit on me and I'm just so tired. Plus he was definitely giving off the vibes of a guy who would only take a rejection as incentive to try harder, but then I realized you were here, and you already hate me, and I'm already fired so what do I have to lose, right?" She smile-grimaces at me. "Oh gosh, you don't look so happy. Are you going to fire me a second time? Here . . . I'll just . . . scootch right over here." She's shuffling her chair farther down the bar. "Consider me thoroughly fired. I won't bug you anymore. In fact, I'll zip it, lock it, and put it in my pocket." Of course she mimes this entire monologue by locking up her lips with an imaginary key and shoving it in her nonexistent pocket.

I watch as Nora sits ramrod straight and turns her face forward as if she no longer notices me. *This woman.*

"Nora, what are you doing?" I ask, trying to keep the laughter from my voice.

She blinks over at me and then pretends to take the key from her pocket and unlocks her lips. "I'm giving you space."

"This is space? You're going to sit an arm's length away from me and pretend I don't exist?"

"Yes—because I'm professional. The peak of professionalism." She's doing something with her hand now. A round-and-round gesture. Nora is a real full-body-conversation kind of person.

"What are you doing with your hand?" I ask.

"Rolling up my window so we don't talk anymore. You're free of me."

"You can have any imaginary car in the world, and you choose one with a manual window crank?"

She still won't look at me. "Of course because this"—she mimes pressing an imaginary button on the bar—"doesn't look nearly as cool."

"I'm not sure *cool* is the word you're looking for."

Nora smiles and slowly turns her face in my direction again. It's like a light has turned on behind her eyes. "You're not mad? You're joking with me?"

"Well, I would if your window was down, but . . ." I shrug and smile into my glass.

I notice the bartender headed our way again with Nora's drink. Against my better judgment, I lean over and hook my hand under Nora's stool, dragging her back to my side. Closer this time. The bartender sets her drink down and lingers a second, hoping to catch her eye (because I guess he feels like dying tonight). But Nora doesn't see him. She's staring at me.

We're both confused as hell.

I don't acknowledge how close I've pulled her. I don't acknowledge how incredible her hair smells. Instead, I continue like nothing out of the ordinary is happening. "Are you going to be okay once the contract is dissolved?"

"Was Matthew Macfadyen the best Mr. Darcy to ever grace the screen?"

"*What?*"

She takes a sip of her drink and licks her lips. "The answer is yes to both. I'll be fine." Except her eyes dart away from me quickly, like she doesn't want me to see the truth. She might not be okay. Her agency might think something was her fault. *Dammit.*

"I'll call them and tell them everything. Make sure they know it's nothing you did but because of my own issues."

"That's okay. I can handle them myself," she says with her usual Nora steel, and then takes a long drink, nearly downing her whole gimlet. She hisses once she swallows.

"A little tart?" I ask with a grin.

She doesn't answer. She swivels on her barstool and her knees push into the outside of my thigh. "So if I'm no longer your agent . . . tonight we're just . . . ?"

"Two people having drinks."

"*People*," she says with heavy inflection. "Right. Not friends. Because you hate me."

"Again—*hate* is not the word for it."

"Okay, well, whatever we are . . ." Her hand wraps around her glass and puts it to her mouth, tipping it back to drink the last swig of it. "Can we be it while drinking? Because I've had a long week and I think I'd like to get drunk safely. And you're a big guy," she says like maybe I didn't already know this. "And a gentleman. I think even though you hate me you'll keep me safe."

"Once again . . . *hate* is not the word."

She throws her hands up dramatically. "Loathe me, are annoyed by me, despise me, abhor me . . ."

Fucking love you.

". . . Have a distaste for me, wish ill upon my soul!"

I raise my hand in the air to catch my least favorite bartender's attention. Nora's gaze slides up my arm and her eyes sparkle. "Ooh, what are you doing? Are you getting his attention? Should I sit in your lap while you do?"

My eyes cut slowly to her, and she smiles wickedly up at me. For some reason—thinking I dislike her is giving her a whole new freedom. Fine. Whatever it takes to get through this last night before we go our separate ways and I make myself get over her for good.

I order us both another round of drinks as well as shots, and a few minutes later, we're raising our glasses in a toast.

"To the official end of us," she says in her usual candidness, making me want to laugh even as my chest hurts at the thought of losing her.

"To the end of us."

Our glasses clink together and then we both toss back our drinks.

18

Nora

I jerk awake from that same damn dream of Derek kissing the woman in the hallway. My eyes fly open to a sunlit room—a direct contrast of the oppressive hallway. I'm dragging in breaths like I just ran a mile, and my face is slick with that familiar cold sweat. *Just a dream.* I blink at the ceiling as a headache powerful as a bolt of lightning strikes through my brain. *Oof must keep eyes closed.* How much did I drink last night?

A lot.

Like a lot, a lot.

Lying on my back seems to be intensifying the headache, so I try to roll onto my side. But I can't because there's a tree trunk holding me down. I swing my gaze to the right, and that's when I realize I'm not alone. A man is in my bed. Oh god, not just any man. My ex-boyfriend turned ex-client is asleep beside me.

No, no, no. This is bad. Very bad.

Also very warm and snuggly. *But no! Don't think like that, Nora!*

Derek's big, heavy arm is draped over my midriff, and I can't breathe. I give it a moment's thought and decide I might be okay with being smothered to death so I don't have to deal with whatever *this* is.

I reach back into the gin-soaked corners of my mind to figure out what events led to this big mistake. Yikes, it hurts to think. Like pounding, throbbing, stabbing sort of pain. The special brand of agony that follows an entire night of drinking and not eating enough or hydrating.

How does a person know if they have alcohol poisoning? Asking for a friend.

But seriously, how did this happen? I haven't let go like that since—well, since I was last dating Derek. I should have known better. He always had a way of pulling me into his orbit of fun until I'm just flying round and round with my hands in the air like I just don't care.

It appears we obliterated rule number fourteen: No drinking together.

I shut my eyes again and make a squeak of anguish before shoving my arm into Derek's shoulder. "Hey! Wake up, you!"

He sucks in a breath like he was just resuscitated. "Huh?" Derek lifts his face long enough for me to see a pillow line slashing down the side of his cheek—almost making him look approachable rather than his usual hulking Thor vibes.

He groans, shoving his face back into the pillow, but doesn't remove his arm. The man is sprawled out like an eagle in flight. A shirtless, freakishly toned eagle, and god he is a sight to behold. His body is impeccable. And somehow even more massive-looking with a sheet draped over his lower half. I'm surprised his arm hasn't broken my rib cage.

Against my better judgment, my eyes trace the curves and hollows of the muscles lining his shoulders and back. The taut skin spreading over those muscles and the faded black tattoos dotting the expanse of his back and arms. And before I know it, I'm leaning toward the heat glowing from his body.

Oh my gosh, wait. Is he naked? Am I naked? This whole thing is going to become sixteen times more awkward if we have to be naked together while sober. It's been a long time since that phenomenon has occurred with Derek. So long it's practically like it never happened. Besides, we were young. Inexperienced.

I happen to know that the man lying beside me is not even in the same ballpark as inexperienced anymore. Nothing about him is like the gangly guy who sweetly took my virginity in college. It almost feels like waking up next to a stranger. And yet . . . familiar at the same time.

I do a quick pat-down of my body under the sheets, and thankfully, I seem to be fully clothed. Still wearing everything but my shoes. I'm nervous to peek under the covers at Derek, but I will because I'm a big girl and can do this.

If I had a breath to spare, I would sigh with relief at the sight of Derek's dress pants hugging his lower half, but I don't thanks to his heavy arm. Is it healthy for obliques to be that defined? I'm not sure you're supposed to be able to see them while someone sleeps and yet, here we are.

I smack Derek's boulder-filled arm a few times. "Derek. Move. I can't breathe!"

He slides it off like he's pulling it out of quicksand, and then flops over onto his back. Silence has never been louder as we stare at the ceiling. From the corner of my eye, I see his chest—so tan against the crisp white sheets—rising and falling. And I glimpse the tattoos there too, although I can't get a good look at them from this angle. Something with wings for sure.

"Am I in your bed?" His voice is sandpaper. Sexy, *sexy* sandpaper.

I need to get out of these sheets.

"It would appear so."

Silence again.

"That's not good."

"Not good at all." I press the heels of my hands against my eyes, trying to relieve the pounding. "What do you remember?"

He groans, apparently feeling as wonderful as I do. "Not much after that first round of shots." Like something hits him in the stomach, he jolts up. "Oh shit, cover your ears."

Derek charges for the bathroom. Unfortunately, hearing his less than graceful consequences of too much alcohol has me catapulting after him.

"Move, move, move!" I yell as he flushes, and then I take over where he left off. *Wonderful. Such a glorious morning. A beautiful day in the neighborhood!*

The bright bathroom lights are harsh and the very necessary exhaust fan sounds like a jet engine. Derek turns on the sink faucet and leans over to rinse his mouth. I can't even bring myself to care that he's witnessing everything that's happening to me right now or that I just witnessed it from him. We are in survival mode. I think I might be crying into the toilet bowl too.

What have I become?

Derek turns off the water and shifts behind me. I'm too concerned with the state of my stomach to wonder what he's doing back there until I feel his hands on my neck. My gin-soaked brain thinks he might be on the brink of strangling me to escape any consequences from last night. But no . . . he's just gathering my hair back and placing a cool cloth against my overheated skin. The sweetness of it doubles my tears.

"What are you doing?" I sit back on my heels and rip off a square of gritty-thin toilet paper and swipe it across my mouth.

"I didn't want you to get puke in your hair."

Now my tears triple. They're fountains, leaking down my face and tasting a little too much like mascara and gin.

I'm in a daze as I watch Derek find an elastic and then gently work his fingers through my hair, braiding it back until he gets to the end and secures it. All I can do is hold on to the toilet seat with both hands like it is a floatie in the ocean as memories wash over me. So many nights where I would sit in front of him on the couch, eating a bowl of ice cream and cereal while he braided my hair. I taught him how when we first started dating, and he did it as often as possible after that.

I whimper as another bolt of lightning strikes through my brain. "Is this death?"

"Pretty close." He presses the cool cloth to my neck once again, and his knuckles graze my skin. "I feel like roadkill. By the way, did we . . . ?" The way he hesitates to finish that sentence sort of undermines his playboy reputation. He almost sounds embarrassed. "I don't remember anything and that worries me for a lot of reasons."

I cut my eyes down to my fully clothed body, and then peek over my shoulder at his half-naked one. He's wearing pants but no shirt. No belt. Just . . . muscles and the waistband of his black boxer briefs peeking out over the top, and . . . tattoos. Two large beautifully detailed hawks are mirrored midflight on either side of Derek's chest. They have broad wings and talons outstretched as if they're about to land or pick something up. Like they're going right for the center of his sternum where they're going to rip his heart out and carry it away. The piece alone is gorgeous, but on Derek with his size and muscles and electric blue eyes, it's downright chilling.

I swallow down the lump in my throat and turn my face away. "I don't think anything happened beyond swimming down the river of alcohol."

Using the toilet seat to help me stand, I wobble like a baby fawn to the sink so I can dash cold water across my skin and smudge away the mascara from under my eyes. Derek sits on the side of the tub, rests his forearms on his knees, and tracks his eyes down the length of my body like he's searching for hidden memories. I nearly shiver from the intensity of his gaze. Is he remembering something from last night, or something from years ago?

"I don't think we did anything besides sleep." He drops his head and runs his hands over his face.

For a moment, my gaze lingers on him and a surge of ugly jealousy rises up. I don't even want to think about how many women have woken up to the sight of this man and tried to lock him down as quickly as possible. He's the kind of person you could easily become obsessed with—I know from firsthand experience.

I turn away from Derek and pick up my toothbrush with a plan to rid myself of this dragon breath and then flood my entire system with coffee. I'll take a shower alone (not sure why I felt like I needed to add the *alone* part) and then pack all my things and book a flight out this morning instead of waiting to fly back with Derek this afternoon like we planned. Derek asked to dissolve our contract last night because he doesn't like being around me, or can't let go of our past, or *whatever's* me, and then woke up in my bed and held my hair back while I threw up; and none of those events make sense to my organization-loving brain, so I'm going to run from them as quickly as possible.

"All right, Pender. We need to get you out of here without anyone noticing. Because if the media were to spot you coming out of my hotel room, it would spell disaster for both of us."

"Uh—"

I shove the toothbrush into my mouth and begin a furious teeth cleaning, talking to Derek through the mouth suds. "In fact, let's just forget this ever happened, okay? We're both grown-ups. No need to make a big stink out of nothing. Most likely you made sure I got back here safely and then toppled onto the bed and passed out with me. No harm, no foul."

Derek rubs the back of his neck while staring at me. "I'm not sure we're going to be able to forget last night quite so easily."

I roll my eyes at my own haggard-looking reflection. My hair is a wild mess of auburn tangles, and I have black streaks under my eyes from my mascara. There's only a faint tinge of pink stain where my lipstick used to be.

I know Derek isn't looking at the woman standing before him and wishing he could have her forever. Not anymore. Instead, he's thinking he got out in the nick of time.

"Derek, there's really no need for you to—"

He launches off the side of the tub and in two strides is directly behind me. We make eye contact in the mirror and the blacks of his eyes are competing against the blue. His hand moves around me to clasp mine, and in the process, his warm bare chest presses against me. He raises my hand, and my jaw drops—toothbrush falling out and hitting the ground with a ceremonial clack.

"Is that?" Toothpaste is dangerously close to dripping from my mouth, so I lean over quickly and spit before whirling around to face Derek. I hold my hand up between us and he does the same with his.

We stare at each other's ring fingers.

"It's possible . . ." he begins with a measured calm, ". . . that we got married last night."

19

Nora

My stomach rolls and I lean against the counter for support. That is not only a ring on my finger, it's a . . .

"A tattoo," I say in a faint whisper. "We . . . got tattoo wedding rings?"

A Rolodex of memories flips through my head. Derek and I were drinking at the bar and then we went drinking at another bar. And then we walked down the Vegas strip and passed a chapel. At that point we had so much alcohol in us that we laughed about how we wanted to get married "back in the day" and then thought about how funny it would be if we went ahead and did it now. *Ha-ha, Drunk Nora is soooo funny!*

So we did. We got married. And then we went to celebrate and have a wedding reception at yet another bar (still thinking what a funny joke it is) and that's when we realized we didn't have wedding rings. But once again, Drunk Nora is such a problem solver, and since there was a tattoo parlor right next door, I had the epic idea to permanently mark this bad decision on my body for the rest of my life, and oh gosh I'm going to throw up again. Or pass out. Or cry. Or all of the above.

Derek sees the look on my face and takes my shoulders in his hands. "Hey. It's okay. So we eloped. No big deal."

"No big deal?" I hold up my ring finger and flip him off with my new permanent accessory. "This feels like a big deal to me. Derek, imagine if the press gets hold of this? Imagine what it will do to our careers! Or no . . . your career will keep chugging along as usual because male athletes literally get away with everything and barely receive a slap on the wrist for it. But me . . . I could lose my job!"

The wings on his chest expand as he takes in a deep breath. "Okay, yeah, you're right. That's not great."

His hand snags back through his hair and I can't help but notice his naked bicep flexing obscenely right in front of my face. It's not my fault. I wouldn't be expected to avoid looking at a comet crashing in front of me and this bicep is roughly the same size. *I'm married to this bicep.*

I need to do something. I need to move. Organize. Sort my life as quickly and efficiently as possible so I can breathe again. A good A-to-Z process always does the trick, and I'll work through it step-by-step until everything is back to normal.

(A) *Pack my clothes.*

I breeze by Derek and fly into the room to pick up my few odds and ends scattered haphazardly all around the room like the wild and fun gal I am (read: neatly folded in various piles and placed in drawers).

Derek leans against the bathroom doorframe. "Nora . . . what are you doing?"

"Running for president. I know it seems like an odd time, but someone's got to do it." The sarcastic words whip out like icicles dropping overhead, aimed to kill. But I don't have patience right now to calmly explain to him that I'm packing my bags so I can (B) *catch the first flight out of here and back home, where I can* (C) *contact a lawyer and figure out how to get this marriage annulled.* And if I hurry and get ahead of this, maybe I can (D) *implement damage control before word leaks.*

What are the rules on annulment anyway? Surely if you've only been married ten hours and haven't consummated it, then it's easy peasy, right?

Derek's hand catches lightly against my arm when I try to pass him. Goosebumps flare down my back. "Nora. I need you to take a breath for a second."

Years of finely tuned smiles and punchy jokes crack under the pressure. I lance him with a look, feeling my heart punch against my chest. My head hurts, the light in here is too bright, and I'm so hungover my skin aches. There's no room to filter words in circumstances like this.

"Unlike you, Derek, I don't have the luxury of taking a breath. For you, this will all be an easy, charming story that everyone laughs at over drinks. In fact, I've been trained to handle situations like this for athletes since day one—it's literally part of my job to help sweep your indiscretions under the rug." My head pulses with each fervent word. "But I will be on the other side of it carefully picking up the pieces and trying not to cut my hands in the process." My voice cracks on the last word, and I hate showing any signs of weakness, so I pull my arm away from Derek and pace to the bed.

"I'm sorry," he says quietly.

My knees buckle against the mattress and I hunch over, hugging my stomach as a fresh wave of nausea hits me—but not because of the hangover. "You don't understand what it's like, Derek. I've—I've worked so hard to prove myself over the past two years. Including going by a name that I hate because you get further in this industry when other men think I'm one of the guys over email." I shut my eyes, hearing how ludicrous that sounds and sad that it's true. "And still, every single one of the men in my office is rooting for me to fail. Waiting for it. They tolerate Nicole because she's slightly terrifying, but they hate me. They hate that I've infiltrated their boys' club with my silly colorful outfits and my bubblegum personality, and they've decided I don't belong. At all times they think I'm an incompetent idiot—and this, Derek, this will prove it to them. Not to mention the fact that I might be outright *fired* when my bosses find out I've drunkenly married my client."

Derek no longer leans against the doorframe. With that trademark thunderous scowl, he strides to me and drops down onto his knees. The weight of his hands dimples the mattress on either side of my hips, bracketing me—cornering me so I'll look at him.

"I do know what it's like to operate differently than those around you and be seen as weak because of it." His voice fades into something raw and tender. "And how bad it feels to work your ass off for something and still come up short in other people's eyes *because* of those differences."

"How do you know?" I ask honestly. "You've always been at the top of your career. Everyone respects you."

A debate runs behind his eyes. "It's a story for another day. Right now, I want you to hear that there is nothing incompetent about you. And I swear to you, I will do everything I can to keep your name out of this. I have incredible lawyers who can be discreet. We can annul this marriage and I won't tell a soul. I swear it, Nora."

Something fuzzy crawls into my heart. All I can do is stare into his blue eyes—telling myself not to wrap my arms around his neck and beg him to hold me. The heat of his body curls around me and it would be so easy to just lean into it, letting his arms smooth away the sharp fear prickling my chest.

I don't get the chance.

My phone vibrates loudly on the bedside table. I sniff and swat away the tears that have leaked down my cheeks. Derek drops his arms so I can get my phone. *It's Nicole.* And if she's calling out of the blue like this, it means she knows somehow.

"Hello?" I answer, trying not to sound like I just barfed up eighteen pounds of alcohol in the rare chance that she actually just wants to know where I filed one of her contracts.

"It's all over the Internet, Mac."

"No." The word comes out as a puff of useless air.

"Yes. Not sure if you know this yet, but you guys posted a photo on Derek's Instagram of you two last night."

"Naked?"

"What? No."

"Oh, right. I'm not even naked now."

Nicole doesn't laugh, and Derek is watching me with pinched brows before he stands, gaze searching the room. "You were fully clothed, but your tongue was down his throat and you two were holding up your ring fingers like middle fingers. A very screw-you-we're-in-love photo. Epic . . . but . . ."

"Trashy."

"Your word, not mine," she says, sounding more empathetic than I've ever heard her.

Derek finds my purse and brings it to me. The sight of this ripped, bare-chested, tattooed male carrying my purse is something I won't soon forget. It's increasingly difficult to fully focus on Nicole's bad news.

"It wasn't a favorable look, and it's going viral," she says. "I shouldn't tell you this, but . . . I've been in a meeting with Joseph over the last hour, and it wasn't good, Mac. You're about to receive an email invitation for a videoconference with us. And because I know you and I'm sure there's more at play here than how it appears, I wanted to give you a heads-up so you're not blindsided by it."

I slump down onto the bed—crumpling under those words. *I'm probably getting fired.* And then like a ghost, I slip out of my skin long enough to stare at this sad lump of a person and judge her for not having the decency to remember what I'm sure was a damn good French kiss with Derek.

Life is deeply unfair.

I'm spiraling out too much to wonder why Derek is rifling through my purse. But when he pulls out my tube of acetaminophen, it makes sense. He's just trying to get rid of his hangover headache.

"So . . . I'm fired?" I ask, all flat and emotional.

In front of me, Derek taps two pills into his palm and then disappears behind me to the other side of the room.

"Legally, I can't answer that question in an unofficial phone call. But I need you to know, I've tried everything to dissuade Joseph from his decision. Hopefully you can come up with something better."

"Why are you even warning me, Nicole? I deserve to be fired."

She grunts a frustrated sound. "I really shouldn't be saying this, but you didn't break any company policies, Mac. There's nothing that says you can't be in a relationship with a client. What you did do, however, was make a spectacle of yourself that reflects badly on the agency. That's the only reason they could fire you. So don't give up yet—I didn't risk my ass calling you to hear you wallow. I called so you could get a hell of an argument ready."

"But why?" At this moment, I don't feel worth it. Maybe all the patronizing comments the jerks at the office have said to me are true. Maybe I'm not cut out to be an agent since I clearly let my feelings for a guy get in the way of my career.

"Don't do that," Nicole says, almost as if she's reading my thoughts. "You're a damn good agent. Yes, you screwed up, but we all do from time to time. Move on. Find a way to turn this into something positive."

Derek rounds the bed and moves in front of me. I'm face-to-face with his navel and I realize after staring for a second too long at his smooth, hard skin that he's handing me something.

Nicole continues talking in my ear. "You're the only other person in this toxic office who understands what we're up against. I can't lose you or I'll have to quit too. So fix it."

Even in the midst of my turmoil, I find myself smiling. There's a man in front of me gesturing for me to take the meds and water I thought he was getting for himself. And there's a woman who I endlessly respect on the other end of the phone looking out for me. The shadow of loneliness that has been creeping over me for a while now fizzles away like morning haze being eaten up by the sun. I'm not alone.

"You're a good friend, Nicole."

She's silent a moment before answering. "We're not friends." And then hangs up. But I don't take it personally because I know it's a lie. A colleague wouldn't risk what she just risked for me. I think Nicole is just as unfamiliar with the idea of friendship as I am. We're both workaholics with big personalities. We're too much for most people and used to facing everything on our own. Two little dramatic peas in a pod.

"Take these. You'll be able to think clearer without a hangover headache," Derek says, and it's this tender offering that slams into my stomach.

My anxiety and nerves hold hands and twirl, forcing me to run to the bathroom and pitch my face back into the toilet bowl, throwing up all of my bad decisions, hoping to anyone above that Derek isn't listening.

This time, it's really not funny. I'm throwing up and sobbing into the toilet bowl because everything I've worked so hard for is gone.

"Please go away," I tell Derek when I hear him enter the bathroom.

"No." He drops down behind me.

"Derek, I'm serious. Please go! I have to deal with my bosses in a few minutes and you don't need to be here for that."

"I'm staying, Nora." He leans around me to turn on the shower.

I want to shut my eyes and slump over the toilet seat and live here for the rest of my life instead of facing what comes next for me. But Derek's arm circles my waist and hauls me to my feet. I don't want to stand, though. I want to be left in my misery. I've never considered giving up before, but everything is a towering monster this time. I'm too tired.

"I can't do it, Derek. I messed up. My career is over, and I don't want to face it all."

"Hey." He spins me around and I sag into him even though I really need to stand on my own two feet. I am usually so good at it. But today, I'm exhausted, and his chest is so firm and warm and capable.

He doesn't push me away. He slides his arms around me and holds me like my soul has been craving. I melt against him, savoring every inch of our connected bodies. This hug is like coming home from a long trip and finally drinking coffee from your favorite mug. Curling up in that plush blanket you've been dreaming about for days.

"You didn't let me give up," he says, his voice a soft rasp in my ear. "And I'm not going to let you give up now. You have a meeting to get ready for."

"A meeting where I get fired." I sniffle against his bare chest. "Oh yes—I should look so presentable for it. What color do you think will pair best with shame?"

Derek takes my jaw in his hand and tilts it up so I have to look in his eyes. There's a new heat there, flaming in the black centers. It looks nothing like hate. "You're not getting fired—and if you think for one damn second I'm going to let you get your fingers cut cleaning up my mess, you don't know me at all. Lift your arms."

I'm so lost and confused and scared of my future that I don't even fight him. I raise my arms above my head. Derek closes his eyes before peeling off my shirt. Goosebumps break over my chest as he reaches around and unclasps my bra. Next he shucks my pants and underwear until all scraps of clothing are like fallen leaves, heaping on the floor at the end of a season. I'm standing completely naked in front of him, but he never opens his eyes. *I wish he would.* Clearly this is Distraught Nora thinking these inappropriate thoughts, and I should be grateful that Derek doesn't share them.

His hand engulfs my bare shoulder blade as he guides me to the shower.

Once the curtain is closed, I step under the warm stream of water and close my eyes, feeling the last of my mascara melt down my face. *Pitiful. You're absolutely pitiful, Nora.*

It's quiet for only a minute.

"I think we should stay married," Derek says from the other side of the curtain, making me startle so much that I nearly slip and fall in the tub. Thankfully there's a handy little shower rail I grab hold of.

"Are you still drunk?" I say over the water. "You'd have to be to suggest something like that."

"I'm perfectly sober."

"Okay then, suffering from some sort of alcohol poisoning to the brain. Call a doctor. Because a few days ago you told me you don't even want to be friends with me—and now you're suggesting we stay married?" I squirt some shampoo into my hand and it makes a gross noise. "That was the shampoo bottle, by the way."

"Mm-hm."

I gasp and clutch the shower curtain to my chest, peeking around it. "How dare you not believe me at an overwhelming time like this?" Should I laugh or cry? I don't know anymore.

He's grinning and leaning his half-naked body against the wall, arms folded—Casanova in the flesh. His eyes are not closed now, and they rake over my wet hair and exposed collarbones. Suddenly, I've never felt more naked in my life.

I let the curtain fall closed again and shield myself from whatever look he's giving me.

"Hear me out," Derek says, his voice sounding a little hoarse. "Most likely your agency thinks this was all a drunken mistake that we're going to annul as quickly as possible."

"And they would win a million dollars because that is correct."

"Okay, but what if we convince them that it's real. That . . . we're staying together and purposely got married?"

I pause with my hands in my hair full of suds. "Why would we do that?"

"Because I have a feeling that they don't want a scandal on their hands just as much as you don't. So if we can let them know it's not a scandal and not something we're ashamed of—maybe they'll let you keep your job."

Wait. Maybe he's not wrong. Maybe this is exactly the kind of plan Nicole was telling me to make.

I don't even care how I look, I peek around the curtain again because I need to see Derek's face. "Why would you even consider doing that?"

His smile curves softly and when he shrugs, the combination is almost sad. "Because it's for you."

I don't know what to say to that. Or even what to make of it, for that matter.

"But you hate me now," I say quietly, and a bubble stream streaks down my face.

Derek shoves away from the wall and moves to me. He wipes the bubbles back from my face and sinks his fingers into my soapy hair. "*Hate* is not the word for it, remember? It was never hate."

No, I don't remember because all thoughts have fled from the way he's looking at me. There's steam behind me, a naked male torso in front of me, and cold air brushing over the exposed portion of my chest and neck. It's a swirl of sensations—all of them mixing to be something dangerous. Something unforgettable.

And for one split second, Derek's eyes drop to my mouth—they hold there long enough for me to wish it were his mouth on my lips instead of his eyes. But then he removes his hand from my hair and steps away, drying his hand on a towel. I can't look away; my body is tuned to his movements, feeling that something is coming.

He gives me a quick hesitant glance before he reaches into his back pocket to pull out his wallet.

A pang of disappointment hits me. "Are you changing your mind and you're going to pay me off? You should know, pal, I'm very expensive."

He only smirks and removes a little piece of paper. It's yellowed, and the creases are so well worn it looks like it could tear into halves from a light breeze. I know what it is without even having to open it, but I reach my arm out from behind the curtain and take it from him anyway. My fingers itch for the memory. To be taken back to the time when I wrote this.

"It's the IOU I gave you."

I remember the day like it was yesterday—waking up almost as hungover as I am now after Derek had taken care of me all night despite having only just met me. And since I'm not comfortable with people helping me out of the goodness of their hearts, I gave him an IOU to redeem at any point.

"I want to use it now," he says confidently. "I want you to stay married to me for damage control—you owe me."

I'm going to cry again. I will dissolve into a puddle of feelings and swirl right down the drain. Of course he would use his IOU to help me. Because when he says damage control, he means damage control for *me*.

I look back down at the little innocent paper Derek has held on to all of these years. Even when he hated me. Even when he thought he'd never see me again, he's carried this with him in his back pocket. Why?

I look him right in his burning eyes, hunting for any signs of distress. There's nothing but assurance. Unwavering dedication that I don't feel I deserve but absolutely need right now. I have no choice—if he's willing to help me, I need to accept his help.

"Well . . . I can't argue with this very formal and binding IOU, now can I?"

"I wouldn't advise it. I do have good lawyers." His mouth tilts into a sideways grin that has Pop Rocks crackling in my belly. He then plucks the IOU back from my fingers, refolds it, and seals it into his wallet once again. *This is mine,* his eyes say.

"Might want to rinse your hair out. You're about to get shampoo in your eyes," he says, and that's when I realize I'm having this lovely, effervescent moment with a bubble wig on my head.

Sexy as always, Nora.

20

Nora

Twenty minutes later, Derek and I are both seated at the little hotel desk with my laptop open in front of us and a videoconference call connecting with Nicole and Joseph.

"Hi," I say with a smile I don't feel. "Is it too hopeful to assume you're calling because you missed seeing my cheerful face around the office and needed a boost?"

Nicole gives me a look. Joseph—the owner—grimaces. They don't like my humor today. Or any day, really.

My knee bounces like a windup toy set loose.

Nicole sighs and her eyes betray no hints that she called me half an hour ago to prep me for this very conversation. She's a good actress. "Mac—you know I like to cut right to the chase."

"I do—yes, it's one of your most impressive qualities." I imagine Nicole is the special breed of person who flips right to the end of a book and reads the last page first. She won't waste her time on a story that takes her by surprise. "But if you don't mind, I'd like to apologize before we get started. I'm truly so sorry. I know that what happened between me and Derek this weekend doesn't look good, and I feel terrible for any bad publicity I might have brought to the agency."

Mr. Newman (Joseph) nods and, when preparing to talk, leans much too close to the screen. It's ninety percent his nose at this point. An ominous little frown etches between his bushy gray brows and my leg bounces at double time now.

"Mac—you know that despite your unconventional ways, we've enjoyed having you in the agency and have considered you as an asset to the team. But . . ."

Oh. Here it comes. The hammer. I hate the hammer.

". . . But this was bad," he continues. "I don't know exactly what happened between you and Mr. Pender—who I see is seated beside you—and please know, Derek, that none of what I'm about to say reflects on the way our agency feels about you." Seems about right. "But, Mac, we can't have an agent on our roster who has a reputation of imbibing and eloping with a client in Vegas on a whim. It doesn't look good and frankly is highly unprofessional."

I wish I could disagree, but he's absolutely right. Of course, there's much more at play here than they understand, but I'm not even sure that makes it better. I should have been honest about my history with Derek from the start and told them it would be a conflict of interest to represent him.

My knee is now its own person with a mind of its own. All my stress and anxiety filter down to that one extremity as I prepare to hear the words *you're fired* come through the line.

But then the strangest, most startling thing happens: Derek's hand moves under the desk to settle on my thigh. The weight of his heavy hand melts against my leg and the bouncing quiets immediately. He squeezes once, and instinctively (as well as irrationally), my body eases. For the first time in my career, I realize I don't have to face this obstacle alone.

Derek clears his throat—not removing his hand from my leg. "But see, that's the thing," Derek begins, and my head whips in his direction. He glances at me quickly, and I get one more gentle squeeze on my knee. *Trust me.*

"It wasn't random or an accident," Derek tells my bosses with all the confidence in the world.

And then he lets go of my leg, just long enough to raise his arm over my head and settle it around my shoulders, pulling me into his body. *Ohmygoshyes.*

"Nothing about our elopement was accidental. It's been years and years in the making, in fact." That's a nifty way to spin the truth.

"Explain," Joseph states firmly but not unkindly. He's intrigued.

"Well, sir, we didn't inform anyone from the beginning because Nora and I both thought it would be a non-issue, but . . . we had a previous relationship. A serious one back in college."

Joseph's bushy, Eugene Levy eyebrows rise. I can't tell if he's happy about this admission or even more set in his decision to fire me. My knee bounces again. I would really like to ask for a sidebar with Derek right about now to make sure he knows what he's doing. This time, his leg hooks over mine to pin it down under the desk.

"We decided not to make it a big thing since our history was so far behind us. And that was my first mistake." His eyes drop to me now and the affectionate look on his face is so convincing even I believe it. "I should never have assumed that I wouldn't immediately fall in love with Nora all over the second I saw her again. I should have been open with Nicole and the agency in anticipation of needing to spend the rest of my life with this woman."

My lips part and I breathe deeply as my eyes search Derek's face. He looks so genuine. So heartfelt. Why does it feel like he's telling the truth right now? *But no.* That's absurd. Just last night he was firing me. Wanting space from me. Hate or not, he didn't want to spend another day in my company.

No one interrupts Derek. "When we were both honest with each other about our feelings, one thing led to another, and we decided we couldn't go another hour without making it official. It's not a fluke, or an accident, or something that's going away. We are married now and not ashamed of it."

Good lord above, what a convincing act. I try not to let my shoulders sag at that thought. Which, hello, is ridiculous because I don't even want a relationship with Derek! *Do I?* Honestly, I've been so full steam ahead on my career that I haven't even stopped to consider that maybe I am ready for the next phase of my life plan. Maybe I can balance all this time.

Ah. No. What's happening to me? I can't entertain the idea of a real relationship with Derek. When we talked everything out before this call, we decided we would stay married only long enough to settle everyone's feathers and then quietly divorce and not make a big fuss. That it would be a marriage in name alone—and fake as the plastic plant in my office. (Real plants don't grow in there from the lack of sun.)

Joseph sighs deeply and I'm on the edge of my seat for his answer. He opens his mouth to say goodness knows what after that epic speech from Derek, but Nicole finally breaks her silence and talks before he can.

"You know, Joseph, I was just thinking . . ." Her red lips tilt in the corner into the most conniving wonderful smirk I've ever seen. And if I'm not mistaken, there's a sparkle of pride in her eyes too. This was the sort of plan she was hoping we'd make. "If this marriage is real and they plan on making it last for the long haul, this could be really good exposure for the agency."

The crease between his brow craters. "We *just* had a meeting about how big a problem this was going to be."

"Yes, well, that was when we expected them to get the marriage annulled immediately. But a marriage based on love and commitment is a completely different story."

My heart is on a white-water rapid. Am I losing my job or not? It sort of feels like not, but also like a very intricate web of lies is being strung out in front of me, and let me tell you, I am not good at lying.

Nicole steeples her fingers in front of her (her nails match her lipstick). "I say we get out in front of this and release a statement in support of their relationship immediately. No apologies. No hints of a mistake, because"—she pauses meaningfully and grins like a sly cat—"because this wasn't one, as they've just confirmed."

The odd thing is, something real and honest in me truly doesn't think it was a mistake. And that's got to be bad, right? In what world is something so messy a good decision?

"In fact," Nicole continues, "I think I could pull some strings and turn this into something great if they're up for it. I have a good friend at *Celebrity Spark* magazine who dies for stories like this. I say we put Derek and Mac on a plane tomorrow for . . . I don't know, a resort on the beach somewhere to celebrate their honeymoon for a week or two," she says flippantly. "We can let *Spark* cover the story of their whirlwind romance and direct the narrative in the direction we want it to go. A powerhouse couple or something."

This time, my hand moves to Derek's thigh that's still paperweighting mine, and I grip it out of terror. This is not good. Not good at all. Derek and I can't go on a honeymoon. We're not really married! *Oh god, I'm committing fraud!* Can I go to jail for this? Actually, I might be thinking of obtaining a green card. Different situation.

Derek's hand covers mine, and we're an absurd Jenga of limbs. He's as relaxed as if we're sitting in the movie theater watching a completely fake scenario unfold that has nothing to do with our very real lives. Still, the warmth of his hand is reassuring.

"You really think this is a good idea, Nicole?" Joseph asks.

Nicole tips her eyebrows in amusement like she knows any idea she comes up with is gold. "It's a fantastic one. I predict it will make a cover story for *Spark,* and even bring in new endorsement deals for Derek once it shifts the spotlight off his recovering injury and onto what a romantic he is—because the public loves nothing more than seeing a man devastatingly in love. Just ask my client Nathan. I had him and his now-wife Bree do something similar a few years ago and it brought loads of attention to him. And as for you, Mac, it could re-establish your professionalism before any unsavory narratives circulate about you. It's a win-win for all of us."

Derek was right. This is really going to work.

"Now the question is, Mac . . . are you okay with having a very publicized honeymoon? I don't want to force something on you that you're not comfortable with."

I take exactly two seconds to respond. But you better believe that in those two seconds, I have entire days' worth of overthinking. I stalk through a maze of possible solutions to get out of this mess and hit a dead end every time. I'm out of options.

If I want to keep my job, I have to stay married to my ex.

"I'm in! Let's do this Hokey Pokey." Everyone blinks at me. Everyone but Derek, who is staring down at my hand on his leg with a look I can't decipher. "And by Hokey Pokey I mean please do contact your people at *Celebrity Spark,* and Derek and I will show up wherever they need us to."

Nicole nods once. "Good. I'll be in touch."

She ends the meeting, and me and *my husband* are immediately swamped in overwhelming silence.

Buckle up, Nora, you're going on a honeymoon with your ex.

21

Derek

As a pro athlete, I have punished my body plenty of times. I've pushed it to the brink of physical failure—including playing a game hours after a stomach flu. But I'm not sure I've ever felt as beat as I do now after waking up massively hungover, married to my ex, and then having to spend hours frantically shopping around Vegas because we didn't pack enough clothes for a spontaneous honeymoon to Cancún, Mexico.

Nicole's friends at *Spark* were very excited about this scoop, and they said it would pair perfectly with a promotion they were already set to run with a ritzy resort.

The plan is for me and Nora to love each other all over this resort and *Spark* will photograph it. *Damn.* That didn't sound right. Essentially my and Nora's honeymoon will be sponsored by Nirvana— a new luxury resort in Cancún. We'll eat at their restaurant, lounge on their beach, swim in the pools, and do a few resort activities— basically, say cheese for ten days while wearing a bathing suit and then make it home a few days before training camp begins.

We landed around nine P.M. in Cancún after five hours of the worst turbulence I've ever experienced where neither one of us slept a wink and barely said two words to each other. And then there was gridlock traffic leaving the airport (because of course there would be traffic at nine P.M. on a Sunday night because that's the way things go when you randomly wake up married one day to the person you were trying to never see again).

And to top it all off, Nora is being strange. Well, stranger than normal. She's dancing around me like I'm a human grenade. However, to be fair, I can't decide how to act around her either. What the hell are we now? And how are we going to survive for ten days like this?

We're finally in the hotel lobby now and I feel like I've made it to the promised land. Not because the place is incredible (though it is) but because I know a bed is only minutes away. I need food. And then sleep. And after those things, I'll be ready to address whatever this is between me and Nora.

Even though it's late, the resort is brimming with wealthy energy and people in white linen clothing. Nora keeps getting distracted by the opulence as we walk.

"Now that is a lion sculpture! We've got to get you one of those. It could be a daddy lion to your baby lion." She gasps. "Mufasa for your Simba!"

"I don't need any more lions."

She laughs one sardonic laugh. "As if anyone can own too many lions. Come on, Pender, use your head."

"Would you just keep walking?" I put my hand to the small of her back, ignoring the way it fits like a lock and key. How I never want to remove it.

The deeper we get into the resort, the more attention we gain because unfortunately my size doesn't allow me to fly under the radar all that easily. Even if they don't know exactly who I am, people generally assume I'm an athlete of some sort and start googling. Doesn't take long after that.

The elopement post going viral hasn't helped either. I opened my social media for ten seconds, and that was all I could take. Most people were supportive, and then a lot of ignorant assholes called Nora terrible names I'd like to jam down their own throats. I guess that's why I'm feeling protective of her now.

As we walk over the marble floors, we both notice two couples milling around the hotel bar staring at us. They have the look of intoxicated fans about to swoop in and ask for autographs and pictures.

Nora notices them too and steps in front of me—her small hand splayed out behind her in the air like she's projecting an invisible shield.

"What the hell are you doing?" I ask the back of her head.

She cuts a look at me like I've lost my mind and pulls herself up to as tall as her five-foot-seven stature will allow. "Um—protecting you. What does it look like?"

She's . . . oh my god. *This woman.* "Why are you protecting me?"

"Because I'm your agent. That's what we do."

"That is not what you do. Bill never once acted as my bodyguard."

She shrugs a single shoulder. "Not my fault Bill wasn't as great an agent as me. Why? You don't think I can do it? There are female bodyguards, you know."

I snag her hand, intertwining our fingers and tucking her against my side. The lock-and-key sensation flares all over again. "Yes—but they're trained. You have arms like spaghetti noodles. And besides, this"—I gesture to our clasped hands—"will keep people from approaching better than your bodyguard scowl. People don't usually talk to me while I'm on a date, for some reason."

"Interesting logic. You should have made Bill hold your hand."

I grin down at her. "Who says I didn't?"

Nora halts and doesn't laugh like I expect. She studies me as her mouth curves into an intrigued smile before those eyes drop to my lips and stay there for one long moment.

"Nora. You're staring at my mouth." It comes out unplanned and maybe a tad too hopeful.

She doesn't look away. "Because you finally smiled. I don't want to miss it if it happens again."

I roll my eyes and tug her with me toward the check-in counter. She talks with the receptionist, but I don't hear a word of it. My mind is stuck back there where Nora stared at my mouth like it was something wonderful that belonged to her.

After checking in, we decline help from the bellhop (because honestly, I'm just sick of people) and step into the elevator with our two suitcases. Unfortunately, a random guy follows us in, and I don't miss the way his gaze rakes over Nora from head to toe. It's been happening all day today actually. She's wearing a pair of tight black leggings, white Nikes, and a boxy purple crop top (all items we acquired this morning on our shopping spree).

Nora is all beautiful curves, strong-looking legs, and soft pale skin that I'm trying with all my respect not to notice but failing miserably. Especially when I'm able to remember—hazy as it is—what all that soft skin felt like under my fingertips.

And it doesn't help that when she reaches up and adjusts the ponytail sitting high on her head, her shirt hikes up, showing a few extra inches of her stomach. At the sight of her navel, a memory rockets back to the front of my mind. Us playing on the couch while watching a movie (using the term *watch* loosely) and her shirt riding up just like this. I smiled and then lightly sank my teeth right there in the soft side of her stomach—just enough to make her gasp and then laugh from her own reaction.

A little white horizontal scar that wasn't there when we dated lives on the side of her abdomen. My nails bite into my palms to keep from reaching out and touching that thin mark.

Nora has lived a whole life I know nothing about, and I hate it.

She catches me staring at her stomach, and I wonder how transparent my desires are. *Pretty damn transparent* given the way she raises her eyebrows.

I cover my ass by meeting her gaze. "I was just thinking about how I'm really going to have to wear sunglasses on the beach, or I'll be blinded by the light of your stomach." It's delivered in deadpan perfection.

"Hey!" She points up at me. "Not nice. Some of us can't lay our bodies out to crisp up like a brown biscuit in the sunshine. Some of us have to lather up with SPF 70 or we turn into a shade of red that can be seen from outer space. Last time I tanned"—she puts bunny ears around the word *tanned*—"the lower part of my butt cheeks were so fried I couldn't sit down for five days. But as a plus, my standing goal was met at two hundred percent that week."

Sometimes I wonder, if I stay quiet, will she continue to talk the whole night? I'd happily let her.

Suddenly, gawking guy peeks around my shoulder to look at Nora, and the scent of alcohol oozing off him speaks for his boldness when he says, "I'm happy to volunteer as tribute to lather you up so you're protected from the sun, princess."

My eye twitches with the sudden urge to shove his body back against the wall.

Nora, however, laughs just as the elevator doors open. "Really kind of you, random dude. Sort of batting a hundred on the creepy chauvinistic vibes, but thanks for the offer." She exits the elevator and I turn and face him, backing him into the corner but not laying a hand on him.

"Speak to her like that again and find out what happens."

I leave him wide-eyed and speechless. The elevator doors close behind me and, finally, Nora and I are alone walking down the hallway. I am officially done with people today. *Except for her.*

We both stop just outside our suite, and she grins up at me. "What did you say to Mr. Princess back there?"

My eyes slit and I fight the smile trying to break. "What do you mean?"

"I know you hung back and talked to him. What'd you say, Dere-Bear?"

I breathe deeply and shrug. "It was so long ago. Who can remember?"

"Try your best," she says, a taunting grin curling her lips. And now I know I'm no better than the dude in the elevator because I want to take Nora's hips in my hands and pin her back against this hotel door, and kiss her until our mouths are bruised. But of course I won't unless she asks me to. Even then, I'm not sure that I would do it because my heart still feels battered from how she left me in college. I'm scared to want her this much again.

"I might have said something like . . . 'Talk to her like that again and find out what happens.'"

Nora chokes out a laugh. "Derek, you didn't. And with that macho voice too?"

"I didn't like the way he was talking to you. It was disrespectful. And 'princess'? Was he serious with that shit?"

Nora shakes her head at me while fighting a smile. "For the record, I'd prefer to fight my own battles. But also—" she looks down, presses her tongue into her cheek, and then glances up again—"Thank you. It's . . . kind of nice to have someone looking out for me."

"Always," I say, because I mean it. Even when I was at my angriest with her, I still would have stepped in front of a bus for her.

We stare at each other now, both seemingly at a loss for what to say, but clearly feeling an old intimacy curl around us like smoke. It's so thick I can barely breathe. Nora's expression mirrors mine. Pinched brows. Thoughtful eyes. Parted lips. How do we acknowledge this thing between us?

We're saved when my phone rings. I answer it immediately—pathetically looking for a way to fill the silence while also delaying having to enter that suite with Nora.

"What the actual hell! Are you married?" Nathan practically shouts into the phone. I've made Dad angry.

"Well—"

"Give me that!" It's Bree. I imagine her jumping for the phone and, when Nathan won't give it to her, jabbing her fingers into his ribs until he involuntarily pitches forward, and it slides into her hand. Because a second later, she sounds as if she's running away as she says, "Derek Pender, you're in so much trouble! You can't just post something like that and then go dark for an entire twenty-four hours with nothing more than a text that says *it's fake—I'll explain later. Keep it to yourself.*" She says that last part in an overly deep voice that honestly gives my ego a boost. "That's a bad friend!"

"She's right, very un-classy of you, Pender," Nora says with a smug eyebrow lift that I don't need from her right now. "Even I found a minute to call my mom."

It's true, she called and told her the news pretty much the second we hung up with Nicole and Joseph yesterday. I asked how she took it and Nora only smiled and said, *Pam lives for stuff like this. She told me to keep her in the loop.*

"Wait, is Nora there right now?" Bree asks, sounding too excited for my comfort. "Put her on the phone! Better yet . . ."

Oh great. Bree is trying to FaceTime me now.

I let the call connect and Nora tilts her head against my shoulder so we can both watch Bree actively sprint through their house to keep Nathan (who's in the view behind her) from getting the phone. She feints right in the kitchen and slides over the counter. "You're a sucker, Nathan Donelson! You're never getting this phone back."

"She seems sweet," Nora says in a whisper to me.

"We call her *Bree Cheese.* If you're not careful she'll try to become your best friend."

"There's no trying, only succeeding!" Bree says with one of her huge smiles into the phone. "So you're Nora?" Now she's hurdling the back of the couch.

"No, I'm his other fake wife."

"Oh my god, she has a sense of humor too! I love you already," Bree shouts just before she runs into something and the phone clatters to the ground.

I hold the key card in front of the lock and the light turns green. That feels metaphorical in an intimidating way.

All I hear over the line is Bree yelping and then a grumbled argument before Nathan's face fills the screen. "How did this happen? You said you were never going to get married. And why is it fake? And how long is it fake for? Also—hi, Nora," Nathan says with a grin that he doesn't even mean to be sexy but probably is. *Fine, it absolutely is.* "Nice to see you again."

Bree hops like a squirrel on a caffeine high behind Nathan's shoulder. "Answer the questions, Derek!"

I would, except Nora and I finally step inside our incredible suite and our eyes track to the same spot in the room.

"Wait—what are y'all looking at?" Bree asks, smashing her face closer to the screen.

"I don't know," Nathan responds more to his wife. "They both look like they've just seen a monster, though."

I swallow. "We'll call you back later."

"Derek Pender, don't you dare hang—"

I end the call, unable to tear my eyes from the unfortunate object in the room.

There's only one bed.

22

Nora

It's a single-room suite. And of course it is! Why would we have expected the agency to book us anything different? We're married, for pancake's sake. But somehow in the mad dash to buy and pack our clothes and get to the airport and slip further into delirium from complete lack of sleep over the last forty-eight hours, I didn't stop to consider that Derek and I might have to share a room. Share more than just the same space, in fact.

I blink at the only bed in the room.

It's enormous—which is good, I guess. But also, somehow daunting. A zing of desire strikes down my spine as I think of sleeping next to Derek again. Should I be having desire zings? I don't think so. *You're his agent, Nora!* Wait, am I? He unofficially fired me.

Dear god, the enormity of the mess I'm in fully hits me. I'm married to my client who fired me. Who also happens to be Derek. Who I also happen to still have feelings for and find myself wondering every ten minutes if I made a mistake breaking up with. Wondering if maybe I could kiss him, and he'd kiss me back?

Not good.

My eyes slip to the man beside me. Up his solid tattooed arms to his hulking shoulders, over his square jaw and to that full mouth a man has no business possessing.

This is going to be tricky.

"Well now, this is a gorgeous suite," I say, stepping deep into the bowels of the beast but away from the offending bed. I drop my backpack next to the big black velvet couch and run my hand over its soft armrest.

"I've always wanted a velvet couch." I'm a blabbermouth with nothing important to say.

Derek watches me dramatically wiggle my butt around and make a big show out of loving this piece of furniture. "This is sublime. I mean, what a couch. In fact . . ." I trail off while unzipping my backpack and pulling my laptop out onto the tops of my thighs. "I think I'm going to claim it, if that's okay with you?"

"Nora." That's Derek's all-too-familiar *what is happening to you now* way of saying my name.

I force my gaze up.

He's still standing in his same place just past the door, but he's so large it feels like he's taking up the whole damn room. Another reason I'm not sharing that bed with him. He seems to be hitting a growth spurt as we speak, and his shoulders are doubling in size. There'd be no room for me on there. Our butts would bump. Legs would tangle. I'd have to lie facedown on his chest because it's so big it would become the mattress. And then I'd somehow wake up pregnant and there's no way I'd be able to birth one of Derek's monstrous babies; therefore, I will claim the couch.

I only glance up at him for a split second before I dive back into the world of my laptop. Even as I begin typing the response to an email that came through while we were in the air, I feel my shoulders relaxing. Some people use fidget spinners to distract their fingers from anxiety. I use work. Work is good. Work is where I go when I feel unsure in the world because for me, work is an equation that has a clear answer every single time. Plus, I'm good at what I do.

Want to guess what I'm not good at? *Derek*.

I feel his eyes on me and my fingers are clumsy on the keys. I backspace four times.

"Nora, I feel like I'm always asking this question lately, but . . . what are you doing?" Derek's voice rumbles at me. Or it rumbles extra at me. It's gritty from his lack of sleep and he's sporting a very nice scruffy jawline.

"Working."

"Yes—I see that, and I'll get to that in a second. But more specifically, I mean what are you doing saying you're going to sleep on the couch?"

"The truth is, Derek, I have a serious lack of faith in anyone else's ability to really appreciate the importance of a great couch. I want to make sure the furniture in this suite is all treated fairly. It's equal opportunity or bust in my hotel rooms."

His head tilts, giving me an unamused look. "You're making sure the inanimate objects have a shot at equality?"

I run my hands over the sofa like I'm searching for its ears. "Shh. You never know when this could turn into a *Beauty and the Beast* situation, and all this furniture might come to life. You want to be on their good side."

Derek pinches his eyes closed and rubs them with his thumb and forefinger. His bicep does that comet thing again. "Nora . . . I can't let you sleep on the couch."

"Why not? Do you want to sleep here? Tell you what, I'll play you for it. We can both balance on our left foot and the first one to drop their other foot has to sleep in the boring bed." I continue to type type type while carrying on a conversation like I've watched Nicole do successfully dozens of times. But it's harder than it looks. I've just written one long line of gibberish.

"Because—can you stop working for a second?"

"Why?" I frown up at him. "The bird that catches the worm never sleeps."

"That's not the phrase."

"It should be." I continue typing.

"Nora, put down your laptop," Derek commands, but it barely pierces my consciousness because now I'm eyeballs-deep in emails and feeling my purpose in the world restored. But then something slips past his lips that has me looking up. *"Please."*

I meet his tired eyes and then gently close the laptop.

He watches me move it aside. "I'm not sure if you've noticed or not, but there's a big elephant in the room." He moves to perch on the edge of the bed.

"Of course I've noticed. She's bedazzled herself and is shooting off fireworks. Frankly, that elephant is an attention hog."

Derek fights a smile with all of his heart and loses the battle right there in the corners. I love it. I'm a glutton for that smile ever since seeing it in the lobby. *Give it to me, Pender.*

"Please answer honestly, Nora. I'm too tired for anything else right now."

"Okay. The truth is, I'm working because I don't know how to act around you anymore. I don't know how to breathe normal when you and I are married and sharing the same air in a room with a king-size bed. I don't know how to make eye contact with you ever since you said you understand why we broke up, but now you don't want to be friends. Because how the hell do we do that? I'm your agent, who was also fired, who is also your ex-girlfriend, who is now your wife, but we also have this long list of rules to follow. There's too much overlap and confusion here. The Venn diagram looks like a hypnotic swirl!" I glance longingly at my laptop and pat the top. "But in my emails, I'm still just your agent for the time being. And that's not confusing at all so I'd rather live there."

He nods slowly. "It's good you brought it up. I'm unfiring you."

I glance sidelong at Derek, all suspicion now. "Why? I don't want to be your agent if I'm only getting the position because we're accidentally married and you feel bad about it."

"That's not even close to the reason. I want you to be my agent because you're resourceful and creative. Because you somehow managed to still cut killer deals for me even when I was running you into the ground with busywork. Because you stood up to me and told me to quit being an ass—something no one else would have done in your situation. *Because you're the best one for the job.*"

I'm not convinced, and I have a chronic need to earn my place in life. "If all those reasons are true, then why did you fire me in the first place?"

He holds my gaze, his jaw ticking once. "Honestly? I thought it would be too difficult between us in the long run. But I'm ready to get over it now and work together. I'm really sorry, Nora, and hoping you can forgive me for it. All of it."

"*Oh.*"

"You're speechless?"

"For the first time in history, yes."

"Then I'll take advantage of it." He pushes the sleeves of his lightweight hoodie up his forearms and then leans over to rest them on his knees. "I really do want you to be my agent, but not this week. This week, I think you should close your laptop and take your vacation days."

My mouth falls open. "It's time to clean your ears out because clearly you heard nothing I said about needing my work to keep myself grounded during all of this."

He leans back, pressing his hands into the mattress behind him and—dammit—his chest grows again. "It's too weird if you're working and we're acting married. For this week only, let's just be Derek and Nora. There're too many spinning plates in this scenario and it's a mess for both of us. So I propose—"

"Ironic word choice."

"—that we close your laptop for the week, and then when we go back to L.A., we can double down on the rules and get back to normal."

I hate to admit it, but I think he has a point. "You want to get rid of the rules also?"

He frowns in thought for a minute. "Where we can, yeah. But I want you to feel comfortable and safe, so we can stick to them if you want. But it might be difficult while trying to sell the relationship in public."

"I always feel safe with you, Derek," I say before I can stop myself. But it's true and I'm not sorry that he knows it. "We could completely dump the rules out the window and I'd still feel that way."

His sharp blue eyes bore into me, and the air feels thick. "I'm glad to hear it. And since we're on the same page . . . I think we can share this bed."

I cut my eyes to where his hand is denting the comforter. "How can we share it without . . ."

He lifts a brow at where I let my sentence dangle.

"Accidentally touching! That's all I was thinking. Not sex. I wasn't thinking about having sex with you at all. Sex never even entered my train of thought. Ever. Not even back when we were having it."

Somehow his entire body is a smirk. "You're saying the word *sex* a lot."

"It really feels like it, doesn't it?" I grimace. "Now we definitely can't share that bed."

He laughs and unfolds his big body like the word *sex* never fazed him. Probably because he's had plenty of it over the years, unlike me who hasn't touched a man in three whole turns around the sun. Jeez, I should fix that.

But not with him!

"We used to sleep together, Nora, that's a fact and not something we have to be ashamed of. Open communication now." He grins at me from where he's standing beside the bed, and it makes my knees feel like they're made of banana pudding.

"What are you doing?" I ask as I watch him add an extra blanket to the bed and then toss his pillow to the opposite end.

"This is how we can share a bed without touching. I'll sleep on top of the comforter, and you can sleep under it. And just for added measure, we'll sleep feet to face."

"You mean sixty—"

"*Don't* finish that sentence," he warns, and the serious note to his voice has me thinking maybe he's not so unaffected after all.

23

Nora

"Okay," Derek says, stepping back into the hotel suite after leaving ten minutes ago to find some food.

The heavy door falls shut behind him and if he thinks it's uncomfortable that I've ventured to the bed while he was gone, he doesn't show it.

I, however, pop up off the pillow like a guilty jack-in-the-box, because lying horizontal while he's in the same vicinity as me feels wrong. Wrong in that it feels amazing, and I want to tug him down beside me and see if all the extra muscle he's put on feels different while he's lying on top of me or not.

Derek walks toward the bed and I sit up straight. Puritan posture.

"I thought you might be hungry, so I got you something too." He raises two bowls in the air as he approaches the bed. The mattress dips almost obscenely when Derek settles onto it, tipping me toward him. I'm resisting the urge to shape-shift into a marble and roll onto him.

He pauses and looks around curiously. "What's different in here?"

He all but sniffs the air. "Ah—you moved the décor around and grouped it all by color."

"It happened before I could stop it," I say.

"As it usually does."

I straighten in defense. "When I feel out of sorts, organizing helps me relax."

"I know."

"You do?"

A soft grin. "My apartment in college had never been so clean and organized than when we were dating. And yours is like that now, I noticed. But the color component is new."

"What can I say, I've evolved." I run my finger over a wrinkle in the bedding. "Is it . . . annoying that I do that?"

His eyes find mine and he tilts his head, searching for something in my face. "I'm not sure I've ever seen you insecure before."

My cheeks flush. "I am a human."

"Debatable. Who told you it was annoying?"

Okay, well, he wasn't supposed to ask that. Or perceive that even. "Just a person."

"Clearly a shitty person to try to tear down something unique about you." He looks upset. "No. It's not annoying. And . . . I struggle with organization so I thought the extra help was nice."

I notice things I shouldn't in this moment: His black joggers wrapping his muscled thighs like a second skin. How I can smell the mix of his deodorant and a hint of sweat from a long day of travel. The subtle brackets on either side of his mouth—evidence that he *has* been smiling since we broke up. And the sharp call of my body to crawl across the bed and press my nose to his neck and drag in his scent. Clearly, I need sleep.

"So what did you forage for us?" *Subject change, initiated.* "I would like to lie and tell you I'm perfectly capable of skipping one dinner, but the truth is, I was two minutes away from eating this pillow."

He grins. "I figured."

Derek hands me the bowl and I'm momentarily incapable of words. I blink down at the late-night snack like it's an offering of jewels. I suddenly feel uncomfortably misty. "You ... got me ice cream and cereal?" *Two scoops of vanilla ice cream and something similar to Cinnamon Toast Crunch to top it off.*

"Do you still like it?"

I nod. "It's my favorite. I guess I just ... didn't expect you to remember."

Soft amusement unfurls on his mouth, making my stomach somersault. "Nora, you ate this at least four times a week in college. There's no way I could forget that."

"It's always represented the majority of my food pyramid," I say before taking a huge bite just so I don't blubber about how much this means to me. The truth is, I forgot what it's like to have someone around who knows me. Or I guess ... who knows me and doesn't think my oddities are over-the-top. Sometimes I get so exhausted from putting in all the effort to know someone only for them to decide I'm not worth it and ditch me. Other than my mom, work is my BFF for a reason.

I clear the knots from my throat. "Did you get ice cream too?"

He answers by lifting a celery stick dipped in peanut butter to his mouth, making a huge crunch between his pretty white teeth. "This close to the season I really try to watch what I eat. Especially when it seems I'm going to need all the help I can get coming back from this damn injury."

"Did you not eat like this before the injury?"

He shrugs lightly. "I did. Not as rigorously, though. I'd still go out and party and drink. But I've cut that out completely now."

I pull the spoon from my mouth. "That's sadder than a wet Pomeranian puppy."

"It's not so bad." His grin is a fragile thing. "Well . . . I do miss the ice cream, but oddly don't miss the partying." He pauses, forehead creasing. "That's been the strangest part. I thought I'd really miss that side of things when I stepped out of the limelight and focused all of my attention on rehabbing my ankle. But it turns out it was a pretty natural transition. Nice even."

"Oh no. Did Peter Pan leave Neverland for good?"

"I've started drinking chamomile tea at night, Nora. *And I like it.*" He says this like a confession of murder. "It's been a weird couple of months for me."

I take another bite of my comfort food. "I can imagine."

"Actually . . . I've been wondering something." He studies me. "You said you've been at the agency two years . . . what did you do before that?"

A mental image of the rules we made together unrolls in my head, and then tears down the middle. Not only are we currently sharing the same bed (bye-bye, rule number ten) but he's also prying into my past (see ya never, rule number two).

"As it turns out, the rumors are true. The sports industry really is full of chauvinistic, narrow-minded dudes who don't think a woman could ever understand sports as well as someone with danglies between their legs. Apparently, that's where all the world's knowledge is kept."

"Why do you think we guard them so preciously?"

I pretend to kick him, and he laughs—like really laughs. It swirls around in my chest and sweeps out all the cobwebs. "Really they're where we store all our unjustified ego. Hurts like hell getting hit down there."

"Duly noted."

"So what happened?" he asks. "You graduated and said you went on to grad school . . . and then what?"

"And then I stormed into the world with eternal optimism and a new power outfit, and spent the next year interning for an agency that made it clear I was never going to do anything for them beyond fetch coffee and push papers." It's honestly sad that Sports Representation Inc. looks like a walk in the park compared to that other agency.

"So I quit and went in search of a new position or internship," I say. "Each interview was with a man named Robert or Michael or Richard who would address me as 'sweetheart' or 'young lady' when they were telling me they needed someone with more experience." I roll my eyes. "Interns don't need experience. Apparently, they just need—"

"Danglies," Derek says, making me laugh. "So then what?"

I polish off my bowl of cereal ice cream and set it aside. "Then I gave up."

"Bullshit," he says with emphasis and completely unsarcastic.

"I did!"

"I don't believe you. I've never known you to give up on anything." But as soon as he says the words, we both register them the same way. There is one thing we both know I gave up on. Derek doesn't mention it, though, and neither do I, but his smile dims a little.

I shuffle my legs against the soft comforter. "My favorite coffee shop was hiring, and I really needed money—so I took that job and licked my wounds for a long time, until one day, Nicole and her fabulous five-inch stilettos waltzed into my coffee shop." I can still hear the sharp clicks of her heels echoing off the floor. "I knew her from my research while sending out applications, and she was one of the people I never heard back from. I introduced myself with a clever coffee pun and then asked her if she would look at my application."

"Did she say yes?" He takes another bite of nature's homemade dental floss.

I laugh a little too loud. "No. She hated me instantly. She said I was too friendly and cute for this business and to stick to slinging coffees."

"Ouch." *I love his grin.*

"No, I appreciated it. Because for once, I was turned down for a concrete reason. The reason was her own internalized misogyny that she was completely unaware of—but it was a reason I could battle against too." Those weeks when I was trying to win Nicole over were some of the best in my entire life.

"Nicole came into the coffee shop like clockwork every day. I memorized her order and made sure it was ready for her when she needed it. And then I started jotting down all the reasons she should hire me on the sides of the cups—as well as stats from college athletes I thought she should take note of."

"And?" Derek asks with glinting eyes, knowing me too well. "What else was on the cup, rookie?"

I smile. "A knock-knock joke."

"Figured. Did it work?"

"The jokes worked against me—but in the end, I wore her down. She came in one day, took the coffee, and on her way out the door called over her shoulder, *Be in my office Monday morning at eight.* And that was that." I shrug a single shoulder, remembering that moment like it was filmed and stored in my brain among my happiest memories. I like to replay it when I'm feeling low or beat down and it reminds me to keep going. Keep fighting for what I want even when everyone else tells me it'll never work.

I don't realize until a few moments go by that Derek is staring at me with gentle eyes. "I'm happy for you, Nora. You're good at what you do. And I'm glad you didn't give up on your dream." A fuzzy little creature curls up in my stomach at his words.

"Same goes for you. I screamed so loud when they called your name in the first round of the draft." My smile fades when Derek's eyes sharpen on me. I realize my mistake instantly.

"You watched for me in the draft?"

His blue gaze pins me down. I want to hide from it so he doesn't get a chance to see the truth. That I have followed every inch of his career. That I have watched him achieve every milestone, career goal, and success. That I have regretted losing him more times than I can count. And that while he forgot me so easily, I've always been hung up on him. That I've learned to live with that fact.

Instead, I nudge his knee playfully with my foot. "Come on—don't make this weird. Of course, I watched the draft. I've watched every draft since I was six, and my dad let me have chocolate cake if I watched it with him."

But I wasn't watching it that year for my dad's attention . . .

"Right," he says, attempting a smile that doesn't make it to his eyes and then sets his empty bowl aside.

The silence is so thick I can't even swallow. Our friendly moment has vanished into something heavy. Surely Derek isn't disappointed thinking I didn't watch the draft for him? He's over me. Literally said he doesn't want to be friends.

So then why does he look like that?

The tension is too much, so I pop off the side of the bed. "It's getting late." I pull my toiletry bag and a change of clothes from my suitcase. "I better brush my teeth before I fall asleep and forget. Because you know what they say about teeth . . . ?"

Derek shakes his head, already regretting that he's indulging me. "What do they say?"

"Clean teeth are godly teeth."

"That is absolutely not how the phrase goes."

I scrunch one eye shut. "Respectfully—I think you're wrong."

"I'm not wrong." He gets up from the bed and follows me with his own toiletry bag. My saucer-eyed reflection says a wild bear is joining me in the bathroom rather than a man.

"Oh. You're going to brush your teeth too?" I look at him over my shoulder as he reaches around me, his chest so very close to my back. He places his brown leather toiletry bag right next to my rainbow-printed one.

He lifts a brow. "Is that okay?"

"Sure! Absolutely. I'm very excited for you to have godly teeth too."

It's terrible beyond reason. Because as I brush my teeth, Derek stands just behind me, also brushing his, and I have to try with my whole heart not to stare at him in the mirror. And once we're both tending to our dental hygiene like two domestic and completely platonic nonfriend/people/exes, my gaze drops away from his intense eyes just to get a break from them. A little breather, you know? A girl can only look into the gorgeous blue irises of a muscular, scruffy, six-foot-four male for so long.

And that's when I really take in the tattoos on his arms for the first time. In the bright light of the bathroom, I can finally see what they are. *A vicious shark shooting through the white caps of waves, baring its teeth.* Cute. That one's obviously for his team. *A skull with a bird perched on the top.* Scary but cool. *A dragonfly. Clouds with a sun peeking out. Vines with little flowers that wrap up his arm and* . . . wait, what's that tiny little black one on his inner bicep? It's like a letter or . . .

Derek pointedly clamps his arm against his side.

My eyes slingshot to his in the mirror and he doesn't make an excuse or even bother looking guilty for blatantly hiding my view of that tattoo. Instead, he leans around me to spit out his toothpaste—his chest brushing against my outer arm as he does. He rinses his toothbrush and sets it meticulously beside the sink exactly where he used to put it at my apartment after I told him how my overly neat brain liked for our toothbrushes to line up.

Without a second glance, he leaves me blissfully alone in the bathroom. I barely refrain from sagging dramatically against the door once I close it behind him. The thirty seconds it should take me to change my clothes takes five full minutes because of the silent mirror pep talk I give myself to not lose my heart to my ex-boyfriend again. *He doesn't want you. And even if he did, it would be too messy. Too unpredictable.* I finish it off by telling myself to go out there and get my butt under the covers without turning this one-bed situation into a big deal.

I crack the door open. "I'm, uh, coming to bed now. Don't look."

"Okay."

"Are your eyes closed?"

"No."

"Derek!"

He laughs. "Come on, don't make this weird," he says, using the same tone I used earlier when saying those exact words. "You literally stood in front of me in your underwear the other morning without batting an eye."

"That's because I was loony, and sleep deprived!"

"You're always loony, Nora." But there's unmistakable affection in his voice that warms me up like a cup of sweet hot chocolate.

"Fine. I'm coming out—but just prepare yourself because I didn't anticipate sleeping in the same room as you this week and I wore my sexiest pajam . . ." My words trail off as I step out of the bathroom and find Derek sitting up against the headboard, hands clasped behind his head, crisp white sheets pooling at his tapered waist . . . shirtless. My bathroom pep talk takes a hike.

Why does he have to be so muscular? And sexy. And tattooed. And . . . mouthwateringly tan.

I want to jump his bones. I need to jump them.

"Those are your sexy pajamas?" he asks, drawing my eyes away from his nakedness to his face, where my gaze should have been the whole time.

I inch toward the bed. "I tried to warn you. They're very seductive."

"I've never seen Mr. Rogers's face quite so large before."

"I know . . . it's really something." I hesitate before lifting the comforter to crawl underneath the covers. To get in the bed. With Derek.

I'm wearing an XL T-shirt with my dear ole pal Mr. Rogers taking up the majority of the front. The text rainbowing across the top reads *I like you just the way you are.* I have zero illusions that this thing is actually sexy. But . . . I'm not wearing pants under it. And unless I'm mistaken, Derek used to think I was pretty cute pantsless.

Derek doesn't bother looking away the entire time I climb under the covers. He watches unabashedly and then once we are both situated and the light is clicked off he has the audacity to say, "I noticed you still wear your days-of-the-week panties."

I choke on my own spit. "Oh my gosh—don't say the word *panties* while we're in bed together."

"Sorry," he mutters, but the grin in his voice tells me he's not sorry at all. It's a quick peek at the old Derek. The shameless flirt. The one who always knew exactly what he was saying and how it would affect me. I love it. And for one jolting, radical second, I wish he wanted to be with me again.

"Just go to sleep, troublemaker." I aggressively punch my pillow into comfort as I rotate to my side. But then I make eye contact with Derek's feet. "'Umm. Derek? You don't still run in your sleep, do you?"

"Sometimes," he says, and then realizes why I'm suddenly worried about it. He sits up and so do I. "This is ridiculous, right? You should move up here. We can sleep in the same bed without anything being weird."

"Right. You're totally right. So right, you don't even have a left." I'm already shifting around so my head and pillow are on the same level as his. "This is no big deal."

"None." He lies back down. "First one to fall asleep wins."

I appreciate his attempt at levity. But when I feel his body heat creeping through the covers. When I shift my legs and my knee brushes his thigh. When I blink my eyes open and find him watching me, just an arm's length away, it all feels like a very big deal.

And when I wake up at two in the morning and realize I'm completely tangled up with him—leg draped over his, stomach against his side and face pressed into the crook of his shoulder with his hand spread over my hip, it feels like an alarmingly big deal.

More alarming is I can't bring myself to move away.

24

Derek

"Let's make this quick, Nora's in the shower but she might not be for long," I say to the laptop screen I'm hunched over at the coffee table. Each of the guys' faces is represented in his own videoconference square. I texted them a few minutes ago and called an emergency meeting.

"All right, then, let's get to it," says Jamal, sitting forward eagerly. "Your hair is too long. Your nose is a little crooked and honestly some plastic surgery would go a long way. And when you walk—"

I mute him and then smile at the screen. "Perks of being the host of the meeting. I get to silence you whenever I want. You're officially in a talking time-out, jackass."

Jamal makes an inappropriate gesture at the screen.

Nathan sets aside the protein smoothie he was finishing up. "Not to be that guy, but Bree and I are about to go on a run. So let's get on with it."

Lawrence and Price both confirm they're ready. Jamal pouts with his arms folded.

"All right. Here it is. You all know I accidentally married my agent who is also my ex-girlfriend who I am still frustratingly in love with."

"And posted your tongue down her throat on social media and nearly got her fired. Let's not forget that part," Price says with a smirk.

"Careful, I'll mute you too."

He raises his hand. "Just laying out all the facts for the people."

Nora starts humming loudly in the shower and it reminds me to hurry this shit up. "Here's the problem. I think . . . no, I know that I want to get back together with her. Not only is she hilarious and smart and gorgeous and so good at organizing, but she's good for me. She's not afraid to call me on my bullshit and I feel lighter when I'm with her. I . . . I can't let her go again."

I wait for the surprised gasps but they never happen.

Lawrence laughs. "Yeah, man. We know. We've known since we met Nora at your place that you'd want her back."

Nathan smiles. "We've been waiting for you to realize it too."

Jamal is gesturing wildly to the screen, begging me to unmute him so he can gloat. *Not a chance.*

"The hell? You guys knew this would happen even after I told you I wanted to move on the other night?"

Price laughs and it's definitely at my expense. "Hard to miss it when your face looks even more annoyingly moony-eyed while talking about Nora than Nathan does talking about Bree."

"*Hey,*" me and Nathan say at the same time.

But Nathan is offended for a different reason. "No one loves their woman more than I love Bree."

We all give Nathan a look and I crash my finger down on that mute button. "That just earned you a minute of talking time-out too. Jamal, you're on probation." I unmute him.

Jamal gasps for air like he's been choking for twenty years. "Derek, I hate you so much it somehow dips all the way into love, and that's why I'm going to skip the I-freaking-told-you-so speech and jump right to telling you that Nora seems worlds out of your league and you should absolutely use this time you have with her to win her back. Fight for her. Who agrees with me?"

Lawrence raises his hand. "I agree . . . but with a caveat. I don't believe in chasing a woman who doesn't want to be chased. Has she put out any vibes that she's into you again? Or does she seem closed off and reluctant?"

"Of course she's reluctant," says Jamal, while gesturing most likely toward my picture on the screen. "Look at his face. Would you want to look at that every day of your—"

I mute him again and unmute Nathan. "We spent a long time just talking last night. And then we shared a bed, and when I woke up this morning, she was sleeping pretty much on top of me." Everyone makes a similar eyebrows-raised hopeful face. "But that could be because I'm twice her size and the mattress just dipped so much that she rolled onto me."

Their brows lower back to puzzled.

"You could always just try being honest right away," says Price.

Nathan hisses in through his teeth. "That's risky. Not only do they have a whole honeymoon together full of potential awkwardness if she doesn't return his feelings, but when they get back home, she's still his agent. I'd rather have at least a little assurance things are tipping in that direction before jumping all in."

"Okay, so that's what you're looking for, then," adds Lawrence. "Really listen to her. Study her mannerisms. And if you start to suspect she still has feelings, woo her."

"Woo her? What are you, an eighty-year-old grandma?"

"*Woo* is a good word. You're not trying to seduce her. Wooing insinuates you're trying to get to her heart, not just her body."

It checks out. Still, this makes me think of the other reason I called them. "Do you guys think I'm being ignorant to consider pursuing her again? Since she was the one who broke up with me and it nearly killed me the first time?"

"Bree cut me out too, right before college," says Nathan. "And although I don't know all the particulars between you and Nora, I know that if I had let myself stay hung up on a choice she made when we were young, I would have missed out on a beautiful life with her."

Lawrence nods. "I agree with Nathan. You've got the perfect week to see what's what. Give it a shot. And although I don't think you have to go all in with her—I think it's brave of you to be open to connection again and see what happens." *What the hell kind of self-help books does this guy read?*

Nathan sits forward. "You know, I still have my old cheat sheet that helped me win over Bree. I can text it to you."

I roll my eyes. "I don't need help in that department, thank you very much. I gave you the ideas for that damn thing."

"You told me to wink. And it did not work out, might I add."

"Not my fault you don't have game."

Jamal is literally standing and yelling god knows what at the screen. I smile pleasantly and flip him a little birdie. Just for fun I use my other hand to give it wings and let it flap all around the screen.

"*What* are you doing?" says Nora, standing just outside the bathroom door I never heard open wearing a big sun hat and swimsuit cover-up.

All I see is a glimpse of the guys' wide eyes (and Jamal howling with laughter) before I slam my laptop shut. "Oh, uh—nothing. I was just . . . doing a hand stretch thing. It's for football." I pause and she doesn't rush to fill the silence. "It's just . . . sports people do it. Athletes. It's an athlete"—I pause painfully again—"hand thing."

She smiles. "That seems like a very suspicious lie, but I'll allow it because we're going to be late for our meeting if we stand here chit-chatting about your interpretive hand dancing any longer."

25

Nora

"We are just so excited to be sitting here with you two!" says Kamaya, the sweet journalist from *Celebrity Spark* beaming at Derek and me from across the table. We're seated in the little outdoor resort café, and if you typed *paradise* into Google Maps the pin would drop here. Warm air, baby blue skies, palm trees around the patio, and an ocean that's so beautiful it must be fake in the background.

Sitting next to Kamaya is Alec, the photographer who will be following us around through the week. They both have beautiful smiles and the kind of personalities that make me feel immediately cozy. I like them.

And I like that our meeting with them gave Derek and me an excuse to avoid talking after waking up in each other's arms (for the second time for me) and instead, rush to get ready and sprint downstairs to make this breakfast meeting on time.

Because avoidance is healthy, right?

"Thanks again for allowing us to cover your love story and honeymoon," says Kamaya. "Nicole and I go way back, and so when she called and told me she had an inside scoop for me, I knew it was going to be good. That woman never misses."

I laugh. "No one rejects a call from Nicole."

"Exactly!" She readjusts in her seat to cross her long golden-tan legs, looking down at her notes with a soft smile. The lady is gorgeous. Could be a runway model if she wanted—not unlike the women Derek used to date actually. I can't help but wonder if he's attracted to her now. If he's looking at her across the table and thinking *Jeez, I wish this woman didn't think I was married.* A sudden stab of jealousy hits me that I have no right to.

But then, as if Derek could sense my thoughts, his knee settles against mine under the table and I glance up at him. He's not looking at the beautiful woman across the table, he's staring at me—with a questioning look. Was I frowning at Kamaya? I probably looked like I wanted to rip her lovely hair from her head and Derek witnessed it.

Not very feminist of you, Nora.

"Okay, so first I thought we could discuss the schedule for the week and then move on to the interview. Sound good?" Kamaya asks, and I try to push all my jealous thoughts aside. It's hard, though, when she looks so lovely and polished and I'm wearing an opaque swimsuit cover-up and a straw hat, because like I told Derek before, the sun and my skin are not friends.

"Ready Freddy. Lay it on us," I say, a little too chipper.

She wrinkles her nose at me with a smile. "You're as adorable as Nicole said you are."

"Was *adorable* the word she really used?" I'm skeptical.

Kamaya shrugs. "Give or take."

"She said *obnoxious,* didn't she?"

"*Obnoxiously cute* were the exact words."

I don't know why it stings to hear that Nicole—my only ally in that office—said that about me to Kamaya. That's exactly what I am, and I've always been okay with it. I won't change to fit into society's idea of a powerful working woman just to make them more comfortable. And yet—I think with Derek beside me and in the face of a woman I really admire, it has me deflating a little. I feel frumpy and silly, and my hat is too big.

But I'll eat this oversized hat before letting anyone know that their opinion of me has me down. Because opinions are not fact. As my mom always said, opinions only become truth if you accept them as such.

"I prefer hysterically funny, or cheerfully outgo—" I was going to say *outgoing* but in that exact moment Derek leans forward and drapes his arm around behind me as his fingers skim down my shoulder and bicep. So the word *outgoing* sort of just comes out like "outgorrgg."

Kamaya notices my sudden machine malfunction and her smile melts. "The honeymoon phase. Love it. Okay, let's get on with this so I can get out of your hair for the day!"

I slide my eyes to Derek and . . . he winks at me. *Holy Mother of Harry Styles.* What was that? My stomach swoops like I'm in turbulence on a plane. He blatantly broke rule number eighteen (not that we're supposed to be tracking it).

I can't believe the way my body responds to him. It's unearthly. I've slept with other men—good-looking men, I might add—and my stomach never swooped. Not once. And all Derek has to do is wink? He's always been able to undo me in a way that terrifies me. When he's around, the rest of the world might as well not exist. It's consuming. And it's exactly why I let him go before.

But what about now? Am I ready for it this time?

Oh my gosh, Nora, now it's fake! Now he's putting on an act to help me keep my job. The swoop of my stomach is irrelevant because now Derek is my nonfriend/client/husband. Stay focused.

Buuuuuuut, my brain argues one more time, he has been keeping an IOU from me in his wallet for years. He remembered your favorite snack. And sometimes I catch him looking at me like . . . like he still loves me. *So maybe let's not be so ignorant, Nora.* Because if I'm feeling this thing between us again, maybe he is too. I think I might be scared to hope for it.

"Here's what we're thinking," Kamaya begins, snapping her papers into a neat stack that honestly gets me a little hot. "This morning we'll get our interview portion out of the way. After that, we'll all hop in the car we hired to take us to the coral reef tour that's provided through the resort. Okay with you two?"

"Sounds good to me," says Derek. "How about you, Nora?" But instead of just asking me, he lays a soft kiss to my temple. While his thumb brushes up and down the curve of my neck, just under my ear. While my heart flatlines.

I swallow, trying not to show how affected I am by him in this moment. "Great!" But it comes out like a prepubescent squeak.

Kamaya grins. "Wonderful. And since this is your actual honeymoon, we tried not to plan more than one photo event for each day to leave you the rest of your time together to . . . well . . . do whatever you like!" She waggles her eyebrows and I try not to choke on the embarrassing implication that what we like is Naked Twister. "You can take a look at each of the events we have planned here." She slides a packet over and Derek doesn't remove his arm as he leans forward. Instead, he pulls me a little closer so I can look with him. I smell his deodorant and it makes me want to lick his bicep. I'm unhinged.

"A spa day?" Derek asks with a lifted brow because he's actually paying attention and not dreaming of inappropriate things we could do together like I am.

Kamaya nods. "Most of these events are amenities provided within the resort that they would like to promote for couples. Alec and I will try to stay out of your way as much as possible during the activities so that you hardly know we're there. And obviously, if any of these look terrible, we'll nix them and plan something different. Sound good?"

Derek and I both take a minute to look over the itinerary and don't see anything that looks too rigorous or uncomfortable, so we agree and begin the interview. Kamaya sets a recorder on the table with our permission and lobs us a softball: "How did you meet?" Derek answers the first question, strolling truthfully down memory lane to describe in perfect detail our first encounter at the party in college.

We get asked a few more easy questions like what was our first date? *Bowling.* And what's our funniest couple memory? *Getting caught skinny-dipping in our college lap pool at night.*

The interview is going so well that I'm lulled into passivity until Kamaya looks me dead in the eye and asks: "What was the reason behind your breakup in college?"

My knee bounces because I don't know how to answer this. I'm not good at lying and I also don't want to dive into a truth that Derek and I have barely explored together as it is. Of course, to Kamaya, for a now happily married couple, this question would be cute and funny to look back on. But in reality, the fractures still live under our skin. Especially for Derek, and I want to be sensitive to that.

Kamaya misinterprets my expression. "I can tell by the look on your face, Nora, that it's a good story."

Um—no, not particularly!

Derek's hand covers my knee. "That's private. Next question." He says it with an authority and protectiveness that makes goosebumps flare on my skin.

"No problem." Kamaya's smile is nothing but understanding. She's not trying to be a prying jerk, just doing her job and digging for details. "What about during the years you two weren't together? Derek, of course we all know you dated a lot, but Nora, what about you? Did you see anyone else or were you pretty hung up on Derek?"

I feel Derek go still beside me and I really wish I weren't having to answer this question for the first time in front of a photographer and journalist. But if I refuse to answer this question too—Kamaya might get suspicious. I also think it's funny that she assumes Derek broke up with me. Because of course a goofy girl like me would be lucky to snag a Derek in this world.

The implication fires up a corner of me that rages for any woman who's ever been told she's lucky to have had a chance with a good guy. Like that is our primary goal in life and once found, he should be her end-all-be-all until he's finished with her.

I sit up a little straighter. "I did date a few men, but those relationships were never serious. Mainly because my fierce single mom instilled in me at a young age to put my dreams and ambitions first—whatever they were. She made it clear that she would never try to hold me back or laugh at how high I wanted to reach. That she'd always hoist my foot up to help me get to the next level, and that unless I could find someone who treated me in the exact same way—as an equal partner whose dreams were just as important as his—to keep moving."

Derek is unnaturally still beside me. His thumb has stopped caressing my neck and I realize with a gripping ache that I wish he'd never stop.

"A wise woman." Kamaya's eyes twinkle. It seems she's been on the same track as me. "And now you've found him."

"Who?" I ask before I realize what she means.

"Derek," she says, with a laugh and nod in his direction. "You finally found the right man to hoist you up instead of pushing you down. And you married him."

That question knocks into me and steals my breath. Because Kamaya doesn't realize just how spot on she really is. My eyes turn to Derek, and I see him in a new light. A minute ago my mind was stuck in the past with a Derek who loved me recklessly but not fully. He fell into the category of men who unintentionally treated my dreams as less important—wanting me to put him before everything else.

But I'm not with that Derek anymore, am I? He's changed. And so have I.

This Derek saw that my career was in trouble, and he was willing to do whatever was necessary to protect it. The difference is unmistakable. The Derek I dated in college was a boy. This Derek is a man. And it would seem he's a trustworthy one.

"I sure did marry him."

Don't get too cozy, Nora. It's just temporary.

26

Nora

"How many?" Derek asks abruptly the first moment we're remotely alone.

"Five hundred." My answer is lightning fast. "Wait, what are we talking about?"

He keeps his face pointed straight out over the helm of the boat toward the crystal-clear, turquoise ocean, but it's clear his attention is zeroed in on me at his side.

After finishing up the interview, the four of us hopped in a hired car and drove to a large boat dock. Kamaya thought it would make for excellent photos to capture Derek and me on a snorkeling adventure in a coral reef with one of the local tours. This seemed like an excellent idea to me as well when I thought a coral reef was something we could walk to from a beach. Not exactly sure why I thought that, but I did. Now, however, I have quickly learned after buckling myself up into a bulky life vest that we cannot walk to it—we ride in a boat across the choppy ocean water and I hope my death doesn't find me out there.

He glances down at me. "How many guys did you date after me?"

I grip the boat railing for support. "Excuse me? Nosy alert. I don't think you get to ask me that."

"I'm asking anyway. I want to know." He cuts his eyes briefly off to the side to where Kamaya and Alec are talking with the captain (driver?) of the boat. I don't know how to refer to the maybe-twenty-something-year-old guy about to steer our boat into an endless roaring ocean who looks like he's barely old enough to drive a car let alone a vessel on the water. I'm not being fair. He's probably a wonderful captain.

I just hate boats so much. Literally every movie ever that features a boat has it crashing and everyone drowning or being stranded on an island. I also imagine my hatred has something to do with the lack of control, but we'll never know since the closest thing I have to a therapist is *The Great British Bake Off*.

Derek hooks his finger into the shoulder of my life vest (one that he's apparently opted not to wear until we get in the water since he's not terrified of going overboard like me) and spins me to face him. He clicks it open and then drags up the fabric of my cover-up to reveal a few inches of my midriff that my bikini doesn't cover.

"Hey! What the—"

"And I want to know what this is from too." His finger softly brushes against the small scar on the right side of my abdomen. The one I got from surgery five years ago.

I yank my cover-up back down and glare at him—not because I'm particularly modest or uncomfortable, but because I don't have my sunscreen on yet and I will fry like bacon. "What's gotten into you? Why do you need to know these things all of a sudden?" *Because he feels what you feel*. A shift. An awakening.

The look in Derek's eyes is burning. "Because you're . . ." He seems frustrated, grasping for how to finish that sentence. His eyes meet mine again and I'm disappointed when somehow I know it's not what he was going to say. "This week you're my wife, aren't you? I should know important details about you. So how many?"

I plant my hands on my hips, suspicion lacing my words. "Derek Pender. You're not . . . you wouldn't be riding the jealous train into Possessive City, would you?"

"Maybe . . . please just tell me how many, Nora. Put me out of my misery." He looks so obstinate. So resolute. Possessive and defeated at the same time.

"I don't think you want to play this game, sir. Especially when I tell you it was only two men compared to your millions of women."

He grimaces but not for the reason I think. "Damn, Nora. Only two? Two is much worse."

My mouth falls open and a laugh shoots out. I peek over my shoulder to ensure that Kamaya and Alec are still in conversation with the boat captain. I lower my voice just in case. "In what world is me dating two men worse than the many, many women you've dated?" And then I shake myself. "No, wait—none of it is bad because we weren't together at all in those years! You were entitled to date who you wanted, and so was I."

He bypasses my pragmatic statement and inches closer until he grasps the buckles of my life vest and clicks them securely together again. "Two is worse because it's so specific. Two means you really knew them—and you can most likely still remember them perfectly." He doesn't let go of my life vest yet. "What were their names?"

"You need to learn manners."

"Please." He grins. "Please, *Ginger Snap,* will you tell me the names of the guys you dated?" I nearly gasp at the sound of my old nickname on his lips. A surge of excitement shivers through me.

Still, I eye him sidelong, half-worried he's collecting names to give to a hit man by the rabid look in his eyes. "Liam and Ben."

"No." He sounds more defeated than anyone has been in the his-

tory of ever. "Ben? You dated a guy named Ben? Which was probably short for Benjamin. Are you for real?" He takes an anxious step away and then whirls back quickly. "Shit . . . he was a good guy, wasn't he? A doctor? Bens are always doctors or baseball players."

I can't help the grin I'm fighting. Turns out, my baser side likes seeing Derek jealous. Likes this new energy running between us as much as it scares me. "Pediatric doctor."

He groans. "Did you sleep with him?"

My eyes flare. "Okay, now I'm putting my foot down." I make a show of raising my foot in the air and lowering it. "See. Foot. Down. You don't get to ask me questions like that."

"You did. You slept with him." None of his distress is for show, he's really losing it right now. And as a result, I am too. Because what is even happening? "God—I'm having the desire to murder someone I've never met."

"You're kidding me with this?"

"Never been more serious."

"Don't you think you're being a little double standard, then?"

He crowds me. "Are you *not* jealous? Do you not hate the thought of anyone else sleeping with me?" he grinds out, more unhinged than I've ever seen him.

And of course I'm jealous! But I don't want him to know that. And frankly, I don't want to be jealous since I know he's had every right to kiss, sleep with, or fall in love with whoever he wants. I like being rational—but I've never been able to stay rational when it comes to Derek.

"Am I the only one who's . . ." He looks torn between finishing the sentence or keeping it to himself. And then his gaze snags over my shoulder and he smiles politely to Kayama who has walked up behind us.

"All right, love birds? The captain is all set, so we're going to take off. If you two want to just stay here and look out over the ocean as we motor, Alec is going to stand over there"—she points a few feet away—"and take some cute candid photos of you two. Sound good?"

"Sounds great!" I say, even though it actually sounds like the equivalent of swallowing cactus needles to have my picture taken while I live through the terror of falling off the front of the boat and sinking to the bottom of the ocean.

The engine revs up and so does my heart as the boat begins moving across the water. I really feel like, at this moment, I should have somewhere to sit, but alas, this boat is not of the sitting variety. Where we are standing is a massive blue deck with a very flimsy railing around it (unsafe), and down belowdecks there's a smallish cabin with a few bench seats, but Alec quickly vetoed those when we arrived, saying it would make for incredible photos if we were looking off the bow of the boat as we cruise.

I bet Alec didn't bank on my look of terror also being in these photos.

"Are you okay there, Nora?" Derek asks, seeing the look on my face and raising his voice above the sound of the boat's engine.

"Yep!" I say loudly and cheerfully with a thumbs-up, but then I immediately regret letting go of the railing and I latch onto it again for dear life.

Derek steps behind me, and his large body presses into my back as he wraps his arms around my midriff, holding me firmly to him. I glance down and nearly choke on my own attraction at the sight of his pronounced veins and tendons wrapping his strong forearms. Manly forearms. *Athlete* forearms.

His mouth is at my ear. "You wouldn't happen to be scared of boats, would you?"

"No," I say quickly, and then when the whole boat dips over a small wave, I shriek like a crow. "Not scared. *Terrified*."

Derek's hold shifts and laces tighter. "You're safe. I won't let you go overboard," he says, and I absolutely believe him. Deep in my bones I know that if this boat were to hit an iceberg and start sinking to the bottom of the ocean like the *Titanic,* Derek wouldn't let go of me. And you better believe that if I found a floating piece of driftwood to hang on to, I'd scoot over and let him on it with me. *There was more than enough room, Rose!*

Distantly I'm aware of Alec moving up to the front of the boat with us and aiming his camera in our direction—but my mind is too focused on the feel of Derek's hand spread out, covering my hip and dipping down to my thigh. His hold is not tentative or restrained. I would ask if it's for show, but . . . after the way he just admitted to being jealous of my past relationships, I don't think it is.

I'm not entirely sure what I'm doing or why my heart is racing out of my chest or if this is the worst idea in the world. But before I can chicken out, I raise my voice above the waves. "Derek. You're not the only one who's jealous."

But he doesn't hear me. "You'll have to speak up! The engine is too loud," he yells over the spray of the waves.

"You're not the only one!" I yell. "I've been jealous since I saw you kiss a woman outside your apartment the week after we broke up!"

Suddenly, Derek is twisting me around to face him, his eyes full of concern. "You were at my—"

But the boat suddenly decelerates at the exact moment we hit a wave and the result has Derek's body swaying into mine as my head jars in his direction—right into his face.

I yelp and Derek groans, and when I look up at him, he's clutching his nose with both hands. "Oh god, Derek, are you okay?" I say but when he pulls his hands away, I see that he is not in fact okay. His nose is pouring blood.

Derek registers this at the same time I do, and his eyes cut to mine, knowing what's about to happen. By this point, the boat has slowed to a stop and our brave captain has announced over the intercom that we've reached our snorkeling destination. But all I hear is *wah, wah, wah*, because at the sight of Derek's blood, the world begins fading out from under me.

Derek calls my name and lunges toward me with blood pouring down his face and shirt, and then everything goes black.

27

Nora

There was so much blood on the boat (and Derek) that they brought us back to the resort. Not to mention the fact that I fainted and freaked everyone out. Kamaya insisted on bringing us back to have the resort's onsite nurse check Derek's nose to make sure it wasn't broken. Thankfully there was no threat of a concussion from me, since Derek caught me before I fell.

Derek's nose and my brain are just fine, but my pride is oh-so-bruised. I made a huge scene. One so big that an entire tour had to reschedule their day to accommodate my unexpected ripple in their timing. Everyone was kind for the most part but definitely displeased by the turn of events.

Of course the one moment I was trying to be vulnerable . . . I slam him in the nose, nearly make him bleed out on a boat, and then I pass out like a dramatic 1800s heroine whose corset is too tight. And it was all captured on camera. I want to cry.

Evidence that Nora Mackenzie (Pender) really is extra.

Derek is in the shower now (washing off my blood) and I'm lying in bed, nursing my deflated ego and wondering if this is a sign from the universe that I need to keep my mouth shut. That what Derek and I had was in the past, and it should stay back there. Buried. With no maps or X's to mark the spot.

It's probably a moot point anyway. Derek had a fresh taste of the realities of what dating me is like.

Except the bathroom door opens and steam billows out around a massive, tan male form clad only in a small white towel tucked around his waist, and I think that the universe can suck a lemon. That towel is barely hanging on and I have an internal cheer section rooting for it to fall.

"Sorry. Forgot my clothes," he says, and I'm definitely staring at the dusting of hair that trails down his muscled abdomen and disappears behind the towel.

I shoot my gaze to the ceiling. "Mm-hm. No problem."

It's dead silent in here except for Derek's naked feet walking over the carpet, reminding me that he's here and we're sharing this room and there's water droplets crawling sensually down his spine. Oh damn, I can even hear the towel brushing against his thighs. Can hear his suitcase unzipping and then the sound of fabric sliding up his legs. His underwear? Did he drop the towel in plain sight? Should I look? No. That would be rude.

I peek and find him already mostly dressed with his back to me, but oh my god the man is still shirtless in black form-fitting sweatpants. His muscles literally ripple beneath his flesh as he raises a shirt over his head and pulls it on, quickly followed by a Sharks hoodie that looks so snuggly I want to climb inside with him.

He turns around and catches me watching before I can look away. I guiltily fall back onto my pillow and shut my eyes.

"Whatcha doing over there?" he asks, amusement running through his tone.

My eyelids remain closed. "Sleeping. I'm exhausted from draining you of all your blood today, so I think I'm going to nap."

It's quiet for a while, and then I jump when I feel Derek's hand touch my forehead. My eyes fly open to find him standing just beside the bed.

"Are you sick?" He's serious.

"I don't think so." But I do feel dangerously close to crying.

"I've never known you to nap."

I raise a brow. "Well . . . to be fair there's quite a few years in there you haven't known me. Maybe I nap every single day now."

"Do you?" he asks, and I refuse to acknowledge the way he doesn't immediately pull his hand away but passes his fingers over my hair first, gently pushing it back from my face and tucking it behind my ear.

I shiver a little. Maybe I do have a fever. "No. I haven't napped since I was twelve years old. But . . . I'm just tired. It's been a doozy of a month and I feel like a goose for passing out on the boat and . . . I think . . . I think I just need a nap." My voice wobbles.

No jokes. No playfulness this time. Just honesty because everything is catching up with me and I'm tired all the way to the center of my bones. I need a reset so I can wake up and stop feeling so embarrassed and flooded with feelings for Derek. I need to get ahold of myself before I start reading too much into him telling me he's jealous. Into his little touches. Into the possibility that he'd ever consider having another shot at this with me, when really, that would be a terrible idea.

Derek eyes me for a few seconds, his square jaw flexing once before he moves around to his side of the bed. I go up on my elbows and watch his every move. "What are you doing?"

"I'm going to nap with you."

I laugh nervously. "What? Why?" That's definitely not going to help me reset.

He lifts the comforter and slides in. "It sounds like a good idea. I never get to nap in my day-to-day back home. So let's nap."

"*Okayyyy,*" I say skeptically, lying back slowly onto my pillow. Again we fall into silence together and all I hear is the soft sounds of our side-by-side breathing and the shifting of sheets every so often. The curtains are open so the room is all sunny and warm. This is nice.

"I'm sorry about your nose," I say quietly. "And the scene it caused."

"Who cares about a scene? I'm just glad you didn't hit your head."

I'm choked up—emotions clogging my throat from how freeing it is to not be treated like a nuisance for something I can't control. "Because you caught me. Even though your nose was bleeding and you were in pain."

He raises an arm above his head. "Quit making me out to sound like a hero. My nose is perfectly fine." A light scoff falls from his mouth. "God knows I've had worse injuries."

I shift onto my side, tucking my hand under my pillow to look at Derek. He's lying on his back, that arm with the tattoo I can't make out above his head still hidden from view, eyes closed. "Were you scared? That day on the field when your ankle snapped?"

He winces lightly and I regret saying it so bluntly like that. His eyes open and they connect with mine, face angled toward me. "I was terrified." He pauses and looks at the ceiling again. "I can still hear the sound it made. The bone literally snapping. I was convinced that was it for me. That . . . I would never play football again and it was all going to be gone before I was ready."

What I don't tell him is that I was in the stands for that game. That

I saw him hit the field and not stand up and I thought I was going to be sick. And then those torturous moments where I had to watch him get carted off on a stretcher and then anxiously refresh my phone over and over again to find out what sort of injury he had—it was hell. I wanted to be there for him. I wanted to hold his hand.

And I guess it's that memory that has me reaching for his hand under the comforter now. When I bump the back of my knuckles against his, his eyes jump quickly to mine, and for a moment he's frozen. I'm barely breathing myself. And then all soft and sweet, he inches his fingers over mine, until our hands are tangled up.

I close my eyes again and let the dazzling heat between us lull me into a restfulness I don't enter easily.

"Nora . . . we need to talk about what happened before the bloody nose on the boat."

I grumble a sound with my eyes closed. "Do we have to?" All my adrenaline has worn off and now I regret the vulnerability dump.

"Yes. We do." And then he turns my hand over so it's palm up. With his index finger, he starts painting lines over each finger. I tingle with every stroke. "Please tell me."

It's . . . hot. And somehow also sweet. And also a very, very bad idea. But it works to distract me from my fear of telling him the truth.

"The week after we broke up, I came to your apartment. You were just getting back from a date and it sounded like you guys were having a lot of fun, so I ducked around the corner." His finger pauses, likely knowing what's coming given what I admitted to him on the boat. "And then I saw this gorgeous woman in an impressively tiny dress kiss you. Right on the mouth. And you kissed her back . . . so I left."

I still don't open my eyes. I can't bear to see whatever look is on his face. Pity, maybe? Embarrassment? Whatever it is, I don't want to see. I just want to lie here and immerse myself in the feel of his fingers tracing my skin like nothing bad has ever happened.

"Why did you come to my apartment?" he asks, his voice softer than velvet.

I breathe in and decide there's no time like the present for the truth. "Because I . . . missed you too much and wanted to see you. I felt like I'd made a big mistake and wanted to fix it." I pause when the rush of pain hits me all over again. "Even though I had no right to feel hurt since I was the one who broke up with you—it stung so bad to realize how easily you moved on from me. How easily replaceable I was."

He breathes out heavily and then his finger moves to my palm. Drawing a pattern now.

"But then," I continue, "I decided that you were okay, and you had moved on and were happy, so it was something I should do too."

He's silent so long that I finally get curious and crack my eyes open. His expression is not one of pity or embarrassment—it's something completely different. It's something like relief.

It's now that I realize the shape he's been drawing on my palm is a heart. *Over and over again.* Just like he used to.

"You left a second too soon, Nora."

"Why?" My heart is thumping against my ribs.

"Because if you'd stayed—you would have seen the truth of just how not over you I really was. How not over you I . . ." He stops himself.

"You what, Derek?" *Say it. Whatever it is, say it!*

He breathes out one long breath, his finger still moving over my palm, branding me with a shape I'm not even sure he knows he's making. "That night, you didn't stay long enough to see me pull away from her and tell her I couldn't invite her in because I wasn't ready to move on from my breakup yet." He pauses as my mind frantically tries to grab onto this new information like it's a piece of driftwood in the ocean.

"I couldn't do it," he continues. "I couldn't move on from you that quickly . . . I didn't sleep with her, Nora. Or anyone else for a very, very long time. Two years, to be exact. Even though I tried to make it look like I was thriving in the media so my friends and family wouldn't worry about me, I wasn't thriving. Because without you, I was lost." A sad smile breaks in the corner of his mouth. "You weren't even close to easily replaceable to me."

Derek's hand moves away from my palm, sliding to my wrist and gently tugging. My body responds without hesitation, scooting closer and closer to him. I know I should be hearing warning bells, but they're nowhere to be heard in my head. Someone has ripped them out and buried them under the sand.

He turns onto his side facing me, and his hand glides around me, settling low on my back. I arch into him, feeling a swirl of heat settle in my core, spreading outward. My eyes close when I feel his breath against the side of my neck, smell the scent of his bodywash fresh on his skin, and before I can tell myself to stop, my leg is hooking around his thigh. His hips press into me and I suppress a groan. His mouth lowers to my neck with the most patient, soft kiss, but his hand slides down further to gently squeeze my ass. I don't know what's happening and I don't care because Derek's hand is—

A loud, firm knock sounds at the door and I catapult off Derek and completely out of the bed like we were about to be caught in some sort of forbidden tango.

"Housekeeping!" someone yells through the door.

Derek is lying there shocked at my sudden spooked-animal stance until his laugh cracks the air. I use the interlude where he's having the time of his life to sweetly yell through the door that we don't need housekeeping today, and then I go back to the bed, where I throw a pillow at Derek's laughing head.

He wipes at his eyes. "The look on your face!"

"Stop it!" I say, laughing a little myself. "It's been a traumatic day for me, okay? And that," I say, gesturing toward what we were just doing in the bed, "was a mistake!" Because it was. It had to be. No matter how much fun I have with him, how much I love his smile, the way he lights me up like a firework, the way I respect him for pausing his day to take a photo with every single person who recognized him, how he took care of me even when he supposedly hated me, how much he . . . wait, I'm losing my train of thought. Where was I going with this? *Ah yes, mistake.*

Because when you strip all the lies of this fake honeymoon away, we're nothing to each other besides people who will have to work together when we get home. People who can't afford to kiss for the fun of it.

Derek is perfectly sober now. His laughter dies and he sits up with a slight frown. "You think it was a mistake?"

"Yes! We can't . . . kiss like that in our situation. Our lines are going to be blurred all over the place, and it just . . . it can't happen again. In private."

His head tilts. "In private?" he asks, a curious spark to his words.

Yes, you heard the loophole correctly, Derek.

"I mean . . . I assume we'll have to . . . embrace at some point in public over this week. And I think that's fine. But in here"—I hover my hand over the bedding in a very Alexa Rose–type gesture—"no embracing. Talking only."

"So we don't get blurry."

"20/20 vision only."

He stares at me a minute and then grins, accepting my silent challenge. *Game on.*

28

Nora

"All right, love birds, we want this to be fun and not take up too much of your time today, and hopefully not end with Derek's nose pouring blood and Nora passing out," says Kamaya, with a little laugh. I can't help but laugh too because the embarrassment has worn off and now I'm just left with a great anecdotal story for a party. "So we were thinking it would be fun to snap some candid photos of you two playing together on the beach. Sound easy?" says Kamaya, smiling happily to us, barefoot in the sand right next to the ever-quiet Alec.

But no. It does not sound easy. And up until this moment, I didn't allow myself to think about being photographed. I'm not just being modest when I say I don't take good photos. The moment a lens is pointed in my direction, I forget how to act like a human. My shoulders go rigid, and I sweat, and my smile looks more akin to a predator with rabies. I've been this way my entire life and I wonder if Derek remembers. My social media is all artful photos of my hand holding a coffee mug or my feet in snuggly socks. Everyone assumes it's because I'm trying to be mysterious and creative. No. It's because

I look like a clown popping out in a haunted house when the camera finds me.

"Why don't you guys go stand over there, just in front of the waves, and do that sort of lovey-dovey gaze you were giving each other on the boat yesterday."

Derek and I glance at each other and our expressions are a mirror image: We were giving lovey-dovey gazes? But more important, my brain fixates on: *He* was giving *me* a lovey-dovey gaze? More and more signs are pointing toward Derek having feelings for me. And here's the problem, I absolutely have feelings for him. That shouldn't feel like a shock since part of me has never stopped loving Derek. But there's a difference between having always loved a man you knew as your younger self, and really *liking* the man you know now on top of that. It's dangerous. It potentially complicates everything.

Derek and I begin walking down toward the water when Kamaya's voice stops us. "Oh uh—sorry to be awkward, guys, but . . ." She gives an apologetic smile. "Mind losing the cover-up and shirt?"

Oh my gosh.

Not only did I not consider that I'd have to be photographed this week, but I also did not consider that I'd be photographed in my swimsuit that will be put in a magazine! Cool. Great. Fun.

"Righty-o, Captain," I say. "But only on one condition. You see, I have cellulite on the backs of my legs and stretch marks on my inner thighs—"

"Oh, don't worry! We'll edit all that out."

"No. That's not what I mean. I have cellulite and I *don't* want it edited out. If you're going to put my body in a magazine, I want it to be mine. I want women to see it and see themselves in the photo too." Another thing my mom taught me: Love your body—it works hard for you every day of your life.

"Huh," she says, and I can't decide if she's impressed by me or already dreading the team of men she's going to have to stand up to on my behalf when they try to airbrush me within an inch of my life. "I love that, Nora. You have a deal."

"Thank you." I nod and then whip off my cover-up and lay it on the beach chair. I set my hat on top of it and then remove my hairband and set my hair loose. I run my fingers through it a few times in hopes that it looks like effortless beach crinkles and not a raccoon who just climbed out of a dumpster. And then I turn around.

Derek is staring at me.

Like *staring* staring. His eyes unashamedly run over every inch of my pink-bikini-clad body. Which listen, I like my body. She's a good body and it's taken me years to come to terms with the fact that I can love her even if the media tells me she's not up to the standards they expect. I simply don't care anymore because I'm happy in my skin and I refuse to spend my days hating it because some person back in the day decided I should have a tiny waist, a big booty, and huge breasts. My body is soft and squishy in places and flat in others, and it's perfect for me.

But the way Derek is looking at me right now makes me feel as if my body is the standard all other bodies should be judged against. Like mine is his ticket to eternal happiness. Like I am a freaking goddess—and I realize no one has ever appreciated my body quite like Derek.

I'm sure every inch of me is turning as pink as my bikini under his gaze. He's not supposed to be looking at me like that. We're supposed to be married, for god's sake! He needs to appear at least a little immune to me by now. Instead, he looks like if I step any closer, he's going to take a bite out of me.

He drags his eyes back up to my face, and it takes him a second to snap back to reality before he reaches his hands behind his head and tugs his shirt off his so, *so* fine body. And now it's my turn to drown in a pool of desire. I rake my eyes over his strong physique and admire not only the shape but the hard work and determination it's taken him to get to this place. His tan skin is already glistening with a nice sheen of sweat, highlighting his massive shoulders and defined pecs. He's all hefty brawn and ropy muscle. A warm breeze rolls off the ocean and tousles his hair. The man not only has glorious abs but a stack of fully visible oblique muscles down the sides of his torso, and . . .

Wait.

He runs his hand through his hair, exposing his inner bicep. My eyes snag on that little black tattoo I've never been granted a good look at. And for the first time I'm able to identify that one blot of ink tucked secretly inside his arm. It's a single letter.

N.

It might as well be tattooed in neon glowing letters for how my attention zeroes in on it.

Derek sees me inspecting it, but this time, he doesn't try to hide it. "Are you ready?" he asks after a moment, slowly dropping his arm and pulling my attention to his face. He nods at the ocean.

Behind us I hear Kamaya whisper to Alec about how we look like we're about to rip each other's swimsuits off right here on the beach. Derek hears them too and glances down at me with an almost apologetic smile.

When we get down to the water, Derek and I turn to face each other, and that's when I make the mistake of looking at Alec. I see the harrowing lens aimed at our faces and the panic sets in. I try to smile at Derek. It feels stale.

"Um . . ." Alec lowers the camera. "Nora, maybe try shaking out your arms really quick."

I do except that doesn't help. I'm just hyperaware of my arms now. I'm a Betty Spaghetty doll from the '90s and my arms are long limp noodles.

Kamaya jumps in to help. "Just . . . breathe out a smile, Nora, and maybe put your hand on Derek's chest, like you're leaning in to kiss him."

It's possible I'm moving in slow motion as I lift my hand and lay it on the hard lines of Derek's bare chest. My hand settles against his warmth and I'm set on fire. "This isn't working, Derek," I say, yanking my arm back. "I can't do it. I'm feeling more awkward than the time I ordered at Starbucks and then realized I had a tampon wrapper stuck to the front of my shirt the whole exchange." Truly it was the barista taking my order who looked the most awkward. Poor guy. "We both know I can't take a good picture to save my—"

Derek's arms suddenly snag around my waist and he tugs me up flush with him, so tightly that my back bends when I look up at his face. All of me is pressing against all of him and I can't breathe. His eyes are dark as the depths of the ocean. "Stop thinking so much and have some fun with me, Nora."

I think maybe he's going to kiss me until suddenly he bends down even lower and scoops my legs out from under me, carrying me out into the water.

"Derek!" I squeal and kick. "I can't swim yet! I don't have my sunscreen on!" It's not even a fake excuse. I can't be in the sun long without protection or we'll need a fire extinguisher to stop the burns.

I manage to kick and wiggle myself out of his grip, landing on my feet with the waves only around my ankles. I don't waste a second before I take off, slogging my way through the water and sand— aiming for my bag with sunscreen up on the beach chair, but really just trying to run from the unhinged joy overtaking me. I'm feeling . . . scared again. Scared to care for someone so much. Scared to recognize a definite shift between us. Scared that I'll mess it up—or he'll mess up, and either way we'll end up heartbroken when my career was just starting to go where I wanted it to.

But also . . . *What if nothing bad happens? What if . . . it's just wonderful?*

I glance over my shoulder and Derek is running after me. His long lean lines and structured muscles flexing with every step. "Get back here," he yells, and I trip my way up the sandy beach, laughing too hard to really run.

It takes Derek all of two seconds to catch me. He loops his arms around my waist and carefully tackles me to the ground, taking the brunt of the fall. I wriggle around laughing until we're face-to-face, him lying atop me, but his forearm and legs taking most of his weight.

He pushes my hair back from my face and then cups the back of my neck. "You're fast. Ever consider a career in football?" he says with a dimpling smile, leaving me dizzy.

Nothing about this feels fake.

"I wouldn't want to show anyone up."

"So kind of you."

Distantly I'm aware that Alec is snapping photos of us, and hot sand is stuck to the backs of my arms and legs. I'll be rinsing it from my hair for weeks, but for once, I really can't bring myself to care about anything outside of this moment. Outside of Derek looking in my eyes—his body heavy over mine.

The grains of sand turn into glitter. It's all *magic*.

"We're in public," he says, quiet enough for only me to hear. "Fair to kiss you?"

My stomach twirls. "Absolutely fair."

But apparently he didn't mean on the mouth because he responds by leaning down and touching his lips to my collarbone. I suck in a breath from the shock of tingles that flood my system.

"I'm glad you told them they're not allowed to airbrush your images." He lingers there and nips at the stringy strap of my bikini like he can't resist. "Because smoothing away any part of your gorgeous body would be a travesty."

Oh my.

My body is putty under the feel of his lips—my skin is so sensitive. He might just be putting on a show for Alec, but I don't think he is. Either way, my core is molten and I'm unable to care about anything other than sinking my fingers into the back of his gold-kissed brown hair. I pull my knee up, laying my foot flat against the sand, and almost automatically Derek's hand goes to that outer thigh.

Alec's camera frantically clicks now and the sun just behind Derek's head is so bright I have to shut my eyes. It's bliss. Pure bliss.

"Derek. Can I ask you a personal question?"

"Anything." He kisses my other collarbone, making it very difficult to focus on my words.

"Is that a letter *N* tattoo on your arm?"

He pulls away enough to look at me. The waves crash below us, and the sun behind his head is nearly blinding when I stare into his eyes. His blue rivals the sky.

"Yes," he says simply.

Huge monarch butterflies launch through my stomach.

"And . . . would that *N* be for . . . Nora?"

His jaws flex before a lazy grin hits his mouth. That hand of his slides up my bent knee and down the top of my thigh—a professional skier on a treacherous slope. He studies my lips and I think I'll remember this moment and the way the sun feels and the waves break and the look of utter affection I see in Derek's eyes for the rest of my life.

"Yes," he says. "I got it for you."

Stunned doesn't begin to describe me. "But . . . when?"

He drops his head again and breathes against the skin of my neck and ear. "The week after we broke up. Or more specifically—the day after you saw me kiss that woman outside my apartment."

"Why? Especially after the way I hurt you? Why would you get my initial?"

"Because regardless of how it ended, I needed a way to prove it existed." He says the words just above my mouth. "I was scared of forgetting what we had. The tattoo was a way to admit to myself that you were important to me and would always be a part of me no matter how much time passed."

I don't know what to say. How to express that my heart feels simultaneously heavy and light. And he doesn't make me find the words either.

Derek's thumb traces up my jaw to tease the corner of my lips before his head lowers, mouth finally covering mine. My body exhales.

I hear the faint clicking of Alec's camera a few times before it stops completely. Alec whispers loudly to Kamaya that they should give us some privacy.

Probably because this is not a sweet kiss. Not like the accidental brush of lips we exchanged in Derek's kitchen. From the second his mouth covers mine, it's consuming. It's years and years of longing, and missing, and needing.

I wrap my arms around his neck and tug more of his body weight onto me because I want him there. Need him there. His hand moves to cradle the back of my neck so he can tilt my face for a better angle.

When he lightly licks my bottom lip asking for permission, it undoes me. I open my mouth, and his tongue sweeps over mine, sending white-hot desire striking through my core. I run my hands down his hard back, reveling in the gritty texture of sand mixed with sweat. I take his bottom lip between my teeth and then suck it into my mouth. Derek groans and I'm desperate for more of that sound. I want all of it. I want to see the man unravel completely and know that I'm the one who did that to him.

Except I don't get more because a second later, Kamaya is somewhere nearby clearing her throat. "Um. So sorry, you two. But I feel obligated to tell you that you're garnering a bit more attention than you'd probably like."

Derek tears his mouth away and looks up toward the top of the beach where sure enough, there's a few people cupping their hands over their brows to give them a sun-shielded view of us. "Shit. I'm sorry, Nora. That was . . ."

"Incredible," I say, touching his face so he knows I don't regret it.

I don't regret one second of it.

29

Derek

I live for this moment every night when Nora steps out of the bath-room from brushing her teeth, because she's sleepy and relaxed and the smile she gives me when she sees me on the couch is just so . . . intimate. It's this little brief second where no time has passed at all and we're still just two young people madly in love with their whole lives ahead of them.

And I don't know . . . maybe we are still those people.

The door opens and there she is in little black sleep shorts and an oversized sweatshirt and that sleepy smile on her lips. God—she's so gorgeous. Sexy and curvy and freckled.

I kissed that woman this morning—I kissed her and she kissed me right back. Nothing about it was fake. Nothing about it for show. If there's one thing I know for certain, Nora is not a good actress, and an even worse liar . . . so what I saw in her eyes, felt in her kiss, it was real. It was one of the signs the guys told me to look for, and I found it.

Was it maybe not the best place to have a kiss that passionate? Most likely. But I don't regret it one bit. We were lying there on the beach and the sand was in her hair and the sun was golden on her skin and I couldn't help it. I wanted her. Still want her. Will likely spend forever wanting her.

But not just in a physical sense. I want her as my best friend, my favorite person to talk to, the one who I walk with through every good and bad season. I want so much more with her than just that kiss on the beach.

The problem arises if Nora doesn't want this too. Because 20/20 crystal-clear lines or not, it's going to be difficult returning to a normal business relationship after all this. Make no mistake, though, if that's what she wants I'll do it. Because I've decided that living a life where Nora is nothing but a platonic work friend is worlds better than a life without her in it at all.

I think she's sorting through all these potential implications and pros and cons too. Because after that beach incident and the truth bomb I dropped about my *N* tattoo, Nora didn't come back with me to the room. Or she did, but only long enough to change her clothes and pack a tote bag with a few books, and then she made an awkward excuse about wanting to go read by the ocean and live her best unplugged life. In other words, she was feeling off-kilter and avoiding me to regroup.

It was a good separation for the day. It gave me time to process my feelings while working out in the resort gym. To replay every damn word I said out there and decide if it was worth it to tell the truth. I don't regret it. If anything, I feel relieved. Part of me is still worried that Nora is going to bolt. That maybe she'll go out on a coffee run and then text me that she went to the airport instead and couldn't do this anymore. But even if that happens, I won't regret having told her the truth and kissing her like I did.

It helps, though, that Nora did come back this evening. She

walked through the door, smiled a soft smile, and then went to get a shower.

And now here we are, me drinking hot chamomile tea and mentally falling all over myself at the sight of Nora leaving the bathroom. Except when she twists back to turn off the light, she winces.

"What's wrong?" I sit up straighter on the couch and set down my mug.

"Nothing." She comes over to the couch and sits, but on the opposite end. *Far away.* Is that a bad sign? Did her thinking on the beach lead to an opposite outcome from mine? "What are we watching? *SportsCenter?* Ooh—turn it up."

"Nora."

"Derek, let it go. I'm fine. Everything is fine. Turn it up, please," she says with a final bite to her words. She's not mad at me. This woman just hates when people fuss over her. I remember when I had to take care of her while she had the flu once and I thought she was going to chop my head off every time I forced her to take medicine. And it's her spiciness to me now that lets me know something truly is bothering her.

I have no choice but to let it go, so I turn the volume up a few notches. Of course, no sooner than I do, my face suddenly fills the screen. Nora and I both tense, instinctively thinking our elopement is about to be discussed on television, but it never comes up. Instead, the two announcers discuss all the potential pitfalls of me returning to the Sharks after my injury.

"I don't know, Blake, do you really think they'll start him? Sure, Derek used to be a heck of a tight end before his injury, but he's thirty now, and it's harder to bounce back from these things. I mean, how many players have we seen come back from an injury like this and play even half as strong as before?" says one of the announcers.

"Very few," the other host adds. "Especially now knowing how incredible of a backup the Sharks have had sitting on their bench. Collin Abbot had a heck of a rookie start at the end of last season with an impressive five catches for 121 yards and two touchdowns."

"As much as I'd like to see Pender make a full comeback, I don't think it seems likely."

The TV cuts off. I turn my head to find Nora setting down the remote. "You don't need those buffoons getting in your head. Collin is a good player"—she smirks—"but you're better."

My pulse floods my ears. "They're right, though. I'm getting old in the world of sports. Abbot is a better bet."

"You're thirty, Derek. A sprightly spring chicken." She nudges me with her foot, but I don't laugh. I can't because my chest is too painfully tight to even breathe. Everywhere I look someone is telling me I'm going to fail. That my career, I not only love but have grown up with, is over.

I look away but Nora is beside me in a flash. Curling into my side and putting her hand on my jaw to pull my face back. "Hey. What's going on? What are you not telling me?"

It's not fair of her to use her softness against me like this. One look in her eyes, one swipe of her thumb against my cheek and I melt for her. All my best-kept secrets fly out like they were never guarded in the first place. "I can't lose it, Nora. I can't lose football."

"You're not going to."

"I might. You and I both know the Sharks are looking at budget cuts. I'm the weakest link with the second-highest salary. I might as well have a target on my forehead. And if I lose it . . ." The words come out gruff and thick—because anger is easier than disappointment for me.

My damn eyes prickle. I won't cry in front of her. In front of anyone really. So I try to get up from the couch with the intent of leaving the suite until I can get my feelings under wraps again, but Nora puts her hand on my chest and stops me. "Oh no, you don't."

"Nora, please let me g . . ." My words die off as she slings one leg over my lap and sits. Two hands go to my jaw, and her hazel eyes sear into mine.

"You're not going anywhere until you tell me the truth. Give me all those ugly feelings swirling around behind your eyes. They look like they're on a teacup ride having the time of their life."

Like it's a fragile thing, I close my hand softly around her wrist. She's straddling my lap, anchoring me down intentionally to get her way. "This isn't fair."

"We can't always play by the rules." Her smile turns to a frown. "Tell me what's bothering you. *Please.*"

I wish I could keep it to myself. But I'm weak under her hypnotic gaze. Drunk on her touch. Spiraling out on her scent.

"I'm dyslexic." It's fitting that Nora is the first person I've ever said that out loud to, since she's also the first person I've ever felt truly understands me.

She looks shocked only for a second. And that's mainly because of my abrupt admission. Her thumb touches my lips and slides away. "How long have you known?"

"Not long. A few months. I had my suspicions, so I got tested."

"And how do you feel about it?" She's tentatively circling me with her words. Feeling me out to see if this is the main issue or if there's something deeper.

I sigh and release her wrist to run my hand over my face and into my hair. "Honestly, having the diagnosis hasn't changed a lot in my day-to-day. I mean, I don't have a career that exactly requires a lot of reading or studying, so it's been more of an emotional shift than anything. And that's . . . been interesting."

She drops her hands to rest between us on my chest. "How so?"

I glance down and close my hand around her fist—holding it like a present. "I guess I've been looking back at my younger self with more compassion. And maybe a little sadness." I feel the need to blink several times. And clench my jaw. "It's nice to know that there was a reason behind all the difficulty. To know that I wasn't just some kid who didn't know how to apply himself like everyone said. But to look back and be able to appreciate how hard I was working, and actually did great considering the lack of support or resources." I pause and swallow. "And I guess that's where the sad part comes in— my brain just works different, and no one saw it. Not even my parents. Not my teachers. Definitely not my classmates who were busy laughing at me every time it was my turn to read out loud." *Definitely never mentioned that particular memory to anyone before.* "Everyone just assumed I wasn't trying hard enough . . . and because of that . . . football really became my ticket to a good future. One where I didn't have to rely on reading. One where I could make something of myself and finally see that look of pride in my parents' eyes."

I pause and have to clear my throat twice. I look away and Nora lets me. "But now, all I have is football, Nora. All I am, and have ever been, is a good football player. And I'm scared that if I lose this—the only thing I've ever exceeded at—I'll lose everything. Who am I without it?" *Because the last time that I lived a life without football, I was nothing but a disappointment.*

She doesn't rush to correct me or to convince me that I'm overreacting. Nora's eyes peer into mine for several breaths before she tilts her head. "Okay. Let's say you lose it all. What then?"

"This doesn't feel like a good start."

She pushes against my shoulder. "Just answer the question. What happens to you if the Sharks call us tomorrow and tell us you've been cut?"

I shake my head. "I don't know. I'll probably get epically drunk, to be honest."

"Okay, after you get drunk and feel your feelings and sober up, then what?"

I don't like this game. I don't like thinking about what's going to happen to me. It's why I haven't let myself consider it yet. The thought is too depressing. But she's not going to let it drop, so I force myself to do it. "I . . . I don't know, I imagine the guys will probably be all up in my house trying to revive my spirits."

"You think your friends are still going to talk to you after you've been cut from the team?"

A defensiveness for my friends sweeps me. "Yeah . . . of course. They would never—"

I cut off and a slow cunning grin pulls over Nora's mouth. Damn. I fell right into that. *You won't lose everything.* That beautiful devious smile of hers shoots down my spine, amplifying my desire for her. But she's on my lap, so I need to not think about how beautiful she is or how much I want her in this moment.

"It doesn't matter how you got your friends; those guys are going to be with you for life, Derek. And they'll be there to help you in your next steps too. It might not be easy to find out who you are outside of the NFL, but that's okay because you've overcome hard things your whole life. You're up for the challenge. Yes—the sport, the people, the fame, it all shaped you into who you are now, but it does not make up the whole of who you are. Football was just the start. You have—"

I kiss her.

I steal the words right out of her mouth. But then I remember that she has a no-kissing-inside-the-room rule and I pull my mouth away just as quickly. "I'm sorry. You said not to kiss inside and I—"

She kisses me.

We both breathe sharply. She hesitates for only a second before rising to her knees to wrap her arms around my neck and get a better angle on my mouth. The kiss is melting and demanding all at once. I spread my hand across her back to rock her closer to me, but she yelps at my touch.

I pull back. "Okay, what's going on?"

She shakes her head, already leaning in to continue where we left off. "I'm fine. Kiss me."

But I tuck my chin back, cutting off her access to my mouth. And then to really seal the deal I cross my arms over my chest. "I'm not kissing you anymore until you tell me why the hell you keep wincing in pain."

"Just let it go!" she pleads.

"No. You didn't let it go for me. Fair is fair."

Her face is all defeat before she twists around, presenting her back to me. She reaches over her head, slowly bunching up the sweatshirt to reveal a very, very sunburned back. Excruciatingly red from our day on the beach.

I drag in a breath through my teeth. "Shit. Nora. I'm so sorry." I feel like a real jackass for pulling her out into the water without sunscreen. "I didn't think you'd burn that quickly."

"It's not all your fault. I forgot to put on more sunscreen before I went out again to think—I mean read," she quickly corrects with a guilty smile. "But it's fine because I've always wanted to know what it feels like to be a stop sign and now I get to find out firsthand."

"All right. Lie down on the floor," I tell her.

Her eyes widen. "I'd like to remind you, Mr. Dermott, ours is a business relationship."

"Huh?"

"It's from *How to Steal a Million* . . . never mind."

It's hard to keep up with Nora sometimes, so I don't even try.

"Lie down on your stomach on the floor." I set her on her feet, and then I go into the bathroom, where I dig through my toiletry bag.

Unsurprisingly when I come back into the room, Nora is standing stock-still beside the couch—noncompliant with my command. I smile, knowing where her head has gone. I hold up a bottle of aloe and realization sweeps her face. "Oh. Aloe! That makes more sense. You just had that on hand?"

"I can't promise it's not expired—but yeah. During summer practices I usually get pretty sunburned on my forearms at least once. I like to keep this around for emergencies. I'm going to use it on your back."

"*You* are going to put it on *me*?"

I look around. "Unless one of your inanimate furniture pieces decides to come to life and help, yes."

She worries the side of her lip, frowning at the floor. "Are you sure it's a good idea? Especially after all the . . ." She hitches her head toward the couch where we were just making out. The blurry lines are concerning her again.

"What I'm sure of is that without this aloe you'll stay in pain and sleeping will be near impossible—and then I won't sleep either, knowing how much you're hurting. So do us both, and everyone who has to interact with us tomorrow, a favor and let me cover you in this nasty, sticky green goo." She hesitates another second. "I know you don't like when I bring this up—but . . . I have touched your bare skin before and I doubt applying aloe is going to affect me given the things we used to do."

Her face flushes a vibrant shade of red that has nothing to do with the sunburn. "Okay, yep, just do it. But make it quick," she says while adjusting facedown on the floor.

"Funny, that's opposite of what I'm usually told."

"Ha-ha so funny, Mr. Sexy Funny Guy. You kill me with laughter." She peeks her unamused eyes over her shoulder at me. "Aloe, if you please."

I kneel down beside her. And push her hair off to the side—it's the color of cinnamon tonight. And even though I talked a big game to Nora about having touched her before, my hands shake as I lift the hem of her sweatshirt, slowly exposing the long expanse of her bare back all the way up to her shoulders. No bra in sight.

As if she can read my mind, Nora says, "The straps hurt too bad against the burn."

It's frighteningly red. Poor thing is going to have to sleep on her stomach tonight for sure. I feel terrible for convincing her to swim without sunscreen. I'm buying her a rash guard from the gift shop first thing tomorrow morning. I'll lather her in sunscreen from forehead to toe. Hold an umbrella over her as she walks.

I dispense a little aloe on the center of her back and then cover it with my hands, softly spreading it around. Her skin is blazing under the cool gel and I worry that even though I'm moving as delicately as possible, my callused hands are too rough against the sensitive silkiness of her back.

This feels like a terrible time to be attracted to her, but I can't help it. My teeth clench as I trace my gaze over her hourglass figure from her shoulder blades, along the soft curve of her waist, all the way down to where her hips flare out. I see the top freckle above the waistband of her shorts that begins my favorite constellation on her ass. We used to joke that stargazing was my favorite hobby.

And as I apply the aloe to the portion of her lower back where the sun especially attacked her skin, my fingers move from tender to worshipful—gliding over the soft divots that bracket her spine and kneading my thumbs up her shoulders. I notice chills spreading down her arms, and then suddenly Nora makes . . . a sound. A familiar sound low in the back of her throat (a moan if you will) that she absolutely didn't mean to make, judging by the way her body goes tense. She abruptly lifts her head off the floor.

I raise my hands from her skin, hovering in limbo until I know what I'm supposed to do next.

"Umm . . ." She swallows. "That sound you just heard was . . . an . . . I-just-remembered-something-important sound. That's all."

"Ah," I say with furrowed overly serious brows. "I understand."

"Yeah. It's like how phones have little dings for reminders. Well, I have . . . that sound. My reminder sound. *Remember to drink a full eight glasses of water tomorrow, Nora.*"

I gently pull her sweatshirt back down over her now-sticky back, unable to keep the smile off my face. Friends don't make sounds like that. And co-workers don't kiss like we kissed on the couch either. I finally have the answer I've been watching for.

I plant my hands on either side of her shoulders and lower my face to her ear. My nose brushes her cheekbone and I watch her eyes flutter shut. "I was hoping the sound was something else. Because turns out, I was wrong. I'm completely affected by touching you. Even with aloe."

She inhales sharply and I want to kiss her while I'm here, my chest brushing against her back, smelling her tropical-scented hair and aloe-soaked skin. But I don't.

I push up and off the ground, leaving a stunned Nora in my wake as I go to the bathroom to wash my hands.

Two seconds later, Nora pops up over my shoulders, looking at me in the reflection. Her eyes are bright, pupils dilated and skin flushed. "Okay, so listen. I've been thinking. It might be time—and this is completely out of the blue, mind you, and not as a result of any person whose pronouns are she/her making any inappropriate noises recently—but I think we should reinstate our good ole faithful rules."

I turn to her, and she sinks back into the corner of the counter a little more, eyes flaring as I reach my arms around her to dry my hands on the towel behind her head.

"Funny you mention it." The same sort of adrenaline I get before running out onto the field floods my veins. "I was just getting ready to bring up that topic."

"You agree, then? We need to go back to the rules?"

I angle my face down to look her in the eyes. "Disagree. Strongly, in fact."

She blinks. "Wait. Huh?"

I let go of the towel and lean back against the counter, folding my arms in front of me. "Nora, in the spirit of full disclosure, I want you to know, I plan on breaking every single one of our rules over the course of this week. Now is your chance to officially tell me not to."

Her lips part in shock. It takes her a few seconds to respond. "Wh—why?"

"Because . . ." I breathe out my nerves. "Because I regret ever letting you go in the first place." If she looked shocked before, she really does now. "Because I'm not convinced that what we had is really over between us. Because when we kiss, it feels right. Because when you smile at me my world feels whole. And I want to use this week where you're not my agent and I have no other obstacles in my way . . . to woo you."

She shakes her head slightly, trying to dislodge her words. "You're going to . . . woo me?"

"Yes—I'm going to woo you."

She shifts on her feet. "No, you're not."

"Yes, I am."

"No, you're not!" she says an octave higher.

"Okay, I'm not."

Her shoulders sag and she looks disappointed now. "Wait—you're not?"

I smile and step closer to her, putting my hands on the outside of both her arms. "Nora. What do you want? Do you want to try us one more time while we have the perfect excuse to do it? Or do you want me to forget I ever said anything, and we can do as you suggested and double down on the rules? Either way, you'll still be my agent when we get back to L.A. Your answer has no bearing on that."

Her eyes meet mine and the air sizzles between us. All I really want to do is press her back into the wall and continue the kiss we started on the couch, but I refrain. Barely. Because I want her to be able to think about this. I don't want her decision to be out of lust—or for her to think it's out of lust on my end either. It's so much more than that to me. It always has been.

And after several long, torturous moments Nora blurts, "I have to make a call!"

She slips under my arm and flies from the bathroom and then the suite. The door falls shut behind her with an ominous and non-encouraging thud.

30

Nora

Fifteen quick steps and I'm out in the hallway. What is happening? I repeat, *what is happening*?

I double over by the ice machines and clutch my stomach. I'm grasping for breath like a claw in a toy machine—can't quite get it.

Derek wants to woo me?

Do I want him to?

My head is spinning. I'm terrified, and yet the smile on my face is drawn in permanent marker. I should find a way to wipe it right off, though, because no good can come from this. First of all, we're married and need to get a divorce. How would we throw dating into the mix? Do we just stay married? Do we divorce so we can date? Second, I'm his agent and I want to continue being his agent. Third, I want him to take all my clothes off and—

Shoot. That's not supposed to be a point. And I'm not really the casual take-my-clothes-off-just-for-the-hell-of-it person. No matter how much I wish otherwise. When my clothes come off, my little monogamous backpack of feelings clips on. I can't help it. It's the law of my body governed by a cute little prudish policewoman that I really wish would go away sometimes.

And therefore I need to call my mom. My best friend. She always knows what to do.

I swipe through my phone as quickly as possible to find my mom's name. Two rings later, she answers. "Hi, honey! How's your fake honeymoon going? Oh, by the way, I got on Instant Gram this morning to see if you sent me any new cute animal reels and my gosh, honey, your face was everywhere! Well, yours and Derek's faces and mostly pressed together making out on the beach. But still. Did you know that you've gone vital?"

Calling Pam is always the right decision. "Mom, first, it's called Instagram. And it's not going vital, it's going viral."

There's music in the background, as well as someone talking loudly.

"Like a virus? Ew, why would we call it that?"

"Because it spreads quickly, I guess."

"I like *vital* better." Someone shushes my mom.

"Agreed—let's change it. But no, I haven't gotten on social media at all, and now I'm glad I haven't." The music on her end is booming. "Mom, where are you?"

"I'm in the movies. But it's just the trailers playing right now." She pulls the phone away from her ear a little to talk to someone around her. "Oh—for pity sakes, it's just the trailers! No one cares about these movies anyway and this is my daughter on the phone. Do you have a daughter? Well, you would know how important it is to not miss this call if you did! Okay, okay, I'm leaving!"

There's a muffled sound like fabric scraping the phone and then, "Nora, you still there? I'm in the lobby now."

"I'm here." The wall is solid at my back. I slide down it and sink down to the floor—tucking my knees up into my sweatshirt. "What movie are you seeing?"

"That action flick where the guy takes off his shirt."

"Oh yeah—the guy with all the abs?" I set my chin on my knees.

"Yes. And good hair too."

"Right. I know exactly the one you're talking about." We both chuckle. "I wish I was there watching it with you."

"Why, pretzel?" she says, playfully using the ridiculous nickname. "Are you not having a good time on your fake honeymoon with your ex-boyfriend?"

"That's the problem." I whine like I would never whine to anyone else but my mom. I'm safe to be absolutely obnoxious with her. "It's getting complicated because I'm having too much fun. And just now . . ."

I launch into a lengthy explanation of every single detail of the last twenty-four hours. Even the parts a daughter would normally leave out from telling her mom, I tell mine because I'm not kidding when I say my mom has become my best friend. Partly out of necessity because either I tunnel-vision on work too much or I'm simply too much for people, and both options leave me pretty lonely at the end of the day. But also because my mom has always given me room to make mistakes and tell the truth without fear she'd use it against me. We're genuine friends, and her opinion is the shiniest gold in my eyes. Which is why it's a little unnerving that she's completely quiet during my story.

It's unlike Pam to be silent. By now there should be a hundred different gasps, and *he didn't!* comments.

After I've finished, my mom asks me one question and one question only. "Nora . . . is your silverware drawer stocked?"

My mouth falls open, but it takes me a second to form any words.

"Is my . . . ? What? Mom, I just told you my ex-boyfriend-slash-fake-husband-slash-client wants to woo me and all you can ask is if my silverware drawer is stocked? You're giving off one-fry-short-of-a-Happy-Meal vibes right now."

"Well, honey, I've seen the state your spoons are in," she says emphatically, like that explanation is reason enough. "Those things have gone down the garbage disposal more times than any spoon should, and I've personally thrown a few of them away—so I'm worried that there won't be enough utensils for two people."

Movement by the ice machine catches my eye and I spot a woman approaching the reusable water bottle filler station. She has five water bottles in her arms and can't figure out how to get the tap to turn on.

"I have two spoons and three forks and one knife," I tell my mom while watching the woman wave at the dispenser like it's motion activated and requires an interpretive dance to work. Solid logic, honestly. Everything seems to be motion activated these days. I often wonder how many hours of my life I've lost while waving at hand-drying machines until they turn on.

My mom hums knowingly. "Thought so. I'll stop by the store tomorrow and restock them for you."

I laugh like she's finally cracked. "Mom! Why are you going to restock my silverware drawer?"

Pushing off the floor, I walk over to the woman and gesture for her to let me have her water bottle. She eyes me up and down speculatively because in my ratty old sweatshirt, and seemingly nonexistent short-shorts underneath it, I must look like a failed influencer who just lost all her money on a shampoo pyramid scheme and is trying to secretly live within the resort.

The lady reluctantly hands over her empty water bottle and I hold it under the fountain, pressing the little pedal on the floor to release the stream of water. The lady gasps and smiles wide. I feel like a top-tier magician. How glorious. Maybe a change of professions is in order.

My mom continues while I work to fill this lady's water bottles one after the other. "Because, Nora, my only daughter just got married. And I want her new husband to be able to eat cereal with her in the morning without cutting his mouth."

"But Mom—right now it's fake. F. A. K. E. You understand that, right?" I say, and then remember the woman beside me and hope she has no idea who I am. I smile awkwardly at her as she hands me another bottle. I'm no longer a magician to her—she thinks I work here. "We haven't even talked about what will happen when we go back home. All he said is he's going to woo me on this vacation."

The lady beside me waggles her eyebrows and nudges my shoulder. "That sounds fun," she whispers. I nod several times because it really has the potential to be a good time.

"Darling, I love you with every fiber of my being, but I'm angry at you for thinking any of this is fake. Or even has been fake since the beginning. And since I happen to know with all my motherly wisdom that it's not fake and that that boy will be sleeping over at your house before you know it, I want to restock your silverware drawer. Don't worry, I have a key to your apartment."

"I do worry, Mom! I worry about the state of your comprehension skills right now. You're not listening. This could go badly a thousand different ways. And besides, where is my fiercely feminist mother who usually tells me to consider my career first?"

"Now I worry about your comprehension skills. Have you not been listening to me all these years? Feminism, my love, is about uplifting women and fighting for our rights to equality and choice. If your choice is to follow your career, I will fight for that until my dying breath. If your choice is to be married and become a mother, or even a combination of both, I will fight for that until my dying breath too. It's not about what that choice is, it's about your freedom to make it. All I've ever wanted—and continue to want for you—is a partner who is going to uplift you as much as I know you will uplift him—and to cut loose anyone else who would dare do otherwise."

The lady beside me must be able to hear my mom's voice through the phone because she gives me moony eyes as she covers her heart with her hand. She shoos me away from the fountain to finish up her remaining water bottle herself and signals for me to go talk to my mom. *Take the day off from your water bottle job,* her eyes say. And this is what I love about women. Movies prefer to portray us as catty—but I know better because of moments like this. And moments where complete strangers have banded together in the bathroom to find me a tampon when I started my period unprepared.

"And Nora, my little butternut squash, you don't make rash decisions. Everything you do has a motive and reason behind it. Even when you're drunk. Honey, remember last year when we accidentally drank a little too much at that wine tasting and then you ordered your pink couch online. You laughed it off later as a frivolous drunken mistake, but you forget that I follow your Pinterest boards and I happen to know you had been pinning pink couches for a month before that. You *wanted* that couch."

I did want that couch. I wanted it more than anything.

My bare feet pad back down the hallway toward our suite before I even realize what I'm doing. "What are you saying, Pam? That Derek is my pink couch? You think I've been nursing a broken heart all these years and pining for him? I'm the one who broke up with him because I wanted to pursue my career, if you will remember."

"I think you already know the answers to those questions and don't need me to point them out."

She's right. I have been nursing a broken heart, I'm just embarrassed to admit it to my strong mom. And it doesn't matter that I ended it with him—my heart was still broken. The only difference is that I'm the one who shattered it myself.

"Nora, you are so excellent at thinking with your head. I've always admired your ability to look at life ten steps ahead and maneuver yourself in the safest most efficient route."

"Thank you. You should see me play checkers."

My mom doesn't stop for my quip. "It's worked for you because you really needed that stability and self-preservation from the way your dad has always come and gone from your life. But now, my darling goddess . . . you're standing on your own two feet. You know who you are and what you want out of this life, and I think it might be time to think with your heart a little bit and give your brain a rest. And if your heart wants Derek . . . well then, my sugar plum fairy, as of tomorrow, you'll have enough silverware to accommodate him."

I'm silent for a minute, digesting everything she said in little bite-sized lumps. And when I can't think of any adequate or profound ways to tell her I love her more than the ocean or rainbows or Sprite from McDonald's after a stomach bug, I settle for a fact. "You know Derek has a mansion, right? Full of spoons."

"But does his mansion have a beautiful woman and a pink couch?"

The door to our suite looms in front of me, and I eye it as if it's a fire-breathing dragon. "I'm frustrated with myself, Mom."

"Why?"

"Because you're right about all of it, obviously, and I do still have feelings for Derek—love him, even—and did when I broke up with him too. But I really thought there wasn't a way that we would work out back then and be able to pursue our separate dreams." *I also might have been trying to beat him to the punch by breaking up with him before he had a chance to break my heart.* "But now that I'm here and we've both achieved our goals and our feelings have lasted all this time, I can't decide if I regret breaking up with him or if I'm happy I followed my career?"

"I think both realities can be true. You don't have to pick. Maybe Derek was always the right person, just at the wrong time." I can hear the smile in my mom's voice because she knows that what she's saying is profound, and she will likely turn it into an inspirational quote for Pinterest after we hang up. She'll take up embroidery just so she can stitch it onto a pillow.

"Now, I'm just your old mom, but I say Derek's right and you could ease up on yourself this week. Use this time to get to know him again and figure out what you really want. Have some fun."

It feels like my stomach grows wings and dashes off a cliff at those words. *Have some fun.* The concept is definitely long overdue.

"Do you want shiny silverware or matte?" she finally asks.

"Matte. Thank you, Mom."

"I'm just a call away if you need me, lovey. But maybe wait until my movie is over because those people in there would be excellent hall monitors and I'm scared to find out what they'll do to me if I act up again."

We end the call after exchanging *I love you*'s and Mom reminding me to wear sunscreen (a little too late for that, lady) and then I lower my phone and eye the door again. I would touch it longingly if I didn't think the security cameras out here would catch me looking angsty.

Before I let myself start thinking too hard about this, I fill my lungs with a breath so big they might pop and then I march into the suite.

Derek is on the floor foam-rolling his right hamstrings when I storm into the room. His eyebrows lift.

"First of all, that is a very scandalous position you're in, sir."

"I've learned not to do this stretch around any cameras for a reason," he says. "Do you have a second following the first?"

"Yes," I say with one final, definitive Nicole-esque head nod. "Let's break all the rules, Derek Pender."

31

Derek

I can't stop staring at Nora. She's like a sexy stick of bubble gum right now. Not sure she'd actually think that comparison is attractive, but believe me, it is. She's wearing a two-piece bright pink outfit that I was told is called a bandeau and trousers fit. All I know is her shoulders are completely bare, still a little red from the burn and sprinkled with cute freckles that have darkened from our day out by the pool this morning (taking pictures for the article), and a section of her abdomen is peeking out from behind the high waist of her flowy pants.

She looks good.

So good that as Alec took photos outside the restaurant and people stopped to watch and snap pics with their phones when they realized who I was, I felt the urge to stand in front of Nora. Her body looks too incredible. Her smile is too wide and sparkling. I want to hide it so no one else can see it. *She's mine.*

But no, Nora is very much her own person. And hiding any part of this woman would be a mistake—so instead, I angled behind her, setting her up front and center where she belongs.

Her lips curl around the rim of her drink now—oblivious to the desire and possessiveness thrumming under my skin.

"What's next when you get home, Nora?"

She eyes me sidelong. "Like . . . next for us?"

"I mean, what's next for *you*." I tilt my head. "You haven't so much as slipped a mention of your career plans for after we're back—which tells me they've been swirling through your head for days and you've been extra careful not to hint at them."

She sits back in her seat, eyeing me appreciatively—hesitantly. "I didn't want to bring it up and risk messing with whatever this connection is again."

"You think it's that fragile?"

She shrugs. "I don't know. It seemed wrong to flaunt my dreams in front of you when yours are . . ." *Hanging in the balance* is what she doesn't say. And now she looks like she instantly regrets those words.

I get it. There was a time when I unintentionally prioritized my career over hers. When I wouldn't have been able to stomach watching her success while mine was fading. And now she thinks this truth might shut me down completely.

I sit forward and smile. "It's Demetris, isn't it?"

Those lips pull into a soft surprised smile. She leans forward too. "What do you know of Demetris?"

"Going into his senior year of high school. Shattered several records by the end of his junior year. Is an all-time leading career rusher in varsity history." I pop a bite of steak into my mouth. "Seems like he's going places and will need a great agent to take him there."

A competitive twinkle opens in Nora's eyes. I could stare at her like this all day. "Seems like he will indeed."

"Speaking of great agents. We never talked about that endorsement deal you got for me with Dapper." I pause. "It's unreal. How did you get them to fork over that much money?"

Her grin—the one so many people underestimate because it comes from a watermelon-pink mouth—turns downright cunning. "Simple. They were asking for my A-list celebrity athlete to star in their commercial and wear their suits to every major function for the next year. They needed to pay like it."

"Yeah, but Bill never landed deals like this for quite that much money."

"Bill was a nincompoop," she says plainly, making me laugh. "Honestly, Derek, I looked at half of your deals and they all should have been negotiated for a higher payout. Bill needed to grow some ovaries and fight for his client."

Mark my words, Nora is going to take over the sports agency world—and I'm just lucky to have gotten in with her from the beginning.

"Back to Demetris." I lean back, crossing my arms. "Everyone is going to be after him. Including Nicole. What's your plan?"

She narrows her eyes and points a fork at me. "Wouldn't you like to know. Unfortunately for you, I don't discuss clients or future clients with my current roster. So put your magnifying glass away, Sherlock."

"Mm. That's fine. I'll have fun trying to get the answers from you later, Ginger Snap."

Her cheeks turn the same shade of pink as her top, but she doesn't look away. "Bypassing that salacious comment. How do you know about Demetris?"

I shrug. "I like to keep up with notable high school and college players just in case they ever end up on my team." It's happened twice. One of those high school players being Collin Abbot, the guy who very well might take my job this year. "I know veteran players don't normally pay much attention to the rookies—or if they do, it's mainly for hazing. But I've always preferred to take a different approach."

"Which is?" she asks.

Suddenly I feel exposed talking about myself. I've never liked it much. But especially not when it's something personal like this. But for Nora, I will. "I like to help them adjust and show them the ropes from the beginning because you never know when one of our starters might get injured and the rookie suddenly becomes a vital part of the team. Also . . . I don't know . . . I just enjoy it."

I pause and adjust my pant legs just to give myself something to do. But Nora the menace doesn't say anything. She just watches me with a smile.

"Don't tell me that you suddenly have nothing to say?" I ask sarcastically.

"Oh I have plenty to say! But I know that there's more, and I plan to stay quiet until you say it all."

I roll my eyes and groan. She taps her foot against my leg under the table, eliciting currents that roll up my shins and thighs and settle low in my stomach. "Fine. I guess I've been thinking about our conversation yesterday and letting myself really consider what will happen if I get cut. And then I realized that even if I'm not a Shark anymore, I don't ever want to fully let football go. It's a part of who I am—but maybe there's another avenue I could approach. I think I'd make a good . . . coach." I wince. "Is that ridiculous? I don't even know if I could find a coaching job. I just . . ." My voice fades out.

"Why would that be anything other than super incredibly amazing? I think you'd make a wonderful coach. And I also think it'll make an excellent option for you when you're in your forties and decide to retire from the Sharks." Her smile is a sharp, sweet dagger. "Because I'm willing to bet you anything, my top client—"

"Your only client."

"—That you're going to come back stronger than ever. So quit your fretting, because I'm a hotshot agent and I know what I'm talking about." I wish everyone else shared her faith in my abilities.

Truth be told, I'm afraid I'm going to get out there on the field, hear the haunting echo of my bone snapping in half, and freeze up. I'm afraid that maybe this really is the end for me. But at least that fear doesn't come with quite as much panic as it used to. I have some options . . .

"Okay, I'm done talking about me. Are you going to visit Demetris when we get back?"

"Why are you so worried about this?" she asks with a curious smile.

I shrug. "I guess I just . . . I've already gotten in the way of your career enough. I want to support you going forward."

She looks at me now like a person in a museum studying an abstract painting and trying to find the hidden meaning behind it. And then a soft smile curves her mouth as she pierces a bit of potato onto her fork. "Don't worry. I've got everything in hand, and I do plan to pay Demetris a visit."

"Good."

"Just not until Nicole does first."

I frown and sit forward again. "Why?"

That challenging glint that sets my body on fire hits her eyes. The one that most people miss because they're too distracted by her bright clothes and innocent demeanor. Those people are fools. I was a fool for thinking I could ever orbit around Nora without falling into her gravitational pull. *She owns me.*

"Because I want him to hear her pitch first, and then see what it was lacking when he hears mine." She is all delicious confidence. "Nicole taught me everything—which means I had a front-row seat to her weaknesses. And before you think I'm a horrible greedy human, she already told me to use them against her. Nicole appreciates a challenge and seems to be excited to have a new competitor in the ring." Her smile drops away when she sees the muscle in my jaw jump. "What? Do you think I'm being a sleazy colleague? You have to understand, Nicole and I—"

"That's not at all what I was thinking."

"Then what is that look for?" she asks, picking up her glass. "Tell me the truth. I can handle it."

"Okay." I rest my forearms on the table and let my emotions reach my eyes as I stare into hers. "That look was the result of me wanting to rip your clothes off with my teeth and do very dirty things to you right here on this table when you talk like that."

She chokes on the water—because whatever it was she was expecting me to say, it wasn't that. When her coughing is under control, she yanks her folded cloth napkin from the table to wipe her mouth but doesn't see that the fold is caught on the corner of the menu. Next thing we know, the menu is launched like a Frisbee across the restaurant. It sails to the table closest to ours, where it knocks over their glass of wine.

Before the waitstaff can blink, Nora is up and rushing to their table. She moves their dishes aside and soaks up the liquid with her rogue napkin, all while murmuring a wholehearted apology. She's blending into the restaurant as much as a pink flamingo would blend into Wall Street.

A waitress comes to her side with fresh linens and is so stunned to see Nora there helping that she silently extends the cloths as Nora asks for them. I go help too, shifting plates of food so Nora can catch the wine trying to roll off the table before it makes more of a mess. No one around us seems to know what to do but Nora—who is on a mission to single-handedly salvage their table.

"Holy shit," the man sitting at the table says when he tilts his head up and sees me hovering over him. "You're . . . you're Derek Pender, right?"

"He is!" Nora says cheerfully. "Would you like to see his ID? It's an unfairly good picture, to be honest."

I give her a flat look.

"No, I—I believe you. I mean . . . damn . . . you are a big dude." He then grimaces. "Sorry, that was a weird thing to say. I'm a little tipsy because I was nervous about . . ." He glances at the table and our gazes all fall on a little red velvet box sitting to the side of the table.

Nora gasps with delight. "Did you two just get engaged?"

"Yes, we did," says the woman with a fond smile at her drunk fiancé.

Nora launches into a series of congratulations, complimenting the woman on how beautiful she looks in her dress. She can tell immediately that it's an antique engagement ring and asks if there is a story behind it. Five minutes later, the man has wrapped up an entire story about how the ring came from his grandmother and that his grandfather purchased it during the war and mailed it to her, asking her to save it for when he returned. He did return, and they had a beautiful family of five. Nora is crying. The woman is crying. The dude is crying. I'm . . . misty . . . but that's all I'll admit to.

"But you two just got married, didn't you? I've seen the story of your secret elopement all over social media!" says the woman. "Can I see your ring? I bet it's . . ." At this moment her eyes drop to Nora's finger, and she sees that it's empty except for the discreet little black line.

Nora's smile doesn't fade a bit, but I do notice that she grazes the inside of the tattoo with her thumb—like she's tracing the line to feel something. Proof that it's there. "We thought a tattoo would be a fun way to commemorate the spontaneous event."

She looks up at me, and the gold in her eyes burns brighter than the green in this light. Even though she's smiling, I see what she doesn't want me to. The creeping reminder that this isn't truly real. That whatever we are now started on a lie. That I never gave her a ring out of love. This was all to keep her job, and yes, a new relationship has bloomed out of it, but how will it withstand real life at home? Do we even have a chance when a lie was our beginning?

I pick up her left hand and bring it to my lips, kissing her tattoo ring and hoping Nora feels what I can't say: *It doesn't matter how this started, it's real for me.*

My gaze moves behind Nora and I realize most of the restaurant is watching us. Not just with their eyes—their phones too. Our time here is up.

After giving my autograph and taking a picture with the couple, Nora asks the waiters to bring the couple any dessert and bottle of wine they want as a congratulations (and apology). Even when she's not trying to, Nora is in agent mode, and it looks damn good on her.

When we're back at the table, she smiles as if nothing out of the ordinary ever happened. "I've been thinking, Dere-Bear. Will you go to a club with me after this?"

"A club?" I ask—hesitancy tugging me. I haven't done anything remotely close to partying ever since my injury. (1) Because I haven't felt like it. Anxiety and stress over recovering to my fullest have been my guiding factors since the day I woke up from surgery. (2) I don't want to appear flippant in the media. No one likes to see a guy with his career hanging in the balance out getting drunk in a club. (3) Because I haven't missed it.

This time, Nora is the one to read my thoughts. She stares at me and tilts her head. "You're allowed to be dedicated to your career, drink chamomile tea, and have fun too."

I extend my hand to her. "Hello, pot? Kettle."

"Exactly. *Takes one to know one.*" Her pink lips curve into a smile as she slaps my hand away. "Come with me. Let's have fun together tonight." Her words seep into my chest and pump like blood through my heart.

"Which version of us is going? Agent and client? Husband and wife? Or friends?"

Her face blooms. "All of them."

32

Derek

After leaving the restaurant, we dipped into an Uber and headed to a nightclub in the touristy district of downtown Cancún.

Inside, it's loud. Blue and purple lights stream through the dark, hazy, sweat-drenched atmosphere and reflect off mirrored surfaces. The place is full but not packed. Still, there are enough bodies in here to have me instinctively reaching for Nora's hip as we walk.

"Let's go get a drink!" she yells over the music. Her eyes are sparkling from the lights, and an addictive energy ripples off her. I haven't seen her like this since college. Old memories and familiar sensations buzz to life.

"Are you sure?" I ask, leaning close to her ear so she can hear me over the music. "Last time we drank together we ended up married."

"All the more reason to do it again," she says, eyes shifting to my lips.

She slips out of my grasp and walks in front of me, taking my hand to pull me with her through the crowd. Every so often she tosses a grin back at me over her shoulder, and I doubt she realizes how weak it makes me. How scared I am that this is all a dream and it's going to slide through my fingers when I wake up.

When we get to the bar, she flags down the bartender and orders us a round of shots in Spanish. It's not perfect but the bartender nods and in perfect English tells her he'll be right back with the drinks. I put my card on file for our tab, and a minute later, she's counting us down before we toss back the tequila.

Nora grimaces with a smile and then slaps her hand down on the bar. She's all freckled and tannish-pink. It's a great look on her. The faint tan line running over her sunburnt shoulder from her bikini strap snags my eye and suddenly it's all I can focus on. I want to use it like a path to take across her body.

There's no use trying to hide my desire at this point. And when her eyes meet mine, I make it perfectly clear. "You look edible in this pink."

"And you . . . must be drunk already."

"Not even close."

She studies me and the solemnness of her expression is at war with the party raging around us. "Can I ask you a question?"

"Anything. Always."

Her expression turns mischievous. "What's in your bedside table, Pender?"

Any question but that one. "Something important to me—but that's all I want to say about it for now."

She looks sad but doesn't press me on it. "Fair enough. I'll try another one, then." We're both sitting on barstools side by side, and she angles herself a little more toward me, our outer thighs pressing together.

"Why two years?" she asks. I don't understand immediately what she's referring to, so she continues, "You told me you didn't start dating again until two years after we broke up. What changed at two years?"

I look out over the pulsing club and back to Nora. "You weren't the only one who saw something you weren't supposed to."

Her brows knit together.

"I saw you in the airport."

She looks like the floor is falling out from under her. "You did? Why didn't you say something?"

"I was going to. But then I realized you were with someone."

"*Oh.*"

I lay my hand over hers on the bar, tracing my thumb over each of her knuckles. Mainly to remind myself that she's not at that airport with that random guy anymore. She's here. With me. In whatever messy-beautiful situationship this is.

"I was about to catch a flight for a game, and I looked across the way and there you were." I smile, remembering how it felt to look at her again after two years. The way my stomach clenched, and it was like light had burst through the room. "You were rolling a bright pink suitcase, wearing tennis shoes, black leggings, and a white hoodie that said *Sesame Street is my happy place.* Your hair was darker then, and you wore it in a ponytail. I remember you smiling over your shoulder, and even from twenty yards away you stopped my heart."

Tension gathers between us, and she doesn't ask to hear more. She already knows what's coming. I didn't realize it at the time but seeing her at the airport that day was just penance for her having to witness me kissing someone outside my apartment the week after we broke up.

"Then a guy walked up and took your hand and you two went to your gate together." I breathe in, bracing against the memory. "I stood there for way too long watching you leave with him until I couldn't see you anymore." What I don't tell her is that Nathan found me like that and said I looked like I'd seen a ghost. I didn't bother telling him that I had. "You looked so happy with that guy, though . . . Ben or Liam, I'm assuming. I didn't want to mess that up by saying hi. And similar to how you felt—seeing you with him helped me realize it was time to finally let you go too."

Except I never really truly did.

Before I can say anything else, Nora grabs the front of my shirt and pulls me to her. She kisses me—and it's desperate. She pours all of her feelings into this kiss. The low bass of the music thumps through us as we simultaneously deepen the kiss. Nora slides off her stool to stand between my legs, and my hands glide up her back, over her warm shoulder blades. She tilts her head and with this better angle, I sweep my tongue through her hot mouth, devouring the sweet, tequila-soaked desperation of it.

Someone bumps into me accidentally and it pulls me back to life. I'm making out with Nora in the middle of a club—and enjoying the hell out of it. When we peel apart, she looks up at me smiling, maybe a little embarrassed. I wish she wasn't. Everything about her is perfect.

Nora pulls out of my arms and takes my hand, tugging me up from the bar. "Come on, let's dance."

Most men my size are embarrassed to dance. There's nothing discreet about it. I don't give a shit, though—I've always had fun making a fool out of myself on the dance floor, and it's good to be out here again with her reminding me of that fortunate night when I met her at the party.

I can't say I've really missed all the partying I used to do that much, but now, laughing and intermittently kissing Nora out here under the colored lights with music vibrating through my chest, I realize I need more of this in my life. I've closed myself off to fun and focused too much on holding as tightly to my career as possible. But not tonight—tonight, Nora pulls me onto the dance floor and reminds me to live.

Plus how much of a fool can I really look if I have the most beautiful woman in the world dancing against me like we're trying out for the next *Dirty Dancing* movie?

There are a lot of people out here with us, but as far as I'm concerned, there's only Nora. Nora's eyes as they glitter against the darkness. Nora's smile as it beams its own light through the room. Nora's body as I curl her into me.

After who knows how long on the dance floor, we go back to the bar for a water and another drink. I leave her there sipping her water for no more than five minutes while I go to the bathroom, and apparently that was too long. When I return, I see an American guy with a death wish aggressively grabbing Nora's bicep as she turns away from him.

"Don't be such a prudish bitch! I was talking to you," he yells above the music, but that's all he gets to say before I grab him by the shoulder and whip his body around, throwing him back against the bar. He's clearly a tourist because he speaks English and has that glazed-over, partied-too-much look in his eyes. Screams erupt around us and just as I'm about to throw my fist into his face repeatedly until each and every one of his damned teeth are on the floor, Nora wraps her hand around my raised arm.

"Derek! Don't!" She says it as a command, and only because it's her do I drag my eyes away from the dude. I'm shaking with rage and she's breathing heavy, looking nervous by whatever she sees in my eyes. "Don't hit him. He's not worth the assault charges. Please. I'm okay—I promise."

I clench my teeth against the anger and adrenaline surging through me. "That's where I disagree. It would absolutely be worth it to make him pay for touching you." And I mean it. I'd go to jail for her if it meant keeping her safe from assholes like this guy.

She squeezes my arm. "I believe you. But I just got you back and I don't feel like losing you to prison bars."

Nora drops my arm, but her words wrap around me and squeeze.

I drag in a long breath through my nose and swing my gaze back to the wide-eyed dickhead pinned under my fist. I crowd him even further, getting so close to his face that he's doing a backbend on the bar. I want him to be able to see the fillings in my teeth.

"Do you see that woman behind me that you just touched without her consent and then called a nasty name?" I ask him in an intentionally low voice that I hope haunts his nightmares.

He swallows and barely manages to get his single-word answer out. "Yes."

"She's my wife. And if it were up to me, I'd have you bleeding all over this bar right now for laying a single finger on her that she didn't invite. When I let go of you, you're going to apologize to her. And then you're going to leave this bar, and if you ever treat another woman like that again, I will know, and I will hunt you down . . . and for legal purposes, I'm not going to tell you what I'll do to you. But I'm sure your imagination can fill in the blanks."

I release him with a shove and step back.

It takes him a few seconds to peel himself from the bar and stand upright again. He looks around at the gathering crowd and shrugs his shirt back into place—rolling his shoulders.

I cross my arms and wait expectantly for him to address Nora.

"Umm . . . I'm sorry for—"

"No." I cut him off. "Don't look her in the face. You don't deserve to look at her. Look at your ugly-ass shoes while you apologize to her."

His gaze drops immediately and he is now physically shaking

while he grounds out his halfhearted apology. And then like a chickenshit, he runs out of the bar.

I take one full deep breath and ignore the gawking crowd—ignore the phones pointed in my direction and look at Nora. Her eyes are misty, and when I open my arms, she steps into them, letting me hold her tightly against me. I want to be her human bubble wrap.

"Are you okay?" I murmur into her hair.

"Yes. I'd drifted away from the bar to watch everyone dance and then he appeared out of nowhere and wouldn't leave me alone. I told him I didn't want to dance but he kept getting in my face and insisting. So I turned away, and that's when you showed up." She pauses and I can't say anything yet because fury is dripping into my veins. "It scared me. I realized very quickly that I need to sign up for self-defense classes when we get home. My wit is sharp as a knife and I could have killed him with a well-timed knock-knock joke, but I think maybe I need to learn to throw someone into the bar like you just did too. Wouldn't hurt to have options."

"I can't joke around with you yet." I take her hand and put it over my heart so she can feel just how forcefully it's pounding against my chest.

She kisses me there, right over my beating heart. I don't even care if an entire club is watching us, I take her face in my hands as gently as I possibly can and look in her eyes. "What he called you . . ."

"It's okay, Derek. He was just a miserable person and—"

"No, it's not okay. Not at all, because you, Nora, are beautiful, rare magic and nothing less." A tear streaks down her face and I kiss it from her skin. "Let's go."

33

Nora

The elevator is so silent I'm worried Derek can hear my thumping heart—but it has nothing to do with what took place at that bar.

"Are you really okay?" he asks for the hundredth time since leaving the club a few hours ago. I was shaken up at first, but then we came back to the resort and Derek worry-ordered me five different appetizers and three desserts and we spent two solid hours just talking and laughing in the nice barroom. Now my anxiety about it has completely faded and been replaced with a warm-sparkly comfort.

"I really am. I promise times a million."

"I just . . ." He shakes his head. "I hope you know. There's nothing I wouldn't do for you, Nora."

"I know," I say, softly. "And I hope you know I'd definitely fight off a guy in a bar for you too."

A smirk slices the side of his mouth. "Oh, I know."

He's on one side of the elevator leaned back against the wall and I'm against the other. You couldn't charge the air between us more even if you were to hook us up to electricity. His arms are folded, one lazy ankle crossed over the other, head tilted, eyes fixed on me.

I'm mirroring him while we calculate each other. Considering briefly all the ways we might royally screw up each other's lives if we act on the impulses zipping under our skin and it turns out to be a mistake. The thing is, I've never felt more certain that this is not a mistake. Not this time around.

And when those ice-blue eyes of his land on me and linger, I feel like I'm free-falling into a pool of bliss. They leave my face briefly to trail down my neck, across my collarbones, over the curve of my shoulders and chest and abdomen. He looks at me as if he's devouring me little by little.

God help me, I want him to.

His gaze catches mine again and he doesn't look in control anymore, he looks desperate.

The elevator dings and a man steps in between us. Derek and I don't move. The poor guy is caught in a dangerous crossfire, and he knows it. He taps his foot anxiously as the elevator advances us. He's the next stop and no sooner than the doors open does he dart out with a nervous look over his shoulder.

The doors shut and I grin.

Derek's jaw flexes. "There's two rules left . . ." He pauses and I encourage him with a lifted brow. He continues in a voice like black silk, "Two left we haven't broken."

"Only two?" I feel oddly accomplished that we managed to break eighteen out of twenty rules since working together.

"Only two," he repeats, holding up two lazy fingers.

I immediately know which two are left:

Rule number 3: No friendship.

Rule number twenty: No sex.

He crooks his finger twice. "Come here."

"Not a chance," I say, wrapping my hands around the railing at my back to anchor me. "You come here."

"Always have to win, don't you?" he says with a pleased grin.

"And you can't keep yourself from competing."

The elevator is almost to our floor, and the look on Derek's face has my heart racketing against my sternum, trying to crack my ribs. "All right, then. What are your parameters for this competition?"

I bite my lip just as the elevator doors open. I can't believe we're going to do this, and yet I'm helpless to stop it. No, that's not true. I don't *want* to stop it. He has been a magnetic force in my life since the day I met him at that party in college—I don't want to overthink it. I just want to be with Derek tonight and hope that I get all the nights after it too.

I step out of the elevator and Derek prowls closely behind as we walk down the hallway to our suite. I'm hyperaware of my skin. Of the way my clothes hug me. The sound of our feet against the luxurious carpeting. Of his hungry expression in every mirror we pass.

"It'll be like the question game," I say over my shoulder, and then face forward again. "Mixed with strip poker."

I'm aware of Derek's steps faltering slightly behind me. But by the time we reach the door and he holds the key card against it, he's completely composed. More than composed, in fact—his confidence is radiating from his large form like he's the origin of all seduction. If there is anything Derek excels at—it's this.

A thrill twirls through me. This particular dance has never been more fun than with the man holding the door open for me.

"Okay," he says, his voice a low gravel after we're both closed inside the room. "So, if I answer the question you take a piece of clothing off, and if I don't answer it, I have to?"

I nod. "Whoever is naked first loses . . . and they have to make the first move."

He stares at me for a beat with a wolfish smile. "I'm in."

Oh. He knows exactly how good he looks with that slanted half smile—and yet he has no mercy on me. He drops his gaze to his wrist, where he unlatches his watch and tosses it on the couch. "A freebie," he says in a tone that makes my thighs clench.

I can't help but feel he's too far away and too close at the same time.

I've very quickly lost the upper hand. He's so much better at this game of seduction than me.

That's why I follow his lead and kick off my heels. "A freebie for a freebie."

His eyes narrow slightly as he holds my grin. "You go first, Ginger Snap."

Okay, I might faint. My heart is beating too fast. My skin is clammy. How did I think this was a fun idea? It seemed exciting when we were in the elevator, and I was still high off adrenaline from the club. But now it's gone and I'm just in this room with a man who overwhelms my senses. Who is sexier than any man has any business being.

There's only two rules we haven't broken.

There was no mistaking his intent when he said those words. And there's no mistaking how much I agree with him. *Tonight, number twenty is for sure getting detroyed.*

But I also play to win every game I ever compete in. So I will not be caving first—which means I need to keep as many articles of clothing as possible. Be prepared to lay my heart on the line with the questions he asks me and think of truly impossible questions to ask him.

"Derek," I say with a taunting tone.

"Yes, Nora?" He takes a step closer. We're six feet apart now, standing in the middle of our suite with a huge window to our right. A more beautiful picture has never existed than the sight of the moon, dipping over the dark, rolling ocean.

I think of a question I know he won't want to answer. *Prepare to lose a piece of your precious clothing.* "What's in your bedside table?"

Derek gives me an indiscernible look. "You're determined to find that out, aren't you? Pass."

A zing of triumph soars through me until Derek's eyes glitter. He leans over and kicks off his shoes.

"Nora," he says when he returns to a standing position, arms folded. "What is your favorite dessert?"

I frown. "You know the answer to that question. Why not ask me something better?" I ask, as my brain scrambles in the dark for his angle.

He gives me a look that betrays nothing. "You didn't say we couldn't ask questions we already knew the answer to." *Suspicious.*

Narrowing my eyes, I answer, "Ice cream and cereal."

He grins. Not just any grin, though—a hot, melting, intentional grin as he works the buttons of his shirt open, one by one, all the way down that gorgeous, defined abdomen. He shrugs out of it and my heart leaps. The tops of his shoulders are deeply tanned from our days on the beach. And nothing is sexier than how his dress pants sit low around his hips, taunting me with the upper band of his black boxer briefs and somehow intensifying the dark detail of the winged hawks on his chest. Even this man's hips are defined. There's a band of muscle that sits where most people have love handles and it trails down into the V at his lower abdomen. It would be easy to hate him for how stacked he is if I didn't know how incredibly hard he works for it.

"You could have taken your socks off instead," I tell him, mentally remapping the route to find his destination.

"I could have." He's amused. A sly trickster. "Your turn."

I don't know what he's playing at yet, and because my brain is just intrigued enough to need the answer, I step closer and try his same tactic. "All right, Mr. Smirky Pants. What's your favorite color?"

If he answers, I have to take off a piece of my clothing, and it's risky considering I'm wearing less than him to start. But it's a price I'm willing to pay to find out what he's up to. I get the feeling there's a second secret competition he's started, and I want to win that one too.

Derek's brows knit together, and he tilts his head. His jaw looks sharp enough to cut a steak. "Pass. That's deeply personal."

"*What!*" Not only am I flabbergasted that he would refuse to answer and forfeit a piece of clothing, but I can't for the life of me figure out what his aim is in doing so. It feels less like the question game and more like putting a little ball under a cup and mixing them all around and then asking me to find it. *Thrilling.* "Not that I don't appreciate the importance you're putting on artistic expression, but how in the world is that personal?"

He tsks. "That sounds like another question. Wait your turn, greedy woman."

I sigh and cross my arms over my fully clothed body as I watch him double over to slide off his socks. As he does, I'm treated to the most exquisite view of shoulder and back muscles bunching and twisting under his tattoos. It's like watching a superhero get cozy for the night. He straightens up and lifts his foot to wiggle his toes in a playful, over-the-top seductive way. But I'm not looking at his toes. I'm looking at his abs contracting as he balances on one foot. *Lordy.*

Whatever he asks next, I need to refuse to answer and take off a piece of clothing. I can't explain why or how—but I can see this second secret game playing out in his eyes and I will be a participant.

"Nora . . . do you feel safe with me?"

I gasp and point a finger at him. "Foul! That's a manipulative question. You can't ask me one you know I'm not going to want to leave hanging."

He shrugs slightly—again not giving any hints to what he's thinking. What his motivation is . . . because as it stands, it looks like he's trying to lose. "We can't always play by the rules," he says with a smirk, and I wonder how long he's been waiting to use my exact words against me.

I'm all turned around now. I don't know if I should answer or pass. So I tell the truth. "I've never felt safer with anyone than you."

His chest expands with a breath and the barest smile curves his mouth. And then, he's unfastening his chinos and dropping them down to the floor. *Step, step*—he's pantsless.

Now, Derek Freaking Pender (that should be his actual middle name but really it's Felix and he hates it) is standing in front of me in skintight black boxer briefs and I'm about to faint. Sure, I've seen him naked plenty of times. But that was different. We were young, and time (that unforgiving jerk) has erased most of my memory.

This . . . this feels like an entirely new experience. This feels like palms sweating. Thighs tingling. Toes curling.

One more question and I win.

He sees the hungry look in my eyes and his grin turns downright wicked. "Ask your question."

I don't hesitate. "Why do you anonymously fund a nonprofit that helps single mothers pay their rent and mortgage?"

His eyes flare. I got him on that one. "You really were digging through my finances, weren't you? *Pass.*"

And then without an ounce of self-consciousness, without a bit of hesitation, Derek steps completely out of his underwear, leaving all of him (and I do mean all of him) on display for my eyes to devour. He lost and I won—but when his eyes lock with mine and I see the arrogant glimmer I love so much, when he steps closer to me to make the first move as defined in the earlier rules of the game . . . it sure feels like he won somehow.

"What's the secret game you were playing?" I ask, my face tipping up, up, up as he approaches. He's powerful clothed. He's unearthly naked. My skin warms and tingles as every cell in my body reaches for him.

"No secret game."

"Don't lie to me, Pender."

"Truly." He glides my hair back, fingertips brushing my shoulder in a whisper. "I only lost because I want to show you in a physical way that I'm intentionally and completely vulnerable to you, Nora. That I'll gladly lose to you every day of my life—because for me, the prize is just being near you." His hand slides against my jaw and a tremble runs through me.

"Now, a few truths." He leans down to kiss my cheek. "I don't want to tell you what's in my bedside table because when I do, it will change everything between us, and I don't think you're ready for it yet. I have no desire to watch you bolt out the door, so you'll have to be content with waiting." Another kiss on my other cheek as delicious heat billows off his body, silently calling to mine. "My favorite color is hazel." He angles my jaw up and his lips find the underside of it. "And I fund that organization because when we were dating, you said you'd wished something like that would have existed for your mom and other moms like her. So when I got my first major paycheck and my CPA asked what kind of charities I'd like to donate to, your words were the first ones that sprang to mind. I did it anonymously because I didn't want you to see it and think it was strange of me."

"I would never have—" He silences me with a finger to the bow of my lips.

"And the first day I saw you again in the conference room, I was *livid*"—he growls that word—"that you were still the most beautiful woman I'd ever seen in my life."

Now tears collect in my eyes and drop down my cheeks. Derek wipes them with his thumbs. "I'm at your feet, Nora. If you want me, I'm yours."

There's no part of me that needs to even pause to consider it. "Yes, Derek, I want—"

34

Nora

My words are taken by Derek's crushing kiss. His mouth catches mine with a force that stirs every corner of my body. It simmers over my lips. It heats my skin and inches its way to my core.

His hand whispers down my side, drawing goosebumps to the surface of my arms and the tops of my thighs, as he wraps around to my lower back, tugging me up against him. Our kiss slips away and comes together again, angling and re-angling. The best geometry class of my life.

My heart is thunder as he carries his breath down my throat, teeth gliding gently over my flesh until he reaches the base of my neck. The inky night slips around us, stars winking out the window, encouraging me that *this* is a very good idea as Derek's mouth sucks lightly at my throat.

More, more, more.

"Happily," he says, because apparently I'd been whispering my sentiments out loud. My abdomen tightens instinctively as Derek's knuckles brush against the skin of my midriff, briefly toying with the waistband of my lovely pink trousers. With an expertise worthy of an award, he flicks open the button, pulls the zipper down, and then drops them around my ankles. It happens in a flash. Cold air rushes my thighs, but I shiver from Derek's large warm hand moving around to my ass and giving one firm squeeze.

He groans a gutted sound that sends need striking through me from all corners. "These are not your days-of-the-week panties," he half growls in my ear.

"No. They're not." My smile is dipped in confidence. *These* are lacy. *These* are see-through. *These* are sexy and daring and make me feel like a woman. Derek's eyes eat me up from head to toe.

"I love them." A dark grin overtakes his mouth. Eyes glittering dangerously. "Now take them off."

His thumbs hook the flimsy waistband and peel them off me—inch by inch. I can't stand to keep my hands to myself any longer. I want to plaster myself to him and never let go. To start, I trace the raised lines of the tattoos on his shoulders and chest, letting my fingertips dance down his hard abdomen and toward other hard places. But Derek catches my wrist, stopping me before I can.

"Not yet," he warns. No—*pleads*. It cracks the moment wide open, reminding us how much this means to both of us. "I don't want to rush. Tonight I just want to savor you."

There's absolutely no arguing with that. So I raise my arms above my head, letting Derek remove my bandeau top. He gives it a few quick tugs, but it won't budge. I'm just about to show him where to find the zip when I hear a sharp tear. My sad little bandeau falls limply to the ground next to my trousers as a discarded scrap of fabric. I'll take this top home with me and frame it with a little plaque underneath that reads *An Ode to Cancún*.

"I thought you said you didn't want to rush," I chide, taking my hands up over these mountain ranges he calls shoulders.

"We have to make exceptions now and then. I'll buy you a new one, Ginger Snap," he whispers against the shell of my ear, teeth catching at my lobe once. Tension gathers between my thighs as Derek's tongue swirls over my pulse. Sensations unlike any other zigzag down through my stomach.

My nails bite into his back, trying frantically to get closer, to feel the rocking pressure of our hips meeting. He swears against my skin before his hands drop to hook under my thighs. He hoists me up so we're face-to-face, and despite drowning in this haze of lust, I'm able to appreciate how very blue his eyes are even in the moonlight.

I clinch my legs tightly around his abdomen, and his skin is blazing against me. His mouth takes mine in a slick, hot kiss, winding me up to a tension so tight I'm afraid I'll snap right in half. My hands chart a path through the back of his hair as he carries me to the bed. But he doesn't lay me down, he sits with me straddling his lap, breathing deep and slowing the moment to something graceful and dazzling. As a perfect contradiction, his massive, rough hands delicately push my hair off my chest and shoulders to fall down my back. His arctic eyes melt over my body as his fingers trace up my ribs like piano keys. I'm not prepared for the sensation of his hands curving worshipfully under my breasts.

The *look* he's giving me right now. Yes, there's desire and promises of how good his body will feel covering mine completely, but there's so much more here too. Something raw and almost painful.

His finger runs a line up the center of my breasts and pauses on the left side of my chest, just below my collarbone. He draws a shape. My shape. *A heart.* And then bends, caressing it with his lips.

"I never told you thank you," he says while standing up from the bed. I squeak and grip him around his neck, even though he seems to have me easily tucked against him without needing my help at all.

One half-turn and he lowers my back to the cushy mattress. It's a white, puffy cloud of luxury.

Finally he's covering me with his weight, and I want all of it. I hook my leg around his back just to make it a reality. But he grins as his hair falls over his brow. "*Patience.* I have something to say."

"Do you want to maybe say it later?" I'm desperate for him. Never been more desperate for anything or anyone in my life.

His hand dives under my back, lifting again until he scoots me up to the pillow. "No. I want to tell you now, while you're naked. It's better this way."

I barely manage to hide my whimper, especially as Derek dips his head, shoulder muscles rippling under his skin, and presses his mouth to the most sensitive skin of my breast. His tongue is a work of art, and I arch helplessly into him.

After a moment, he has more to say. "Everyone in high school and college made me feel inadequate when I was pursuing anything apart from sports. Even as an adult, the relationships I've had have been purely physical and surface level. I've never felt particularly wanted or cherished. Except . . . with you."

As he's talking, his hand is skating down my belly, drawing tiny hearts with his large fingertip on my inner thighs, and then moving between them, *finally* touching right where I want and need him most. His words alone buzz over my skin like a dangerous current of electricity, but paired with his touch, it's like taking a direct hit from a bolt of lightning. It's an overload. An onslaught. And he's right—these conversations are better naked.

His mouth presses into my neck as his hand keeps its pace and I'm dizzy from the pleasure he's coaxing from my body. *He still knows me so well.* I don't want it to stop. I don't want it to end. I want to live here in this cushy cloud with Derek for eternity.

"Thank you for loving *me* back then, Nora." His voice is ragged. "It was the right thing for us to have time apart, but *god*, I'm so lucky that we still ended up back here somehow."

"*Derek*," I pant, so close to the edge. "Words. Can't. Form . . ."

He smiles like this is the best reply I could ever give before his mouth catches mine in the devouring kiss I crave. The feel of his tongue and hand and body all culminate to release that delicious pressure rolling inside me. Sparks fly behind my eyelids like crunching a wintergreen mint in the dark. I grip his back as a shudder corkscrews through me, curling my toes and wringing me out. He kisses me through it—groaning like he loves the feel of me coming undone from his touch.

I don't think there's anything better than this.

Except a few seconds later, after a brief pause for Derek to put on a condom, I realize how wrong I am. There is something so much better—Derek whispering my name, kissing my neck, my face, my shoulders, anything his mouth can reach as he slowly pushes inside me. *This. This is how it's supposed to be. How it's supposed to feel.*

Being reunited with Derek nearly brings tears to my eyes because it's so right it's a relief. My body letting go with the only other person I've ever truly felt comfortable with. He moves slowly in and out, letting me adjust to him again and I want to sob from how much I missed him. How much I missed doing *this* with him.

He grabs the headboard with one hand for leverage as his hips push into mine. Sensation peaks and a new wave of need rushes me. I match his movements, rolling and lifting my hips, and together we build toward that approaching height. That bright burning thing in the distance. I lock my leg around his hip and he groans, dropping his head in the crook of my neck.

"*Shit, Nora*," he rasps as his free hand laces with mine, pressing it into the mattress.

His rhythm picks up, carrying mine with him. "*Derek* . . ." I don't even know what I was planning to say. I don't have real thoughts at this point. Just a body. And he has a body. And we are working them together so perfectly, so obsessively I think I might die.

I lift my head and open my mouth against his neck—tasting the sweat from his skin. I swirl my tongue and I hear my name on his breath one last time before he grips my hand harder. The sound of him unraveling has me tumbling right after him. A rush of electric pleasure surges through my veins before I go limp with delight.

We breathe together a minute, settling and savoring. After a minute, an hour, a year, who knows . . . Derek shifts his weight onto his elbow, releases my hand to tilt my chin up and kisses me so carefully it splinters my heart into a zillion pieces. "Are you good?" he asks in a low rasp that make me wiggle my toes.

I smile, lean up to kiss my initial on his bicep, and then push his hair back from his damp forehead. "I can assure you, I've literally never been better."

He leaves me only for a minute to go clean up, but I'm too sleepy to move yet, so I lie here with a big cheesy grin on my face. And after he climbs back in bed, he pulls me up against him so he's the big spoon and tucks the covers around me. I'm a warm little caterpillar in a cocoon of comforters. I live in a cloud of delight where no trouble can reach me.

His big bicep is draped over my shoulder and I kiss it. Nip it. And kiss it again. "It's never been like this with anyone but you for me too. Not just the sex. But everything." I pause and listen to the ocean roll in the distance mixed with the pulse of Derek's heart. "Even when I've been in a relationship, I've felt sort of . . . lonely. No one understands me like you do."

And it's because of this understanding that he doesn't push me to explain more. So I keep the rest close to my heart—that being replaced became such a common experience in my life that I stopped pursing relationships and even friendships altogether.

He kisses my temple. "I'm sorry I said I couldn't be your friend. It was only because I didn't trust myself to not want this if I got close to you again."

"It makes sense. I'm very irresistible," I say, twisting in his arms to face him.

"Is the offer still open?"

"To be my friend?"

"Mm-hm," he says, closing his eyes.

"That's trickier now that we're naked. And married."

He pulls me in tightly against his chest. "No—it's better now. Please say yes. I'd love to be your friend, Nora."

As if there were a chance I'd ever want to say no.

I draw a heart on his ribs. "Yes, you can be my friend, Derek Pender. But this breaks rule number three."

35

Nora

For the last few days, Derek and I haven't left the room once. Just kidding. Truthfully, we've been jam-packed busy at the resort. We finally took that coral reef snorkeling tour. Had an afternoon shopping adventure in the local open-air market. A day trip to visit and swim in the most beautiful cenotes that seriously were too pretty to be real. And a spa day where we got couples massages and had an unfortunate incident with the sheet that I'd like to put out of my mind for eternity.

All of it feels like I'm living in a dream because I'm getting to experience it with Derek. We've spent these days completely wrapped up in each other—relearning who the other is now. I don't think I've laughed as much as I have over the last week in my entire life. Not only that, but we've sat under the stars at night on the beach filling each other in on all the life events we've missed out on over the years. Like how Derek's teeth are so perfect because they're actually veneers he paid thousands of dollars for and hasn't regretted once. And how he and his friends helped get Nathan and Bree together through a romantic cheat sheet. And how I'm completely obsessed with *The*

Great British Bake Off and secretly dream of going on the show one day even though I'm American and have zero baking abilities.

In quieter moments, he's also opened up to me more about what living with dyslexia has been like. How hard it was to be treated like he wasn't trying when endlessly *trying* was all he was ever doing. I want to fix his hurt—take away the wounds, but I can't, so I whisper how proud of him I am and cuddle him into oblivion, shifting through his feelings together as best we can.

But our nights . . . our nights have nothing to do with the article and are completely our own. We spend them in each other's arms. It goes something like this: We stumble in dead tired from a day of exploring and smiling for a photo shoot, and shower and then get hit with a second wind that we absolutely burn off in the most delicious ways.

Which is why now, it's late and we're both sweaty and exhausted as I fall into Derek's arms for the most epic snuggle of my life. He trails his fingers softly down my bare spine and my body shivers in response.

"Are you worried about going back? To the office?" Derek asks me, his voice so lazy I can tell he's as sleepy as I am. I know why he's asking, though. Marty emailed me a link today of an online tabloid with a picture of when Derek and I first kissed on the beach. He was careful with his wording in the message—but the slight was unmistakable: *Thought you might like to be aware of the sort of image your honeymoon is giving off, so you don't jeopardize your professionalism. Would hate for other male athletes to get the wrong impression of you.*

I nuzzle in closer. "A little." I pause. "Okay, a lot."

Derek casually offered to end the man's life for me (he was kidding . . . I think) but I declined. I did, however, forward the email to our HR department. Unfortunately, they said there was nothing in the email that was strictly offensive or inappropriate (due to his strategic wording and that it was a link to a photo rather than an actual screenshot). It probably doesn't help that Marty plays golf with those same guys from HR either.

I curl up closer to Derek. "Or . . . I guess it's not really that I'm worried, as much as I am maybe sort-of, kind-of dreading it."

Derek's fingers continue to track over my skin like they're blazing a future trail. "You know, if you wanted to quit and find somewhere with a less toxic environment, I'd follow you wherever you go. I mean, not sure how much that means coming from an athlete who might be out of the job in a few months. But you have options."

"Quit being a tuna sandwich! Of course it means a lot. In the next few months, rockets are going to want to be you when they grow up from how high you're going to soar." He laughs a quiet rumbly laugh. I close my eyes and savor the feel of it vibrating through me. "Truthfully, though, I'm starting to doubt that anywhere less toxic exists. I'm afraid it's just the world of sports and if I want to live in it, I'll have to get thicker skin."

He hums and pulls me tightly against him. "That doesn't sound very Nora Mackenzie–like to me."

I angle my chin up, resting it on his chest to look at him. "What do you mean?"

"The Nora I know doesn't adapt to something she doesn't like. She changes it." His hand strokes over my hair.

I breathe out. "That Nora is tired. She's ready for someone else to take on the world."

Derek wraps his arms around me and flips up over so he's pinning me in. He kisses my jaw and nuzzles his face against the crook of my neck. "Keep resting with me, then, and when we get back, you'll figure out how to bring those assholes to their knees." He kisses my neck and then pulls back to look in my eyes. "And if you need any help, just say the word and I'll be there."

I smile and he dips his head to capture it against his.

Unfortunately, no sooner than his mouth claims mine does his phone begin ringing loudly on the bedside table. We both startle and Derek's hand dashes out to fumble for it. "Sorry, I thought it was on silent," he rasps as he retrieves it and holds it up to his face.

That's when I really think it through. It's the middle of the night and someone is calling Derek. There's no way this can be a good thing. I sit up as I watch Derek's brows pinch together.

"It's Price," he says, adjusting to rest his back against the headboard, and flips on the light. He answers with a quick "What's wrong?"

Derek listens silently, staring out at the room as I stare at him. I search his face for any hints to what his friend is telling him, but his expressions are made of stone. Derek's eyes shift to me for a fraction of a second and then he looks away, sending his hand through his messy bedhead. "*Shit.* Is she going to be okay? What about the baby?"

Now, I'm fully on my knees, clutching the sheet helplessly to my chest as I stare at Derek.

He hums a few times while listening before throwing the covers off his legs and swiftly standing up from the bed. "Yeah, man. Of course. I'll see you tomorrow regardless."

Derek goes to his suitcase and searches through it. Even though I don't know what's going on, I run to the bathroom while throwing on one of Derek's T-shirts and then swipe everything off the counter into my toiletry bag. Even though it makes me cringe to see everything all mixed together haphazardly, I can feel it in my bones that there's no time for organizing. We can separate our things out later.

"Like hell," Derek replies aggressively to something Price says. "I'm coming back no matter what, so go be with your wife instead of wasting your time arguing with me." Price says something else to Derek that has him responding quietly, "I will."

Derek slips on a pair of athletic shorts after ending the call and joins me in the bathroom just in time to find me aggressively winding up the cord of my curling wand. We make eye contact through the mirror, our gazes a mash of emotions. I whirl around to face him, and the plug on the end of the cord bangs into my leg. "What is it? What happened? Are they okay?"

Derek nods but looks shaken—scared. I've never seen him like this before, and it bothers me. I want to fix whatever this is because suddenly I have the distinct feeling that Derek makes up my entire heart. I've never doubted that what I felt for Derek back in college was love. But now . . . I feel *love* love. It's different somehow. Inarticulate and elegant all at once. Soothing and aching. Before, my love for him lived on the outside of my skin, and now he's wormed his way into my chest cavity and pumps through every chamber of my heart. When he's hurting, I'm hurting.

"Price's wife, Hope, went into labor several weeks early."

"Is she going to be okay?"

He nods. "She's all right and her doctor is confident that even though she's a little early, she's far enough along for the baby to be safely delivered. Price is mainly freaked out because it's finally hitting him that he's going to be a dad."

"*Oh*," I say with a relieved sigh, and then swat him in the chest. "I thought . . . by the look on your face . . . I thought something was wrong."

"There is something wrong." He pauses, a furrow gathering between his brows. "I need to ask you if we can cut our honeymoon short and go home early. I want to be there for him . . . but I don't want to end this yet either."

It's on the tip of my tongue to say something like *We can always go on another honeymoon when everything settles down*, but I stop myself. We haven't precisely figured out our future yet. And

I'm too scared to ask him if I'm going to be in his. Old wounds rear their heads and tell me there's a chance he'll replace me. Someone easier will come along. Someone who's not already mentally reorganizing the toiletry bag and cringing with every second that passes where our things are swirling together like a toddler's fingerpainting project.

So instead, I step up to him and wrap my arms around his bare waist. "Turn that frown upside down, because I wouldn't have it any other way." I kiss the front of his shoulder. "Let's go home. This is important for your friend, and you need to be there for him."

Derek's lips press to the top of my head and I hear him drag in a deep breath. His arms tighten around my waist, and maybe I'm projecting, but I feel so many unvoiced concerns in his hold. Neither of us says them. We're both too scared, or worried, or afraid of pushing the other too far too fast. The communication that felt so open and free over the last few days suddenly seals up, airtight.

36

Derek

We're in the air and it's tense. Ever since I broke the news about coming back, we've been mirroring weird smiles at each other. The tight kind that have too many teeth in them to be honest. The pageant grins started after I broke the news about needing to come back early. But I don't think that's why Nora's smile is painted on like Travel Barbie.

My mind likes to kick me in the shins, to tell me she's regretting everything now that we're getting back to the real world, and run off with my favorite backpack. It's a little shit and it's doing this on a loop. But we've shared so much over the last week. There's no way she can be having second thoughts. Right? Because I'm not. Then again, I wasn't the one who left the first time either.

Shit, just talk to her about it, Derek.

The closer we get to L.A., however, the more dread settles into my stomach. After wheels down, I pretty much have to hit the ground running. First up is the hospital to check on Price and Hope. And then I have a million and two things to do before training camp starts in a week. I have several intense bodywork sessions scheduled to make sure everything is limber and ready to go for the intense rigor of the NFL season. Because once it begins, my life becomes devoted to football again and my body won't feel one hundred percent from then until next offseason (or until I get benched if I play like shit).

When we land at LAX, I get some good news in a text from Price: *Meet Jayla Price. 6 Lbs 2 oz. Healthy and strong like her mom.*

An anchor lifts from my chest while reading that text. I don't know a lot about babies or birth—so I had no idea what to expect. Especially after hearing Price's shaky voice last night tell me Hope was in labor early. So this is good. (Understatement of the year.) It's great. And I feel antsy to get off the damn plane, get a minute of privacy with Nora to ask her why we look like two ventriloquists talking through our teeth, and then to take *my wife* with me to the hospital to officially hang out with my friends.

Doubt creeps in. *Maybe she doesn't want you to think of her as your wife.*

Why the hell didn't we nail all this down in Cancún? I hate the uncertainty.

Once we're off the plane, Nora and I wait in baggage claim surrounded by people tossing not-so-subtle glances my way every few seconds. Nora's bright yellow suitcase comes around and I step up to haul it off the belt, but she beats me to it. Her movements are choppy and agitated, pulling her suitcase down like she's practicing for a professional hay-baling competition. But when she looks up at me— *bing,* I'm treated to a megawatt fake smile again. This is weird as shit.

"Nora," I say once our bags are in hand and we're finally leaving the airport. "Can we talk about—" I cut off when we step through the sliding doors. The smoggy L.A. air pummels us, and my career grabs me by the neck.

"*Shit,*" I hiss after seeing the small mob of media waiting for us just past the doors—most likely someone who saw us at the Cancún airport tipped them off to our departure back to L.A. I'm not ready for this. We're not ready for this. I don't even know if we're actually a *we* at this point and I don't like the idea of facing cameras and reporters with that uncertainty between us.

I glance at Nora, and she only appears caught off guard for a second before I watch her agent mode slip over her like a second skin. She smiles up at me, and my shoulders relax a little when it doesn't look painted on. "I hope you put your makeup on today, Pender, because it looks like you're about to get your picture taken. Stay behind me."

I swear. This woman who has had zero security training being willing to walk in front of me to take the brunt of any potential trouble is the sweetest damn thing I've ever seen.

"I appreciate your sacrifice, but I'd rather have you beside me than as my bodyguard." I hold out my hand to her. "Ready?"

Hesitation creases her forehead, but she eventually nods and links her fingers with mine. I feel them curl all the way around my heart. For a brief second, worry dissipates and it's just me and Nora with our whole lives ahead of us.

I glance at the gathered media and recognize most of the journalists. They're obnoxious but not a threat to our safety. Nora and I are both wearing hats (hers says *Go, Mac and Cheese!*), tugged low over our eyes so the cameras don't catch our expressions as we walk through the crowd.

We walk double time, suitcases bobbing over cracks and bumps in the pavement like a ski boat chopping through waves in the ocean. It feels wrong to not acknowledge other humans, and even worse to just plow through them without stopping, but that's the nature of this business. If you stop, you get ambushed. If you get ambushed, you almost always say something you regret. And on the heels of an injury that I haven't publicly discussed yet and a marriage that started in Vegas while drunk—it feels way too probable.

We're halfway through and my grip around Nora's hand is lock tight. That's when I start to register the questions.

"Derek! Derek! Over here! Is it true you married your agent?"

"Nora! What led to your spontaneous elopement with Derek?"

"Is it true you didn't sign a prenup?" It never ceases to scare me how these people get such personal information.

Most of the questions are all in the vein of the elopement. A few make me angry on Nora's behalf as they start questioning the integrity of her position and whether she's going to fraternize with all of her clients like she has with me. She must feel me about to respond because her gaze shoots up to me and she smiles. "Don't do it, big guy. I know who I am—you don't need to defend me right now."

I nod, forcing some of my anger to dissolve.

We've almost made it through the media cloud and are at the door of the waiting, blacked-out SUV Nora scheduled when I hear it:

"Derek! Can you comment on the rumor that the Sharks are officially cutting you in favor of Abbot?"

I freeze.

"Some people are speculating that taking time off from training to go on a honeymoon shows carelessness for your career in a time when you should have been doubling down on your training. What do you have to say to that?"

Several more similar questions fly at me like hornets. Each stinging in a different way. All saying they've heard from a source that my career is officially in jeopardy.

I don't even realize that I'm just frozen staring at the SUV until Nora wraps her arm around my waist and discreetly tugs, reminding me to keep moving. In my peripherals as I'm loading into the SUV, I watch Nora turn and address the media. Even though she has every right to feel as bombarded and cornered as me, she is every inch the professional agent. Her tone is set to dazzle.

"This was so sweet to throw us a welcome home party! But we weren't expecting company, so you'll have to give us a raincheck. In the meantime, we're registered at Target and my favorite color is pink!" she says playfully with a wink, making everyone laugh and proving she was born for this. Leaving a bewitched crowd in her wake, Nora climbs into the SUV behind me and shuts the door.

Only then does her smile slip as she sinks back against the seat, taking a deep breath. I guess I should do that too—breathe—but my lungs are full of sand. This shouldn't come as a huge surprise since everyone in the media has been talking about it, but this is the first time I've heard any sort of supposed confirmation of me being cut. And it turns out that no amount of preparing myself to hear those words did anything to lessen the burn of it.

"It makes sense for them to cut me," I say in a daze as I stare out the window, feeling those old insecurities hover over me like shadows. *You're not good enough and you never will be. Now you have nothing.*

"Don't say that," Nora snaps. There's urgency and something else in her tone. Protectiveness, I realize. "Those gossip columnists don't know what they're talking about. It's rumors, that's all. If any decisions had been made, management would have contacted me first."

My eyes are trained out the window. Sunshine and blue skies feel bitter. "But they've leaked it to the press before. This wouldn't be the first time they put it out there unofficially to drum up buzz around the team. Around the new star player they want to highlight."

"You and Nathan are their star players! They're not going to cut you."

"Unless I suck," I say, finally rolling my head in her direction. I know I'm being moody and unreasonable. I'm like a teenager with his hood up.

Nora knows it too because she sits up straighter and smiles tauntingly at me. "Okay, fine. Are we officially giving up on football already?"

"Seems like the reasonable decision."

"You could go into finance."

I grimace. "Too sedentary."

"Well . . . you have a fine body." She gestures to said body, which is slumped over in my seat.

I shrug like the consolation prize isn't enough. "Thank you."

"How do you feel about stripping? I bet you'd make some real money if you started your routine in your uniform and pads. I'd pay to see it for sure."

"That's nice of you," I say with a sad smile. "But it'll never work. I can't gyrate."

"Well, not with that attitude!" She toes her shoe against my knee. "But with a good teacher and a can-do spirit, I believe that you, Derek Pender, will be able to gyrate your hips and make your penis wave to a crowd like it's the queen of England!"

I love Nora.

I want to tell her too. But this doesn't feel like the right moment. And why the hell didn't I say it in Cancún? I thought I made my feelings clear, but the more I replay everything we said, the more I realize how vague it actually is. She knows I've always had feelings for her. But love? *Never said it.* Commitment? *Was scared to even think it in case she heard it whisper in my mind and bolted for the door.*

She shifts closer to me now and grasps my jaw, tugging my face to look at her. "Believe in yourself, Derek. And I don't just mean on the field or on the *Magic Mike* stage. Believe that no matter what happens, you're going to be okay. You're strong, determined, and a hell of a good time in the sheets." She grins playfully, and the tightness in my chest loosens. "You're not alone. You're not a kid anymore, facing obstacles without help. And this career is not all you have or all you are. Not even close."

Her face softens and she slowly leans in to brush her lips over mine. It's the first real contact we've had since last night. I need this—and she senses it. Her lips press into mine over and over until my mouth softens.

"*Breathe*," she whispers, and I breathe in deeply through my nose for the first time since we boarded the plane this morning. She knows how to unwind me—and just as I'm reaching to tangle my hands in her hair, she pulls away, lips swollen and dark pink.

"But as your agent," she begins in an altogether different tone. I like getting a taste of what everyone else gets from Nora Mackenzie too. "I need you to know, I'm going to do everything I can to make sure you don't lose this job you love until you're ready. You saved my ass, and now I'm going to save your deliciously firm butt cheeks too."

I nod. "Thank you, Nora."

"Of course. What is a friend-slash-agent-slash-accidental wife for!" Her grin softens. "Go to the hospital and be with your friends today. Try not to worry about any of this work stuff and I'll go to the office and sort it all out."

Wait. She's not going with me to the hospital? The tightness in my chest coils up again.

"I thought you were going with me to see the baby." There's no way to say that without sounding miserable and clingy.

"I want to. But I need to get to the office and figure out what's going on. Is that okay?"

I stare into her green-gold eyes for a beat, emotions tugging me both ways. This is the first moment we'll separate since we got married. The first moment that real life will try to rip us down the middle. Last time that happened, I lost her. Anxiety fizzes in my stomach like a carbonated soda. I don't want to lose her. But I can't sink my teeth into her and refuse to let go either. I've got to give her space and find some trust if this is going to work. Plus, she's my agent. She has to do her job. I'm just now realizing, though, how tricky this is going to be going forward.

After an awkward amount of time, I answer, wishing it were honest, "Of course it's okay."

My ventriloquist smile is back, and as I hold her hand in the car, I can't help but run my thumb over the little black tattoo on her finger, wishing we'd spent a little less time talking about our past on our honeymoon and more about our future.

When I enter the hospital, I check in at the front desk and am told my friends are all gathered in a private waiting room and given instructions on how to get there. It's pretty typical to be given a room off to the side anywhere we go because when me and the guys are all together (especially with Nathan present), we tend to garner a lot of attention. Attention the hospital probably doesn't care to have.

I open the door to the waiting room expecting to find a somber environment, because we were all up the entire night waiting to hear word about Hope and the baby. I am dead wrong.

All I get is a glimpse of long curly hair before I'm grabbed by the wrists and tugged abruptly inside the room, where a shower of confetti rains down on my head. All the guys plus Bree cheer and whoop at the same moment that Nathan pops a bottle of hospital-appropriate sparkling grape juice and the Bruno Mars song "Marry You" ignites through the portable speakers.

I feel like I'm experiencing this moment through a funhouse mirror. Or high on an edible.

"Mr. and Mrs.—" Bree cuts off suddenly with a scowl. She's holding a tacky veil attached to a hair clip in her hand.

I grin at the veil. "Is that for me?"

Everyone's smiles fall when they realize my "other half" is not in attendance.

"Where the hell is Nora?" Nathan asks with something close to a glare. Like maybe I forgot her in the car or something.

Price crosses his arms. "Dammit, Derek, did y'all already break up? Is this because you cut the honeymoon short? I told you not to—"

"Would you shut up for a second and let me hug you?" I say, walking up to Price. His arms go around me the second mine extend to him. We've hugged before—after winning a big game mainly. But this is different. Price doesn't let go of me right away and I don't let go of him. He hugs me like a brother. Like a brother whose life has just changed for the better and he wants me to feel the terror and wonder swirling around in him. I hang on until he's ready to let go.

"I'm a dad," he mumbles into my shoulder, and emotion rips through me. I'm grateful I'm here for this.

"Hell yeah you are," I say, squeezing him harder.

"And you're married."

"Hell yeah I am." I chuckle. "Sort of." We pull apart and I eye the mess around me. "Speaking of, what is all this?" I ask Nathan when he steps up to hug me next and then Lawrence after him. You'd think I was the one who just had a baby. Bree is still put out that Nora isn't here.

"It's a wedding reception," says Nathan. "Or it was supposed to be if you'd bothered to bring your wife."

Bree slaps my arm. "For real. Where is she? Did you break up?"

"You guys have zero faith in me."

"Because you're a big baby," Jamal says from the side of the room with a grin while holding a teddy bear the size of his body.

"Tamara finally get sick of you and leave you to your girlfriend?" I say, nodding toward the bear.

He flips me the bird. "This is my epic present for Jayla. Tamara and Cora are up there with Hope right now lavishing her with take-out food." Jamal smirks at me. "I see you came empty-handed like a dipshit."

"I literally just landed back in L.A. And what's a baby supposed to do with that monstrosity? It'll smother her."

"Enough!" snaps Bree with a clap of her hands—clearly used to gaining the attention of children when she needs it. A spark enters Nathan's eyes because he loves when Bree goes into teacher mode. Unable to help himself, he falls in behind her and wraps his arms around her middle as Bree says, "I'm only going to ask you this one last time. Where is my new best friend? We threw this little party so she'd feel welcome and she's not even here to see it."

I can't help but smile. They did this for Nora—so she'd feel welcome. Because they're my family and Nora is my family now too.

"She would have loved to be here, and see this," I say honestly. She really would have gobbled this shit up. Nora loves nothing more than outward expressions of joy. "But she needed to get to work to save my ass." They all frown. "We were met at the airport by a media circus. They seemed to think I'm . . . about to be cut from the team."

A heaviness settles over the room at my words.

Surprisingly, Jamal sets down the bear and is the first to say something heartfelt. "They'd be idiots, then. Surely they're going to at least give you a shot to play first?"

I shrug. "That's what Nora is going to find out."

No one is ready to acknowledge quite yet that I may no longer be a Shark. Although I have to admit, I think I'm starting to come to terms with the idea more every second. Being here today, hugging Price, and seeing what all my friends did to make Nora feel welcome—it has nothing to do with me being a Shark. They're my family. No matter where life takes us, we'll always be close.

Nathan thankfully changes the subject. "We could FaceTime her and do it all over again if you want? So she can see it."

I consider it briefly and then disregard the idea. Whether it's because I'm truly respecting her space or because I feel awkward as hell after the way we parted is a toss-up. "Nah—I don't want to bug her at work today."

"I doubt you'd be bugging her," says Lawrence.

But all I can think about is how in college, I didn't see that she needed space. I didn't prioritize her success. I *always* interrupted her to see the cool thing or go to the fun place with me. And those things pushed her away the first time; I'm sure as hell not going to pick up my phone and FaceTime her an hour after parting from a weeklong trip.

And that's when I feel it—all the little fractures cracking through our fragile little relationship. Damn, I need to talk to her later. Awkward or not, we've got things to figure out.

In the meantime, I snap photos of everything to show her later.

Price squints in the direction of my ankles. "We really gotta find out what's happening with your pants, man."

37

Nora

The minute I step through the doors of our agency, I feel a hum of excitement mixed with anxiety slither under my skin.

My year interning here felt like sitting on hold for a call I was dying to make, just having to listen to the same elevator music loop endlessly and hope that I wouldn't get disconnected along the way. But now, I'm here with the freedom to act as a full-time agent, and it's like the call has finally connected. I have a purpose and a future, and I could sing from the joy of it.

The anxiety comes from knowing I have to interact with the jerks in this office while enjoying that freedom. But I don't want to think about that now.

Two things happened when I heard that journalist's question about the Sharks cutting Derek. (1) My heart sank for him—the man I love. Seeing how he believed them instantly, how his entire demeanor shifted into despair—I hated it. I wanted to do whatever I could to secure his dreams. (2) My blood lit on fire. How dare they try to cut my client from the team. Or to leak the information to put us in a groveling position. After all the years he's devoted to them—all the games he's helped them win, this is how they're going to treat him? Unacceptable.

Mr. Rogers has a saying I've always lived by: "There are three ways to ultimate success. The first way is to be kind. The second is to be kind. The third is to be kind."

And that's why I'm going to kindly ask if there is any truth to those rumors. And if they confirm them, I will kindly tell them they can shove their underhanded gossip-leaking manipulation up their asses, and then I will kindly remind them that if needed, we would have been happy to revisit contract terms and salary had my client been shown the respect of approaching us first—but when that respect is violated, they can go suck on gumballs as far as we are concerned.

I have an entire email mentally writing itself through my mind as I move down the hall. But the second I open my broom closet office and find it utterly empty, my thoughts are wiped.

Where is my stuff?

And then another appalling thought.

Oh my god, did they fire me?

A chuckle sounds behind me. I spin around to face Nicole.

"I can practically hear your terrifying thoughts as you're thinking them," Nicole says with a grin on her red lips. She's looking fabulous in her expensive wide-leg trousers, shiny pink heels, and a white silk blouse tucked in. I'm sure there's a matching jacket draped over the back of her desk chair. "Welcome home," she says with a mischievous lilt. "I knew you'd see your office and assume you were fired. And by the look on your face, I was right."

I sigh with relief, thankful I'm not finding out I'm fired while wearing leggings, an oversized smiley face T-shirt, and a hat that expresses my support of macaroni and cheese. "I'll be honest, I don't enjoy this pit of despair you're dangling me over for your own twisted fun. But I do like seeing you happy, so by all means, carry on."

She groans. "Follow me."

We pass a few male colleagues in their starchy gray department store suits and they do not look happy to see me. I mean—to be fair, they've never been overjoyed to see me under normal circumstances. But definitely not after returning from my honeymoon, apparently. And none seems more unhappy I've returned than Marty—who is watching me from his desk as I pass his office. His pasty white complexion is full of disdain that I don't think I deserve. Actually, I know I don't deserve.

"Marty," Nicole says as we pass. "Might want to wipe that look off your face and then do the same with the mustard on your shirt."

I almost wish I had been drinking something so I could have done a dramatic spit take.

Nicole is my queen. She doesn't take anything from anyone. I would go to the ends of the world for her. And I hope that one day I can have skin as thick as hers—because part of me is a little afraid that if I have to work in a building surrounded by so many unkind people every day, I'll crumble. Derek's words echo in my mind. *You have options.* But do I really? I worked so hard to get to where I am now. If I quit and go somewhere new, will I have to start from the bottom again?

Ugh—Derek. My anxiety is like building blocks, layering one after another, forming an endless, daunting tower of misery. This morning was weird. Awkward and uncomfortable and I can't decide if it was me making it tense or him. What happened to our breezy openness from Cancún? My honesty felt tied up and locked in a dungeon. I couldn't even bring myself to ask him if he was upset that I was going to work instead of the hospital. Somehow it felt like saying those words out loud would infect a healing wound. I was unprepared for how quickly life would slam into us, and I wish . . .

No time to think of all that.

I follow Nicole down the hallway to a closed office door. My eyes bounce from Nicole's smiling red lips to the door she's gesturing for me to open.

Tornadoes take over my stomach as I touch the handle and tug it down. The door opens and I stand rooted—speechless as I stare at the beautiful office. The office that now houses my desk and my belongings. The office with enough room that Derek, Jamal, Nathan, Price, and Lawrence could all fit in here comfortably with me. *And look!* It has a window. A huge picture window that overlooks the city and is bursting with sunlight. There are even fresh flowers in a vase on my desk.

Nicole got me an office. A real, honest-to-goodness office.

"You know I have a no-crying rule," Nicole says, interrupting the moment.

I sniffle. "That's unfortunate because I'm about to blubber all over you." I turn my face to her, and Nicole takes a retreating step back.

"Oh no you don't."

But I do. I practically leap for her and wrap my arms around her fabulously dressed body and squeeze her like a lemon. "Thank you. Thank you. Thank you."

"You're welcome. Now, let me go or you're fired," she wheezes out.

I release her so I can finally step into my new grand office. It feels so official when I take a seat at my desk. So important. Everything I've ever wanted, and . . . I'm immediately sick with guilt over it. I lied and I manipulated things in my favor so I could come out on top—and it worked. I have the sudden distinct feeling that I don't deserve any of this.

"I need to confess something."

My hands bunch into nervous little knots under my desk. "The marriage . . . we lied to you about it. The elopement wasn't on purpose, contrary to what we told you and Joseph. We accidentally got drunk and eloped, and then he saved my butt by suggesting we sell it as true love for a while. Long enough to let the scandal fade. The only part that was true in our whole speech was that we dated in college."

I pause, waiting for Nicole's anger or feelings of betrayal to show. But instead, she smirks. "Yeah—I figured. And it was smart."

When she doesn't say anything else, I show indignation on her behalf. "No. Not smart! Cunning. Manipulative. Wrong," I pronounce with conviction.

"I literally called you and told you to come up with a hell of an argument. And you did. Job well done."

I shake my head. "I don't deserve any of this. I got it through deceiving others, and now I'm going to have to sit in here every day on my throne of lies and know what I did to achieve it! I should quit. Better yet . . . you should fire me! Go ahead. I can take it."

Nicole runs her tongue over her teeth and then gracefully takes the seat facing my desk. She leans back into the corner of it and crosses one perfectly creased pant leg over the other. "Listen to me, I never, ever want to hear you say you don't deserve any of this again."

The quiet ferocity in her voice has me keeping my mouth shut—but I know my eyes are saucers.

"You did not earn this job because of who you are or are not married to. I could honestly give two shits about your marital status. It's true, lying about your marriage helped you keep your job because the world is still very cruel to women and would have eaten you alive if you admitted to getting drunk with your client and accidentally eloping. They wouldn't have been able to see any of the nuance in the relationship." She uncrosses her legs and leans forward. "But I know you, Mac. I know you better than you realize. And if you didn't already love Derek, your college sweetheart, you never would have gone along with the plan. If you didn't know deep down in your heart that Derek might still be the one for you—you would have come clean immediately. But part of you knew he was a safe bet."

I open my mouth to argue but she continues, "Besides all of that, you weren't breaking any company policies. The only reason you were going to be let go after you married him was because of the scandal it would have caused when you divorced right away. Because it would look sloppy. And would have made the agency look sloppy. But you salvaged it by selling your love story—just like I hoped you would."

She does have a point. But my conscience is still screaming at me. "I don't feel good about keeping this job under false pretenses."

"It's not false pretenses though, is it?" she asks with a conniving grin, and I know exactly what she means before she even clarifies. "Are you and Derek still planning to divorce?"

I pause. "No." *At least, I don't think so.* Dammit. Why didn't we hammer out those details?

"And did you two by chance exchange declarations of feelings at any point on your honeymoon?" she asks with a raised brow. *All-knowing sorceress.*

I fight a smile, because at least we did do that, even if I didn't tell him the extent of my feelings for him. "Yes. Declarations were exchanged."

She rolls her eyes and waves off my fear with a flick of her hand. "Then put it all behind you, Mac. We all make choices in life and some of them are necessarily more gray than others. This is one of those times. You're a good person and I don't think for a second you would have eloped—or even gone out drinking—with anyone other than Derek. You did what was needed to extract yourself from a messy situation, and it was honestly brilliant."

My moral compass is spinning out of control.

"I've had to make gray, self-preserving choices too," she continues. "I think every woman fighting for equality has or will have to at some point to be honest. And we need each other's support along the way. You have mine, not because of who your husband is, but because even before all of that, you were the best intern and associate we've had in years. No one has worked harder than you, and I truly believe you're going to be one of the best agents in the business. That is why you deserve to be in this office—and that's why I never want to hear you say anything contrary to it ever again. Understand?"

I press my quivering lips together and nod. "Thank you, Nicole."

A kind smile pulls at both corners of her mouth. She really does like me.

The sound of a muffled sneeze outside my office door yanks us both from our conversation. And then panic hits. My door was open during all of that. And even though Nicole is understanding about it all—who's to say that anyone else would be.

Nicole must have the same thought as me because she shoots from her chair and goes to the door, peeking her head out to look both ways down the hallway.

"There's no one out here. We must have heard someone in their office."

My shoulders relax and I let out a whoosh of air. "Before you go. Can I get your advice about Derek?"

Nicole closes my door this time and retakes her seat in front of me. I tell her everything that happened at the airport this morning and we spend the next twenty minutes talking strategy and wording for when I go digging for the truth. This. This is what I love to do. And knowing I'm fighting for the career of the man I love makes it even more tantalizing.

After a while, Nicole stands from the chair and heads for the door.

She hesitates before leaving, though, and turns around. "I'm glad to have you in the office, Mac. You . . . you make the tough environment here more bearable."

I grin proudly. "It really cost you to say that, didn't it?"

"Thank you for noticing."

"I don't care what you say, you're a great friend, Nicole."

She narrows her eyes. "*Work* friend. We're work friends only, got it?"

"I would honestly die for you," I say solemnly while standing up from my desk and moving around it without having to press my back to the wall. "We'll be best friends by next week."

"I already have a best friend."

"Which is me," I whisper.

"It's not you." She rolls her eyes. "It's my husband."

I gasp with genuine shock. "You're married?! Why did I not know this?"

Nicole grins—proud of the secret she's apparently kept from me for goodness knows how long. "I don't mix my personal and work life."

"What will you tell me next? You're a singing governess for the von Trapp family on the weekends?"

She's already walking away from me. "Goodbye, Mac. I'm leaving now."

"Nora, actually," I correct for the first time. "I'd like to go by my first name from now on, because I've honestly never liked Mac. It doesn't feel like me."

Nicole pauses to look back at me. She smiles (or in the special way that only Nicole can smile where it's really just a minuscule lift to the corners of her mouth) and nods. "Nora it is."

"Thank you, bestie."

She disappears down the hall into her office and I turn to look at mine again, trying to convince myself that the hesitation I feel about working here for any length of time is just nervous jitters. I put my hands on my hips and force a smile. "Yeah. This is going to be okay."

My phone starts ringing and I'm hopeful that it's Derek, but then I register my dad's contact photo and my stomach drops to the earth's core. This is it—the call I've been dreading. The one where my dad will expect me to be so happy for him even though I haven't heard a peep out of him in months. He'll also expect me to offer my wedding planning services in some way like I have in the past. He'll want me to be happy for him even though it'll mean him trading me out for another family until he moves on from them too and circles back to me.

Normally, I would be compelled to answer this call. I would be afraid it would be my only shot with my dad—and if I missed it, I wouldn't get another one. But not this time. The more rings that go unanswered, the easier it is for me to completely let it go. To finally see with unflinching clarity that I deserve more than this. And from now on, I'm not going to dangle off the edge of his halfhearted communication. I'll call him back when I'm good and ready. And then I'm going to tell him I won't be making it to his wedding, and that after the wedding, we need to have a real talk.

I reject the call and then look out over my office and smile.

38

Derek

I'm driving home from Nathan's house where we all hung out after leaving the hospital when Nora calls me.

Tension in my shoulders unravels just from the sight of her name. All day I've been considering what to do about Nora, and I think I have a good plan.

"You must have felt me thinking about you," I say as a greeting.

"My nose *was* itching earlier . . ."

I grip the steering wheel. "That's not the part of your body I was daydreaming of touching."

The line goes silent.

Grinning, I ask, "You there, Ginger Snap?"

She clears her throat. "Mm-hm. I'm here. Just . . . had to have CPR for a second there. I'm revived—everything is fine."

God, I love her. Miss her already.

Turning on my blinker, I switch lanes. "How's your day been?"

She sighs contentedly and I imagine her soft lips smiling. "It was . . . good. I got a new office. You didn't see my other one, but if you hold up your thumb you'll have an accurate representation of the size."

I smile. "And the new one is bigger?"

"Definitely. And has these big, glorious windows and doesn't even smell a bit like cleaning supplies." She pauses. "You'll have to come see it."

"I'd like that."

"But you'll have to behave," she says, accurately reading my thoughts through the line.

"When do I not behave?"

"You're purring, Derek."

I laugh. "So why just good and not great? Was Marty a jerk? Say the word and I'll be the worst surprise he's ever found in his office tomorrow morning."

She chuckles, but it's not convincing. "I didn't interact with him much. I stayed buried in my office pretty much all day."

Alarm creeps over my skin. "You sound sad, Nora."

"I don't mean to . . . I guess I just—actually can we circle back to this question? I want to fill you in on what I learned today. About your position on the team. Are you where you can talk business for a minute?"

Her tone of voice is throwing me. I wish I were with her right now so I could see her face. Check to see if there are lines beside her eyes when she smiles or if her mouth is pressed flat.

"I'm just driving home. So yeah, let me hear the good news," I say with unmistakable sarcasm.

"I spoke with the team execs and everything we heard today at the airport really was just a rumor—and not one leaked by them." *That's a relief.* "They want you to know there are no immediate plans to cut you, and that the Sharks have always valued your position on the team and are going to give you the shot you deserve."

"But . . . ?" I ask, knowing full well that there is one.

"But," Nora begins gently, "you already know the rest. Your job is by no means safe and will depend heavily on how you perform those first few games. They want to see how your injury affects your performance—and if it's for the worse, we might be looking at a bench, a cut, a salary renegotiation . . . or even a trade."

"I don't want to play for anyone but the Sharks."

"Even if that means not playing at all?" she says, cutting right to the meat of it.

I allow her question to sink in before I answer. And for a minute we both listen to the soft sounds of my blinker. "I don't want to be traded. The Sharks . . . the guys . . . they're like my family. I want to end my career as a Shark."

"I understand that. And respect it," she says, and I wish more than anything I were there with her—could be having this conversation with her in my arms. Preferably naked. "Okay, then I have more to say, and I want you to listen and not respond until I'm completely done. Promise?"

"That doesn't sound good."

"Promise?"

I sigh and it rushes into all the little cracks of our relationship I've been feeling today. "Fine. I promise."

There's an awkward silence before she says, "I'm going to give you an out from our relationship right now."

"Why the *hell* would I—"

"Hey!" she cuts me off. "No interrupting, remember?"

"Sorry," I growl, hating this promise I've made already.

"As I was saying, I want to give you an out. All day I've been thinking and realizing our entire relationship is unfair to you. You did this as a service to me and my career, and I'm so grateful, and the last thing I want is for you to feel stuck."

I have to clench my teeth together to keep from interrupting.

"We fulfilled our honeymoon obligation and will be out of the public eye for the most part while everyone expects you to focus on training camp and preseason. If you need to pretend that everything that happened in Cancún was just a fever dream—I'm willing to do that for you. Because I put my career first all those years ago, and I won't fault you for doing the same for yours now if you need to."

I wait a beat after she's stopped talking to answer. "You finished?"

"Yes. I think so."

"Okay. My answer is *hell no.*"

"But, Derek—"

"No, listen. Because there's one thing you said that was completely wrong." The gates at the front of my neighborhood open when I flash my key card at the receiver. "I didn't go on the honeymoon with you as a favor. I stayed married to you because I'm selfish and I was glad to find any excuse I could to be near you as much as possible. So no . . . I don't want an out. *Do you?*"

I pull into my driveway and that's when I notice Nora's car parked in the guest parking space. But I don't see her anywhere. "*Wait.* You're here?" I ask.

"I used your door code to get in. I'll see you upstairs," she says before hanging up.

Knowing she's here has me racing into the house and taking the steps two at a time. I fly into my bedroom but then stop short at the threshold when I spot her sitting on the edge of my bed. She's still wearing the same clothes from this morning, that huge yellow smiley face tee and leggings . . . but now her hair is piled up in a cute bun that makes my heart stop.

"Hi," she says, with a soft smile, but then I notice she's holding something. A big cardboard box. And suddenly this feels too much like the day she broke up with me.

39

Nora

Derek pockets his phone, and when he spots the box on my lap, his steps slow. He looks hesitant to get near me and I know exactly why.

"*No*," I say firmly, trying to put him out of his misery as quickly as possible. "I don't want an out. I want the opposite of an out. I want an in but I needed to make sure of what you needed first."

His brows furrow as he takes in the box once again. "I'm confused."

I stand and set the box on the bed. "I realized something at work today."

Derek's mouth is tight as he leans a shoulder against the doorframe and crosses his arms. Unwilling to take a single step into this room with me and this cardboard box.

"I spent the entire day doing what I love," I say. "Sending strategically worded emails. Reviewing contracts. Playing word chess with your team's executives. I basically sat at my desk and didn't surface for air until everyone else had already cleared the building and I was there all alone. And that's when I realized it . . ." I pause and Derek's brows pinch together. "It didn't fulfill me quite like it used to. Instead, I opened my phone and saw the pictures you sent of what your friends did for us at the hospital and my heart ached."

The glue holding him in place loosens at my words. He pushes off the doorjamb and strides toward me. "I'm sorry, Nora. I didn't mean for it to—"

I hold up my hand and he freezes. "I mean my heart ached because I wish I had gone with you. It ached because I realized I've apparently entered a new season of my life where my career isn't all I need anymore, and I keep trying to live as if it is. I need and want you, Derek. I need and want a life with you. With friends. With better balance to my day."

I pause and Derek lets me take a minute to gather my thoughts before I continue. "Back then, I wasn't ready for us. But now—you're so good for me. You've championed me and sacrificed for me and reminded me what it's like to have fun. And I want to be good for you too."

"You are . . ." he says, inching closer, filling my body with that sweet, warm anticipation I've become addicted to. "You always have been."

"Then I want to be good *together* too. I don't want our past to dictate our future. I don't want to be so scared of making the same mistakes as before that we hold back honesty from each other now." I notice his hand flex at his side, and it makes me realize I struck a chord. I wasn't the only one feeling insecure today.

"How do we do that?" he asks, a raw sadness lacing his tone that makes my heart turn syrupy. He was holding back from me today. Worried and hiding it for my sake.

I breathe in. "Well, like today. I don't want you to be afraid of asking me to pull away from my work if you need me around for something."

"Only if you promise to be honest with me when it's something you can't get away from. I don't want to have that whisper in the back of my head, always wondering if you're sacrificing something you love for me."

"I can do that."

Some of the structure in his shoulders relaxes. He tilts his head, eyes slanting to the box. "Okay, now I need to know why the hell you have a breakup box with you, because I feel my blood pressure rising each second I have to share a room with it." This little brown box is a living, breathing monster to him.

I grab his hand, pulling him closer to the bed. I stand and face the box as he wraps his arms around my abdomen. I want to moan from how good it feels to be reunited with him in this small way. To have the fake smiles and terrible tension gone.

He leans over my shoulder to see inside the box, but I slam the top folds down so he doesn't ruin the reveal. And okay, maybe I am being a little extra with the theatrics but I don't care. Derek likes my extra-ness.

"This is not a breakup box. *This* is me realizing that you were completely honest and vulnerable with me on the honeymoon, but I've been holding back from you. *This* is me leveling the honesty playing field."

He kisses the side of my face. "Okay, let me see all your kinky sex toys."

My laugh cracks the air before my heart leaps into my throat. My tongue feels dry as a paper towel at the thought of emptying all my secrets. He squeezes me lightly in encouragement, the veins in his forearms growing even more pronounced. With one deep breath, I peel open the box.

There's a shift in the air as I pull out the first item. Derek's body straightens a little behind me with recognition.

It's an old jersey, worn and faded—numbers cracking. I lay it on the bed.

"Is that . . . the same jersey you wore to my games in college?" His voice is gritty with emotion.

"The very same one." I say. The sparkle glue I used to outline his number is still clinging beautifully to it.

Before I lose the nerve, I pull out the next one, a jersey with his number from his first season when he played with the Colorado Trailblazers before he was traded to the Sharks. At the sight of it, I feel Derek's chest fill with a deep breath. I throw it on the other, forming a little pile and dig in the box for more.

Derek is silent and statue-still behind me as I reveal the older jersey style from Derek's first year with the Sharks—his number as well. And then two more follow from where the jerseys updated through the years. Each time I told myself I wouldn't buy a new one—that I needed to let these feelings fade and burn them all in a heap. But something in me couldn't let go. Some part of me knew deep down that I shouldn't. We'd find our way back to each other.

When I reach the bottom of the box, I twist around in Derek's arms so I can look him in the eyes. In his eyes that look suspiciously misty-blue. "I watched every single game you played with Colorado. I've also gone to every home game you've played for the Sharks. Not because I loved the Sharks—because I loved you. *Every. Single. Day.*" I wet my lips and he watches. Emotion tugging his brows together at the sound of the word *love*. The Big Important Word we've yet to say to each other since finding our way into each other's arms again.

"And now—prepare yourself for my speech. It's a good one. I've been making notes."

He grins. "Is each bullet point a different color?"

"Heartfelt is purple. Relationship history is red. Everything pertaining to you is cornflower blue."

His thumb tracks a circle on my back. "I'm ready."

I adjust my shoulders, trying to remember my topic sentence. "My whole life I've felt like nothing but a stepping-stone for people. Whether it's that I'm too much for them or too little, I'm not sure. All I know is that friends only stick with me until they find the better, less obnoxious version of me. The one who doesn't have weird catch-phrases and compulsively organizes their linen closet." *And pantry*. It's a big one for me. "Even my dad continues to try out fatherhood on me until he gets a new stepchild and then dumps me to the side." I breathe through a rush of emotions. "And my last ex-boyfriend, Ben, he couldn't stand how incapable I was of sitting quietly in a room. He was always commenting on how much attention I brought everywhere we went. And after I passed out at the sight of his blood, he told me this was just too much for him and ended it."

Derek looks like he'd like to tear a mountain in half, but I continue. "I was so afraid back in college that I'd give you everything and in the end, I'd be your stepping-stone too. So part of me broke up with you to beat you to the punch. But I'm not afraid anymore, and I want you to know that I'm so completely in love with you." His hold around my waist tightens and I've never had a more captive audience. "I don't want an out. I want this—me and you—for real if you're up for it."

Derek's blue eyes are dark right now. A blue cornflower dropped in the belly of the ocean. His hands find my face and he cradles it. "You are not and could never be a stepping-stone, Nora." His lips slip into mine and even from this small touch I want to groan my delight. He pulls away too soon, but his words make up for it. "You're a gem-stone. Rare and unique and vibrant. And anyone who can't see that doesn't deserve to have you in their life."

A garden of joy blooms in my chest—warm and full of color as Derek lays me back on the bed so my ankles are hanging off the edge.

He only gives me half his weight as he leans over me and traces a finger down the curve of my neck and over my collarbones.

"If it wasn't obvious before, I love you too. I love you more than you love cereal on ice cream and more than the sun loves to fry your pretty skin." His eyes crease in the corners. "You deserve the whole world, and I'd try to give it to you, but I think you'll enjoy fighting for it yourself more."

I want to wrap myself completely around him and squeeze like a python. "You're not wrong. But if I get tired or dehydrated running *The Great Race,* can I request assistance from the sidelines?"

"Of course. I'll bring electrolytes." He's a softie.

"What if I want you to piggyback me over the finish line because my legs are too cramped?"

"I can do that." His lips find my jaw.

"What if I want you to just hold my hand while I cross it?"

He hums against my skin, the sensation buzzing my nerve endings to life. "I'd be honored."

"You're so lovable, Dere-Bear."

"That's honestly such a bad nickname." His hand is playing with my fingers beside my hip. "But I actually have an idea to run by you?"

"I'm listening," I say, wiggling my fingers free from their captivity of his big hand and sliding them under the fabric of his shirt. His skin is a hot iron pulled right from the fire.

"What do you think about letting me date you for a while?" He nips at my earlobe before his lips slide down my jaw, headed back for my mouth. "You live at your place, and I'll live at mine, and I'll pick you up for dates. We'll have sleepovers. We'll take things slow just purely for the fun of it because we can. Because we have forever. Because I hate that I didn't get the time you deserve to win you back before we inked these bands on our fingers—and I want to give you that time now."

I pull away slightly to look him in the eyes. "I think that's an amazing idea. Especially with training camp coming up."

He cups my face—smiles, and then presses another kiss to my lips. Harder. The intensity growing with each one. "And I have a feeling you're going to be very busy over these next few weeks jetting off to sign every athlete under the sun. Dating is the practical solution right now. And I know you love being practical." He takes my bottom lip between his teeth.

"*Practical* is the sexiest word in the dictionary," I say before wrapping my arms around his neck.

He puts his mouth right next to my ear and whispers, "And maybe we could even . . . coordinate a calendar schedule."

I moan theatrically. "You're so dirty."

"You haven't even seen the beginning of it, Ginger Snap."

It doesn't take long before my hands are in his hair and his hands are fisting the front of my shirt, dragging it higher and higher each second. His tongue sweeps over mine and an explosion of heat rushes through my stomach, my limbs, my head. I put my hands under his shirt and run them up his muscled abdomen and over his pecs, feeling the raised lines of his tattoos under my fingers. He presses me firmly to him and his kiss melts me from the inside out. Every sweep of his tongue, caress of his hands, press of his lips seems to say *I love you, I love you, I love you.*

"I've missed you all these years, Nora. My friend. My love."

I want to swim in a pool of those euphoric words. I want to turn them into blankets and nap inside them every day. "I've missed you too, Derek. All's well that loves well."

He whispers in my ear, "That's not the phrase."

"It should be." I'm arching. More, more, more.

"One more thing. I know you hemmed each of my pants up an inch on one leg."

I press my lips together, frantically trying to gain control of my expression. "I will not answer any further questions without my lawyer present."

"Menace." He kisses my temple once, then rises to stand in front of the bed with a smile. And then a heated, promising look flares in Derek's eyes before he grasps my hips, pulls them to the edge of the mattress, gives me his trademark wink, and drops to his knees.

The next morning, Derek goes back to my place with me, where we eat breakfast with my lovely new utensils while I sit in his lap at the table.

40

Derek

It's finally game day.

My game day.

We're all in the locker room getting ready to enter the tunnel and then run out onto the field. The crowd is wild out there. The first game of the season is always nuts—especially when it's at home like this. We won two preseason games and lost one, all of which I had to watch from the sidelines. They rarely start veteran players for preseason games, and especially not when we're coming off an injury.

Today, there's a lethal undercurrent in the locker room while everyone suits up. It's a fresh season. A clean slate. You can feel the anticipation of it like a cloud of smoke in the air. But for me, it's even more intense. I finally get the chance to prove myself for the first time. And I feel ready.

The last two months have been . . . incredible. Not just because my job has been ramping back up again and filling my days, but because my mornings and nights have been devoted to Nora. Nora. I can't think her name without smiling. Without heat gripping my spine.

We've both been wildly busy—Nora even more so than me. And it's been the greatest privilege to watch her absolutely shine. The magazine article was published last month, and ever since, athletes have been banging down her door for representation. Not because our love story has gone viral and put her on the map—but because of the advice she gave to young women during the interview. Since then, her roster has been filling up with eighty percent female athletes. Because of it she's been out of town a lot, traveling all over the country to scout athletes and take meetings with others. I didn't see her once this past week because she was in Illinois scouting a female college soccer player—the last one she wants to add to her roster before closing it off to new clients.

Yeah, I miss her like hell when she's not around, but I'll sacrifice getting to see her every day in favor of witnessing that beaming smile on her face each time she returns home. She's living her dream and it shows in her laughter, in her smile, even in the way she makes love with me. Nora is truly happy. And I'm happy too because of it.

We haven't moved in together yet. We've been operating more like a monogamous, serious dating relationship than marriage just to give ourselves time to adjust. We did literally everything backward and so it's been fun to simply date Nora these last two months— forgetting entirely about the tattoo rings on our fingers sometimes. But even though we don't technically live under the same roof, we spend most nights we're in town together. Either at my place or hers, but rarely separate. Her mom comes over a lot for dinner or a game night along with the guys and their wives. Pam is honestly one of my favorite people in the world. She gives us all shit over everything in the way a friend would. She's great.

And maybe that's why I'm excited today and not worried. My life feels more whole than it ever has before—and I've been thinking more and more about my future away from the Sharks . . . getting excited about it instead of dreading it. I have Nora to thank for that, because watching her pursue this new season in her career has inspired me to want my own.

Whatever the outcome today—even if I play my shittiest game ever and get cut immediately after, I know I'll be okay. There's more out there for me than just football.

Still . . . I plan to play a hell of a game.

"You ready?" Nathan asks, coming up beside me and slamming a hand into my shoulder pads. He's already in uniform, helmet in hand, grinning like he can see into the future.

I nod and reach for my helmet from my locker. "More than ready."

"And if you play like shit?"

"Still ready."

He nods with a smile and gets ready to walk away when Jamal interrupts, looking in the mirror in his locker. "Tell me, you guys . . . does it suck waking up every morning knowing you'll never look as good as me?" He smirks at his reflection, diamond earring glinting in the light.

Price, who's sitting on the bench in front of his locker looking more exhausted than I've ever seen him, looks up at Jamal. "Do me a favor? When you get tackled today, picture my smiling face the whole time."

Jamal pretends to pout. "Someone a little grumpy from not sleeping with the new baby around? Don't worry. I'll pick up your slack on the field today."

Price stands and towers over Jamal. "Go ahead, little chicken nugget. Taunt me some more."

Jamal pats Price's chest, not at all intimidated by his height. "Oh good. You're awake now."

Nathan shakes his head. "Jamal, one of these days you're really going to get the crap beat out of you."

Jamal only grins wider and runs a hand over the side of his head. "And I'll still look good."

"All right," Lawrence says, stepping into the circle and drawing all eyes to him. "It's almost time. And I just want to say . . ." He looks at everyone and his eyes fall to me last, holding my gaze. "I'm proud to play with all of you. And proud to call you my friends."

I frown and cross my arms. "The hell, Lawrence? Is that supposed to be my farewell speech?"

His face flushes and all of the guys laugh. "No. Not at all. I just wanted you to know that no matter what happens—"

"What's going to happen?" I interrupt, lifting my chin and letting my arrogance fuel me.

Lawrence sees it and nods with a smile. Everyone does. It's been a minute since I've felt this familiar confidence pump through my veins, and clearly, they've noticed its absence.

Nathan smirks. "Oh damn. Derek's got his bedroom eyes."

Jamal cringes. "Is this what Nora has to look at right before you—"

"Oh, yes. Please do finish that sentence, because I would love to respond to it."

"So many threats today, gentlemen!" Jamal raises his hands with an indulgent smile. "Does no one appreciate my attempts to liven you guys up before a game?"

"I appreciate you," says Lawrence, with such tender gratitude there's no way it could be misconstrued as sarcasm. No one would guess that this man is about to become feral in the stadium in a few minutes.

"All right, all right," says Nathan, stepping in the middle of all of us. "Real speech time . . ." We have a formal huddle with the whole team on the field—but this one is tradition for the five of us. A minute for us to regroup and get ready. Nathan gives the first speech of the season each year, and we rotate every week after that. And just in case this really does end up being the last one I hear from him, I savor it.

"There's been a lot of change for each of us this year. We've had babies." He looks at Price. "We've gotten married." He looks at me. "We've gotten a second ear piercing." He looks at Jamal. "We've had poems published." He looks at Lawrence and stops there, oddly not adding any monumental moments for himself. "It's been a good year and I'm thankful to have walked with each of you through it. And today . . . I'm thankful to walk on that field with you too. It's going to be a good season. But mainly because I'm playing beside my friends . . ."

There's a beat of silence because no one trusts themselves not to get emotional. Everyone's eyes have suspiciously dropped to the carpet and there's sounds of throats clearing and aggressive sniffs.

Finally, Nathan finishes while looking right at me. "Let's give 'em hell today, boys."

We run out of the tunnel and the crowd's cheering rips through me. The sun is hot and the sky is as blue as the day I kissed Nora on the beach. The memory of her has me squinting up into the stands to find her. She has use of my private box, but she didn't want to sit in it today. She wanted to take her usual seat in the stands—the seat I had no idea she'd been occupying for the last several years.

I was all for her sitting there until I realized that seat was up at the tip-top of the stadium. I selfishly vetoed it. It didn't take much to convince her—I just told her the truth: I wanted to be able to see her face from the field during the game.

So now I search the seats just behind our sidelines, anxiously trying to spot her. To find the woman who's my tether to happiness.

The crowd roars around me and several of my teammates jostle my shoulders as they fly past me and onto the field. Our coach slaps my back and tells me good luck before he jogs over to his position on the sidelines. But I'm preoccupied looking for *her.* Nora Mackenzie Pender.

And then there she is, my wife.

Her auburn hair glints in the sunlight and her smile grows eight sizes. I missed waking up to her this morning after having to spend the night in the hotel with the team. I'm starved for the sight of her. Hungry for her touch.

Nora blows me a kiss and then points down to her new jersey I had secretly delivered to her apartment this morning. It's the newest black-and-white design for the season that she doesn't have yet. She spins around so I can see she's painted the number with glitter glue and she holds her hands over her shoulder, making a heart.

At the sight of her, the rest of the stadium falls away and it's just her standing here—her pretty mouth smiling as she turns back to me, silently calling me to her. I jog my way over and drop my helmet beside me on the turf. I grab the railing and jump up to stand level with her. The people beside her are family of the other players and don't make any moves to touch me. But Nora, she leans forward and dives her hands right into the back of my hair.

"Well, hello there, handsome," she says in that fake southern accent she once used on me at the bar in Vegas. The night we accidentally changed our lives forever.

"Kiss me," I half demand, half beg.

She obliges, pressing a tame yet intoxicating kiss to my mouth. I'm vaguely aware of cheers and catcalls rising around us. "I missed you last night," she says, breaking the kiss with a twinkle in her hazel eyes. "But I used my time well and made this epic sign."

My gaze drops to the thick cardboard she holds up for me.

PENDER, LET ME SEE THAT TIGHT END.

I shake my head. "Is that drawing supposed to be my ass in uniform?"

"It's an uncanny likeness." Her eyes glow with happiness—or maybe that's just all the glitter reflecting from the sign.

"I love you." I lean in to kiss her one last time, but just before my lips touch hers, a hand grips my back and rips me off the wall.

"You two kiss too damn much. It's time to play football."

"Jamal, you have a death wish today," I tell his retreating back. He's sprinting out onto the field with a shit-eating grin, holding up a middle finger behind his back, specifically for me.

I glance at Nora one more time and point at her before I go join the guys on the field to stretch. *This one's for you.*

41

Nora

The crowd loses it the second the clock runs out with Derek having just caught his twelfth catch of the game in the end zone—making it his third touchdown. The winning touchdown.

My mom and I both scream and launch ourselves at each other, hugging and jumping up and down like kids. Derek throws the ball to the ground and jogs to the fifty-yard line, stopping to face me. He smiles, drops to his knees, and fans a bow like I'm his queen. Like he did it for me. The rest of the guys quickly follow suit and before I know it, most of the team is bowing before me like I had anything to do with the incredible game Derek just played.

I'm laughing my head off, gesturing for them all to stand up, all the while feeling so relieved and proud, I could explode. He did it—and I knew he would. The entire team played like champions, but Derek was unstoppable the whole game. No one could cover him. And Nathan's passes were flawless today.

Speaking of Nathan, when the guys all rise back to their feet, I see him cast a silly face to one of the boxes above me. Sure enough, there's Bree sticking her tongue out at him in return. I love them. I love that I get to call them my friends now.

"Let's see them try to cut your man after that game!" my mom says, taking my hand and squeezing it because she knows how worried I was for Derek. I didn't want to show it, because I know that even if he played terribly today and got cut, he'd still be okay and find something new to love. Derek has too much to offer to ever truly be out of options. But I know how much he loves the Sharks and thinks of them as family. I wanted with all of my heart for him to get to stay with his friends on this team. And thanks to how he played today—there's no question the Sharks will keep him on. It was like his ankle injury never existed and I can't wait to listen to those assholes on sports radio eat their words.

Derek stands, tosses off his helmet, and runs full steam for me. I lean over the railing as he approaches, wrapping my arms around his sweaty neck and placing a kiss to his smiling mouth. "I'm proud of you," I tell him, happy tears clinging to my lashes.

"Thank you for being here for me," he tells me, his breath coming quickly. "For always being here for me." Several people behind us are shouting his name trying to get his attention. Their new football god dropping from his throne to lavish us with attention. He kisses my cheek once and then looks past me to the crowd, taking off one of his gloves and tossing it back to a little boy about ten years old in the stands.

He then snags my hand and kisses my tattoo ring. "See you in the media room?"

He'll have to go do a postgame press conference now—and I wouldn't miss it for the world. Not when I know he's going to get to gloat over how well he played.

"I'll be there."

He hops back down to the shouts of the crowd, and my mom beams at me. She's told me repeatedly over the last several weeks how much she likes Derek. It means the world to have her blessing.

We pack up our things and move against the crowd, heading to the second level to Bree and Nathan's box. It'll be a bit until Derek's press conference because the players will shower, and then most likely Nathan will go first with his interview. I plan to hug Bree and then eat all her free food in the box while I wait.

Except when we make it into the box, Bree is staring at her phone with a frown. And then those eyes lift to me, and somehow, I instinctively know something is wrong. Something that has to do with me, judging by the way her eyes fill with a mix of fear and pity.

"What?" I breathe out.

There are a few other people in the box: Bree's friend Dylan and her sister Lily. They each look at me like I've just been announced as the newest tribute in the Hunger Games.

Bree opens her arms to me. "Come get a hug first, and then I'll tell you."

My stomach falls, but I comply, stepping into Bree's arms and letting her squeeze the life out of me before she releases me, handing over her phone.

I hold it but can't bring my eyes to look yet. "Do you think if I avoid looking at whatever you're trying to show me, it'll just . . . go away?"

"Not likely," Bree says with a frown that makes me even more nervous. "And you should read it quickly."

My mom steps up beside me to read over my shoulder—scanning the online article that just dropped a few minutes ago on the heels of the Sharks' win. The article isn't about the L.A. Sharks, though, it's about me. And Derek . . . but mostly me.

The title of the article is *Conniving Agent Marries Football Legend to Further Career.*

Wow, how original. But then the terror sets in because as I read, I realize a lot of what this article says is truth. I mean, it's spun to make me look like a manipulative witch, but the foundation of the truth is there. It states that although Derek and I presented a romantic front, it was all a lie. That our spontaneous elopement was nothing more than a drunken mistake on Derek's part.

The source has the audacity to suggest that I purposely got Derek drunk and used him as a way to get ahead in my career (that part an obvious lie). It then goes on to spell out how our honeymoon was nothing but a publicity stunt that Derek was forced into to cover our butts so he didn't ruin his reputation. Which . . . is not at all true either. Derek's reputation has withstood far worse. (Including the time he got drunk in a club and stripped completely naked in the center of the dance floor. He was escorted out and put in a car and all that came of it was a lot of blurred-out gifs. His endorsements still flowed in.)

No, it was my reputation that Derek was voluntarily protecting.

"How dare they write this," I say, shaking as I near the end of the horrendous article and see that the source is cited as anonymous, but this is undoubtably the work of a jealous co-worker. And then I remember the day I spilled my guts to Nicole in the office several weeks ago and us thinking we heard someone in the hallway. Apparently, there was someone listening in.

I'm going to barf.

"Are you okay, hon?" my mom asks, wrapping her arm around my shoulders.

"Yes . . . no . . . somewhere in the middle maybe."

"Do you have any idea who wrote this?" Bree asks, concern etching her brow.

"Someone jealous enough about the sudden spike in my career to want to see it end," I say, knowing exactly who it is. It's the same person who's been whispering behind my back for weeks. The same one who has been upset watching the office slowly accept me as one of their own. And the same one who has tried to poach the athletes I've been in talks with right out from under me—claiming he's seen my work ethic and it leaves much to be desired. *Your work ethic leaves much to be desired, Marty, judging by how poor a job you do of cleaning up your trash in the break room.*

I hand Bree's phone back to her when my own begins vibrating in my back pocket. I pull it out and find Nicole's name on my screen. She must have seen the article.

"I just read it," I tell her in lieu of a greeting.

She doesn't bother with one either. Instead, she cuts right to the point. A point that makes a cold sweat break out down the back of my neck. "Derek's press conference. You need to get to him and prepare him before he steps in front of the cameras."

I mutter a curse and take off in a sprint out of the box.

I jog as fast as I can through the stadium, accidentally bumping into a few people in the process. One guy holding a beer is not watching where he's going and clearly doesn't expect a woman running toward him at the speed of light because he steps out directly into my path. That beer ends up all over my beautiful new jersey and if I weren't already in a frantic hurry to make it to Derek, I'd (1) stop and buy him a new drink because courtesy is the currency of my life. (2) I'd feel buzzed with excitement to try out a new stain-removing hack. But there's no time, so I keep pushing through the crowd.

I manage to dash off a text to Derek while moving, but upon a second look, I realize it reads *Trbl. CLL mE.*

When he doesn't call me immediately, I call him on repeat while zigzagging through the crowd and flashing my media badge to security guards as I rush down tunnels until I'm field level. After the fifth time Derek doesn't answer his phone, I'm fairly certain he must have left it in his damn locker.

There's a security guard posted outside the media room, and when I race up to it dragging in breaths like I'll never get another, the man looks as though he's debating throwing me in handcuffs out of precaution alone. I try to push past him, but he stops me with a sharp frown. "You can't go in, ma'am. They're in session right now."

"I know—that's why I need to get in there."

"No one goes in after they've started."

I summon my inner Nicole and hold up my badge three inches from his face. "I'm an agent and my client is participating in a press conference right now without me. Kindly step aside or find yourself without a job next week when I speak with the GM about your conduct."

He still looks a little torn but ultimately decides not to risk it and steps to the left. I'm in a hurry and have no seconds to waste, but . . . my conscience is so obnoxiously loud. So I pause and smile up at him. "But you're doing a fine job keeping everyone out. Next time I throw a party and need a bouncer you better believe I'll be calling you!"

And then I walk through the door of the media room and my panic swells to a new height. It's a packed room full of reporters with cameras and recorders pointed in the air. The constant soft clicks of pictures being snapped fills the air, and they're all aimed at Derek Pender. He's on the stage already, standing behind the lectern with a mic in front of his face. Behind him is a backdrop with the Los Angeles Sharks logo.

His hair is still a little damp on the ends, peeking out from under the hat he's wearing. The stern set of his face has my thighs clenching because I love this look on him. His all-business face. I also love the new black team hoodie he's wearing right now. I might have to abduct it tonight.

Right. Not here to jump Derek, steal his hoodie, and then climb him like a tree. I need to get his attention before someone can ask him about the article.

"Excuse me," I whisper frantically, pushing past a man hovering in the aisle. Jeez, it's congested in here. So much liberally applied cologne and perfume that I'm nearly choking. I try to catch Derek's eye as I move slowly toward the front of the room, but he hasn't seen me yet.

My shoulders tense as a hand goes up from a man in the front row and Derek calls on him. "Congrats on playing an incredible game today, Derek. How did your ankle feel while you were out there?"

An easy one.

I sigh with a little relief as I continue moving around the perimeter of the room to get to the front without drawing too much attention to myself.

"Thank you. I felt better than ever. No problems at all from my ankle."

Another reporter speaks up. "We've seen other athletes sustain similar injuries and not come back half as strong as you played today. What do you attribute the success of your recovery to?"

"Yeah—I owe it all to my trainers. They worked just as hard as I did to get my ankle back in good shape." The agent in me swells with pride at his answer. And the part of me that's in love with that man is even more proud knowing that the gratitude he showed for his trainers and the people he works with isn't just for show. He means it.

Derek calls on another reporter and something about the way the man's shoulders straighten before he rises from his seat—which is completely unnecessary in here—has me catapulting myself toward the stage. But I don't make it in time.

The man's low voice booms through the room. "Derek, are you aware that an article was published just after the game stating that your and Nora Mackenzie's relationship is a fraud?" I freeze in place as blood roars in my ears. The clicks and flashes of cameras are as frenzied as a lightning storm. I'm going to faint. Everything I've worked for—everything I've accomplished—is going to go up in flames from this article. And I doubt Derek will take a hit from it— but if he does, I'm not sure how I'll live with myself.

But Derek, bless him, is stone-faced. He betrays no hints of emotions or surprise at the question, showing only his years of experience in media training by not letting his eyebrows so much as twitch. But his eyes move swiftly over the room, hunting for me. And like he can sense me in here somewhere, his eyes slide straight past everyone else and land on me.

The moment our gazes lock, I feel his tenderness like a tangible caress. It's him briefly taking a time-out from this circus and acknowledging the turmoil I'm swimming in. It's a language only we can read, though—no one else realizing the silent conversation taking place between us.

When Derek doesn't answer immediately, the reporter continues with a smug grin like he knows he's just gotten the scoop on the story of the week. "The source reports that the elopement was due to a night of heavy drinking, and that Nora Mackenzie only used you and your status to launch her career. Do you have a comment?"

I want to shout across the media room that I would never use him. That I love him more than I've loved anything or anyone in my life. But like in my recurring nightmare, I'm frozen and silent. Probably for the best since my comment or sudden appearance would only make it worse. Because as it stands, they've phrased the question in a way that doesn't hurt Derek—only me. And I can live with that.

I hate to admit it, but in this moment, I have no idea how to fix this. If he doesn't comment, we look guilty. If he does comment, there's a possibility it will come out all wrong and blow the entire thing up into a bigger deal than it is. Which is exactly what the media would love. He needs to tread very carefully and I'm just holding my breath that he'll know how.

Derek's eyes settle on me again and even though I'm a swirl of terror, he looks utterly calm and confident. And then he flashes me a subtle grin. Of course my skin curls with anticipation before he turns his eyes back to the reporter and leans toward the mics. "Listen up, because I'm only going to acknowledge this once."

I clutch my hands to my stomach as it bottoms out. The room goes utterly silent except for the sounds of cameras snapping pictures. Recorders are raised in the air all over the room to catch each and every word that comes out of his handsome mouth. "First, her name is Nora Mackenzie Pender now, but don't be mistaken. She might share my name, but she owes her success to no one but herself. My role in her life has nothing to do with how hard she's worked for years and years to get where she is now. And I swear to god, anyone else who dares question my wife's integrity or work ethic is going to have to deal with me, but more terrifyingly, you're going to have to deal with her. Don't be fooled, she can be ruthless as hell."

I can't breathe. Can't blink. Can't look away from the blazing fury in Derek's eyes. I watch as they shift to me once more and then I see it—the wink.

Oh, Derek. What are you about to do?

He leans forward slowly; he's holding a winning hand of cards and he knows it. "And now . . ." he says in a stern, no-nonsense rumble. "We can continue talking about that joke of an article supplied by some desperate source . . . or . . . we can discuss how I'm officially retiring from the NFL."

I clutch the back of the nearest chair. Voices rise. The energy of the room uncaps and now everyone is practically falling all over one another to get Derek to notice their raised hands and shouts of questions. Cameras are flashing like fireworks. And Derek—the smug devil just stands there and lets it erupt around him with a quiet grin on his face.

42

Derek

Shit.

Nora left during the press conference directly after I announced my retirement. We had locked eyes and I hoped she saw what I was trying to tell her—*It's okay. I want this.* But judging by the way she bolted, I don't think she picked up on that memo.

I couldn't follow her out because I had to finish answering questions that I really didn't have answers for. And now, finally finished with the seemingly endless interviews and trying to avoid any team executives or our coach, who will absolutely cuss me out for announcing the news before telling anyone else, I step into the locker room to grab my phone. Except I find the guys waiting for me. Arms crossed. Scowls tight. They had no idea I was planning to do this, because I had no idea I was going to do it.

Before they say anything, I lift my hands, palms up. "I don't regret it."

"Were you planning it?" Nathan asks, voice cooler than I've ever heard it.

"Yes and no. I realized I wanted it after the game. And then it seemed like the perfect time to announce it to pull attention away from that bullshit article." Their shoulders slacken a little.

I'll never forget the look on Nora's face when that prick asked if I'd like to comment on how she used me to get ahead in her career. He said it like a statement, not a question. Like everything someone reads online should be held as gospel. I wanted to tear him limb from limb for insinuating he knew anything about what my wife has done to gain her position. None of it had anything to do with sleeping with me.

If anything, I stepped in her path, and she found a way around me.

"You're really okay with this?" Price asks.

I smile. "Never been more okay with something in my life."

"Okay, then." Nathan hugs me first and the rest of the guys follow.

Jamal whispers in my ear. "I still think you're a big-ass ugly baby, but . . . this was inspiring."

I put my hand over his entire face and push him back. "Thanks, pipsqueak."

He throws off my hand and shoots me the bird.

"We'll let you get a head start home," Nathan says, subtly reminding me that our friendship has nothing to do with my position on or off the team.

I try calling Nora the second I'm in my truck but it goes straight to voicemail. Rocks drop into my stomach, and I worry that my move today upset her. That it was too grand a gesture and I scared her off. But then a text comes through:

I'm at home waiting for you.

Home.

I text her: Which one?

Her response has my chest loosening a bit. Your house.

She called my house her home. That has to be a good sign, right? I've been trying so hard to play it cool the last couple of months. To not push too hard or ask for too much because I don't want to make her jumpy. But I've been noticing small things too. She bought a second toothbrush that stays at my house. She has more clothes at my place than her own now. She brought her pink toaster from her place, and it lives on my kitchen counter now.

It feels so right seeing her things slowly mingle with mine.

And maybe that's why I feel completely at peace after announcing the end of my career today. Because when I looked out at the crowd and locked eyes with her: Everything just clicked. I'd never been able to picture the second part of my life after football. And then suddenly it sprawled out in front of me—and I felt ready for it. Ready for the change. Ready for what's to come.

I pull up to the house now and find Nora sitting on the ground by the front door. Waiting. Even from here I can see the tear stains down her cheeks and I'm worried. So damn worried. Is this because of me?

Or is it because—

I open my truck door and she launches herself from the ground, sprinting full speed for me.

43

Nora

Derek drops his duffel bag on the driveway and takes two steps to meet me—where I throw myself into his arms and he catches me with zero hesitation.

I've done nothing but cry for the past hour. He gave it up. It can't be for me.

His arms wrap around me so tight I can barely breathe, and I bury my face in his neck. His fingers sink into the back of my hair, and he whispers in my ear. "Why are you crying, Nora? What's wrong?"

This jolts me back to reality and I wiggle out of his arms, landing once again on my feet.

And then I shove him in the chest. "What were you thinking? You retired! Derek!" Fresh tears well again. "You can't retire for me! Tell me it wasn't for me! That's too much. You played so incredibly today. You broke your own freaking record; did you know that? You . . . you can't give this up because of some absurd gossip magazine article. It would blow over on its own!"

Derek smiles and cups my face, wiping my tears with his thumbs. "Are you done?"

"No. I'm not done. You should have told me first. Run this by me!"

"You would have told me not to do it."

"Exactly! This is a mistake. I could have found another way."

Derek bends and presses a silencing kiss to my lips. "It's not a mistake. You know how I know?"

I eye his beautiful face. His sharp cheekbones, the scar above his eyebrow. My heart aches with love for him. "How?"

"Because on the way home, I felt a knot in my chest loosen for the first time in years. It's true, I didn't plan for this—but I'm grateful it happened the way it did. I've had such a great career in football, and now I'm ready for a change, Nora. I want it. A new adventure. I just needed the push in the right direction. And I know you could have fixed this yourself another way. I know it likely would have blown over just fine in a few weeks. But I didn't want you to weather a storm for any length of time when I had a perfectly good solution right at my fingertips."

I want to weep. In fact, I am. "You can't do it for me, Derek. It's too much. You'll resent me."

"I could never resent you, Nora. And if it helps you sleep better at night—remember that I'm an arrogant asshole and I'd much rather end my football career on the heels of playing the best game of my life than when I'm washed up." He smooshes my cheeks together. "I'm happy, Ginger Snap. I'm so damn happy. I want this for me. I'm so ready for this change. Ready to see what else I have to offer in this world."

"But if you're not . . . if you're regretting it—I will . . . I will go to the Sharks right now and tell them you made a mistake."

He kisses my forehead. "No mistake, Nora. None. This is what I want. Even if you break up with me here and now, I'll stay retired. I'm so tired of striving at max effort every damn day. I've loved my football career, but I need to see what else is out there for me. It's just time."

I sigh, wanting to protest more. Feeling like I should do everything I can to make him change his mind. But I have to admit, his eyes are convincing. He seems like he genuinely wants this.

"Okay, but just know you're allowed to still change your mind tonight. Or tomorrow. Or even next week."

"Noted. But right now, all I want to do is go inside with my girl and lie on the couch and watch something chill on TV."

He takes my hand, ready to pull me with him into the house.

But I can't move. I can't do anything other than what I've wanted to do since the night on our honeymoon when he told me hazel was his favorite color.

Derek pauses when he feels the tug of my hand and turns around—finding me down on one knee. The cement is sharp and hot under it, but I don't care. I love the bite of it in this moment.

His brows pull together and then immediately soften when he realizes what I'm doing. "Derek Pender . . . I know we're already married but—"

His hand juts out and covers my mouth. "*Wait*. Is this happening because you feel guilty about my retirement?" I shake my head. "Did you want to do this yesterday? Before any of this drama today? Or did the idea only just occur to you?"

I nod, and then frown and shake my head. He releases my mouth so I can answer. "Yes, to wanting to do it yesterday—no to it being a recent development. Can I finish proposing to you now?"

"No," he says simply, and bends to scoop me up in his arms and carry me inside. *Confusing.* He marches me all the way to the living room and then deposits me on the couch and tells me to stay here. But then he turns back, brackets my body with his hands, and kisses me tenderly. *"Please."*

And then he's jogging up toward his room and I'm left here on the couch to twiddle my thumbs, thinking this must be the weirdest proposal ever. He doesn't leave me here long, though. And when he emerges from the top of the stairs, the look in his eyes has my heart shifting into fourth gear.

"I had to get something from my bedside table," he says meaningfully while moving to stand in front of me.

I know my eyes are lit up like stars right now. Who cares if he interrupted my proposal . . . I finally get to see what—

Oh.

Derek drops to one knee. And then he pulls a little black velvet box from behind his back. "You don't mind if I pick up where you left off, do you?" He smiles, and every drop of blood in my veins rushes to accommodate my bursting heart. "I know we're already married, Nora. But it would mean the entire world to me if you would stay married to me. For real. For always. For eternity. Stay with me. Let me love you fully and desperately forever and ever."

He pops the top of the black box, and a shiny diamond ring sparkles up at me.

My lips tremble as I look between the engagement ring and Derek's sharp blue eyes. "This was what the guys found in your bedside table? This is the embarrassing thing?"

"I never said it was embarrassing. I said when I gave it to you, it would change everything. Because this . . . this ring belongs to you— and it always has. I bought it for you in college."

"What?" I breathe out. "You . . . you were going to propose?"

He nods. "The day you broke up with me actually." He grins at the horrified look on my face. "There was a proposal waiting for you on the other side of my apartment door with way too many flowers. It's part of why I didn't ask you to come in and talk it all out after you said you wanted to end it. This ring"—he raises it—"was in my back pocket."

"*No.*" The word comes out as a breath. "Derek. That's heartbreaking."

Sensing my guilt, he tips forward, clutching the ring box in one hand and my face in the other so he can kiss me back into the present. "No shame—no guilt, Nora. Everything happened exactly as it was supposed to, I'm confident of that now. If I had proposed to you back then, everything would have been a mess. We weren't right for each other then, but I plan on working every day to be the right person for you now."

I loosen a breath lodged in my throat. "You've held on to this ring all this time?"

He nods. "I could never bring myself to get rid of it. And now I know it's because we were always going to find our way back to each other." His fingers bite into my hips and he pulls me to the edge of the couch. We're eye-to-eye with my thighs cradling his hips. "I'm yours, Nora. I always have been. Always will be."

I'm struggling to find the words to convey the gooey mushy center of my heart. I wish I could just give him a peek inside; it's exploding with color and confetti. There's sprinkles and glitter. It's a mess.

Instead, I smile with tears in my eyes and lean forward to nip at his bottom lip. "*Mine,*" I whisper before pulling away so I can slide the ring onto my finger. It's a perfect fit.

Derek ruins the moment by grimacing down at my hand. "Damn, it's small. I forgot I didn't have money back then. We can get you a new one tomorrow," he's saying while reaching for my hand, but I hold it away from him.

"No way! I want this one."

He goes for it again. "You can wear this one on your other hand. Let me get you a new one."

"Absolutely not. This one is perfect. And if you take it, I'll scream." I scramble away, standing on the couch to evade him, but he stands too—nearly eye level with me without having to stand on a cushion. He's laughing.

"I can make you scream if that's what you want . . . but I'd prefer it be my name over and over again."

I gape. "What a dirty mouth you have, sir."

He leans closer to lace kisses up my neck and I secretly eye my ring over his shoulder as he does.

A minute later, as Derek has me pinned to the couch and is just about to remove my shirt, the front door bursts open. He groans and drops his head into the crook of my neck as the song "Kiss Me" plays loudly over someone's cellphone.

"Y'all thought you had the evening all to yourselves to make luvvv, didn't you?" Jamal laughs one loud laugh and points to our position on the couch. "Wrong!" His wife, Tamara, just waves as she takes an armload of snacks into the kitchen along with Lawrence's wife, Cora—clearly already used to the way things are done in this friend group.

"Get out!" Derek yells, but no one listens.

Instead, Nathan comes up to the couch and smiles. "Sucks being interrupted, doesn't it? Payback is a bitch. Where do you want me to put this cake? Bree had us stop and get it at the store on the way here. Said you'd probably propose. And . . ." He peeks over Derek's shoulder at my hand. "Bree Cheese!" he yells back at his wife. "You were right. He gave her the ring."

We hear Bree's squeal before we see her. And then she's running into the house and jumping on the couch with us like it's a dog pile.

She wraps her arms around both of us and squeezes. It's delightful. "Ah! I knew it! What a good day."

Price and his wife come through the front door next, kicking off their shoes and setting the car seat with Jayla inside on the floor.

"Maybe if we stay very, very still, they won't see us and they'll all go away," Derek mumbles in my ear—his voice still dark with unresolved desire.

Bree pops over his shoulder with a wide smile and whispers, "Not a chance." But then she pushes off the couch and stands with a wicked gleam in her eye when she sees her husband and waves him toward her.

"Besides," she says as Nathan walks up to her and wraps a possessive arm around her waist, pulling her up close to him for whatever she's planning to say next. "Since it seems like the perfect day for big revelations and truth bombs, I thought I'd go ahead and share with you all that . . . I'm pregnant."

Derek and I both sit up quickly, ready to cheer for them with the rest of the group when we all seem to notice Nathan's face at once. His shocked face. And that's when we realize . . . Bree hasn't told him yet.

"Surprise," she says, looking up at him with so much love and tenderness it feels as if the entire room has just been blanketed with sunshine. "We're having a baby, Nathan."

"Bree . . ." He blinks and looks for all the world like he's just been crowned king. His jaw flexes and his nose wrinkles, as he tries and fails to keep his emotions at bay. And then he's taking her face in his hands and kissing her as they both cry. We're all crying. Even Derek is rapidly blinking back moisture.

"Aw—hell no!" says Jamal, wiping his eyes and then taking his wife's hand and pulling her toward the front door. "We gotta go, love."

I blink at the door after they disappear through it. "Where are they going?"

"I'm guessing to make a baby," Derek says with a grimace. "Jamal hates to be left out of group events."

"Group events?" My eyes widen at Derek, and I scoot away from him meaningfully. "Don't get any funny ideas, Pender."

"Oh—I've got ideas," he says, pulling me from the couch and hoisting me over his shoulder. "But all of them include protection, don't you worry." He carries me to the stairs.

"Derek! All our friends are here! You're not being a hostess with the mostess!"

His laugh rumbles through my body as he continues carrying me up the stairs. "And those friends have exactly sixty seconds to get out of my house if they don't want to hear some things."

And approximately sixty seconds later, we hear the front door slam—leaving Derek and me alone in our home.

EPILOGUE

Nora

The water sloshes over the edge of the tub, bubbles scattering onto the floor as I lean back against Derek's chest.

"Mmm," he moans. "Why . . . have we never done this before? It's so good."

I smile around my spoon. "You'd think we were doing the hanky-panky in here by all those sounds you're making back there rather than just eating ice cream."

It's been two months since Derek played his last game—and he hasn't seemed to regret it once. Believe me, I've been watching closely for any signs pointing toward disappointment. Instead, I've seen Derek come alive. He smiles wider, laughs louder. He's still addicted to exercise, which I fully support because those muscles are too sexy to quit. But now he does things like eat ice cream topped with cereal with me in the bathtub on a Tuesday night.

His cold lips touch the side of my neck, making my back arch. "Who says we're just eating ice cream in here?"

"Do you have other plans?"

"I have so many plans, rookie."

"You can't call me that anymore—I'm a business owner now."

Derek sets his empty bowl on the floor and pushes lightly against my shoulders, signaling for me to sit forward. I do—cradling my bowl of melty ice cream and cereal against my bubble-coated chest as Derek's thumbs knead into my lower back and glide all the way up my spine to my neck. "You're right. Want me to call you *boss*?"

"Ooh, I like that," I say even as I shiver in the warm water from how delicious his hands feel pressing into my sore muscles.

So much has changed over the last few months. One being I no longer work at Sports Representation Inc. It's true that all the public gossip around Derek and me died down immediately once he announced his retirement, and his news overshadowed pretty much any other headline in sports that week—and who knows, maybe it would have died down even without his help. We'll never know. But inside the office, no way. Marty was like a villain straight out of Disney Channel movies from the '90s. I was never able to prove that he was the source behind the article—but there was no one else it could be. The man couldn't let my relationship with Derek go.

One Tuesday afternoon, I had enough. Marty was talking with some co-workers in the break room about a client he was in talks with, and when I walked in, he said, "Actually, maybe I'll just send Nora to sleep with him, so he'll sign with me."

Joseph was there . . . he heard the entire thing. And yet—he chose to say nothing to Marty. I would have been fired on the spot for a statement like that, but Marty just got a quiet chuckle from the men in the room.

So I quit then and there. I couldn't work any longer for a company that doesn't value me or women in this industry. And because *I'm extra,* I waited quietly until all eyes were on me, and then I went to the bowl of fun-size Skittles I had refilled earlier that morning, tucked it under my arm, and strode toward the door. "Consider this my official resignation," I told Joseph. And then I looked right in Marty's beady eyes. "And since my contract lacked a noncompete clause, please know it will be an absolute pleasure stealing every single one of your clients, Marty Vallar." And then I dropped my gaze to his nose and flared my nostrils before grimacing. He swatted at the nonexistent booger and I took that as my cue to leave for good.

In the most epic turn of events, later that night as Derek and I were sitting in my living room discussing my next steps, the security guard at the front of the community called, saying a Nicole Hart was asking to be let in. I assumed she was there to tell me I was making a big mistake and should come back. Boy, was I wrong. She burst into the house carrying her leather laptop case and the name plate that used to live on her desk. She set it on the coffee table in front of us and simply said, "We're going to need an office space."

Yes—Nicole left the company and that's how the two of us started our own agency, one founded by women and ready to provide a safe, affirming atmosphere for female athletes. Of course, men are welcome too, and when told our mission statement, Nathan was all too happy to stay on with Nicole and help promote the cause. As were each of my clients. It was so lucky that Nicole was badass enough in her early days to demand that all noncompete clauses be removed from her contract before signing with Sports Representation Inc. and taught me to do the same.

And since I no longer need my apartment, it's been converted into a makeshift office space until we find an official location we like more. Needless to say, it's been a busy few months.

Derek leans forward now, and I glance over my shoulder to look at him, my husband, as his dark damp hair falls over one of his brows.

His lips graze the shell of my ear. "You've been working so hard. What can I do to help you relax?" I love that seductive voice of his. It's smooth like honey on fire.

I also love his hand as it emerges from the bubbles to rest on the top of my bent knee—unmoving. Taunting.

I grin at that hand. "You're the one with the early morning tomorrow, Coach."

That's the other big change. Derek accepted a position at our college alma mater (USC) as an offensive line coach. A job that he's very excited about and I have no doubt he'll excel in. It's perfect for him. He's also made the brave decision to talk openly about his journey with dyslexia and being diagnosed as an adult—hoping to bring awareness to more parents and teachers, as well as the athletes that he coaches on the field.

We've had many late nights together recently, his playbooks scattered around his side of the bed and my contracts taking up the other. We work in tandem until one of us eventually pushes all of it aside and jumps the other. It's a good system—10/10. Highly recommend.

But these moments . . . these quiet moments where work is far away and I'm alone with my husband, best friend, and yes, *client* (because I also represent coaches, for anyone wondering)—they're my favorites. As it turns out, celebrating our successes in the bathtub with a bowl of ice cream and wandering hands is the best way to spend an evening.

Speaking of wandering hands, Derek's hand trails oh-so-slowly up my thigh as his teeth nip at my neck. "Hey, remember that rule book we made?"

"Yes," I say, and it accidentally comes out like a purr. I can't help it, though, when Derek's muscled body is wrapped around mine, his breath caressing my heated skin and his hand headed to caress another favorite location.

"I thought of a new rule we should add to it . . ."

"You realize we broke every rule on that list, right?" I lay my head back against his shoulder as his lips press against my throat, dragging up and down like he's obsessed with me.

"Mm-hm. And now that I know how much you love to break those rules . . . I'd like to add one."

"And what would that be?"

Those fingers. That mouth. His grin. "No sex in the bathtub."

I laugh—happiness fizzing in my heart. "And here I thought you'd say something romantic like 'No loving Derek for the rest of your life.'"

He leisurely kisses the bubbles off my shoulder and neck and chest like he has all night—like he's perfectly content to shut out the world and soak in this tub with me forever. "Sure—we can add that one too."

The Rule Book
(est. by Nora M. and Derek P.)

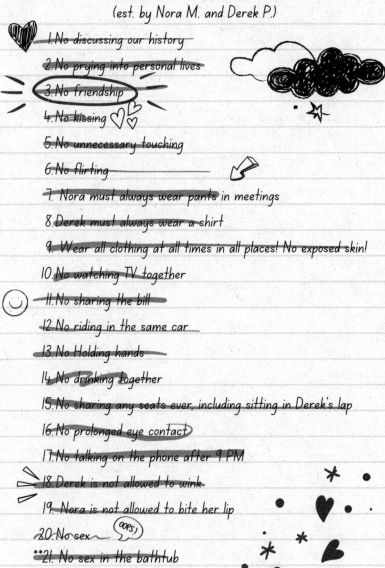

1. No discussing our history
2. No prying into personal lives
3. No friendship
4. No kissing
5. No unnecessary touching
6. No flirting
7. Nora must always wear pants in meetings
8. Derek must always wear a shirt
9. Wear all clothing at all times in all places! No exposed skin!
10. No watching TV together
11. No sharing the bill
12. No riding in the same car
13. No Holding hands
14. No drinking together
15. No sharing any seats ever, including sitting in Derek's lap
16. No prolonged eye contact
17. No talking on the phone after 9 PM
18. Derek is not allowed to wink
19. Nora is not allowed to bite her lip
20. No sex   (OOPS!)
**21. No sex in the bathtub

ACKNOWLEDGMENTS

Allow me to start by saying I am the luckiest writer in the world, because I absolutely have the most magical, kindhearted, creative team on the planet. My heart gets mushier and mushier for these people after every book we put out together because of how good they are to me.

To Shauna Summers, my editor and shining star, I have the most fun working on my stories with you, and I wonder how I ever did it before you came along. I'm endlessly grateful for you and the beauty you add to my books. Sometimes I think we are soulmates in this publishing world because no one understands where I want to go with a story or how to help me get there like you do. I adore you!

And a big, *huge* thank you to the rest of the incredible team over at Dell! Kim Hovey, Taylor Noel (adore you forever), Corina Diez, Mae Martinez, Brianna Kusilek, and everyone else who worked behind the scenes to make this book possible!

There's no way I would even be typing this without the endless support of my incredible agent, Kim Lionetti, who has been such an anchoring presence in my traditional writing career. Thank you, Kim, for your many hours of work on my behalf, but also for reminding me to not overtax myself and to prioritize my mental health when I try to take on more than I should. I'm so thankful for you and everyone at Bookends Literary!

Additionally, I'm so grateful that this book gets to be read in

Europe thanks to the hard work of my wonderful UK publisher, Headline eternal! Thank you all from the bottom of my heart.

And now, I want to send so much love and gratitude to The Book Shop—one of my local indie bookstores that has championed me and worked for hours and hours on my preorder campaigns for the last few releases, including this one. Joelle, you are a rock star and I'm in awe of you and your kindness. Thank you!

To my friends and family, it feels so weak to say thank you when you all literally hold me together on a daily basis, but . . . thank you. Specifically, my husband and best friend for life, Chris, who has given so much to help make my dreams come true. It's a joy to walk through life with you—ups, downs, and squirrely unpredictable middles.

And finally, to you, my readers: You are what turns these stories into magic for me. They feel real when I write them, but they come *alive* after I see you read them. It's one of my greatest joys to experience my stories through your eyes. Thank you for your reviews, your emails, your DMs, and your posts. I hope this book brought you so much happiness.

ABOUT THE AUTHOR

SARAH ADAMS is the author of *Practice Makes Perfect, When in Rome,* and *The Cheat Sheet*. Born and raised in Nashville, Tennessee, she loves her family and warm days. Sarah has dreamed of being a writer since she was a girl but finally wrote her first novel when her daughters were napping and she no longer had any excuses to put it off. Sarah is a coffee lover, a mom of two daughters, married to her best friend, and an indecisive introvert. Her hope is to write stories that make readers laugh, maybe even cry—but always leave them happier than when they started reading.

authorsarahadams.com
Instagram: @authorsarahadams